Glorious Verve

By Tennison Long

Smashwords Edition

Dedicated to my girls…

SAN FRANCISCO — A female suicide bomber detonated a vest loaded with explosives on Monday in a busy San Francisco farmer's market, killing at least 136 people including dozens of children on a field trip.

The Islamic State later claimed responsibility for the attack.

The bomb went off in a produce market that was packed with commuters and children, a police officer said, adding that another 82 people were wounded.

During a news conference with San Francisco Police Chief Ed Hardly, first responders said the suicide bomber had pretended to be asking for directions to the ferry terminal. Once the commuters gathered around, she detonated the vest.

The Islamic State, also known as ISIS or ISIL, claimed the attack in a statement circulated on www.sharia4ever.org, a site often used by the group. It was the third such attack in three days in or near the Bay Area, underscoring the lingering threat posed by the extremist group despite a string of setbacks for it elsewhere in the country over the past year, including in and around Northern California.

Blake Hampton, 32, an organic cheese vendor, described how the children had gathered around the bomber when she asked their chaperone for directions.

“Then a big boom came, sending everyone up into the air,” Mr. Hampton, who was injured by a piece of flying debris which severed his right ear. He blamed religious fanaticism for this “cruel and unnecessary event.”

“We have no idea who will attack at any moment and who’s supposed to protect us,” said Bobby Johns, a 50-year-old BART conductor and father of two who was hurled over a panini stand by the blast. “If SF fire and PD cannot protect us then send in the military, it’s as simple as that.”

Several smaller bombings elsewhere in the Bay Area over the last 2 weeks have killed at least 18 civilians and wounded 23, according to medics and police officials. All officials spoke on the condition of anonymity because they were not authorized to speak to reporters.

The Governor of California and the President of the United States condemned the attacks.

Separately, the FBI announced digital surveillance of Caliph8, the infamous jihadi propagandist, has been put on indefinite hold as the digital ping to his online activity has been lost, without providing further details.

-Ten Months Earlier-

I certify under penalty of perjury under the laws of America that the foregoing is true and correct…

Taking the approach that I can dress as I please, my look and style today could be called raw but glamorous. I am wearing a snake-print shirt, a stretch-leather jacket, boot jeans, Prada shoes. To sum it up, it is international and of the moment. It all fits very well and the style endures.

Laugh at inappropriate times.

With each waking morning, the reinstated potency, I undertake a semblance of normalcy. Away from the pornographic imagery, away from the varying positions, away from fashion photography, away from wounded phantasm. Within moments from arising, I attempt to suppress this debauched parade of cerebral facsimiles.

Usually it overcomes me and has the better with me. I am left succumbing to all of its sweet trappings, deviating from undistorted focus. I am a victim, victimized by libido, dichotomies, incident and chance. Taken by the evils of carousal, indulgence, debauchery and luxury, I attempt advancement, full passing an outcome, ending in self-savagery. Beyond the delirium of women, flesh, stockings, retail, arriving at a calm place, free of the confines of the aforementioned. Liberated to paint a clean picture from a blank canvass, to follow a pure thread of thought, a pristine wilderness realized and an unpolluted stream of unconsciousness.

I sit here now in a state of composure, I am on the clock, and nails are filed, peering at the office women, cooking the illusion. Paid to undress women in my mind. On payroll to defecate and masturbate. Free office supplies, new Bics with each day.

The money produced covers superfluous costs, the most minimal of overheads, such as rent, transportation, cheap packaged food. The other money pays for fine clothing, seduction and vice—both physical and mental. Widespread intellectual corruption is the main preoccupation, which is always free. I venture to wipe clean my introspection and sustain it throughout the day.

The temp business's appeal: it is a perpetual state of displacement, a continual state of flux, I am bound by no one, nothing, and I play by no one's rules. I come and go as I please. I am afforded an invaluable liberty in a stifling age. The humdrum for others is transient movement for me. It can happen that I don't like an assignment, and I make one call and I am gone from there forever, the next day working elsewhere—new location, different supply closet, new break room rules and new women. There is nothing more invigorating than a new workplace—it alters all perceptions exorbitantly. Life theory: an individual human existence should be like a waterway, at first insignificant, narrowly contained within its shores, rushing passionately past boulders and over waterfalls, gradually the waterway expands, widens, the shoreline recedes, the water flows more quietly, and, in the end, without any visible break, the waterway becomes one with the high seas, and painlessly loses its unique essence.

Correspondence in transit. A piece of mail—a letter, junk ads, an invoice, a magazine—is mailed from an unknown place and put through the circuitry until it reaches the receiver's hands. It is then habitually discarded. This constant perpetuity is prophylactic, a continuum of ideas, sales, discounts, flash and rebate, offers—another epitome of consumerism's glory. Receiving mail makes me feel alive: somewhere someone is under the assumption that I am a participating player and my demographics warrant their correspondence, hence this excerpted letter: *I'm an airline stewardess looking for sexy fun, travel, and a little extra pocket money. I do phone sex for free. For a gift of $10 or more I will write you a truly personal letter (not Xeroxed), send you sexy color photos, and really get into your hottest fantasies with you. I'm really wet for you. Please write me soon.*

The thrill of eavesdropping…a quick departure from the tedium…slow thoughts of hope that some woman somewhere will speak of her sex life, or lack thereof…she may hint in passing how she doesn't get enough, or about the *fuck boy* she picked up over the weekend…she may allude to a neglectful husband, or generic dissatisfaction with a lover of the same sex…she may go into detail about an exploit or reveal her heartbreak when talking of an ex…most is allusion and illusion, either the facts are masked or the reality bent, regardless, it is all very good…the process of the process, her allusions inspiring my illusions…this goes on incessantly, coming full circle recurrently.

As for real women, they run the full gamut of expenditure, sexiness, intellectualism, ethnicities, silhouettes and hues. For this puts them beyond categorization—the reason I am perpetually drawn on, never tiring of their presence, manipulation or charm...except when foul odors are present. Their assortment is more rousing than morning sunlight, than religious moments, than escape into film, than drunken debauchery, at times even the release of orgasm—nothing more entrancing, more engaging and ongoing as the women and all of their accessories. Mocking terminology, they still are my subject, however feeble my exertions, when I note my failing muse, energy, heartache, surrender, desire, motive and hope. A journal of worship. A ledger of appreciation. The annals of devotion.

My inspiration exists in the clamor of public places. The spectrum of things which appear: public dress, the gamut of emotions, multi cultures and multi races, street failure, street victory, whispered revelation, hushed gossip and blinking eye secrecy. The air is afire, unseen charges about the crowded room; the light is dull and buzzing. Telephones ring amid the chatter of voices. Women parading abound. The attitude and ambition on their sleeves. Unwilling to pause momentarily. *Hey, stop and smell this.* Unknowing of their own seduction's prowess. The sexiness when they are oblivious to their own charms. Those work outfits. The business suits in dark blue, somber grays and funeral black. The faux leather high heels, but never too high. Try to avoid the slutty look, it does nobody any favors. The panty lines then the attempted imagery of the panties, and their form and texture and fabric and color and levels of cleanliness. Are these out of the fresh laundry or have you worn them for days. All of this and more. To sit surrounded by such abundance, allowing the evolution, the cultivation, I may not see you again, this may be the last stare, will you miss me—all to start up again the next morning.

Maddening.

Irritating.

Renewed vigor.

Rest for my exhaustion.

One could detect the slightest of residual lust, simultaneously sensing the reverberations which drag me into the streets. The city of fog: comfort in the cool breeze, the tremors under foot, the traffic ever congested, inhaling generic smoke, gasping for the possibility of a voluptuous moment, all blurred into the intangible blue of the deepest night (imagine this peculiar craving in its uncanny details and hideous continuity). I hope the photo (included in this letter) may restore some exuberance within you. What I really like about this picture is not only the possibility of her having a shaved muff (which is definitely possible) rather how solemn and sober she seems to debauch in those sweet torments of bondage.

These are my aesthetics.

Infinite shine.

The new minimal.

La vie en rose.

From: caliph8@sharia4ever.org

Hi friend! I know you don't know me but can we make acquaintance here? This is not a virus. I am safe to open. I am here for you as much as you are here for me. I want to share with you my religion, Islam. And to let you know that if we stick closely to the Straight Path that Allah has created to protect us from slipping and from losing our way then we will be rewarded tenfold. Every human being is required to follow this final message of Islam and leave all other paths. Everything else is just an ancient religion that has been corrupted or canceled with misleading ideologies and philosophies. You see, there is the path of decadence that most go down, and their negligence is hypocrisy. These non-followers are painfully conscious of the void and it is not through their faultings. The West is so sore and raw. It is hard to exist here. Write me back if you want to make friendship and to learn more...

With warm regards,
Caliph8

The fashion magazine and lingerie catalog thing, based in glazed aesthetics…not the sexual gloating, rather the shapes, the lighting, the colors, the manipulations, the staging crew, all enticing me in…the girls become more and more exotic, erotic, opposite and foreign as a species, bordering on madness…to see the magazine in its entirety and all that it embodies—the ads, the articles, the advertorials, the sweet smelling perfume tear-outs—is to condense the current state of women: the advertising of their own goods, and the chatter ranging from pap smears to 12 steps of getting Mr. Right off…trashy and recurrently unsexy—something for a cross-dressing step-father, something foreign made…spending the budget on one top model for the cover…photos meant to seduce the working man, relying less on good judgment by a burnout photographer…the emphasis put on padding breasts and good angling

A few seconds past two-thirty-seven on a sizzling afternoon.

She just left. Was wearing the ivory wool barathea dress from Thursday. Hair was pulled back, brown tortoise sunglasses. Smoking three cigarettes in the forty-three minutes she was seated. Along with her unattractive girlfriend (borderline DUFF) she got up—flirting like she always does—and flashed me a wink from behind those knock off designer eye frames, all the while passing within a foot. She was on her way to class—it starts at thirty after the hour (she likes to be late).

I am left playing with a spent wet lemon tea bag.

Sets in 60 seconds for all-day wear.

Eyes should show mischief not your age.

Sharia4Ever Mission Statement

The worldview of Sharia4Ever forms the basis of its ideology as follows:

1: Muslims are under attack by everyone.

2: Sharia4Ever and its followers are fighting the oppressors of Islam.

3: If you are not supporting Sharia4Ever, then you are supporting the oppressors.

Sharia4Ever sees its mission to be the vanguard of the uprising of the oppressed.

Sharia4Ever knows it cannot achieve these goals by itself, so it needs to inspire the masses with an uplifting message intended to create a revolution. Jihad is war. It is an obligatory act for all Muslims. Permission from parents or other relatives is not required if the jihadist is of an age

of understanding. The aim of jihad is to achieve Muslim dominance and total sharia forever. Armed jihad is the highest form of jihad and should be undertaken against all enemies of Islam, including the infidels, polytheists, fornicators, as well as those who support them. The bayat is a pledge of obedience given to the Emir, the leader of a group. The bayat to the leader of the group is the same that one would give to the Prophet Mohammed. Once a bayat is given, it cannot be broken. Anyone who breaks the pledge is guilty of an exceptionally grave sin. One who does so is not only guilty of sin, but then becomes a kafir (non-believer) as well. If you have not made a bayat, you can be considered less pious and less Muslim than those who have. Daru Islam or an 'Islamic state' mandates that in order to establish the religion, it is first necessary to establish an Islamic state, which, in turn, will then lead to the re-establishment of the Caliphate (Khilafah Islamiyah). It is obligatory for all Muslims to contribute both financially and physically to this end. Sharia4Ever strongly advocates becoming a shaheed or 'martyr' by the act of suicide bombing. This istimate (suicide act) is part of the hirja or "migration to God." You will be rewarded in heaven for this action. Sharia4Ever volunteers should leave their homes, properties, jobs and families for the sake of God. You do not need permission from your families to do this. We also advocate that you should disregard the needs of your parents, wives and children for the sake of the struggle. You should migrate (Hijrah) from worldly inclinations to heavenly goals. You can achieve this and obtain beautiful virgins through suicide bombings. Sharia4Ever wants sharia in the economy, in the politics, in the judicial systems, in the borders and in foreign relations...and when do we want it, we wanted it yesterday!

"The best jihad is the one in which your horse is slain and your blood is spilled..." - Caliph8

Be your own modern classic: the statue of her begins with the rouge painted toe nails…the small nails, the small toes, crooked and soft…the curved feet, callused and tender…her strong heels, statuesque in their base formation of those calves…like antique neo-classical furniture legs, those calves take the completed feminine shape, imposingly bleeding into the knee, with its two sides: the beaten and stone-like front with a baby fist-sized cap, and the yielding, supple, hyper-sensitive backside, unwrinkled and unfrayed…the upper-legs enlarging, fatter from knee on up…the femininity taking figure, the four sides of her lower body competing for the splendor: the sides, the thighs, magical in their ability to expand, swell, take on the most feminine of formations; the backside, the ass, those full cheeks, broad and padded in their glory—like a budding yellow daisy, small and concealed, growing to expansion, bending to expose; or the anatomy of survival, the birthplace, the shrine, in the wake of her baptism: the womanhood standing alone, encased by the oval-shape facade spared the obligation of homogenizing itself fluidly with the rest of the body, allowed to be as foreign and obscured as it wills; or, like tranquil lagoons, rising and fading with the tide; the front side, a woman's truest asset and attribute, shielded by a jet black fleece, expensive silk, a temple in a jungle, the jewels crowned…the inward turn of her hips to her paunch, the muscles of the lower-back, the small part, an arid and mysterious desert…the softness of her tummy, the belly button, the small hair, the tight pores…the narrowing ascent to the bosom, the under hang of her breasts, the outward dangle of hardness and texture—overcoming contour by the rosy-tinted nipples…like untouched mountain tops…the depth of her cleavage, voluminous and endowed, encased in blue veins, glands of life, bags of thrill…the trail to her pronounced neck, the rigid collarbone, an outline in the flesh, grids on a canvass, carpet-laden sand dunes, forming her shoulders…the long arms, elegant dizzying railways, the skin and bones relaxed, hanging, dangling like earrings from a lobe…the dignity in her finger bones, the refinement in the nails like freshly-groomed flower beds…the fingertips, willowy as an unhurried insect's moving legs… her elongated neck, that delicate jaw-line…the instrumental outline of the ears…the topography of an oasis and the elevated full lips…her mouth, a brightly painted red boat, bobbing at its mooring, ready to sink if commanded…her face framed under that unruffled hair, the sum and theme of chamber music, the hygiene of her sustenance…the aloft bone structure and the piercing luminescence…the high of black brows, her nose, the nostrils as the artist's final touch…the revelation in her forehead, the hint of a widow's peak…her eyes gleaming as the sun shines off a mirror…her after-dark charms, intoxicating like bottomless carafes of red wine…the cool breeze of her virtuosity, her fervency nearly tangible, her verve almost attainable…she is the doorway between befitting and improper…the curves formed like shadows in fall…inlets along a coastline…when walking, swaying in tango spirit.

Around four-thirty in the afternoon.

Knowing she wants me but she can't stop staring. W*hy* does she perseveringly glance over at me (like I haven't noticed) and play it off as if she is looking—or waiting—for someone that, like a ghost, lingers somewhere beyond me. Girls! That's why I love them so: they think they are so sneaky; they think I don't know what they are up to; they hide behind their sunglasses, as if I can't see them. Nuts—they're all nuts!

Today she is wearing a chiffon dress that travels down her legs, but, of course, she has the slit of the side going up her front side instead of her thigh, exposing myself (she thinks that I will be turned on by her frivolous, girly tricks) to those long, brown legs, the tan never breaks, the edge of white cotton panties, an odd combination for sure with such an evening gown. She pretends to read a book (she knows that I like smart women, so she has taken it upon herself to entertain my desires). I cannot see the cover, but I am sure it is chick lit; women like this—I know them—they are into that sex-talk literature. She is fingering the tea bag in the paper cup, metaphorically paying homage to the little man in the canoe.

My tea is cold and I make my last note to surveil.
Feel naked yet covered in perfection.
Free the fantasy.
Let your you shine through.

From: caliph8@sharia4ever.org

Hi friend. I am an Arab because I believe in God and not in matter. I sanctify the prophets and my strength is the basis of our existence. I have a human mission which calls for the good of all, for social justice, and mutual help among the classes. I am here for you my friend. I will advance and I will take the hand of anybody who wants to advance with me. I maintain a bond with my past and with my traditions. I honor the heritage of our fathers. It is our duty to guard it so it can be passed along, whole and pure. We must believe in the eternity. Because the foundation of these values is true. They are beautiful and good, my friend. In these attributes there is something of God. We must not adhere to the view outside of our horizon. Such views can shatter our existence, and injure everything that is sacred to us. It is of us and we are of it. Are you with me?

Daily lesson for female knowledge. Behind the fast-food bag, I see her pick the pickles off the juicy meat. She can't keep herself from playing these little sexual games with me. Again—and I don't know how many times today—she is sucking on that straw as if it were a plastic replica of my penis. The off-red lipstick from her naturally brown lips remains on the clear plastic, encircling the small orifice, my metaphorical corn hole. Brown drops from diet coke procrastinate on the inner edges. While she eats I pretend to look away—but, in reality, I am only watching her watch me, back and forth. Under the table I see up the short skirt she is wearing (whenever she wants to provoke me she simply uncrosses her legs, slowly, deliberately, pausing for effect, then crosses them again: only exposing to me her white panties, cotton indeed). Crumbling the paper wrappers slowly and neatly into little balls, she deposits the waste into the trash can next to me (there is a reason I sit here and not somewhere else).

Through the side window, I see her get into her car—continuing the flashing but this time only upper legs—then teasing me once again: the lipstick, this time bright red, she slowly applies and, flirtatiously, she smacks her lips to me through the rearview mirror.

Won't kiss off on your teeth, your glass, or him.

Warmer, more sensational for every skin tone.

I last see the car at the corner; the time is 12:52.

From: caliph8@sharia4ever.org
Hi friend! How have you been? Me, I been ok. I am a little down, been thinking too much on the endless occupation of our sacred lands by the great USA. Twenty years of control over the holiest of territories, that which is Arabia. The grand plundering of its riches, the puppet government, the humiliation of its people, the threatening of its neighbors, and using its bases to fight against our brothers. The continuous aggression against Iraq, Syria, Palestine, and Yemen. All of this at the hands of the biggest super power and the crusader Jewish alliance. So much destruction inflicted. Anyway, enough about me. Write me soon, let me know you're alive! LOL Bye.

Reluctant to go to the street corner and buy the newspaper, but today she is walking her dog so I make like no big deal and just do it. Her magenta hair is pulled straight up, smooth legs *just* shaven, mediocre tropical breasts with hard nipples, her butt round and protruding at times (hidden well by an extra-large denim shirt). The jungle lips are what get me. Those damn lips...I have never seen such things. What wonderful things lips like that can do. While she walks by I ask her if she has change for a one dollar bill and she tells me to hold on a second while she goes into the café which we are in front of. She gets the change for me (I hold onto the dog's leash while she goes in).

"Tricky won't bite, she's a good little girl, aren't you sweetie?"

One good turn deserves another.

I thank her and hand her a dollar bill with my phone number written on it with a red sharpie—she didn't see it—and I hand back the leash; she slowly strokes my fingertips with hers. It won't matter if she calls: *Tricky—if found please contact: Sophia, -2000 Jones Rd. #13, 456-7832.*

The new laws of lips.

Become inspiration.

Mind over muscle.

Lizzy was being a naughty minimum wage girl today. Usually she makes my cappuccinos with an extra shot of espresso; today she didn't. I know this fit of refusal and deprivation is because of the lingering jealousy from the other day when she didn't get to make it for me. It doesn't really matter, because the complaint card to the manager clearly explains the problems that inherently arise when the help fucks with the customer. I hope Lizzy learns her lesson: *jealousy ends with no winners.*

Will you bring me your chastity in a black cup…will you let me go down on you right here and now, clean or dirty, ready or not…will you stop time just to let me go again…will you take it from behind just to please me…will you wear those ankle-length stockings and that panty girdle…will you take off your undergarments, slowly and gingerly, just after you have soiled yourself, under the restaurant table, then pass them to my jacket pocket…will we do it standing up, in an alleyway, offering a dancing silhouette to the occasional passerby and the dumpster lifestyle set…the sequence of the procedure, the procedure of the sequence.

Appropriately, the newspaper is a week old and the black guy doesn't understand a word I say when I ask him if his newspaper is from today or not. Lint is everywhere and I am forced to run the clothes a second time through the dryer because she has yet to arrive. On the fourth try, the change machine accepts the dollar bill. I find a copy of Vogue, the cover is gone, and I begin leafing through the wrinkled pages as she walks in.

Exactly seven twenty-one, three minutes after her median time. She smiles an infantile smile, flashing those white cap teeth. So white it seems unnatural in a natural way. I watch her put the soiled clothes into the machine. At the bottom of the pile are her panties in a blue net mesh bag. She is quick to move them and she innocently hides a blush of embarrassment. White, purple, red, and even green—each pair a different design and cut and maker. Tempted to approach her while she fumbles with the panties and confuse her and maybe get off with a pair without her knowing it. But I don't.

The best ammunition against her is to simply enjoy her.

Expect a change, love the transformation.

Bring on tomorrow, start tonight.

She takes a seat across from me—positioning herself directly ahead, allowing me a view up the baggy sides of her dolphin shorts. (How dirty are her panties?) She leafs through her own copy of a fashion magazine and I hide my growing erection with my copy of Vogue. The black guy hums a melody and the girl smiles cordially. I see drops of sweat in her Lululemon cleavage.

I ask her if she would ever really wear any of the crazy fashion that is in these magazines and she tells me of course not, but that she likes looking at the beautiful girls and to dream of being so beautiful and I tell her that, frankly, she is actually more beautiful than any of the girls in those magazines. Blushing, she tells me that that's very nice and my mother must have taught me good manners, but that really she was not that beautiful. She continues by revealing to me her stomach—lifting her athleisure shirt—pinching a little flab and asking me if supermodels really have that kind of fat and I lean forward and touch her skin and gently pinch for myself. (I note she likes to be touched—that she *needs* to be touched.)

I fold my laundry and watch her watch me. She informs me that it is Saturday night—as if I didn't know that—and if I would like to, maybe, "I don't usually do this," go up to her apartment, we could open some champagne or wine or something...

...I pour my flute full of bubbly into her cleavage and then lick the fizzle from each nipple…slowly…one...at...a...time. Her hard body—toned with incredible thigh muscles (where they are most needed on a woman)—was too much at times.

I left my address on the bathroom mirror in black eyeliner pencil.

All girls have dreams, which is why I want to make sure each and every one of them has my number.

New ways to blend in.

Savor the simplicity.

Get with the brogram.

At the beach. The girls are always up for flashing me some of their bush. When they get hot...*real hot*...that's when they start playing the mind games. Why the girls just don't come up to me and approach the awkward inevitableness...it would make life a lot easier.

She is precisely on time. The coffee, the fashion section from the Sunday paper, the small backpack (lipstick, tanning oil, light cigarettes, half-liter bottle of water, emergency tampon). Kicks off her flip flops and places herself twenty feet from myself. White hotel towel spread out, she pulls off the cutoffs. Underneath she wears the same black bikini bottoms as each Sunday. Smiles my way, an invitation. Shrug an indifferent smile in return. Rubbing the tropical oil on her belly she provokes. I rub the oil evenly around her stomach, starting with the little puddle in her belly button, from there I playfully study each hair that scarcely blankets her brown skin. She gets excited and playfully runs her left hand through my hair and I tell her to stop.

A full-page advertisement for a grand opening of a large department store covers the final page of the fashion section. Can't see her right now, she is hiding behind the paper. She wants me too badly and regrettably for her she accepts the reality that all I am to her is a fantasy which will never become fact.

I rise to go to the snack shack on the boardwalk. I torture her with the question, would you be so kind as to look after my bag while I get an iced tea? She tells me *of course*, that it would be her *pleasure*. Two children are playing in the shallow water of the shore, I am sipping on my iced tea and, with squinted eyes I see her write a telephone number on the back of a receipt. I play busy, checking my email.

From: caliph8@sharia4ever.org

You see, in the year 20 of the Muslim era, Caliph Umar decreed that Jews and Christians should be removed from all of Arabia. Our Prophet uttered on his deathbed "Let there not be two religions in Arabia." This my friend is why we have been tasked with the fulfillment of this injunction. I found a picture of you my friend online.

Handsome devil LOL. If that is you I suppose, prove it with something more. #inshallah

Are you 2 legit 2 quit? Wanted: male, any age, any race, for two girls who just want to have fun, less talk, more action—sexually clean, UB2, call box 3SKIN.

I call from the pay phone and am charged seventy-five cents for the first minute. The two voices sound very effeminate. First girl is a secretary, second is a junior college student.

They tell me to leave the best message I can and if I am the lucky boy, then they will call me.

You have reached a recording, you know what to do.

Coffee is cold and weak on caffeine and I light a cigarette. Stevia is spilled over the counter and with my ring finger I draw a vagina in the sweet white sand. The red plastic stirrer is tied into a knot and plays the role of the cherry. A virgin's cherry, or course. An ash from the cigarette abstractly, regrettably, fills in for pubic hair. Perhaps this is what they call mixed media. Checking my pockets for belongings, I leave my art for the next patron(s).

I slip the note under her windshield wiper. In a white envelope. Much like a parking ticket. Oh how her mood will change when she sees what's really inside:

And you keep giving and giving and I just want to give into you, hold you hard and still and close, warmth on skin and pressed under me, and let you move yourself up against me while I give myself to you through fainted breath and love strokes, and I feel your slow turning pain and welcome the tears as they fall down your face which cleanses me for the ritual when I am kneeling down in front of you, you my shrine, you my temple, you my pilgrimage, you my holy place, as you flood my garden with your daylight and I downpour your back with my tidal wave of you know what and the flowers that bloom they bloom for you and they are yours alone to smell and they are so fragrant, you keep leaving me disheveled, tossed, trampled, trodden, doused into the flames, bleeding from the inside, your snake oil heals me, and I see there is a future time and it is nearly perfect for me and I think you will be very happy there...all this consuming has made me tumble toward the cellar door, and I ask to have the ambulances bring me in because I am undernourished and the soundtrack that plays is just violins, and like a lonely child I try to unlock the door, and map out this new geography and these new longings, with my x-ray vision I see through your heart and I ditch the magnifying glass then I realize what I really want is to colonize you, lay claim to your wonderland but then I want to spill your drink on me, then kiss my lips and break my heart, lick off your lipstick and sugar cane textures, and before you abandon ship that you let me know it is sinking, all we ever do is wait and in the waiting is the suspense and in the suspense is the survival and the thrill, particularly when you run with me and your hair is blowing backwards while your lips are pushing outward from the smile across your face, when you light me up and the image of you is burned into my retinas so that when I close my eyes you are still there, it is then that I wish I could unravel it all for you and you could take shelter within me, from the outbreak and the fumes, I am a man who has not laid down in days, and my reckless heart is shaped like a parachute to guide you to a soft landing, then stumble like pirates who have captured the lighthouse.

Women are tricks by sleight of hand, which are to admire and we should not understand. Everybody has a secret that they keep. Mine is going through garbage while other people sleep. I will find them if it's the last thing I do. I have to have them—she is too fine to let those beautiful things go to waste.

I get up every day, walking often, enjoying enjoyment, seeking meanings, touching people, daydreaming, believing, laughing, dancing frequently, resting comfortably, looking to see, traveling somewhere, and waiting till the day breaks. Look for me, I am among you. A genuine American flavor.

How to reach perfection. Why be yourself when you can be somebody else? Transform your race, tits, ass, nose, biceps, sex organs and everything else. I like the way she is, more than the way she was. I like her because she doesn't crowd my way of doing things. I like to think that I am free to take life one day at a time. When I start sweating in the sun I just wet myself down. So*, how was the head? Like a vacuum, you say.* We are sensitive to manipulation. Whether it's advertisers or just a pretty girl. When was the last time you saw anything so authentic look so good. *Instinct over intellect.* When you really care about a woman, you inevitably end up putting your hands on her and messing with her because you have ambitions for her. But, the real shit happens when you don't mess with her—when she just comes. Fiction needs friction. Remember the immediacy of now. It's not enough to win; you have to look good winning too. *Humor is the evidence of freedom.* Fear of the devil leads to devil worship, but if you mock the devil, he will run. There is myth and there is mystery. Celebrate uncertainty. This society, trapped in a perpetual present, so preoccupied with irrelevancies and missing the fundamentals. I could feel the wind in my toe hair. For women, masturbation is an act of defiance; for men, a sign of failure. *The magic of a kiss.*

Seduced on the cordless telephone by an anonymous woman.

I am wearing a double-breasted four-button wool-and-silk suit, viscose-and-acetate shirt, and a skinny rockabilly tie (black with hints of smoked gray).

The telephone rang, I answered, and her overture was so immediate and blunt that I was either going to succumb or hang up. I poured myself a cold non-European beer from the Viking stainless steel refrigerator. She described herself for me, word by word, inflection by inflection, moan by moan, whimper by whimper, sentence by sentence—like a slow and patient stripper revealing herself thread by thread: her blond hair, her black roots, her natural breasts, her shriveled and dark nipples, her awkward legs, her *peculiar* (her word) eyes (though this self-portrait may have been entirely fiction, like the adult entertainer's stage name...I was hard nonethesame). After her verbal rundown she asked if I was alright and I told her sure and lit a cigarette.

Who says you can't have it all.

Emit an aura of attraction and success.

The genius of a new luxury.

The girls encountered in my wild wanderings have been reluctant to reveal all the things about them I would like to know, even *not know*, to be *alluded to* or *misguided toward*, directed down the wrong path, *happy to get lost.* The type of girl which impresses me the most, the one I find myself liking more and more, is the girly type. No sight encountered in public is quite so stirring as her ways.

No sight is quite so impressive as that of the Girl walking across a room with Her gestures so feminine, so youthful, so naïve, so nonchalant, so nymph-like, so full of girly spirit. *She* is a dignity and a power matched by no other female. Her demographic the most desirable. To share Her presence for just a short while is a privilege and an adventure like no other.

I have followed Her tracks into an exalted hell, purely to see what She had been doing, and come to the abrupt end of the footprints when the Girl would turn to me with a sudden gesture. To see a Girl wandering and lounging with a cigarette in one hand, a cup of coffee in the other, a thin silk camisole strewn across Her bosom, a red or pink flower upon the unsteady table for which She sits, a waggling naked leg crossed over at the knee, is to see life at its optimum.

The Girl's association with other females is a mixture of enterprising action, an almost magnanimous acceptance, and just plain willingness to ignore. There is a great strength and pride combined with a strong mixture of inquisitive curiosity in the make-up of the girly character. This curiosity is what makes trouble when men penetrate into the realm where they are not known to the Girl. The Girl can be brave and sometimes downright brazen. She can be secretive and very retiring. She can be extremely cunning and also powerfully aggressive. Whatever She does, Her actions match Her surroundings and the circumstance of the moment.

It is no wondering that when meeting Her in this realm it is a momentous event, imprinted upon one's mind for life. Like a study into prehistoric gender roles and attributes.

(It's a whole new game since red has returned to beauty's fore.)

Sun is hot on facial skin; I feel my enlarged pores closing and tightening. My rosacea becomes flush and accentuates...the vitamin D nature's invisible ointment for my ails.

She is coming on to me in direct and indirect manners. A smoke screen of confusion, I do not know where to cross over. She is *accidentally* kicking my leg under the table. It is becoming *difficult* to be with her while she pulls this mundane psychological and physical torture without having sexual fantasies permeate my mind and bloodstream. Wonder what she's like in bed? Wonder what she tastes like clean? What she tastes like dirty? What she tastes like at different times of the month? Salty, alkaline? What her skin looks like down there, close up, with enough light on it?

Am I sexy? I ask myself.

I am wearing a six-button wool-and-nylon coat, zippered mohair sweater, wool trousers and lace-up camel brown leather boots.

I ask her if jealousy is an issue in her relationship. She asks me "what relationship?" I say: So you don't have a boyfriend and she says no. She asks me if distance in a relationship helps keep it fresh and I tell her definitely. We both laugh. I tell her that the most important part is companionship and she disagrees, telling me that disagreements are the most important part. She kicks off her knock off Louboutins and adjusts her lavender Maidenform push-up bra.

Ask her for her worst butt fear; tells me that she has no fears, that she loves her big butt. Tell her it's not so big and she shrugs saying that if she had a butt fear that it would be too many dimples. Asks me what I think makes a good butt and I tell her that a nice roundness is always a prerequisite and that it needs to stick out a bit, have its own profile, more African than Asian, the opposite of a young boy's.

She is intensely feminine and an instinctive exhibitionist is proud of her body and feels that it was made to be seen and admired and shared, at least visually. Understands that seduction is an art, not a physical assault. If approached the right way, the one true way, she will find it very easy to say *yes*—and that means yes to anything, and everything, if you know what I mean, because she can go for bizarre lovemaking.

Has unusual control of her vaginal muscles. Has unusual vaginal muscles, as well. She can constrict to hold me fast, or loosen me at her pleasure. She can bring me to climax without using any other muscle in her body. I have a certain affinity for this woman—she is dressed well and her hair is long. Her clothes look as though they are easily removable—I find her very hard to ignore. And very hard to forget when I am not in her presence. She tells me that she is “inquisitive, searching and experimental," that "eroticism consists of more than the physical act of lovemaking." I have an erection and light a menthol cigarette. Offering her one, imaginations and mental imagery run wild and amuck.

She tells me that she may look like a prim and proper, even dashing, young lady, but that she dresses like, and behaves like, a wanton and somewhat wild whore in the bedroom. Ask her what she means and she tells me that she likes to wear the sheerest of panties, that color or shade does not matter, as long as her female parts can be distinguished at a distance, i.e. her landing strip of pubic hair, or the dolphin tattoo, or her refined labia majora. Or she may wear a pair of French cut panties which is open at the crotch, commonly referred to as crotch-less—as risqué as that sounds she says that they can be found in any mall lingerie shop. "I never take no for an answer," she informs me. Even if sex is not on our itinerary, moves can still be made, evocative advances pondered. Her powers of suggestion: a sexiness which is confident and poised mingled with an almost hidden sensuality and edge-of-your-seat guile. A covert sex appeal. Doesn't reveal much of her breasts or her bottom. Her cleavage or lack thereof a mystery. Her ass crack and its dimples and ridges and convex symmetry unknown. Her sensuality is conveyed by the movements of her hand; her nuances with the words she chooses not to use; her looks at things...and looks at you.

The art of being unique.
The art of essence.
Make it your signature.
What's sexy now.

From: caliph8@sharia4ever.org

Hi friend. I still haven't heard back from you, but I am sure a popular guy like you is extremely busy. It is my hope that you are reading this so I shall continue.
Because of the caliphs the community of Medina, where the Prophet did his thing, grew into a vast empire, and Islam grew to be a global religion. Religious truth sanctified political power and political power sanctified religious truth. Islam is politics or it is nothing. God is concerned with the political realm. This is confirmed with Sharia law. The absolute authority, acquirer of power,

exerciser of legitimacy. Forget the USA constitution. That is the child's play. Sharia forever my friend. #inshallah

Sex is a rounded experience, something tangible and memorable, not merely a quick tumble between the 1,400 thread count sheets. A silk jersey taffeta halter dress with tulle and horsehair trim. Off-black garter thigh highs.

Kinky side and a tendency toward voyeurism and other acts of passive surveillance. Get pleasure from watching other couples have sex, straight or lesbian only. Often strategically place a large mirror at the proper angle to watch my own lovemaking; usually she is in the cowboy position on top. Even tape record bed sessions with a small dictation audio recorder. Love being in the center of a ménage-a-trois. The last man on earth fantasy. The drive borders on obsession. The urge exists on the margins of fixation. Similar to when your heart is set on European time.

Lives to the fullest, and she is slightly chancy. She has a surplus of high spirits. Modernity on display. Telling her fantasies could get one hot. Bothered, even. Enjoys biting and sucking, a self-proclaimed master of any and all oral sex. Inflicting delicate pain turns her on. During foreplay may pinch one's nipples, or the inside of one's thighs. Never hard enough to cause swelling or bruising. No need for a secret password or safe word. Another technique is to meet one coming from the hot tub, then have one take her and press her warm naked back against the cool wall tiles and enter her, unprotected, standing up. She is a water sign, after all. Which explains her desire to help others. Says that she has a special trick to make men go absolutely freaky: inserting her nipple into the opening of the penis. Her real specialty though, she tells me, is the "wink job."

Light a cigarette.

That is when, continuing, she puts on artificial eyelashes. And then runs her blinking eyelids up and down the shaft of the penis until the man reaches orgasm. Asks me if I have ever done that and I tell her no. The Andre brut champagne is room temperature and I ask her if she would like a refill.

Prefer a variety of foreplay acts before getting right down to the whiskers. See a girl through to climax. A woman that knows what she wants can make a man do anything—and everything. If, for example, she was to suggest a ménage-a-trois one night, any man would be happy to join in. Would make sure everyone reaches climax twice—once orally and once genitally. One's only warning to leave such a heavenly and divine situation is when one crazy fuck would bring out the matches. Know how sadistic women can get: *they don't like to be denied.*

Very near is a girl; thought to maybe wake her up by the smell of burning hair. Last night she liked playing out some of the sexual acrobatics she saw on youporn. Fantasies coincided with mine—the action became torrid. Scorched earth. Set the scene like a play: proper lighting with the light meter, musky perfume, black silk underwear, various sized and shaped vibrators in skin hues of brown and pink—whatever would suit her tastes. At least tonight. Because there is only tonight.

Will take the lead on lovemaking and become impatient if I do not get a swift response. Indifferent to sexual restrictions, both moral and legal; prefer an experienced partner with a tremendous craving for sexual activity and goings-on. Like to be slowly and admiringly undressed by a woman. Like sex in a chair, a large chair with plush upholstery, with the woman sitting astride my lap facing me, a side cowgirl if you will. Most fantasies revolve around a dominant woman who makes excessive and unreasonable demands, with my vanity attempting to satisfy her. Become addicted to anything that will give pleasure, diversion and release. Lengthy and luxurious oral sex. Enjoy the sensual comforts of life—food, music, wine; like to pour a few drops of Jesus juice on her bare skin and lick it off slowly.

The Guatemalan coffee is too hot to drink and, when she asks me to enter her, she rests her head on the floor, lying face down, and she raises her legs into the wheelbarrow position and I enter her from behind, as I hold all 130 pounds of her. She tells me that she likes it when the blood rushes to her head, that it is good for her complexion. While smoking the day's first cigarette, she tells me that she loves positions where her buttocks are exposed. To feel the ambient room air down there, to feel the slight forced breeze from the air ducts in the ceiling. Will go almost to the point of orgasm, withdraw, allow her to fellate me, and still hold off until she is ready to scream...I believe this is called edging. Even if the scream is well-acted I do not pay her mind. An expert at clitoral manipulation with fingers; an exquisite, sensitive touch; like to initiate women into the true mysteries of sex and Far East thought and practice.

But, then again, it remains to be seen.

Be your own modern classic.

She makes me kneel for my meal.

I check the light switches, water faucets, the stove, the door locks, and the emergency brake. Counting, arranging, evening-up behaviors, making sure that socks are at the same height. Often I collect useless objects and inspect the garbage before it is thrown out. Rarely do I repeat routine actions—such as: in and out of a chair, going through a doorway twice, re-lighting cigarettes, all until it feels just right. Once in a while, I will unnecessarily re-read or re-write letters, as well as re-open envelopes before I mail them. In the shower, I *do* examine my body for signs of illness. A lump here and subcutaneous pain there. Often inappropriate or taboo sexual thoughts overcome me like the fear of groping a coworker or being gay for a night. Dissect all relationships, friends, lovers, strangers, family members, dwelling on them, alienating them with unbecoming comments and dealing with the uncertainty. Sometimes I feel a need to confess and ask for consolation that what I say or do is correct and proper. Seeking out reassurance to further enable and justify my obsessions. It is all about the consequences if I were to stop.

I have heard of people who avoid colors like red, because it means blood, numbers like 13, because it is unlucky, and even names which started with, say D, because is signified death. And there are those that "preen," the painful behaviors that must be done, like cuticle biting, picking at sores, pulling hair, clearing off dry skin.

From: caliph8@sharia4ever.org

It is all about the Arab Awakening baby. We are done with the spiritual stagnation that has paralyzed the Arab spirit since the last classical Arab age. This current shake up started on 9/11 and may last 400 years. Yes, that is right. Long term squad goals my friend. We have been directed to turn our attention inward, toward our hearts for inner peace. Our quest for meaning is an act of liberation and calls into question all forms of alienation. Western society addresses their deficiencies by maintaining a culture of fear and insecurity. Got to go, talk soon! #inshallah

Her smell is something I will not soon forget.

When she entered a room—any room, any size—I knew it was her, without even seeing her silhouetted profile or hearing her opaque mumbled voice because she had a fragrant breath that was exquisite and extraordinary. I do not know its chemical composition. But it was sweet and saccharine, like crushed and slightly fermented exotic equator fruit. During the daylight, we played constantly. At nighttime, we slept together. She was nude, as was I...and it was a lovely experience. She was a deep sleeper, and I can visualize her now lying in the bed while the moonlight burst through the window and the draped sheers and illuminated her skin with a soft, magical amber glow. I sat there looking at her body and fondling her breasts, and arranged myself on her and crawled over her. In those moments she was all mine; she belonged to me and me alone. Had she known of my blinding worship of her I would have taken her in my chariot made of flawless diamonds beyond the stars and time, further than light to eternity.

Inside of the bar about to kiss the girl.

I am wearing a fur-lined beige and red plaid maxi-coat, introduced in 1968. A tilted fedora. I feel like an ass as the room is so hot. My sweat dampening my wifebeater. A brought on look of a flesh peddler.

People pass by in drunken stupor haze or amped up on amphetamines, all the while I play with the bottom hem of her Catholic school girl dress.

It is getting late, the bar clock way advanced; now is the time, no more procrastination…will she cover me with cheap Wet N Wild Silk Finish lip stick…take her neck in a tight grip with my left hand while my right hand cups her breast. I am right handed and have more sensation in that hand…pull her fixed against me, tightly pressing our thinly veiled crotches…let her lead me through the game…so easy to just kiss her, as I have kissed others, many others, but even so, the implications of the act itself expand around us, like dead spirits of the lovers before us.

Final drag on a waning menthol before dropping it to the wet tiled floor. Her lips surrender and yield to mine. The reaction is not what I expected. Battles with my tongue: a sensuous combat, an oral warfare, as she has done this before so many times…invariably, both sides are rewarded with victory. After, she tells me that she was really worried about kissing a boy for the first time. I will spend a number of evenings with my mouth open trying to instruct, yet still be the consumer, the evaluator, the art critic if you will. (The endless draining durations left my lips ruptured.)

No, it's better if you move real slowly at first. Slower, even still. Right, good. There you go. You are almost there. Yes…

Initially, during these sessions, her tongue will just swab at the lips, as if it is taking a tissue sample from me, but then she will learn to dart with it—to dart lustfully. It will be late on a Saturday night when the meaning of lust will come to her, and in her roommate's room we will hear her roommate fucking her boyfriend, and I will enter her virgin pussy and through the thin walls we will hear: *Yes, oh, faster, oh, yes, deeper, deeper, God, oh, oh...*

Everything she will learn from me she will put to good use with someone else.

And here ends the reading.

From: caliph8@sharia4ever.org

Hi friend. It has been a minute. I hope things are well. I just wanted to drop in and let you know about the ulema. *This is basically the Arabic word for knowledge, but it means more than that, it means with this knowledge it is our duty to uphold and interpret the Holy Law. You see, it is on us to decide. There are those among us who just don't get it. The 'I can't even tho' crowd. But you my friend you get it or you wouldn't be here reading this. I know it is a big task but are you up for it? Talk soon, ok bye. #inshallah*

Desire is as bizarre as it is widespread.

Desire is preference and motivation.

Desire is a wild animal in the room that you cannot ignore.

You can be moved by a voice, a form, a type, an arrangement, a kind of smile, a simple gaze, sometimes a name, a family name, a made-up name, a stage name, the curve of her backside, an image or phrase she has spoken, by some unexpected vulgarity, even one that is impulsive or foreseen. All of that can sum or fade to a woman who, by all the usual standards, might be regarded as a monstrosity.

Desire, or the unconscious, makes a choice; it does not do so according to some imbecile or voodoo logic. It pulls the trigger without logical contributions. Beautiful women, ugly women. There you have the whole enigma of desire and its fetishism. You think you love a woman, but you really love only a part of a woman, one of her features, a detail, an inflection. And there is the opposite too, a reverse fetishism, which is the woman who is truly desired, truly desirable, even lovable, but who suddenly ceases to be so because of some word, some gesture, some small detail. Desire can be as fragile as it is sudden. The fluctuations of desire—and therefore, among other paradoxes, the startling way that ugly women are often very charming. The way it functions is that there is a touch of masochism: self-disgust, morbid self-regard and inverse narcissism. There is a touch of sadism: telling a really unattractive woman: *"You, too, have charm, and I am here to reveal it to you!"* And then there is the urge to perform, to show off. To take it to the stage. The announcement: *I am here.*

It is much harder to seduce an ugly woman than a beautiful one. The beautiful woman is used to it. She is experienced and clever as she has been broken in. She knows the tricks and rituals of seduction. One always knows very quickly whether it is going to happen or not. Whereas, with the ugly woman, she is so flustered and caught off guard, surprised at what is happening to her; she begins by being suspicious and incredulous, telling herself that there is something going on she does not understand, that someone is setting her up. And then, afterward, when she has understood, when she realizes one is actually quite serious and that it is indeed for real, she finds that she does not know the rules, she does not know the passwords, she does not have the map.

Ugliness can be seen as exciting because it adds to the difficulty of seduction. Likely is the fact that the ugly woman has complexes. Her body, with which she is all too familiar and disgusted—her wide hips, her bad posture, her sagging breasts, stretch marks with their own zip codes—all of those afflictions that she is now going to have to reveal, to share, to allot, to bring out into the open. Desire is not all that strong; it is not so irresistible that she can forget her distress and concern. That is why it is often more difficult to seduce an inexperienced and untried and untested woman than a woman who fulfills all the standards of taste and attains to exquisiteness.

The real question is whether ugliness is on the way to becoming society's major prohibition. Into a new realm where life in a society is based not on consumption but on arousal. On provocation. Of all the methods of stimulation, ugliness is the most unacceptable. Life in a time that is setting ugliness up as one of its fundamental taboos. A set up to failure.

(I am preoccupied with acting on an unwanted and senseless urge and/or impulse, such as pushing a stranger in front of a bus, steering my car into oncoming traffic, inappropriate sexual contact and poisoning dinner guests.)

Return to the beautiful women. Even they are keenly aware of their imperfections and deficiencies. They have convinced themselves that the whole world has its eyes glued on some minor flaw, some defect that only they themselves regard as enormous. That is with the exception of a few highly narcissistic women who are literally crazy about the way they look. Generally people don't feel comfortable with themselves, which is why they have such a great response when seduced—a raw evolutionary need to be reassured.

In the mirror I grimace while I pluck hair from my left nostril. To avoid further oil to skin contact I leave the puss from the black heads that I squeezed on my nose for when I will shower which is momentarily (as soon as the hot water gets from the water heater to my floor.)

Free the fantasy.

Life is about moments.

Ignite something.

From: caliph8@sharia4ever.org

You see, we are prone to conflict, or at least that is what the Western media wants you to think. You see, it is all fake news. But the people of the USA they are the most savage. I would not trust many except you my brother from another mother. They are like wild beasts that fear everybody that comes near them. That is why our people are armed and willing to fight and even kill. Allah said "Do not take Jews or Christians as friends, if you do you are surely one of them." You see, our God will not guide the evildoers. They are branded with the mark of the wrath and malediction...do you really want that for yourself? Talk soon. Write back bro! #inshallah

Lipstick and lip liner are seen quite a lot. Women open their mouths slightly and draw their tongues over the lips. (Sometimes exposing a tongue piercing. Sometimes just the indentation of a past piercing.) This is the most common technique. Some women use a single lip lick, wetting only the upper or the lower lip, while others like to run the tongue around the entire lip area. Another behavior is the lip pout. The lips are placed together and protruded. Lower lip is extended somewhat farther than the upper lip so that it is fuller in appearance. Whispers are very common: the woman moves her mouth near the man's ear, and soft vocalizations are produced. When there is a sexual message involved (direct or indirect), the woman will involve her head and neck when moving. There is something called the neck presentation. When she tilts her head sideways to an angle of approximately forty-five degrees. The ear almost touches the shoulder, thereby exposing the opposite side of the neck. The skin tight against her neck muscles, strong like safari game. Occasionally she will stroke the exposed neck area with the fingers. When feeling a little more daring or risqué she will pat down or smooth her clothing, although her clothes do not need adjustment. The skirt hike is performed by raising the hem of her skirt with a movement of the hand or arm so that more leg is exposed. This behavior is usually performed when it is directed at a particular man. When other men might look, the skirt is hurriedly pushed into place. Sometimes she will play with things. Keys or rings are often fondled. Sunglasses are caressed, while she usually slides her palm up and down the surface of a wine glass. Cigarette packs are frequently toyed with. Many women like to touch men in a caressing fashion. She might move her hand slowly up and down the man's whiskered face and rough neck area or tangle her hands in his hair. She might stroke his thigh and inner-leg while they are seated facing each other. While they stand she might tap his ass, usually while dancing. Maybe move her hand, palm side inward, up and down his glutes. Often it is obvious when she will walk across the room, perhaps on her way to the lady's room or the bar. Rather than walking in a normal manner, with a relaxed attitude, she will exaggerate the swaying motion of her hips, as if her world is a runway and all eyes and cameras are on her. Her stomach is held in and her back is arched so that her breasts are pushed outward and appear bigger than they really are; her head is held high like a debutante. My favorite is when she comes straight to me, faces me off, and then whispers into my ear to take her from behind.

The shower from the neighbor's apartment stops running after twenty-two minutes. I wait for the hair dryer to run but it does not come on.

The couple this afternoon will be walking home after catching the first matinee film of the day, heading home for a hot fuck on the roof of their five floor Mediterranean apartment building. In all likelihood, she will be wearing a floor-length floral skirt.

I will watch them from my sixth floor window, across the street. They will not know that I watch; the man is much too prudish to allow something so taboo into his sexual realm. The woman will love it and she will fantasize that there is someone out there, just like me, several of us, watching, with the naked eye, binoculars, telescopes, drone cams, reacting and being turned on, getting excited quickly, intrigued, dreaming that we could be the one with her.

She always mounts him while laying low on him, not drawing attention to their frolics. I have been so fortunate to live directly west of them—allowing an undeviating view of what appears to be hairless genitalia. Two weeks ago, I filmed their lovemaking with my GoPro HERO. There was no zoom and from such a distance the smallest of trembling shook the end product film in amplified proportions. I planned to make a zip file and send it to them, but I refrained. I didn't want them to stop their outdoor play. My time was too fun when spent with them.

A horny couple they are indeed. She likes to run her hand up and down his ass crack while they walk. Today they watched a rom com. Now they stop and enter a liquor store. They stay inside for three minutes and forty-five seconds, then exit with a bottle wrapped in a white paper bag, the woman nibbling on a chocolate bar, hand feeding the man. Unfortunately, I do not know their names. I haven't had the time to go through their building's dumpster or intercept their mail.

As the door closes behind them, I stand nearby and close the paperback, check the time on my Submariner (1:17 p.m.), unfold my sunglasses, cross the street against a red light and enter my building. Take the elevator, resist the urge to touch myself even though I am hard, imagining taking her from behind on the roof while her bf watches from the lonely confines of my apartment.

No one has called, but I still play back archived messages from last night. The Bose is playing electronica music on 8. From the kitchen I take three squares of paper towels and position myself on the sofa that I have placed in front of my window.

(I worry a lot about fire and burglary, hitting a pedestrian with my car while texting, releasing the e-brake and casually letting my car roll down a hill; spreading an STD knowingly, losing something of value like my small but satisfying pubic hair collection, and harm coming to a loved one because I wasn't careful.)

At 1:24 they arrive (each Sunday is different, as the timing depends on the running time of the film they come from viewing [the matinee typically starts at 11AM]). She pulls down his chinos, drops to her knees and begins sucking his flaccid penis. Embarrassed that someone is watching, he nervously looks around and drops to his own knees and positions her on his lap and enters her while she comfortably mounts him. She is extremely wet for such a smooth transition. I can see from my window her round and pillowy buttocks rocking back and forth on top of his swollen gland. She begins to slow down the pace by rising to allow only the head of his penis to remain in her, slightly faster dropping down to fully envelope his manhood. This usually goes on for eighteen minutes. My land line is ringing but I don't answer it. When he finally comes (she does not seem to climax) they will lay, with him still inside, under the sun for about twelve minutes. When she rises drops of ejaculate will dribble from her port of entry (that is usually when I use the binoculars). He will appear embarrassed and pull his clothes on, remaining flat on the ground, whereas she stands, stretches, does a couple yoga moves, hoping there is someone watching, longing for unknown eyes upon her unfulfilled and unforsaken skin.

From: caliph8@sharia4ever.org

Do you want to understand the true meaning behind the "Muslim attitude?" Well, basically it is that our faith is stronger, and our practice of religion more devoted. Islam is our identity and 100% receiver of our loyalty. This transcends all others, my friend. You cannot find this in modern society, it just isn't there. Can you see the honor of being part of something so important and so much bigger than you? #inshallah

On the Samsung 59" is QVC. A bracelet for sale. The model's slow moving hands. On porn sets nobody gets paid if there is no money shot, hence the eager fervor and verve in the actresses. During the program I drink three beers and crank call ex-girlfriends during the commercials, dialing *67. Speed redial called Gabrielle thirty-two times during one extended feminine hygiene commercial. She knows that it is me, and I know she knows, perpetuating the enjoyment and that lover's rush.

I just returned from the grocery store where I invited a girl from the vegetable section over for a glass of wine. Shiraz or cabernet. She was hesitant at first, but gave in when I told her I was totally sane and that I would simply like to enjoy a drink with a beautiful girl. And that I usually don't talk to strangers (she will be over in less than half an hour). "There are no strangers, only friends we have yet to meet."

I have slid the sofa back to its usual spot, away from the window. An open beer sits on the coffee table. Spanish rock plays at 7 on the Bose.

I forget her name while masturbating to a big tits jpeg on my cell. Landline rings and I reach to answer, thinking it would be her, but remember she doesn't have my number only my address so I let the machine answer it; they don't leave a message. This unsettles me.

She arrives wearing a black summer dress with white fringe frill along with brown combat boots and has brought a three flower bouquet of white carnations wrapped in newspaper. I wear faded True Religions with holes in the knees and a flannel military fatigue green shirt and am casually barefoot. Pouring her a glass of Australian shiraz wine (her choice), she nonchalantly walks through the apartment, gently lifting things (a pen holder from Tangier, a pair of Ted Lapidus readers, binoculars hanging from the wall by the window, a fashion magazine on the glass coffee table, a remote control for the stereo, a paper weight I found in the garbage, a Czechoslovakian book translated into English which I am one hundred and eighty-three pages through).

We sit on the sofa. Approximately two feet separate us.

She tells me that she is a bit nervous and I tell her I don't blame her a bit, that, in this day and age, we must be careful going to strangers' apartments but, hell, what other way can we meet good people anymore—definitely not through those hook-up dating apps. She interrupts me to say that is not why she is nervous, that I make her nervous because she has seen me before in the grocery store and that each time she sees me she always wants to meet me and that she has deliberately tried to bump into me many times, but that I never responded.

I blush and fill her empty glass. She is already onto her second one in less than five minutes. Everything is hopeful and going as planned. The night is mine for the messing. If things collapse I am solely to blame. She tells me that she likes Spanish music and I ask her if she happens to speak Spanish and she tells me *un pocito* and I tell her *yo tambien* and we nervously laugh. With the remote control, I increase the volume of the music to level 9 to make conversation impossible...this is cue to self to make moves on her now.

I whisper into her: *So we tried, and died small deaths, realizing that we cannot fight the smells, nor the sounds nor the feel of it all in the face of this infusion of loyalty and the disregard for the dismissal of betrayal, leaving behind the old maps as I chart out your inside motions, and watch close over you with that lurking stare, dazed by your opulence, resigned to your majestic finery...I want to taste your sea salt at the entryways and the exit ways and feel the hunger for better days when we won't squint for the dark, a place where you are the female lead, the so called heroine, a place where we are guilty of the worst crimes, a place of failed addiction and half-hearted recovery, a place where you can bite me and scar me for the sake of legacy, and when I read your skin it is with a blind man's fingertips, and when we arrive there are no bad camera angles as we run along the bridged memories of our unshared past.*

Resigned to the moment.

Capture the day.

Live for the now.

Late for work. Call in to tell HR that I will be taking the rest of the day off.

She and I make love again. Not before a little brunch 69. Always nice when your breath is so foul from a night of drinking and smoking only to munch down on smelly genitals that pay no mind. Then onto our sides, what I believe they call spooning. My face pressed against the lavender-scented sheets. Fall victim to her sexuality; exciting me too much; turning my lust to fervor; must think about anything but her and anywhere but this moment and setting now. Her chipped acrylic fingernails dig into my entire backside; must think of other things: reading the newspaper obits, cleaning the bathroom floor, cleaning the bowl of the toilet, wiping down an empty but well used ashtray with my tongue, etc. Abstract thinking makes me go back down on her again. This time it is me focusing on her. She is the one and only passenger on this commercial jet. I spell out the alphabet forward and back with the tip of my tongue against her throbbing clit. Attempting to capsize the little man in the canoe. Doing this I can allow myself to go limp while she can catch up to me.

Says she smokes very little, but this particular morning she smokes one full cigarette while I devour her downtown nether regions then three cigarettes with the two accompanying espressos in bed.

Her vagina is peculiar. First off she still has her pubic hair. It is quite outstanding, each strand a bit longer than usual, while her labia majora are a tad protrusive. Note: her mane is fully natural, no maintenance whatsoever and this is a good sign because she is so well kept and manicured. Similar to a model's untainted pouting smirk—alive and moist. She tells me that she is embarrassed by her body in general. Examining her body moreover, she continues smoking and blushes with each compliment I give. She has to get going, she informs me, and when fully clothed she writes down her number on the cover of a magazine. I lay naked and she tells me that she will let herself out, that she wants to imagine me lying in bed all day thinking of her and playing with myself. She kisses me good-bye and I hear the door close behind her.

The feminine divide.
Look hot tonight.
Indulge your senses.

Appointment time: 9:45AM
Arrive early, there's loads of paperwork to review and sign.
Dr. Hause. "You will love her." (yelp)
The end of unwanted hair.
Reveal your natural beauty.
Get the best out of life.
There is a way to get the hair-free look you deserve.

When you feel attractive, life is more vibrant and fulfilling.
I was nervous still.
Word is the pain lingers for days.
Especially when performed on the beard area.
I was naked but for the gown and black Lacoste boxer briefs.
I didn't shave for three days. I downed four ibuprofens and a shot of Jaeger in the car.
Dr. Hause prefers to be called Ashley.
I admire her big blue eyes through the clear goggles, and the chest puppies under her scrubs. It took 45 minutes as she slid the hair-thin metal probe slowly and precisely into each hair follicle without puncturing the skin, the electrical charge traveled through the probe, damaging the area that generates the hair. "Killing the formation of caustic sodium hydroxide with overheated thermolysis," she says. The long-term success all depends on the destruction of the hair matrix cells and if the follicles are left incapable of regrowing. I resist the urge to grab her tits with both hands as I have put all focus onto them and away from the pain. Each zap is a positive ground supply delivering 3 milliamperes through my body, the voltage maintaining a constant, while the radio frequency runs at 8 watts on a distribution level of 13.56 MHz, emanating from the probe tip to the tissue, burning the hair matrix to 118 degrees resulting in electrocoagulation.
I will need to return once per week.
"Dr. Ashley, please go easy on me next time, doll."

A full day has passed so I call. Knowing she doesn't arrive home until after five so I dial her landline and leave a message with her roommate. Befitting voice: girly and sexy, even flirtatious.

Oh, I know who you *are, she couldn't stop talking about you last night, she kept wondering when you would call.*

Would you be so kind as to tell her that I called and that I would love to see her soon. Sure, she tells me, and I ask her for *her* name. Jody, why? she asks. Is that with a y or an i? y, she informs me. I write her name down. Just curious, I tell her. Nervously giggles while I tell her thanks again for conveying the message.

In the kitchen I microwave a pre-packaged frozen enchilada and down a shot of bottom shelf tequila, light a previously lit but still salvageable cigarette and finish the letter to the editor which I started earlier today:

Dear Editor:

My issue of LIPS *arrived in the mail today and I tore into it immediately. Now I want to make a one word comment about Tia—Wow!! I don't know if those are her real tits or not, but just looking at them made me hard. I jerked off imagining myself fucking them. I am not normally a fan of shaved beaver, but Tia looks good with a hairless clam. If you have to show shaved pussy every issue, please show the girl actually shaving. We guys who aren't into bald bottoms would at least be able to get off on watching what is otherwise a female's secret ritual. We can only guess what women do in the bathroom for hours! Keep up the good work!!* ________ .

The center of the enchilada is still hard, so I microwave it more and stare into the spinning center of the buzzing machine.

I am bothered by images of death, religious iconography and horrible events.

From: caliph8@sharia4ever.org

Hello friend, how are you? I been busy, but not too busy to write you. You see, radical Islam is getting a bad name. What is so radical about it? I think everyone is afraid of the state-sponsored stuff. We are not like that at Sharia4Ever. We are a homogenous movement yet we do not exclude, in fact we are all inclusive. Supported by kind and outgoing people like you. The other groups they have some government behind them pulling their strings, trying to protect themselves. Look no further than Egypt or Pakistan. Anyway, with that said, nobody controls us but our God almighty. Are you ready to meet for mint tea soon? Bye for now. #inshallah

In these somber days, premonitions of the impending apocalypse, of darker days and more solemn times. I need to get away. A boost from some sustained and uninterrupted sunlight against my face. Against my three precancerous moles. Against the clogged pores. Causing tingling where my adult acne dwells. My rosacea on hiatus.

I loathe this job. Work bores me. The mundane act of repeated mindless motions. Crank call some of the secretaries in the office. It is difficult to keep a straight face when they come to me and tell me that some sick pervert keeps calling them and asking them what brand of tampon they use, that he fantasizes about being their tampon (*thank you, Prince Charles…and Camilla*), that after eating a big meal at Sizzler he likes to wipe his mouth clean with maxi pads, discreetly from a corner booth, asking if the new pads on the market, the ones with deodorized panty liner wings, are helpful and as absorbent as advertised.

I am wearing a variation on the leisure Safari suit. Four flapped patch pockets. A casual appearance. The hunter man.

Do I prey on wounded game?

Do I have sympathy for extinction or endangered species?

I leave work early as my assignment here ends today.

Indian stop-and-rob liquor store on the way home. I buy a bottle of tequila, a bottle of red/rose wine, a pack of generic light menthol cigarettes (I like to mix it up sometimes), a browning and deteriorating banana, two twelve ounce cans of domestic light beer, a pornographic (lesbian themed) magazine and an Italian fashion magazine. Pay with cash and leave the three pennies in a penny tray. On the way out I hand one of the beers to a black homeless guy who I see every day and have come to know over the recent months.

"God bless you," he says.

In front of the neighboring apartment building, I stop and rip a page from the fashion magazine. It is a picture of a girl, around seventeen years old, red overgrown pouty lips, wearing a black summer dress and standing in front of a white backdrop. I write on the white part with a pen I stole from the liquor store:

If I ever touched you with my eyes, I should have done it with my lips, because now I know how it feels, and I know I want it even more. Was it a dream or was it real, if I was dreaming, don't wake me up, if it was real, just love me! Don't be a lonely child, be a friend forever.

I place the note in the mailbox of two girls who live there. They are young enough, and homely enough, to lose their minds over it—wondering for whom it is, asking the building super, being overly excited and even masturbating to the fantasy.

I walk on. Hurried to avoid a confrontation.

Once inside my building I check my mail and open a letter from an overseas girlfriend. Crack open the one remaining beer from the store and light one of the new menthol lights, dry gag a bit then sit on the third step of the stairs:

Dear _____ ,

How long has it been? How many letters have I written? How many nights have I thought of you—my dreams keeping me from my sleep, keeping me anxious for that day when I would lay in your arms once again? You are the most important person in my life—you give me energy and ideas and new ways of thinking. You know I have said that you don't support me. Well, in a way you are the lifeblood for me. The light in a dark night. Every time I think of you, I forget about all my problems and just focus on you. I choose *to do that. No one forces me. So I am not blaming you for my desperation, or for anything that happened between us, because finally in the end all of it was my choice...*blah, blah, blah...*Sometimes I wish you would open up more for me. I have always been open for you. I am so in love w/ you, I will do anything for you. I cannot quite figure out what you think of me...I know there is something but it is never defined. Your reactions are so cool, and unaffected. I spill my guts in trust for you. You should let your emotions come up to the surface—because those are what makes us human:* the emotions. *Without them we are dead...*blah, blah, blah...*For some reason—I* *am sure you are bored by this point, maybe you are not even reading it—I needed to write this. You are always in my heart and I will always love you, love you too much.*

Love, life and eternal happiness, please come see me in _______ , all of my love, I love you so much, ______ , xo xo xo xo.

While I unlock the door to my apartment the telephone rings and I screen the call. I listen to a girl nervously ask me if I would like to meet her for a coffee or something, maybe rent a movie and watch it at her place, oh, I don't know, just give me a call when you get in, or, you know, when you can, okay bye, bye for now, ciao.

Natural prostate relief.

Improve bladder control.

Prevent uncontrollable wetting.

Ennui hits hardest on Wednesdays. The hump day.

I call the girl who left the last message. She studies at a local private university. Studies religion, tells me that she focuses on Buddhism—particularly Mahayana, "you know, the one the Dalai Lama practices"—and that she hasn't studied the Western religions yet, "you know, Christian stuff." I once asked her, after a few drinks, what she thought about cunnilingus and she told me that she hasn't read the Old Testament yet.

She is coming over to my place with white "fetzer" wine—the "only thing alcoholic" she drinks. I place the pornographic magazine I purchased earlier between other varied magazines I have on the table—preparing a set-up for her embarrassment when she finds it, looks at it and, slowly, gets turned on.

Two shots of hard hallucinogenic liquor warm me for the shower. On the Bose plays a soundtrack from a

90s film. When she arrives I will be wearing only jeans. Under the table I find a piece of condom wrapper and wonder where it came from. Across the street, three floors below, I see two people kissing in the windowsill. With binoculars, I can see the man fondling the woman's breasts, even through the thickness of what seems to be a padded brassiere he is advancing increasingly, eventually to pull her left breast completely out of her blouse and then out of her bra (which I now see is skin-toned in color). Provoked and motivated, I crank call a woman from work who—I learned earlier this week—likes being the victim to perverted crank calls. With a handkerchief over the telephone, I tell her that I would love to take her from behind, while softly touching her perfectly shaped ass, continually paying attention to her breasts which hang to large proportions. Hearing her gasp for breath, I can imagine her touching her moist self under a ratted bathrobe. My doorbell rings and I hang up. Binoculars go back on the wall and the blinds are twisted closed. Placing my wet erection up and under the belt of my pants the excitement is still noticeable.

From: caliph8@sharia4ever.org

People ask me all the time, "What is jihad?" Well friend it can mean many things but what it means to me is striving. *The Arabic root is j-h-d. Whether a crusade of one or a personal struggle in devotion, the outlook of my jihad is in its aspirations. Gotta go now. Hope you are feeling better. #inshallah*

Sunny and a forecasted seventy four degrees by one pm.

I am wearing a regimental-stripe tie, bringing to my look connotations of tradition and white privilege. It is somewhat thin, but not ultra-skinny nor too dated.

The most beautiful things about her are what one cannot see.

What is left to the imagination, endlessly.

The mental projector, you as the director, her as your willing nymph actress. She has made it clear that she is willing to do whatever it takes.

She has worked with me for three months, and it is only now that I realize how sexy she is, how much I want to take her, how much she wants me. I have imagined her in every position—bent over the top of a sofa, lying spread eagle on a plush white mattress, up against the white tile in a hot shower. She is very anonymous and low-key—much like myself—hiding her figure with certain discretion, usually a peculiarly cut dress, stifling the sightlines into her eyes with thick glasses, keeping her long hair from flowing by bunching it above her head (the look could be called *librarian chic*). Instead of the usual lines from lingerie or plain old granny panties, she wears a certain brand which does not show through her clothes, giving a gorgeous, seamless look. She also looks rather healthy. Once I saw her with her blouse unknowingly untucked from her skirt, and I viewed her shallow, oval-shaped belly button—this is when I first realized her beauty and took unfailing notice at the office after that. I even stayed in that day instead of going out to lunch. I waited in the lunchroom but she did not show. I believe she has a boyfriend, as I found in her desk a photo of a guy—he could easily be her brother—pictured with a German shepherd in front of a lake. Other than that, I only know her name and that she lives on the other side of town.

The other day she wore a pair of spiked stilettos. Apparent is the fact that she is enamored by the possibility of increased legginess, of finding herself on a rather precarious perch. The stiletto game can be difficult for women to pull off—the four inches require precision walk and exact balance. When she wore them it appeared that her feet were smaller and that the ankle and calf were shapelier. Her profile even had more curves. This is because she must arch her back to compensate for the added height. She looked even thinner than she already is which I suppose can be attributed to the elongation of her frame.

Today I asked her, in a private corridor, if she could make me some copies. Coarsely, I continued: By the way, why did you only wear the stilettos that one time? She answered, blushing, that she read somewhere that high heels, like *those*, cause contracture of the calf muscles and the Achilles tendons, which can ultimately lead to limited ankle motion.

Asking her where she is from, she tells me here. Should I be so daring as to ask her out? We *are* coworkers after all. If I do do something deviant or so, then, perhaps I will be faced with a walk of shame return to the office and I *cannot* afford right now to lose another job.

She tells me that the copies will be ready in a few minutes.

"If you don't mind waiting," she answers, coyly (pure innuendo).

"Just bring them to my desk," I reply coldly.

We share a curious smile and I leave to the restroom to find all the stalls empty. I come rather quickly, masturbating to the thought of her but visually stimulated by the centerfold photo which I have waiting for me, wedged behind the ass gasket box.

At my desk are the copies. A Post-It is taped to the second page, it contains, in female handwriting, her telephone number with *if you dare* in parentheses.

She is due here any minute.

Play list for the evening:

U2, With or Without You
Prince, Controversy
George Michael, Careless Whisper
True, Spandau Ballet
The Scorpions, Winds of Change
Soft Cell, Tainted Love
Soul II Soul, Keep on Movin'
Billy Idol, White Wedding
Julio Iglesias, Begin the Beguine
Dolly Parton w/ Kenny Rogers, Islands in the Stream (house remix)
Human League, Don't You Want Me
Culture Club, Do You Really Want to Hurt Me

Queued up in this order and set to repeat twice then go into random shuffle mode. I calculate that will be approximately 48 minutes after she arrives.

If I call her now she won't be home yet and because of that she would be forced to call me back. She would excite me very much and I would fantasize about making love to her from behind while she wore the stilettos. My thighs tight against her thighs. My hairy skin against her soft skin. If we sleep together it will be difficult avoiding her and equally impossible to get her to leave me alone. I couldn't just simply not give her my number. I couldn't just give her some poor excuse. I couldn't just not do a lot of things. She is in a position to get me in trouble at work. My job could be jeopardized. The other secretaries and female admin associates I have slept with there would find out. Word would hit the street. The lies would begin. The gossip would not cease, but grow. And the exaggerations would replicate.

I dial her number and listen to her machine playing a country western song and I am disgusted and hang up. Redial.

Opening a Chinese beer, I light an unfiltered French cigarette.

I hope she calls and we get together tonight. Imagining the stilettos poking me in the knees, imagining her fingernails digging deep into my back while I run the sharp four-inch heels up and down the crack of her ass—as I think about sliding the unlubricated stiletto into her, the most unforgiving of butt plugs.

Telephone rings and I allow it to ring six times (just one less ring before the machine automatically answers) and it is…

Some kind of erotic frenzy.

Sitting at the glass coffee table, I am watching her clip her fingernails—while effortlessly letting the clippings fall to the floor and disappear in the thick chocolate brown rug. She is wearing a black silk crepe slip dress with charmeuse and velvet insets. She moves like a sex goddess. At the office, her true sexuality is stifled. A bit nervous, she seems to be cooling down with the white wine, leftovers from the other night. A domestic beer sits on its wet circle in front of me. Neighbors are situated at the dinner table. I ask her what she finds truly revolting and disgusting—since I think I need to put some kind of damper on the heated passion between us—she tells me:

"Probably when my doctor uses his gloved hand to give me a vaginal examination."

And I say, "What do you prefer—when he *doesn't* wear the glove?"

She laughs, I giggle, and she says:

"Yes, I would prefer to feel the real skin."

"Bareback," I reiterate.

One of her stilettos sits on the Brazilian cherry wood floor in front of her.

"I find incest to be a pretty disgusting thing," I say, fortuitously.

"It is a good thing we aren't related," she responds, skillfully.

I pour her some more white and light myself a cigarette.

"You don't mind if I smoke, do you?" I ask.

"As long as you don't blow it my direction."

She slowly slides off her other stiletto shoe and reclines, chest protruding outward. Her skirt is hiked up around her waist and black panties tightly fill the hoof-type gap between her legs. Her stockings are crotch less but not the panties.

From: caliph8@sharia4ever.org

Hi. Jihad is our duty. A day and night of fighting on the frontier is better than a month of fasting and prayer. It is better than a debaucherous night with beautiful prostitutes and child brides. Jihad is more welcome than cold water on a hot summer day. He who dies without having taken part in the campaign dies in a kind of unbelief. God marvels at those dragged to Paradise in chains. Learn to shoot my friend. The peaceful battle for self-control and betterment. Strive for the utmost endeavor. Paradise is in the shadows of swords. #inshallah

Gridlock abounds.

Hasten to the cafe.

I am wearing a three-button hacking suit, a cashmere turtleneck (purple) and Italian leather boots.

Also I am commando.

Being late is inevitable at this point; I hope she is too.

I arrive to find that she is not here so I hurry to the restroom and rinse my mouth for a second time, running fresh water through my hair. I walk out of the restroom, picking up my house coffee.

Outside I sit and wait for her arrival. I begin sweating lightly on my forehead and my armpits. The suit was a bad choice. Leafing through a magazine, I read an article on killing sprees.

The terrace of the cafe is crowded, various pretty girls—some uncannily alone—being good little people, unlike myself: the lush. Sweat permeates my forehead while I wipe it down with a white napkin.

She arrives, waves to me, and enters through the cafe's main doors to get herself an iced decaf coffee.

I play things cool. It is a façade and I know it is a façade but denial is part of the façade and in order to pass off the show *one must believe* (this is sometimes called sociopathic behavior but is more accurately *impostor syndrome*).

She joins me, kisses me on the cheek and lights a cigarette. She is wearing a gray cotton-and-polyurethane mock-crocodile jean-style jacket over a white ribbed tee, her dark brassiere apparent through the deliberate see-through cotton. She tells me that she enjoyed last night very much and I tell her I enjoyed it even more so.

"So what did you do before working at this office?" she asks me.

"I was a _____ ," I tell her, "And yourself?"

"I was a call girl," she informs me, rather candidly "Don't laugh, I know it seems pretty crazy and all, but you gotta realize it *is* the world's oldest profession. It pays the bills. I did stripping in college then side jobs in private parties, and it went from there. I can be rather *detached*."

"More power to you."

"But now I am done for good. No more of that business."

"Why?"

I look around us, hoping that our conversation is inaudible.

She tells me that she moved here from somewhere in the east, where she was running a massage service in her house. One day some guy answered the ad she had placed, came over, and ended up holding her hostage for four hours, raping her at least twenty times. Informing me that only about four percent of prostitutes who are raped report the crime, she didn't go to the police because she didn't want to be arrested, resulting in her protecting the rapist from facing justice.

"Do you know what it's like being a hooker and filing a rape report?"

I tell her no.

"Every woman who has ever been held responsible for a man's bad behavior—whether she's accused of dressing too provocatively or walking down the wrong street or sending out mixed signals—has tasted the kind of contempt that I faced all the time."

She sips from her coffee and smiles, I light a cigarette and she says that she can smell alcohol emanating from somewhere.

"It must be rough," I say, still not sure if she is pulling my leg. "You know, having to deal with men who are sometimes twice your size?"

She drags from a cigarette and smiles.

"Well, if he is going at it too roughly, I just reach behind and grab his balls; think of them as the reigns."

We laugh.

"Sex work isn't for everybody, but you have to give people the choice when it comes to their own bodies. Sex work can be dignified, honest and honorable." Nodding in agreement, I hear an ambulance siren some blocks away, which, in turn, sets off a car alarm within the next block from where we sit, which in turn, causes a dog to start barking, each time more loudly and ferociously.

I tell her that it should be legalized.

She reaches under the table and gently massages my knee, I am aroused and embarrassed.

She tells me that legalization would be a good thing for her and her former colleagues, but that legalization would take away a lot of the things which drove women into being prostitutes in the first place.

“We would not be able to act like independent business people. We would have to work in a specific district, kick back part of our fees to the city or state, and register as prostitutes—which could go on a woman's public record and affect her ability to travel, get health insurance or an apartment, *and* keep custody of her children. We worry about being faced with a 'sex factory' situation to have to work in.”

The idea of a 'sex factory' works me up. Although I just found out that she was once a hooker, I still would love to get it on with her tonight.

“I consider myself to be providing a service,” she tells me. “I don't see anything wrong with giving people pleasure and comfort, and I actually enjoyed some of these men. They come to me because I am professional. This is not something someone is taking from me, but something I am giving. There are so many ways that I allowed myself an alternative to the grim ways that it could have been.”

I smile toward her, allowing my eyes to fall on her lips.

“For me, sex work happens to be the best alternative, it's better than being the president of someone else's company. It's better than being a secretary. It's the most honest work I can think of.”

I tell her my coffee is cold and that I would like to go home and change before we go anywhere. As if on cue, she stubs a burning cigarette out on the stamped concrete floor below us.

From: caliph8@sharia4ever.org

Everywhere, in the capitals and in the provinces, in the Bay Area and in the hinterlands, on the banks of the coastline, the shores of the East coast, and the borders of Mexico and Canada, this ancestral fight has been brought to you...it has made itself felt. You see they may have been able to arrest and slow the Muslim progress over time. They may have ended the Andalusian caliphate. But that is the past, we are here and the time is now. Divine law has our backs and our protest is valid. Do you feel me bro? #inshallah

I drop the envelope along with this note in her purse. No response expected or needed. Her thrill is just the same:

Our vital signs and recovery in the smell of a vacant motel, the heartache on our lips, as I took a detour to your downtown, and we run anew on a moonlit midnight path as I roll into you and swivel your backside just so, pausing you there through the gentle steps and the shallow water on the shore although we cannot quiet the dragon within you, your arched flared back like a peacock, caught up in my mind we cross the threshold into the sanctuary and savor the aftertaste of tomorrow, I watch the footage of you in my mind and the girl inside your woman and never want for more, these slowing crescendo moments when scarred remnants will be all that remain in the rotation around you, and the bathing in the forever alterations of our lives, you float through my mind on clouds of princess beauty, atop the underside of all our yesterdays, reveling in the glory that slowly drips in and fills us up, I listen to the ancient melodies of your soul, and feel the desert heat when you straddle me, and I regard you from the floor up, and your body spinning in an unconscious blur, I am killed in the distortion but awakened by your mouth and the slow beat rhythm of your heart, I have fallen through your trapdoor, I am drowning in your turquoise sea, I am sleep dreaming of you, I am perishing within you.

Went out dancing tonight and now she is back with me.

Attempting to get her to pick up some girl at the club—after she told me that she does women too—she told me that I was too precious and valuable to be shared. She has fallen onto the bed and I have helped her in pulling off her leather pumps before I went to the bathroom to brush my teeth.

In her purse I find: a seashell-shaped Pill case (half full of pink tablets), a tampon (XL and a brand I have never heard of), two lipsticks, an address book, a pink condom, a small hair brush full of her black hair, a pair of clean silk panties (purple), various keys, a copy of the same picture which sits on her desk, a transit card.

I brush my teeth and notice a hair growing from within a pimple on my forehead.

She mumbles something to me from the bed.

Wearing her panties gives me the stiffest of hard-ons and I quickly rinse out my mouth and dry my wet face with a towel stained from lipstick and makeup.

The octopus hunts at night.

Give yourself the finger.

Hints of the jet set.

She is next to me in bed, our legs are entwined under the sheets that cover our bodies from the waist down. Her hair flows freely over the pillows and I wonder how I will pay for this one: a sex disease, become her victim while she stalks me desperately at night, get fired because of her...*what will it be this time*?

I have never slept with a prostitute before. I would *never* pay for sex.

She mumbles in her sleep and tepidly strokes my leg. She appears awake and conscious, but the mumbling confirms her dream sleep. She is ravishing. A bit jaded. I cannot believe that she ever did *that* for a living. But, she did make it sound very business-like: she had a commodity, her body, and it was in high demand. I actually feel quite good about things. Like that feeling one gets when receiving something for free, like winning a sweepstakes or finding twenty dollars on the sidewalk. I feel like that now, like I just received a lay that usually would have cost X amount, but I got it for *free*. Imagine all those suckers who paid for the same exact thing.

The sunlight peeks through the shades and the floor is cold to my bare feet. I go to make coffee. The neighbors appear to be out and I am tempted to pay their apartment a visit. I know access is possible from the roof (it is always possible via the rooftop), but I haven't done the necessary homework.

On the answering machine I see there are fourteen messages (an increase from last Friday night's twelve) and I rewind the tape but do not press play. In the refrigerator is a carton of half-and-half and I pour a splash into an empty coffee cup. My horoscope reads that—once again—I am a very well balanced person and that no need to worry, that money is in my future as well as an opportunity for travel, but that family is important these days. I open the window nearest to the coffee table and light a book of matches. In a large ashtray I burn her address book. One book of matches does not suffice. A lighter I find in a kitchen drawer finishes the job.

I burn incense and I spray the air with anti-perspirant deodorant.

Temptation to burn more things fills me.

She is awake and I first see her when she comes out of the bathroom. I will have a cup of coffee waiting for her next to the bed. Then I will take her up onto the roof and we will make love, while I hope that the higher elevated neighbors are awake to watch.

From: caliph8@sharia4ever.org

Islam is a community. It is a brotherhood. It is in the name of Allah. He is the living truth to which it owes its life. He is the center and the goal of the spiritual experience. He is the reason for the state's existence, therefore he is the principal, the godfather if you will. He alone justifies all continuance. This makes the Muslim army the Army of Allah. This makes the US government the Government of Allah and all the laws. The laws of Allah. Life and all of its entirety is in the hands of Allah. You see friend, the picture is very big and it is all much bigger than us. The remembrance of God and His divine presence. Something you definitely want to get behind. #inshallah

Making the actual contact is of a higher level, it means I have to designate a particular woman, make her acquaintance, and gain access to her. This could involve following her for a few days, accessing her apartment while she is at work, hacking her phone and blackmailing her, following her and her friends to a bar or nightclub—countless things which I don't have the time for. License plates are a great source for information. In fact it is the source. Address, social security number, parents' names, age. It opens a variety of other possibilities for the gathering of the intel.

Most men like to look back boastfully and stress the names of women they have made love to; but I prefer to look forward, toward the unknown. Necessity is to look forward to all the women that I have left to see for the first time, to make contact with, and to make love to.

I have agreed to come over to her apartment for champagne. On the phone I told her "Possibly more, but I can't promise anything, you must understand, I am quite tired."

On the second floor of a run-down Spanish revival building, she answers the door in her usual lethal-to-the-fingertips look: *statuesque and dripping wet.*

Sitting on a black leather sofa, drinks in hand, she tells me how she has enjoyed these last days "so very much."

Four minutes in and she tells me that she has lost her address book and that everybody she knew was in there and since moving from the East she has not had time to write anyone and tell them where she had moved. With a truly sad and frustrated frown I tell her that I am sorry and that maybe if she misplaced it at my place that I could find it and everything would be okay. She is relieved and pours me more Cordon Negro champagne. She tells me that she wants to give me a little tour through her apartment.

"Excuse the mess," she tells me, "but boxes are everywhere."

If she pulls any manipulation to lay me this early in the evening, I will avoid her. (Earlier, I masturbated twice).

In her unpacked room, I see diamonds, high heels, scanty bikinis, plastic pistols in garter belts, rhinestone knuckle rings, a slashed black satin skirt. Some of the items are awkward and embarrassing.

We return from the bedroom to the kitchen then to the sofa.

"I like to call myself an antifeminist feminist. One of the ways I began to see the limits of the current rhetoric is through dressing like this and going out to clubs, or even dressing down a bit and going to work."

I see beyond her and through an open window, into an ideal view of the second floor apartment across the alley.

"With the current rhetoric all you see is sexism—I like to take on the Amazonian woman image, I try to pull off a fantastic front for myself and all women."

She drags from my cigarette and ashes for the first time.

"Very powerful, physically active, and very sexy—that is the way I want to be perceived." We look into each other's eyes. "How do you think I went from being a call girl to being a secretary at your office?"

Shrugging, I pour the remains of the champagne into our stemless flutes.

"I want to be portrayed as libidinous—to create an easy environment where I will always say *yes*."

Finishing the bubbly I rise and go to the refrigerator.

She continues...

A box of ten AA batteries, a box of unopened baking soda, a variety of beer. Opening a beer, I ask her if she would like one and she tells me yes. The freezer holds two trays of sickly-looking ice, one bottle of Russian vodka and a bottle of gin.

On the sofa I find that my beer bottle is not a twist off and she must rise and look for an opener which she goes to search for in her bedroom. The neighbors have returned but they are away from the window. She returns with the opener. Under the coffee table is a pair of rhinestone handcuffs.

I am wearing a double-breasted eight-button frock coat and a stand-up-collar cotton shirt.

She tells me that she lives a life under a dictatorship of pleasure.

She is wearing a copper silk moiré dress with crinoline.

She tells me that this dictatorship of pleasure is about the pleasures of the senses that take over when one's eyes are tightly closed, and the pleasures of believing, with open eyes, things that are not so: that a rundown, infested apartment is a palace, say, or that a man can be a woman. She tells me that she thinks, too, of despair, addiction, disease, violence and death. She asks how she can dabble in those essentially invisible and terrifying depths and come out unjaded? The bartender pours each of us another shot, she gulps hers down, makes a pouting grimace and wipes her mouth with a blank, white napkin. Reaching from behind the bar, the bartender lights my cigarette with a shiny, silver lighter which he carries in his black, uniform vest pocket. He smiles a slimy smile and pretends to be southern European even though he is clearly Arab. I decide not to leave him a tip and wait to pocket the change which sits in front of our drinks, but only when we are ready to leave.

She continues on and I inform her with hand gestures that I am going to the restroom.

In the hallway she is waiting.

From her moist hand I take the matchbook. She attempts to say something but I continue on my way into the restroom and urinate a hot and dark, golden yellow piss.

In the uber she continues in a loud voice: “I perceive myself as a casualty, even a victim, and it would be quite accurate to call it a criminal act, but I took these risks on purpose, these were the costs of pleasure's dictatorship.”

At her place I am tempted to call the girl from the club, but don't want to appear too desperate, so I drink a glass of water and watch her strip to the purple panties which I wore to bed the other night. Opening a window and allowing a breeze to permeate the room, I light a cigarette behind a cuffed, trembling hand.

From behind she slides her satin gloved hand up the inside of my thigh. Without looking back, I tell her that I find gloves to be trashy whore attire and she takes them off and continues. I pass the lit cigarette from my fingertips to hers. She drags slowly on the butt and places the lipstick-stained tip in my mouth.

Two floors below, on the street, is a black homeless man walking with a bundle of dirty clothing, a dog in tow. Behind them flashes a red neon sign: KIDS EAT FOR FREE.

From: caliph8@sharia4ever.org

Hi friend. It has been a minute. I wanted to share with you this: the jihad has not ended. In fact it never ended, it just entered a new phase, a new phase inaugurated by the new recruits of Islam. Now you may think this phase started on 9/11 but in fact it goes back to 1453, when we captured Constantinople and made it the capital for the Ottoman sultans. So it is fairly new. But not as new as your involvement my friend. You see, the selfish ego must be removed to make room for the uplifting state of joy, satisfaction and companionship with the Most High. #inshallah

Streaming talk radio.

A teenage boy with a crackling, pubescent voice: *...I considered myself an outlaw. I know now that I was an addict, a thief, an armed robber, liar, fornicator and a dealer. I broke all the Commandments but one. I never directly killed anyone, but I tried. Speed does kill. Everybody I know is dead, killed by meth and crosstops and booze and stupidity and greed. My little brother got me started on speed, when he was twelve and I was fourteen. We were walking down a street and he just went up to this dude and gave him five bucks, and we went into the alley. My little brother was packing the works man, at the age of twelve...*

The batteries of the remote control are dead. I don't want to replace them with the new ones from the vibrator in the night stand. I pour a tall glass of gin and tonic (lots of crushed ice).

...First time meth hit my guts, I messed my pants. A year later I was popping myself in the side of the neck, getting the rush that much closer to the brain. I weighed a third of what I weigh now. Look. I ground my molars smooth, just walking around. I was busy. Speed freaks need money. No mon, no fun. In the early years I got mine out of adult movie houses. You walk into the back room of a girly joint, you rip back one of those little curtains, you put a gun to the head of some guy who has his unit in his hand, take all his money, his watch, his eyeglasses,

sometimes his shoes. Nobody who gets heisted in a porno shop is going to report it to the cops. I got plenty of money for drugs and candy bars. There wasn't much else to life...

On a piece of paper in front of me, I note: be quicker and more alert while visiting adult shops.

...We had to manufacture the stuff, so we moved and started the "Bros in the Basement Crystal Meth Factory." It would take eleven days to make the shit and then we would drive it through three states. Everybody knew the Bros. I liked big motorcycles and bad dogs. I kept pit bulls. Our trouble was that we were addicts and didn't separate the buzz from the bucks. On the day we got busted, we had been drinking and shooting up for six days, getting a delivery ready. We were lost and crazy. My little brother was driving and I was in the backseat with my big pit bull, "Breedin' Bitch," and a sixteen-gauge Winchester pump shotgun, sucking on a fifth of Fireball. Lost and crazy, man, cruising down the highway and I am blowing away freeway signs with the shotgun, at seventy mph...

In the kitchen I make a sandwich and ponder crank calling her.

...My little brother was even crazier than me. He wheels out an exit, leaves me and the car idling in front of a drug store, then comes running out five minutes later, tosses a whole garbage sack full of prescription drugs in my window, downers mainly, Seconal, Demoral, codeine—then peels back onto the highway. I mean you don't do that, man. You don't do that, but we never thought about that, we were invincible. Then, a ways down the road, my little brother has got to take a dump, so he pulls off the road at some gas station. He leaves me and Bitch and the trunk full of drugs, the garbage sack and the shotgun just sitting out in the open, like turds in a punchbowl. First

thing I see in the mirror is the top of a trooper's car. The windows of the car are smoked, way smoked, so I know that the cop doesn't see me. I pump a shell into the shotgun. When the cop steps out of the car, I level on him, through the back window, and fully intend to remodel his face with safety glass and number six shot, but when I jerk the trigger there's just a big hollow click...

Telephone rings, I don't answer it. The neighbors have turned the lights off in their bedroom, but I aspire that the flickering light from their television will suffice for lighting if they decide to make love.

...I'd fired a thousand rounds through that gun, and that was the first dud shotgun shell I'd run into. I now believe that our Lord and Savior Jesus Christ came into that car and saved me from the gas chamber and the fiery furnace of Hell and eternal damnation by seizing the gun and causing it to misfire. So, I give up and open the car door real slowly, sticking my hands out first, but, when the door comes open far enough, Bitch blows through the hole and takes the cop by the hamstring, big time. Pit bulls earn their reputation. He starts yelling and screaming and pounding Bitch with his revolver. Bitch ain't lettin' go. There is only one sure way to get a pit bull to stop biting. You grab it by the tail and you put about half of your finger up its butthole. So, that's what I did...

Touching my pockets—making sure I leave my wallet and money at home—I leave myself a message on the rewound mini tape of a Dictaphone and exit my apartment.

From: caliph8@sharia4ever.org

Those who are killed in the jihad are called martyrs. The English word martyr *comes from the Greek word* martys, *meaning "witness," and in Judeo-Christian usage it designates one who is prepared to suffer torture and death rather than renounce his faith. His martyrdom is thus a testimony or witness to his faith, and to his readiness to suffer and die for it. How are you friend? I been good but busy. I saw your new profile picture, very nice! Hit me back, it has been too long. #inshallah*

Bleaching, chemical depilation, epilation, fatlah, flashlamp, intense pulsed light, khite, photoepilation, phototricholusis, plucking, rotary epilators, shaving, sugaring, threading, trimming, waxing.
Dissolve unwanted hair, leaving your skin smooth for days. A painless and cost-effective way to reveal beautiful bare skin.
The chemical depilatories work by breaking the disulfide bonds that link the protein chains that give hair its strength. The thioglycolic acid breaks down the structure of the keratin to weaken the hair and dissolve it so it can literally be wiped off. Like the effects of chemo your hair will begin to fall out on its own.
Targeted areas: Armpits, arms, legs, chest, back
Non-targeted areas: Head, eyebrows, eyelashes
To be addressed with waxing: Pubic areas (back, sack & crack)
Adding the pill Vaniqua, with its active ingredient of eflornithine hydrochloride, will inhibit the enzyme ornithine decarboxylase, preventing new hair cells from producing putrescine (which stabilizes the hair's DNA).
Antiandrogens, including spironolactone, cyproterone acetate, flutamide, bicalutamide, and finasteride cocktailed with 5a-reductase inhibitors will result in the desired feminizing side effects. This is not recommended

for men but I signed the waivers. At-home treatments involve the handheld Intense Pulsed Light (IPL) machine for DIY targeted maintenance. You can also use the IPL to try and minimize your sun spots and freckles, especially on your decolletage, which will be more exposed going forward.
Concerns: Permanent pigmentation changes and bulge integrity: within the hair follicle stemcells reside in a discrete mocroenvironment (the bulge) which is located at the base of the part of the follicle that is established during morphogeneseis but does not degenerate during the hair cycle, the bulge contains multipoint stemcells that can be recruited during wound healing to help repair the epidermis. No scented products, no swimming, no sunbathing or tanning bed for at least 72 hours after.

Sun has fully set.

I am wearing a three-button leather sport jacket (loosely), a satin shirt and plain-front wool trousers.

With my fourth beer and second shot of tequila, I write the letter which I have had planned for three weeks and four days now:

I would like you to wear panties with a high, seriously high, cut from the sides, exposing as much possible thigh, a nice edge to the silk, precisely where the panties cease to exist and the skin is first exposed. I don't want anything with frills or any extra fabric which would interfere with the shape of the entire area which is covered, nothing school girlish, nor shabby with a certain lace bordering. I want them tight *around the legs, and so* thin *that the flesh shows between them, with (like all good panties should be) a bit of room and loose fit around the bottom, with small escaping patches of hair. Heavily perfume the panties, with your own scent if you like...I expect some of the things that I write will make you blush—at the same time excite you...goodbye,* my *darling.*

Folded and placed in the envelope, I add a card with the name of a restaurant and a time. There are two girl roommates. If I am lucky one will respond (both are gorgeous), if really fortunate they will both arrive in two nights.

Time to step out from the ordinary. Time to take charge and emerge from the confines and the soft lines.

Through the last pages of ____ Weekly, I find singles who are in search of the following: slaves of both genders and all sizes; fellow lovers of lingerie; strap-on sisters; all kink all the time; swinging into action; Asian gangbang warfare; hotties with actual tails; white girls with overlapping toes; albinos need luv 2, and so on. The charge for the response call alone keeps me from further action.

Sex, and the pursuit of it, should not involve money.

Drinking a decaf with cream, I refrain from smoking. In my mouth, I orally fixate on a small red plastic stick. On the paper's final pages I discover the desires of the *anything goes* people: a true love of douching; fetishes for boots (any style); a longing to drink urine (male or female ok).

Sitting nearby are two girls in their twenties. The more attractive one has very round features: round hips, round head, full breasts, eyes, lips, everything round; a Super Lustrous Certainly Red lipstick. The other is unattractive. No lipstick, no war paint. From behind the newspaper, I blur my vision. I appear delirious. I stare at the gorgeous curves of the pretty brunette. The coloring she chooses for her clothing, makeup and hair are all perfectly appropriate. Brown mom jeans (tight all around, a tad loose around the ass, her cheeks not quite filling the high cut, no trace of cameltoe), tight sleeveless white shirt (shaping her exquisite B-sized breasts), white Lacoste tennis shoes (appear to be first time worn, I could be wrong), golden colored jewelry around each wrist and half of the fingers, actual three-in-one bracelets, bangles which link circles of white, yellow and pink gold (to show men that she is either [1]: a well-taken-care-of girl by her wealthy father, or [2]: she has a rich boyfriend from seekingarrangement.com.)

Her trashy friend is explaining to her that when telling men *no* that you don't necessarily need to *mean* no, but that it helps to let them have their way in the end, and something about the coffee, and that this is America and that blah, blah, blah. In the singles section there is an advertisement for telephone sex with pregnant women.

With girls like this brunette, there is no chance of blatant sex appeal toward them as a device to get them. For these types encratism is essential. Deliberate abstinence from sex is not in my agenda; especially for a long enough period of time for my sexual energy to build so strongly that it would magnetically attract this type of girl. Perhaps an onanistic less day would avail. A conundrum of appetite and embarrassment is what she is. That is all she is; and she is everything.

Bare necessities.
New romantics.
Any way you can cut it.
Let desire lead the way.

Girls are everywhere and acting girly, too.
At last, intensity for your lashes.

I am wearing a wool-and-nylon military coat, plain-front trousers, a cotton shirt, silk tie, and leather lace-up boots.

I frequent the malls and shopping centers during the weekends; there is no better place. Blackout lens sunglasses cover my eyes and allow free roaming vision movement (FRVM). In a shopping bag is a video camera and an audio tape recorder. It is possible, with all the practice of late, that today will reap worthy footage.

Last week, in a very chic and high-end women's department store, a tall blonde woman changed right in front of me. She was trying on dresses—various takes on column dresses (one notably wrapped with a keyhole neckline and button detail)—but did not bother to close the door to her stall—allowing me full view with added angles from the mirror; I know she knew; she had to have. Even bent over, fully nude, in my direction, exposing her behind in the mirror. She either thought I was gay or it was for her own thrills. Maybe she thought I worked there. Maybe she was blacked out on prescription meds. Maybe her exhibitionist game runs strong.

In the lingerie store I am running my fingers through the demi-bras. These are my favorites, although I find it very tacky when women go out into public with them on. The black one which interests me the most happens to be called the *Rendezvous* and consists of stretch satin and lace, the small tag says that it is made with Lycra brand spandex. Demi-bras like this one usually offer a beautiful push-up styling and easily convert to two other styles: the halter and the crisscross. A waif sales girl—wearing a luxury matte red lipstick and a crinkled sand-washed silk habutai skirt in black and white floral (high elastic waist)—approaches me from behind and conveys, with a smile, that there is also a matching European-styled bikini.

"Could I get this and one of the bikinis?" I ask her with a smile and inform her further that I will look around a little more. She tells me that the *Chantilly* collection is on sale and I tell her that I don't like to buy sale items, but that I would like to look at them anyway.

"They are this Fall's new exotic mood," she educates me, smiling and shaking her bony hips while strutting one step ahead of me. The line of a black thong creeping above her skirt gets my attention. The dressing rooms are full, while an obese woman rummages through a pile of marked-down clearance floral-patterned cotton panties.

"See, here," she continues, pointing affectionately to each piece of undergarment, "we have these demi-bras with printed lace trim, high-cut briefs—also available, in the back, I don't know why there aren't any up here—"

"Maybe, because they are selling fast," I interrupt.

"Yeah, they must, 'cos they are really *hot*, I mean they are these lace-front string bikinis," she blushes and looks to the ceiling.

"What is so funny?" I ask.

"Oh, nothing, well, I am not supposed to tell you, but, I, um, am wearing a pair right now," she says, shrugging her shoulders, causing tight skin to roll over her collarbone, like small ripples over the sea.

"You wouldn't, by any chance, be able to show me," I ask, in all seriousness. "You know, like in the dressing room—you would only need to pull up your skirt."

She tells me some kind of excuse, but I don't listen, only think about how I can get the camera in the bag to film up and under the partitions of the dressing rooms.

The hole I cut in the bag should work if the camera does not shift.

Approaching a sales girl on the other side of the store, I pretend to be homosexual and/or a crossdresser and ask her, apologetically, if I could possibly try on something. "It really isn't for me, it is more of a gag for a friend." She tells me it is against regulation but that it is okay because her manager is on her lunch break.

In the center stall I rest the camera just under the separating wall from the stall to my left. A sweater in the bag covers the camera from sight. The woman is oblivious and for two and a half minutes I film her change into two different panties.

The next one to change happens to be a younger girl, from her voice likely fourteen or fifteen. She rapidly changes into three different panties.

I stop filming, ruffle up my shirt and untuck one side. Exiting, I smile to the salesgirl and tell her I will take whatever it is that I have taken into the dressing room with me and also the demi-bras that the waif helped me with.

Drinking an overpriced coconut water from a food kiosk, I record (with full audio) a conversation between three girls who talk about rainbow parties and slutty boys and drinking to be cool and I stop the tape after a few minutes. Later, I will ask random salesgirls to help me while the audio tape runs in the bag. At home I will mark the tape with the date and location and in all likelihood never revisit the surveillance. But alas one never knows when such things will be of use.

Once in a while, something comes up that requires no discussion, no compromise, and no debate. Except perhaps with the question of wardrobe.

A scoop-neck shell. A twill jacket with white topstitching. A feather boa. A black thong.

I drop this note in her purse in a full length envelope as I pass her table to the cafe's back exit:

If I could write a line or two for you just a secret between-us note I scrawl out for my lover on a table in the back of a cafe then drop it in her gaping purse, the luxury in the proximity, a guided tour of the travels my tongue takes along the inside of your ear and details of the flooding on my fingertips and the smell trapped under my nails...of how beautiful you are now, forever and ever, your perpetual and evermore divine face and the images I see when I see the wind swirl around you and your curves, the verve and the vigor, the stakes always bigger, and how when I dream of you I dream of you in cinema, with big angles and the soft light, all the jewels of the world and history are no match for your twinkle, you are a throwback to rebellion, of the heart and of affection, of the misconceptions, lost in you the evolving distraction my muse, as you shed your clothing to reveal more foreign lands to visit for an afternoon in flickering light, with all your urban sophistication, when we get there you will post bail for me while untroubled I continue to fall off this cliff of you...

Ideologies into incidents, processes into people; symbols to help us order and make sense of an increasingly complex world. She is an expression of a culture in transition; she is the struggle that accompanies old assumptions clashing against the new. Tonight she is wearing a combination which practically shouts glamour: a rhinestone-buttoned satin jacket and a meant-to-be-seen bra under a slightly sheer shirt (a surefire way to highlight her body). Further focusing on the curves: a shiny, slim belt that cinches the waist. An Ultima Lip Sexxxy Reckless Red lipstick. Her hair shaped with the smooth touch of L'Oreal Simply Straight Sleek Ends gel (I asked).

Pure glam; city slick.

She is seated and smoking a cigarette which I have offered her. In front of us is one bottle of Möet and two flutes which are nearly empty and I wonder if the waiter will return to fill them, or if I will have to do it.

The less we look the more we see.

Experience the relaxation sensation.

The choice is yours, and it's simple.

Strippers say that eye contact is a big money maker…she wears frigid things with potency…she lip sings her letters with lipstick kisses…each breath of her air was another ravished bang at the door of my distress…the sunlight from the glass ceiling casts a beam bright enough to bolt a white silhouette up between her legs with each step…I refuse to come down…she lies and says she is having fun…this hour of edification...oh, I have found a flaw…she overwhelms the devil, speaks in tongues…in search of a better doctrine, her doctrine, one must always be on one's guard toward too much cleverness…I had heard stories about her, only second- and third-hand stories…in the room there was a stir of voices…from the outside cafe, I watch the girl lock her keys in the car and then play it off…all just an eternal chain of exalted beauty…her eyes were glazed, I was filled with longing…plucking, mustering the audacity…she radiates sex…I feel the torment…the hour was inevitable that she would have to leave…she requested my allegiance….she stank of disillusionment, reeked of empty facades…before it was all over, I left her…she did not make a sound, crippled…her entire nude attitude moaned…rubbish, like a beautiful dead lady…need to keep the mad men away from the dance, away from me…she exudes licentiousness…a vamp spirit…*guess what—you're off the hook, I got my period*…she likes to get aroused and then scrawl obscenities on the sides of parked cars.

Sublime with dimensions…dying to hold on and obtain more essential splendor…slow blink superiority to female design, redeem me…she is subversion to my complacency…those who have not seen her, shall see; those who have not heard her will understand…this perennial hunger…whispering into the ear magical pamphlets of all who relentlessly chance a future—and that's not such a bad escape…the utmost…expectation is tension…from a little sprinkle to a huge gush…pure gluttony…hours melt down to habitual instances while longing for a long vanished epoch.

From: caliph8@sharia4ever.org

The renegade is the one who has known true faith yet has abandoned it. For this offense there is no human forgiveness, and according to the jurists, punishment is death. Death for males, for females it is flogging and imprisonment. You may think this is harsh but in God's eyes His mercy has limitations. This is why we are at double jihad: at war against foreign infidels and at war against domestic apostates. You see, sometimes the enemy is amongst us. I know that you my friend have chosen the righteous path. Chat soon, k bye. #inshallah

I am wearing a rust-plaid double-breasted suit and charcoal grey wool sweater.

In a new-to-me coffee shop waiting for a woman whom I contacted through the back pages of the weekly paper. She says that she is a "Born Again Virgin," naturally I had to see why. If she is unattractive I will tell her that I am not who she thinks I am when she approaches me.

Dangerous curves ahead.

She is wearing a dramatic, close-to-the-body, forties-style checkered suit; pencil-straight black skirt to the knees; sheer black stockings; shiny, sleek, black patent leather high-heeled shoes. A Lovable®: The Icing on Your Birthday Suit (*It's not the bra you'll find uncomfortable-it's the way he'll start to beg*) bra. An Aveda Uruku Annatto red lipstick.

"Hel*lo*, you must be..."

I interrupt her: "Yes, and you must be who I think you are—how *are* you?" I ask with sincerity as she is quite ravishing.

"I am fine," she excuses herself. "Sorry for being late but I haven't been here before and kinda got lost."

I tell her that everything is fine and still standing from the introduction I ask her what type of coffee she would like…

…As I talk with her I am surprised to discover the degree to which her language and emotions are contrary to those of the zealots of her following. She doesn't talk about God, but she does talk about love, tenderness, commitment—and about not having sex without it. She is not strictly a virgin—although that would turn me on tremendously. She says that she has had sex twice before. She is what she likes to call a "Secondary Virgin." She says that she wishes she wouldn't have done it before. I tell her that she should try it with me; that all women are virgins until they sleep with me. She laughs, hoping that I was joking.

Picturing kissing her passionately, pinching the lobes of her ears with my front teeth. Getting her excited to the point where she will easily collapse at the exhaustion of her temptations.

While replacing the coffee cup in the saucer, I ask her if she will kiss men, "men like myself."

"Oh, definitely, no problem with that—I love kissing," she explains. “For hours at times."

She tells me that kissing doesn't make her feel dirty, that actual sex is somehow lonesome, and she is determined not to have it again short of a wedding or engagement ring—or, at the very least, true love.

A female employee wipes down a table next to us. Her breasts hang and wiggle loosely, free of the stifling constraints of a bra. She looks at me—in those pigtails—and awkwardly smirks when it is apparent that I had been watching her. My date is talking about her past sex life.

"The thing that really bugs me is that I didn't love him. I don't feel bad about it, but I think that I must wait to be engaged or married the next time. I've had it; I know what it's like; it's no big deal. I'd want something permanent before having sex again, some stability, a reason he won't leave or I won't leave," she says, looking down, struggling with tears.

Hers was a tender and lurching confession, full of pathos and judgment. A retreat from sex that was more convoluted than simply a fear of God and disease. Other intense emotions were rolling around this secondary-virgin's soul. She was full of regret and resolution, blame and more self-blame.

(The shortest line from sophistication to grandeur is simplicity.)

Your look, your body, your happiness.

Unstoppable youth.

Yes you can.

In the mail is the usual trash and I toss it—except for a letter with a local postmark and address written with a female hand. On the stairs I open it and find a letter from the girl on Saturday night.

Warmth overcomes me:

Dearest my _____ , I think I am becoming insane*! It's late in the evening Saturday...*

Perhaps she is the one from Friday.

...I can't move, I can't do anything, except think of you. Every time I try (to move), my mind pulls me back to images of your beautiful face, your eyes: Every time the phone rings, I jump to answer it, hoping it might be you. You probably hate me. I don't know why, I just got scared and ran...I guess the intensity of my feelings was more than I knew how to handle. Why is life so complicated? You are literally driving me crazy. I wish I could see you again before I sleep. Please call. Well, the phone isn't ringing, so I guess I'll go to bed. Sorry this is so broken...Thinking of you, _____ .

The answering machine has four calls for today and the cold beer down my throat tickles with bitterness. I didn't include a telephone number and, after reviewing the messages, she didn't call—she doesn't have my number; but she did have my address, how could that be? She must have had me followed.

Freshness that won't quit.

A real game changer.

The new mandate.
Make memories tonight. Sleep tomorrow.

It is time to disturb the equilibrium.

We went up a badly lit staircase. On the landing before the second floor a group of drunk teenagers were standing near the restroom. I caught hold of the girl from behind so that I was cupping her breast with my hand. The boys in the group saw this and began to call out. She wanted to break away, but I told her: *keep still.* Several dirty remarks to the girl could be heard from the group. She and I reached the third floor. I opened the door of the room and switched on the light.

It was a narrow room with two beds, a small table, a chair and a washbasin. I locked the door and turned to her. She was standing facing me in a defiant pose with insolent sensuality in her eyes. I looked at her and tried to discover behind her lascivious expression the familiar features which I loved tenderly.

She differed only on the surface from other women. Deep down she was the same as they are: full of all possible thoughts, feelings and vices (which justified all my misgivings and fits of jealousy). The impression that certain outlines delineated her as an individual was only a delusion. It seemed to me that the girl I loved was a creation of my desire, my thoughts and my faith and that the real girl now standing in front of me was hopelessly alien, hopelessly ambiguous.

"What are you waiting for?" I asked her. "Strip."

She flirtatiously tilted her head and said, "Is it necessary?"

"Yes."

She had never undressed like this before. The shyness, the feeling of inner-panic, the dizziness. All that she had always felt when undressing in front of others overcame her (and that she couldn't hide in the darkness), then suddenly all of it was gone. She was standing in front of me, self-confident, impudent, bathed in washed out LED light and astonished at where she had all of a sudden discovered the gestures, heretofore unknown to her, of a slow, provocative striptease. She took in my glances, slipping off each piece of clothing with a caressing movement and enjoying each individual level of this exposure.

But then, suddenly, she was standing in front of me completely naked and at this moment it flashed through her head that now the whole game would end, that since she had stripped off her clothes, she had also stripped away her dissimulation, and that being naked meant that she was now herself and I ought to come up to her and make a gesture which would follow with the most intimate love-making. So she stood naked in front of me and at this moment stopped playing the game. She felt embarrassed and on her face appeared the smile which appropriately belonged only to her: a shy and confused smile.

Now I longed only to treat her as a whore. But I had never had a whore and the ideas I had about them came from literature, porn and hearsay. So I turned to these ideas and the first thing I recalled was the image of a woman in black underwear (and black stockings) dancing on the shiny top of a piano. In this little hotel room there was no piano, there was only a small table covered with a linen cloth leaning against the wall. I ordered the girl to climb up on it. She made a pleading gesture and I told her *please*.

When she saw the obsession and longing in my eyes, she tried to go along with the game, even though she no longer could and no longer knew how to. She climbed onto the table. The top was scarcely three feet square and one leg was a little shorter than the others so that standing on it she felt unsteady.

But I was pleased with the naked figurine, now towering above me, and the girl's shy insecurity merely inflamed my tyranny. I wanted to see her body in all positions and from all sides, as I imagined other men had seen it and would see it again. I was being vulgar and lascivious. I used words that she had never heard from me in her life. She wanted to refuse, to be released from the game. She called me by first name, but I immediately told her—in the softest of voices—that she had no right to address me so intimately. And so eventually in the confusion and on the verge of tears, she obeyed, she bent forward and squatted according to my wishes, smiled, and then wiggled her widened hips; during a slightly more violent movement, when the cloth slipped beneath her feet and she nearly fell, I caught her and dragged her to the bed.

We had intercourse.

She told me she was glad that at least now the unfortunate game would end and that we would again be the two people we had been before and would stay loving each other. She pressed her mouth against mine. On the bed there were two bodies in perfect harmony, two sensual beings, yet alien to each other. This is exactly what she had most dreaded all her life and had scrupulously avoided until now: love-making without emotion or love. She knew that she had crossed the forbidden boundary, but she proceeded across it without objections and as a full participant; only somewhere, far off in a corner of her consciousness, did she feel horror at the thought that she had never known such pleasure, never so much pleasure as at this moment beyond that boundary.

From: caliph8@sharia4ever.org

Hi friend, nice pic you sent me! You see there is a new internal enemy, it is this new age of ignorance. All this fake news and bullshit all over the social media webs. And the extinguished candle of so many souls. This is the burnout era similar to the times in Arabia before the advent of the Prophet and of Islam. This is not your path. This is not the righteous way. Your choice now is not lost on your brethren. Your salvation awaits. #inshallah

Dearest ______ :

I thought I'd drop you a note. A note to get you going again. It's a note to inform you of an experience I recently had. An experience you would, most likely, take a liking to. I recently discovered how liberating masturbation can be. I did know of its dimensions when I was first with you, but recently I have taken it higher. This empowerment came about through a girlfriend of mine. She and I always had talked about our sexuality, our lovers and other people's lovers. Recently she seemed hung up on talking about it. I was reluctant to talk too much about this topic, as it is something I do alone, in the dark. But, after her stories, I eventually relented. She went on to tell me that she loves *to masturbate in front of full-length mirrors, exploring herself, her body covered in baby oil, fully naked on lush carpets. After that story, that night, I came across a full-length mirror and did the same. I took off my shirt, revealing my breasts. I watched my* *breasts for the very first time. I took off my pants, then my panties of course. I had seen myself naked before, but I never had lusted for myself like that. I sat spread-eagled and imagined my friend doing the same. I felt so nasty, yet so alive and free. Later I told my friend about this. She was very happy for me. I confessed to her that I had imagined her while pleasing myself. She enticed me into going to her mirror with her. To disrobing and lying next to each other, there in front of the mirror. Her body was extraordinary, the very opposite of mine. (You know all about mine.) Her breasts were quite large, while her ass was small, maybe too small. We masturbated together, looking at the other then back at ourselves. I came and still continued. She rose and went behind me. She reached in front and gently touched my small breasts, hardening my nipples with her fingertips. She whispered some things, but I didn't hear what she said. I penetrated myself with two fingers, then three. I even put my hand to my mouth and tasted myself for the first time. I noticed in the mirror that she was masturbating herself, this time standing up, exposing her wet lips just behind my head. For a moment I thought of kissing her vagina. She was fondling her own breasts at this point. We came to orgasm nearly simultaneously. It was extremely uninhibited. She kissed me sensually and hastily, like a thief. Nothing more came about from this. We do share an intimate giggle when we see each other out, or at school. Otherwise, there is an Indian summer happening here in Stockholm and the cafés are full with blonde people well into the night. I don't have a boyfriend right now, but there is a guy I like, but he does have a girlfriend. Any chance of you coming to visit me soon? All my love, _____*

The Great Wheel of Hip.

She is the pleasure and the pain.

Her living room an homage to the rococo way of life: velvet couches in the entryway, bevel-rimmed mirrors, vast space and painted hardwood floors. I hand her a glass of champagne. Her hair up in bobby pins, talking excitedly. She wears an olive silk taffeta trench gown. When she takes her hair down it flows and puddles like a stream around her face and shoulders, looping gracefully over one eye.

We have a cocktail party in one hour, and I still have not done her. Meanwhile, she is creating an Impressionist masterpiece on her eyelids. (I recall an advertisement for the particular eyeliner she wears: *Stays on your lashes through 1,000 splashes!*) Looking down, looking up. Open. Shut. Getting glamorous graciously, like the manners and attitude and double takes that go along with it, is a learned skill. Her sexy sweep of hair keeps getting in her way. She brandishes her yellow red lipstick (Givenchy's Red #5) like a sword. She throws on the cotton-and-velvet suit, pulls on the fishnets, buckles up the stilettos and takes a deep breath.

At the party I watch her. She does not feel like herself. She feels...*costumed.* She feels like she is not answerable for her actions. She sashays around the room, staring at people from behind her hair-sweep, then props herself against a wall, thinking how great her nails would look with a silver cigarette holder. An ex-lover of mine goes up and starts talking to someone to her right; she gives me a party scan and does not recognize me. When I raise my eyebrows in acknowledgment, she shrugs, depraved. Then a famous guy that I have never met goes up to her and spontaneously starts chatting with her while a photographer from his entourage takes pictures.

Someone hands me a glass of champagne. An older lady I know looks at me with shock and then stammers, "You look handsome." I attempt, unsuccessfully, to think of a brilliant retort.

She returns to my side and I tell her that I am renaming her Veronica. I realize there is no going back.

She is an enchanted spirit. She has a sixth sense of style. If one were to kiss her mouth, she would become the most beautiful of women; if one were to marry her, she would be eternally faithful and bring one power and riches and knowledge one never dreamed of.

It's obvious that she seems to know intuitively what is of the moment. Like some master of invention.

Mission statement.

Pump up the volume.

Give a hint.

But one must have faith in her.

The female of legend.

In lieu of the monotonous work, I retreat to a long overdue letter:

Dearest Lola, I love you. I have watched you for months, and I love and worship your every movement, your powerful body, your skin, the movements of your legs when you walk. Never in all my thousands of years have I seen so perfect a female being. I will do anything *for you—.*

Before sealing the envelope, on the lower right corner of the page, I add: *Do not reject me.*

Walking to the mailroom, I stop at the copy room and see her. She asks me if we could, maybe, get together later?

...Late evening. Open air café...

Magnesium Illumination Light Flare.

At this point I can stop following the conversation for a while (they went on uninterruptedly discussing the hierarchy of Hindu deities) and mention that all this time I had been trying to catch the woman's eye, for I have found her quite attractive since the time (it was about a month ago) I first saw her. The sublimation of her thirty years dazzles me. A short black radzimere dress. Until now, I have only known her in passing and today for the first time I had the opportunity of spending some moments next to her in this small coffee place. It seemed to me that every now and then she returned my look, and this, excited me.

After one such exchange of glances, she got up, without reason, walked over to the window, and said, "It's gorgeous outside...there's a full moon," and then again reached out to me with a fleeting look.

From: caliph8@sharia4ever.org

People ask me all the time, why do you jihad when you guys in the Middle East cannot even get along. Well you see it is a blood feud that runs very deep. It is the inevitable consequence of the intensity of our Arab ethos. Mostly societies which emphasize the kin group but not the individual and subordination to the family and the lineage and one's honor is top priority. It is all about the blood revenge and the trigger chain reaction that always involves large groups of men. You see, how does USA individuality work for you? Is there something missing? Do you feel like it's you against the world, my friend. When some talk of USA being the Great Satan, they mean Satan as the seducer, the insidious tempter who whispers in the hearts of men. Gotta run, let's talk soon! #inshallah

She emerged from the small car wearing a soft rayon georgette shirt and skirt. For shoes, a quilted leather sling-back with buckled straps, a three inch covered heel. She skirted onto the sidewalk, and abruptly strode down a few storefronts to enter a beauty salon. I remained where I was seated and wrote a quick note. I rose and went to her car. I placed it under the windshield wiper, much like a parking ticket. I walked toward the salon. I reached the salon and looked in the front window to see her there. The beginning phase of a manicure. Her wrists limp, fingertips elegantly submerged.

The note said: *I want to lick your pristine pussy. Drink the juice; let it fill me up. I want to nibble on every tender spot you possess. Leaving you quivering and shaking and trembling, wondering if there will be more. I want to give you a long kiss. Ample time to let our tongues adjust to the other and make magic. I want to make love to you under a hot sun. Feeling the warm rays against our flushed and pumping flesh. I want to run my fingers through your hair. Scratching your scalp with my nails. I want to watch you on the toilet, peeing. Making small talk about fashion, or so.*

Then she put her hands on her hips and slid them up both sides of her body and all the way up above her head. Then she ran her right hand along her raised left arm and then her left hand along her right arm, then with both arms made a gesture in my direction as if she were tossing me her blouse. It startled me and I jumped.

Then she put her hands on her hips again and this time slid them down both legs. When she had bent down entirely she raised her right and then her left leg. Then, staring at me, she flung out her right arm, tossing me an imaginary skirt. At the same time I extended my hand, and with my fingers blew her a kiss.

After some more wiggling and dancing she rose onto her tiptoes, bent her arms and put them behind her back. Then with dancing movements, she brought her arms forward, stroked her left shoulder with her right palm and her right shoulder with her left palm and again made a gliding movement with her arm, this time in my direction.

She straightened up and began to stride majestically about the room; she went around to all four spectators in turn, thrusting upon each of them the symbolic nakedness of the upper part of her body. Eventually she stopped in front of me, once again began wiggling her hips, and bending down slightly, slid both her arms down her sides and again (as before) raised first one, then the other leg. After that she triumphantly stood up straight, raising her right hand, as if she held an invisible slip between her thumb and index finger. With this hand she again waved with a gliding movement in my direction.

Then she stood on her tiptoes again, posing in the full glory of her fictional nakedness. She was no longer looking at anyone, not even myself, but with the semi-closed eyes of her half-turned head she was staring down at her own twisting body.

Over the past week, I have experienced all of the following symptoms: inappropriate elation, manic irritability, severe insomnia, grandiose notions, increased talking, disconnected and racing thoughts, increased sexual desire, markedly increased energy, poor judgment and inappropriate social behavior. Last week—being much worse—I experienced: persistently sad, anxious and empty moods, feelings of hopelessness, pessimism, feelings of guilt, worthlessness, helplessness; a loss of interest and pleasure in hobbies and activities I once enjoyed (excluding sex); appetite and/or weight loss, overeating and weight gain; decreased energy, fatigue, and a general slowed down pace to things; thoughts of suicide and death (no suicide attempts); a difficulty concentrating, remembering and making decisions—and persistent physical symptoms that do not respond to treatment, such as headaches, a digestive disorder and chronic pain.

As she turns to smile, she tilts her chin to be kissed, to lift my brow in quiet wonder.

I assured her that she was still beautiful, that in fact nothing had changed, that beauty always remains the same, but I knew that I was deceiving her and that she was right: I was well aware of my physical super-sensitivity, my increasing fastidiousness about the external defects of a woman's body, which in recent years had driven me to ever younger and therefore—as I bitterly realized—also ever emptier and less educated women.

Yes, there was no doubt about it: if I got her to make love it would end in disgust, and this disgust would then splatter like mud not only the present, but also the sacred image of the beloved woman of long ago, an image cherished like a jewel in my memory.

I knew all this, but only intellectually, and the intellect meant nothing in the face of this desire, which knew only one thing: the woman whom I have thought of as unattainable and elusive, *was here*; at last I could see her in broad daylight, at last I might discern from her body of today what her body had been like then, from her face of today what her face had been like then. Finally I might read the (unimaginable) expression on her face while making love.

I put my arms around her shoulders and looked into her eyes.

"Don't fight me—it's absurd to fight me."...

...On the wood floor: an A-line skirt with side zipper and side slits; fully lined cotton voile; a bra in soft microfiber with stretch satin trim; a black thong with a stretch mesh back (tag tastefully removed).

Two miniature black hair are visible: one actually *on* the aureole; the other peculiarly placed off to the lower left—the one I like to call *outlaw*. Stifled between the upper-arm and torso is a small area of shaven black whiskers, a few actually longer than the others—neglected during the last shaving.

From the upper-edges of the panties to the bottom of her navel are numerous and ubiquitous hair (barely worth mentioning): light brown, interestingly positioned, in a thoroughly spread manner, a very thin carpet patch, resulting in a fusion of the existing soft skin ever softening.

On the backside, in the small valley directly above the spine, there is no hair to be found, rather, on the backside of the upper-legs, notably sized blonde hair permeate the creamy white skin—an obviously virgin area afterthought to the razor.

The toes possess small hair which have been bleached (rather than shaved).

Note: the eyebrows and pubic have not been touched.

Out in the wilderness of our games, we are the prey, the livestock. Nature will have her way and we will owe the results to the feminine. The most vicious, omnipotent femme. A welcome warmth and solace arrives with this thought. Surrounded and engulfed by the placenta of our actuality. Succumb to overthrow and socialism and the full circle of time's sequence. The repercussion of our components, the extra ingredient. We will always know what we know, and strive to trivialize that which is certain. And good. Dancing on the tombstones of our scenery.

I decide to meet with her. Admittedly, I was indifferent to her. Since turning her down, I found out that she is western European and wealthy. This combination of woman is as abstract as is infrequent.

I hope she wears that lace chemise with the lavish lace bodice.

Lust, passion, perversion…all species of madness, although they are not enumerated among diseases.

I will wait for her under the street light, against the brownstone, the movement of red light the backdrop. Perhaps a yellow tulip or a sunflower. Concentrated cologne and cufflinks. A whispered voice, bedroom grace. An inclusive exactness to the execution of gestures. Modern chivalry, raw conversation.

The concoction to her demise and abandonment. A fulfillment to something for which she always wondered. A love ideal she won't refuse and return to after being set free.

I dispose of three magazines, a button-down shirt and a broken glass. I call her and the machine answers. I leave a message detailing where it is she is to meet me...

...What makes her so potentially fascinating is her general indifference to everything. She does still have an unjaded spark in her—a longing spirit of hope for something that will excite her. She uses her formidable skills to good effect. But, ultimately, they could be her downfall. She is a fusion of mystique, intrigue and enticement. An unsheltered mix. She reminds me of a girl which I once loved; *she drove me absolutely mad.* She never let me know how she felt—although, to be fair, I never asked. As well, she must have known what was good for her, for she never sunk in my consciousness. She was always there, floating on the surface, never to slip below.

Her taste is very evident; tonight she wears a scoop-neck flared dress in forest green crushed velvet (her makeup changes with the light, like the velvet). A Moisture Whip Classic Red lipstick. Under the white linen table I raise my right foot which is bare and place it gently between her inner thighs. She gives a subtle jump and blushes, looking about the room nervously. I am not suited to be super-civilized. She is shocked—on the surface—but it is apparent that she likes it. Her panties are warm and smooth. Satin. I tell her that her perception of what I have just done is entry-level, and not to worry. Relax. With her slowly-approached acceptance of my barbaric advances, I know she has joined the dance. I ask her why she is so cool, so reserved, almost prudish.

"Look, when savage things come my way," she tells me, looking down at her lap, "they come in such tremendous proportions that they are always…*weltschmerz*, the English word fails me now."

"Can you give me some kind of idea what it means?," I ask her, pressing my toes daringly deeper between her legs.

"It is like, when you expect something to be so great, so wonderful," she gesticulates, "an ideal state, then, suddenly, like that," she snaps fingers from both hands simultaneously, "one goes into a sentimental sadness."

We are sitting in a badly-lit restaurant. Terra-cotta floor, human-sized ferns, ultra-Baroque objects hanging from the ceiling, a plentiful sum of glass and mirrors. Beyond her is a dining group of two couples. Our waiter waits on six tables. I pour the sparkling wine. From yelp: “The decor and ambiance could be considered alluring (if one were blind).”

She continues: “You see”—she pouts her lower lip, under the table she places her hand on my foot, where the concave connects with the opposing cut of the ankle—“it takes me a long time to allow a male into my life."

I think of my erection, of manhood, prowess, potency, mass fornication. I respond:

"It is quite possible, though, if the man were right—let's say, similar to myself—then you would eventually realize it and then click, opening up—opening up totally."

With both hands she massages the edges of my bare foot, where the tenderness of the virgin skin merges with the rough, worn rind. The other dining couples have glanced in passing at us three times, commenting twice.

"Did you know," she asks me prudently, "that the Oktoberfest is not in October?"

"No,” I say with a wide smile and squinted eyes, “but if this is a joke, you are going to get it," I tease her coyly.

"It's in September."

From: caliph8@sharia4ever.org

Allah’s Apostle said: The souls of the martyrs are in the bodies of green birds dwelling in paradise wherever they like and there is all that the souls could desire, all that the eyes could delight in! You see my friend, there is peace eternal where we are headed. We shall not grieve, we shall not lose our hearts when facing death. If compared to the pleasure of Allah all things are possible. Awaiting us will be the pleasant hereafter and everlasting grace. You see, what you are burdened with now will vanish, and whatever is left Allah will endure! The weight on your shoulders eternally lifted! Can you send me a new selfie? #inshallah

Anonymous inhabitants, floating between conversation and glances. Trifling constant static in the air, the faint smell of freon. The casual degrees of laughter's tonality. Stripes and polka dots, pastels and charcoals. I am handed a martini.

I can think of nothing except her most beautiful of measurements: hip size, twenty-seven inches; thighs, sixteen; neck, ten and one half; chest, thirty-six or seven; upper arm measures at seven; weight, one hundred and thirty-five pounds; height, seventy inches; intelligence quotient, I surmise to be around one hundred and thirty.

She was fuller and a bit shorter, even her face seemed less pretty, more masculine, adding a cutting edge to her gorgeousness—it all seemed to be as I remembered, just tiny details (which go unnoticed with continual observation) were different and changed. The cheeks were more colorful—perhaps it was a blushing nervousness—and full, not just in fat quantity, but overall area. The eyes now appeared to be a little more wicked, more diabolical; turning upward at the ends, a characteristic which did not exist before. The eyebrows *do* add the devilish element to her mischievous look; they begin to exist just at the point where the upper nose ceases and the lower brow of the forehead merge—resulting in the most beautiful of brows. Perhaps it was the black crocodile stamped patent leather coat she wore. Or the silk charmeuse bustier and sarong. The lips were fuller—coming upward and downward to fully envelope the actual area of the lips—a pouting peculiarity has come to arrive with the seductiveness of the tender and sensuous rose petal-shaped skin. A Chinatown red lipstick. Lost is the extra fat which once hung from the dull tip of her chin to the upper-center of her neck. *Her neck!* One of the best around. Surely wondrous, leading downward to the section where the collar bones meet, under a thin sheet of white skin. Of course, with age, especially during these important years, her legs are a little longer (the torso remaining the same length; although, now I do recall that she always had been hip long), sensuously shaped in the most feminine of ways, very little muscle revealed to the eye. Her hips curve upward and inward at the area just above the navel and lower stomach brawn.

The ends of the white socks she wears are rolled downward. Her legs are now crossed and her two long hands are at rest, one on top of the other, on her left knee. She begins to work her mouth forcibly as she tells me that *so* much has happened since we last parted.

I've not been alone for what will be three days.

Now naked, except for the two white socks and gold hoop earrings, spread-eagled on my bed, she pinches between two fingers a newly-lit cigarette and talks to me through the bathroom door.

In the bathroom I fluff my erection. She tells me that she had so much fun tonight and I think that the fun has yet to begin. Exiting the bathroom I stare her down, feeling self-conscious at my comical pose in the nude, with a full-blown hard-on, noting the beauty of her brownness, of her ineffable sensuality which flows across her skin like water from a spilled glass.

She tells me how she will miss me. As such, beggars cannot choose, I tell her, we should luxuriate and wallow in the contemporary. Forget about next week. There is not much to say, plus we don't really care. Life is not an experiment. The telephone rings and there is a backlash, the soap drops and it gets picked up.

Introspection swarms, actions are dictated by plan, and life remains amiss.

So much for the necessary.

You. Only. Better.
Like the principle of architecture, much of our approach involves meticulous planning combined with an appreciation for beauty, the laws of mother nature, balance, and perspective. A small price to pay for a beautiful new look that will last a lifetime!
Reasons: your nose appears too large for your face; there is a bump on the nasal bridge; nose is too wide when viewed from the front; nasal tip plunges; nasal tip is enlarged; nostrils are excessively flared; your nose is off center; you have an airway obstruction that impairs breathing.
Risks: bleeding, damage to the septum, a decrease in skin quality, obstruction of nasal passages, deep vein thrombosis and anesthetic complications.
The osseo-cartilaginous support framework divided into vertical thirds from the glabella to the bridge to the tip consisting of the upper third which is relatively distensible but then tapers adhering tightly to the thinner skin of the dorsal section, bridging to the mid-dorsal section nasal skin, segueing to the most sebaceous glands at the nasal tip. That moment when the mucous membrane of squamous epithelium transitions to become columnar

respiratory, a pseudo-stratified ciliated tissue maintaining the nasal moisture. If we plan this well we need to map and execute the correction you refer to as the "Eva Longoria" of a nasal deformity, dividing the aesthetic subunits into nine segments, providing me with measures for determining the size, extent and topographic locale. The right alar base subunit is swollen. The dorsal wall unit is flared. The hemi-lobule segment is rather dry. The columellar segment is frayed and torn, either by age or the elements. The common cartoid artery permits minimal discharge but is not lost. The lateral nasal wall segments left side are diminished to a point requiring a regional tissue graft. We can harvest from the buttock region. The principal arterial blood vessel supply is two-fold, branching from the internal carotid artery to the anterior ethmoid, deriving the ophthalmic artery, essentially supplying all vascular function to the nose, converging on the Kiesselbach plexus, adjacent to the anteroinferior-third of the nasal septum.

No smoking post-op, friend. Tobacco therapeutically compromises the healing. Nice looking drainage of the lymphatic system and superficial mucosa, posteriorly to the retropharyngeal nodes, to the upper deep cervical nodes, down to the neck and jaw. Good movement of the lacrimal nerve. Please blink your right eye. Now your left. Good, it seems the intratrochlear nerve activity is normal. On a scale of 1 to 10 how strong is the sensation of my fingertip running along your cheek? Seven is good. Zygomatic nerve is strong. This has been the Cottle Maneuver Test and you have passed.

So this is how it will go down on Tuesday:

A local anesthetic mixture of lidocaine and epinephrine will be injected into your nose.

You will feel a slight numbing.
Reduced vascularity will limit bleeding.
Full general anesthesia will kick in.
I will part then separate the nasal skin and the soft tissues from the osseo-cartilagenous nasal framework.
Then reshape them as required.
Suture the incisions.
Apply an internal stent and tape to immobilize your new nose.
Reduced dissection.
Reduced post-op edema.
Decreased visible scarring.
Decreased iatogenic damage.
Quicker convalescence.
Your Eva Longoria delivered as promised.

Less than three inches from my face is hers, passionately exhaling exhausted breath onto my sweaty and porous skin. After flashes of feeling her breath, I slowly edge my left leg further up between the two of hers. She grips my leg with hers, as if managing a defiant hug. I contrive to place my bare sex against the panties that she wears. Her naked chest collapses against mine and she mumbles something in her native tongue, while her eyes remain shut. On the floor I spy a seamless, underwire bra with stretch lace. For a quick moment I kiss her forehead, actually *feel*ing my lips against her soft skin. The nails of her toes scratch the top of my right foot. All so natural as, with my left hand, I slide the unwanted panties to her knees. In my mouth I taste the salt of her neck.

Rushed forth with the fervor of two colliding commuter trains. Unchecked by the conductors of our elegance. Willing to fall victims of unjustifiable motive and filth. Coaxed by an ever-mutable push to one apex or other.

It is this quagmire of an uncontrollable infidelity which permeates the soul and the loins and drives one farther and further into a pursuit, a hunt for the opposite sex, of what may seem to be a temporary companion for only moments counted by the clock, but rather—something only the one which is not monogamous can understand—is a trapped image, a blurry Polaroid which remains internalized for an eternity.

A softened linen and cotton suit with contrast trim.

Try to be judged by the maneuvers, by the pitfall in the eyes, by the cocktail in the hand. To see the sequence in fly by motion. The breakdown of topical argument, firm for the degrade of response, shared with a compromise's donation.

Living room, on the sofa. Dressed in a polyester fleece suit, cashmere vest, cotton shirt and silk tie.

"When we love, there is sex," she explains, wine glass in hand. "It's our thought that gives it pleasure, the images that have been experienced, or, in the case of modern day"—she drags on a cigarette, coming to realize it had burnt itself out—"have been installed in us by media, and the repetition of what goes along with it tomorrow, or what *doesn't* go along with it tomorrow."

She arrived yesterday and has yet to change outfits. A black mesh skin dress made from thirty-five percent lycra (created by a German über-designer), a satin blouse, quilted leather vest and black quasi-high heels (Italian). On a chair a pink polyester-Lurex single-breasted jacket with white tulle overlay. Fading Rouge Rouge lipstick. She accepts a fresh cigarette which I offer her with a smile.

"There is this joy in repetition that is delectation which is not perfection," she resumes with the lit cigarette. "Perfection, sensuality and the true meaning of love don't *exclude* sex."

I uncross my legs and rise, asking her if she would like something different to drink.

"Now, with this modernity, people in the world have discovered sex and all of the sudden *boom*," she exemplifies the importance of the point with drunken hands. "And it's the most important fucking thing in the world."

In the refrigerator I take a bottle of beer. On a plate, I place a wedge of brie and a knife. I return to the sofa and tell her that if she wanted to get ready before going out—*if we are still to do that*—that she should be getting ready soon, also because we have finished the beer and I don't feel like drinking any of the hard stuff from the bar. She laughs and calls me silly, informing me that she is already ready.

"I believe that is the only escape left for woman…and man." She looks into a gilded Napoleonic mirror across the room, touches her chestnut balayage hair gently, not altering a thing. "It's the only true freedom."

With the remote control I increase the volume of the Bose. The bass falls in accordance.

She continues: "In all other facets of life we are pushed around, treated condescendingly by politicians, violated as humans, emotionally destroyed by animals called people, we are enslaved with the trivial many, broken down by the vital few, and where do we fall into this, I must ask myself"—she waves to the pack of cigarettes on the glass table, batting her eyelids for approval, a coy smile like that of a little girl—"I don't think we even exist, and, you know what, that's fine with me."

I rise again and ask her if she would like to continue this conversation in the bedroom, *as I have to get ready, and all*, and that I can listen to her while I prepare myself in front of the bathroom mirror. She takes the hand I offer her, and rises, leaning forward, into my face, where I kiss her, considerately. We walk hand in hand down the hall. She sits on the edge of the bed as I enter the bathroom. The dividing door remains open and I run the sink.

"The only time we can be totally free is in sexual experience," she says, asking me if I agree.

"Fully...you have a very good point," I reply. "Please go on." The hot water runs over the backs of my hands, her figure buries into the black of the unlit room.

"Where was I?" she asks herself. Her face, I can see, contorts in intrigue and puzzlement. "Oh, yes, it is in that freedom we come across a certain delight which we want to strive to repeat, for there is joy in repetition."

Splashing drops of puissant florid cologne onto my left palm I raise it to my neck, then onto my stomach and crotch. I view my profile in tedious motion.

"But, when we look at this, where is love?"

I arch my shoulders and feel my toes against the tile floor.

"I think we can love a person momentarily, in a split second if that person gives us felicity and regard and passing reverence."

She asks me for another cigarette and I tell her she can find some on the table next to the bed, and if she would be so kind, would she light one for me.

"What is wrong with some fast-food love," she approaches, strutting runway-style, hip gyrating side to side, handing me a cigarette. I slide the wet part of my lips along the lipstick stains she left on the butt.

"If I can buy a hamburger and some fries and a big fat fucking chocolate milkshake for the change I have in the ashtray of my car while driving through and listening to some poor, exploited teenage girl who has to work just to buy tampons, and hear her voice distorted over a malfunctioning intercom, then I better be able to love a man if I feel like loving him, even from the first instance I meet him."

She spins a hundred and eighty degrees while kicking up her left leg, shaking her head from side to side, the mahogany hair falling softly to each side. The cover of a fashion magazine on the floor reads: SEXPIONAGE, How the KGB Trains Women Spies.

"I don't need all this pre-coital rhetoric that is just as frivolous as the how-are-you-doing-today from the traffic cop that pulls me over for surpassing the speed limit by four fucking miles an hour."

She spins once again, bending forward at the waist, allowing her hair to tease the floor. She flings her torso upright and her breasts bounce lightly, the left nipple blatantly adamant. I finish buttoning the teal dress shirt she has chosen for me. She smiles faultlessly and shows me the burning cigarette butt in her hand and I offer the empty beer bottle as an ashtray. I take her long hand and kiss it lightly with wet lips.

"All this instant love I am talking about," she says with an undertone, inches from my ear, "is simply…verve."

From: caliph8@sharia4ever.org

Hello friend, it has been a minute! Been busy with so much interest in the website. And you? I must share with you troubling info about US government. There has always been the sense of betrayal with this government, never being able to trust any administration, like in 1991 when the US called on the Kurds to revolt against Saddam Hussein and when they did the US did nothing while Saddam's helicopters rained down bloody suppression and group by group slaughter. You see, also the 9/11 blame game and the occupation without end. Who can we trust? What is it that we should do? You see, nothing is at it seems. Are we nothing more than puppets to the puppet masters? I have evidence of some new stuff but I will save it for next time. Kk by for now. #inshallah

I have returned to the same place, at the same time, as 48 hours ago. I did not surveil it yesterday. I hope she will show today. I did not know her, but she still told me of her intimate experiences. She came to me appearing very normal and sane, and asked if I had a light for her cigarette. She was wearing a raw-at-the-edges tweed dress which brought out the tender quality of the hyacinth-colored mohair V-neck sweater, and black boots. Her hair was short, straight and black; perfectly falling to form a frame around her beautifully small-featured face. A Rouge Absolute red lipstick. I lit her cigarette and she asked if she could sit on the bench next to me. She began with small talk, then, without any lead up, went into a fully detailed story about her sexuality, the lingering alcohol from last night the truth serum for today:

"...I have to fantasize that I am receiving cunnilingus from another woman. See, my husband is very effeminate; he prefers sex like that. What my therapist has told me is that what I want from him is simply the *experience* of having my mother love me, being kissed by her. What this oral sex from my husband—his name is Mick—does for me, is it fulfills the needs that produce an ability to *feel* sexual, and ultimately to feel *alive*. But, what I have found out, unfortunately, is that unreal fantasy can never fulfill real needs, so this symbolic behavior has become repetitious and a bit compulsive. Whenever he attempts to penetrate me with his penis, I become completely frigid, and intercourse is extremely painful. My therapist tells me that my body is telling me that there is pain inside. Although my therapist did not tell me to do this, one night after a session, I went home, took off my panties, and physically opened my vagina with both hands so that it was wide open. Then I allowed myself to experience whatever there was to experience. This prying open of my vagina allowed for the *clearing* of a certain road block. For weeks I felt crazy, you know, masturbating all day, playing with myself. My clitoris was totally swollen and I honestly thought it might even fall off. But, in the end, it has all paid off nicely, I have a perfectly good sex life. I mean, if some time you would like to get together for some fun, you know. My husband doesn't mind, he even told me that I should go out and experience all I can—he is truly happy for me..."

She doesn't return. I regret the encounter. The course taken in discretion mode. The abstractions and absorption as by-products to such trifling eruptions by an integral acquaintance.

From: caliph8@sharia4ever.org

The statement of Allah's Apostle, "In Paradise there are beautiful women chained in pavilions, some of these pavilions are sixty miles wide, in each corner there are wives who will not see those in other corners, and the Believers will be able to visit and enjoy these beautiful women, and the wives will not know." You see my friend, the Believers will be clothed with garments of faith, and the tender-aged and full-breasted Maidens of Paradise with large eyes will bestow thee with the Crown of Dignity and a cup for ever-flowing wine, the combs will be of gold and our sweat will smell of musk. The virgins will be satisfied with glorious triumph. #inshallah

Four-o'clock on a weekday morning. The latest addition to the bedroom a white porcelain vase, a lacquer red storage cupboard and a new color scheme of orange and brown.

Time passes like a silent electrocution. I experience echoes of the past with each blink. Memories of her are now vague and distant, like a faded snapshot of a cigar box on the floor. No negativity or bitterness will flaunt their ways, no voices to extol the ripening fruits of a past experience or affair—no, not next to her.. where her gentle breath is a hymn to life.

Last night she told me how it happened; and, now, I cannot help but to recall the story with intense vividness: a banana was involved and a guy she had been seeing (not her boyfriend). He was suffering a bit of performance anxiety and could not get it up, so in the heat of passion and ill preparedness and half drunkenness, she had to resort to the use of the banana.

"Let me assure you," she told me, "it was not delightful."

In the street, through the cracked window, I hear garbage trucks. I rise, gently removing her soft arm, the peeling separation of our skins merged in the night—placing it on the stained sheet. In the bathroom mirror, I see two curious red veins cross the white of my right eyeball. The light is on in the neighbor's kitchen: the man sits with the television, waiting for the coffee to finish making itself, while a newspaper goes unread on the table—these are the obvious things.

The woman in my bed is not as obvious. She is very complex; she had *become* that way, although she never was before. Once, in the beginning of what seemed to be all time (for before then, I cannot recall much else), she was simple, predictable, comfortably boring. Now she consists of many sub-categories and sub-personalities. Not *actual* personalities, but, rather, the subtlest of consciousness of different beings. Beings not all necessarily human. She can be childish, preferring infantilism games; she can be very old and mature and wise, offering words of sagacity; she can be super-feminine, cat-like, full of passion; the best is when she is pure animal, believing she is no longer human, but down one step on a staircase of evolution, mumbling words which are far from meaning, using improper syntax, convinced of her animalness. These moments are the most intense and the most frightening. She doesn't recall it after the fact (allowing for all types of playful recollection, sometimes ending with arguments about her mental health).

He pours his coffee.

She is on the bed. Fully covered by a several thousand thread count goose down comforter, except for the face and hair which evenly cover the three pillows (the fourth pillow is on the floor). She had entered my world with a simplicity, a joyfulness to life. She shrugged off all my distaste with amusement. She never understood me although I tried painfully to understand her. I shook her, vibrated her, striving, crazily, to get whatever is was out of her, the ingredients to her happiness. I didn't get it; it wasn't there. I don't know where they were but I do know they weren't inside of her.

For one stage of life her beauty was transgressed, gaped at with visionless eyes. Now, with veneration and insecurity, onlookers are dismayed by her. She consummates any muse I might have of self. Looking at her, I lose my contemplation; talking with her, I relinquish the next word. What is her most tender and precious attribute, or highlight, is as well her most venomous and unscreened.

From: caliph8@sharia4ever.org

You see, it is not difficult to see that the powers that be want to disrupt us. They see us for what we are, a genuine popular uprising. And instead of causing an implosive coup d'etat they are getting the blow back of a full revolution. So much uncertainty now. They thought we were dangerous before. They have a surprise coming. Hope all is well friend. Sorry to vent like this but much is on my mind. #inshallah

The drone of intercoms and systematic announcements. White courtesy telephones. She has already come and gone. Left at a loss, I felt like hiring a bloodhound to track her down. I would have the bloodhound come over to my place, sniff the bathroom towels, the sheets, my crotch. He would then depart on a search for her, setting out to find you with your smell in his nose. If he finds you with your lover, he is instructed to bite off his genitals. If he finds you in lingerie, he is instructed to bring that soft fabric back to me.

In anticipation, there…crossed legs, yellow-dripped cashmere sweater…looking off to the nothingness, to herself and the complications involved—the musings, the brain fog, the apologies, the lovers, the decisions…at high speeds through her mind…her breasts are remarkably diminutive, sufficing existence to contribute a mere presence on her chest…adequate to perk a second devilish and curious look to ponder, inevitably, how the nipples must fare: large, dark, light, rough, gentle, fair, succulent, sharp, dull, missile-like.

How is my hair…is my makeup working well with my coloring…do I look heavy in these jeans…can he see the panty-line around my ass…should I change into a thong...the high black heels are too tall, but do set a deft mood for her legs: propping up the calves to ascend the intensely-shaped rear end whooty…the sweater is cut perfectly at the top of her waist…sparse stomach and lower-back bared, the belly-button unexposed, and alas tattoo free…when will I meet him…will it be today, here, now…when will I need him so badly that even if it is not *him*, it will be another one…she uncrosses her legs and looks down at her feet….her left hand raises as to lift the blonde hair back from her eyes and face…the lips of her mouth jut out for a teasing special effect…on the wall of her foreground is an oil painting…the image is of a woman in a yellow wedding dress…in her hand, a bouquet of white carnations…as she lifts her hand to her face, one sees the cohesion of her palms…an oversized ring and a boyfriend watch…the latest over-the-top fashion.

A flickering tepid breeze cowers into the room.

At the height of being in love—or lust, for that matter—the borderland between one's selfishness, self-concerns, and the object of one's love is in peril of vanishing. When a very young child sucks on the mother's tender nipple, that child does not realize that she, or he, is separate from the mother—they believe they are one entity. That, oddly enough, is what I feel with her.

She is framed in the shadow cast from the open door to the bathroom. She is dripping with warm shower water, scarcely knowing anything about life yet knowing everything. I begin by advising her to slowly close the door behind her. The light fades with the creak of old hinges. Dropping the towel to the ground, I tell her to pick it up—that I did not ask her to do that. On the edge of the bed she slowly and timidly places her knee, while the foot of the other leg remains on the wood floor. Her hair is long, and with the wetness it has become straight, reaching down to the breaking delta in her torso which becomes her waist. She reaches forward and rests her hands on the bed, her fingers fanned out, looking away from me. The shape of her bent hips and buttocks expand, curving outward then inward, beyond my sight, her hair and chest stifling the vision. Lowering her head, I take in my hand her wet hair. With gentle roughness I push her head down, further down, until, sideways, she rests her head. I feel the hot breath from her small lips in the coarse hair of my lower torso. Beyond her head rests the animal-like body: feminine and sissified like a cat; rawboned and gaunt like a bird or giraffe; gentle and faint like a newborn; vicious and malevolent like a reptile. She asks me if she can have a cigarette. I tell her no, smoking is bad for you. When I see the tear, I light one and place it between her lips.

A few hours ago, while falling asleep, she (wearing a gold Venice lace bra) told me: *It was your face I looked into, unflinchingly, each time I orgasmed, your eyes...*

From: caliph8@sharia4ever.org

Insight from the Qu'ran baby, keeping the perspective legit! "Men are the managers of the affairs of women...those women you fear may be rebellious, go ahead and admonish them, banish them to their couches and beat them." You see, a husband will never be asked why he beat his wife. It is understood that his actions were for her benefit to keep her in her place. If she obeys, no problem. A righteous woman is devoutly obedient and punishment will not be necessary. Indeed Allah is Exalted and Grand. #inshallah

Her innocence and lack of experience can be seen on her pubescent-like nipples: gentle, pink, unsucked, unworshipped. They have been spared the hunger of a man's mouth, the thirst of newborns. She picks up where conventional breasts leave off: rather than succumbing to gravity and hanging, hers do the opposite and oblongly take shape upward.

Earlier this evening she wore a cocoa wool jacket, silk vest, silk charmeuse shirt with tie, brown wool pants with black men's shoes. A parallel red lipstick.

The candles have fully burnt themselves out. Complete darkness fills the room, except for the backlit elongated beam which spans the ceiling above. She is laying, in a fetal position, backside to me, on the other side of the bed, wrapped within a clean white 1,400 thread count sheet, her hips shooting sharply upward, bent skyward. I am lying on my back, nude, staring at her shape, her design.

To use the word Muhammadanism is a misnomer. This is to incorporate the name of the founder, like what happens in Christianity. Islam is the better choice—the word itself meaning *complete surrender to the revelation and to the will of God.* Islam is the infinitive form of an Arabic verb meaning "to submit," and followers of Muhammad therefore call themselves Muslims or Moslems, which is the past participle of the same verb and signifies "those who have so submitted themselves." The founder of Islam—The Prophet—is also referred to as Mohammad or Mohammed, Muhammad or Mohomet, and the followers, Mohammedans, Mahometans, Muhammadans or Muhammedans. The sacred city Mecca also goes by Mekkah or Makkah and the shrine it is home to, the Cabaa, Kaabah, or Ka'ba. The book of Islam, the Qur'an, also can be identified as the Qoran or the Koran. The religious head goes by either Caliph, Khalif or Khalifa(h). All of this is a result of various dialects within Arabic, and, of course, the translating into English seems to always dilute the true meaning of things.

She rolls over onto her stomach, then onto her other side, ending, ultimately, to face me. Within two fingers, I pinch a tender nipple, kissing her lips with mine, docilely. I rest my head and ears to abut her tame mouth. Each breath of her air is another rapturous tap at the door of my undoing.

From: caliph8@sharia4ever.org

As the dominant power in the world, we can blame the USA and all of its infidels for the suppression of our Islamic movements, the slaughter of our followers, and the establishment of anti-Islamist dictatorships throughout the west, especially in Europe, where the people are more than ready for Sharia. When you can no longer trust your government where do you turn? #inshallah

Wanting to know all her details of feminine splendor. Hygiene, birth control, tampons. I want to know what deodorant she uses. What makeup covers her face. What brand and cut of panties she prefers. What panty liner. What yeast infection medication. What size maxi-pad. What type of applicator. Are her periods heavy or light? Does pool sex give her infections? Does she douche? How does she masturbate? A simple pressing of a finger? Gushing water from a bathtub's faucet? A firmly pressed pillow?

Hot sun rays on my face.
Tingling breezes against my hair.
A gas pedal under my foot.
Light's reflection on calm water.
A telephone ringing.
The movement of hands on a clock.
A woman to look after me.

She pushed me into the darkest pit of desolate perplexity, crushing me by her absence. This time, though, I feel the burden of unachieved temptation. The *must* that eventually leads to pleasure, maybe even those moments to die for.

Amidst the sadness, there are still the traces of my own game. I met her casually, beautifully, impeccably. I stalked her address, sent her the object accompanied by the proper writing, setting time and the date of return: a museum of contemporary art, second floor, an installation in a sinister room of absolute darkness, seeing nothing, hearing voices...a vibrant and occasional rush.

A place beyond time and space.

There was a cut in the line of events. The flame died. Progress will reign and there must be another ultimate test of resistance to the seductive forces of suspense leaving any form of surprise absurd.

The drunk sex epidemic.

Freshness that works.

Red handed.

Too many dimples is the largest fear, according to a recent poll, among women and their anxiety of the buttocks. The second most widespread concern was actually not having concern but, rather, accepting the degradation of nature and age and stating that they love their backsides. This is welcome talk from women. I know one woman who had fat extracted from her buttocks via syringe and injected into her face. "I was presentable within twenty-four hours," she informed me, smiling assuredly—going so far as to extend her ass outward, bending at the hips, wearing a pleat-front, full-leg pant with side buttons and zippers. I joked with her that she should have had it injected into her breasts. "God knows how much work *they* need," I laughed with her. She became neurotic over the comment. I then had to explain that they were beautiful as they were.

She is open to any suggestions. She loves sex. She is my friend and she turns me on tremendously. Writing to her could turn out to be quite the erotic journey. The recollections of her. A ponte-knit chemise with floral appliquéd sleeves and faux pocket flaps. Seductive looks passing by over an opened and unread novel. I see one crossing the street. Nipples fully erect in the cool sun.

Hair blowing and ass protruding. A silk-and-polyester filled coat. Images of female genitalia flash mob into my consciousness. Standing there, pulling apart the lips. Inviting a quick lick. Easy penetration. A dangling gold clitoris ring, existing solely to receive one more dollar. Intellectual advancement is uncertain. I must advance. I must advance.

I must advance.

Find your inner badass.

A hint of skin.

Refuse to be ignored.

Rock your body.

Much like any other night, much like this night, I fantasize about her. About that worn-out body-hugging cotton tee with a touch of spandex. About those threadbare triangle sling sandals she insisted brought her good luck (she told me how she wore those sandals out walking and taking trains across Europe six times in four years). When I think of her, I dwell on her fullness, her sufficiency. She was remarkable like that. It was as if her skin would, at any moment, break the fragile confines of printed textiles. As if she were near fracturing the proportions of an unwanted second skin. Of course, though, as I know now, it was an act of well-planned, and well-executed, female artifice. She would never bulge from those seams. She would never give away the mystery to reveal, blatantly and by design, the obvious. Again: she knew the tricks of womanhood yore. One might find her there, lying in wait, wearing the same hook and eye stretch velvet top as the days preceding—but that is all we could undergo. One would be lead to believe that, at any moment, the attire would give way to her endowments, confessing her plenteous sum and substance, her brimming underlying cause. She understands how to tease a man, how to lead him to the chasm's void, mockingly pushing him into a non-reciprocal leap of bribery.

Now, in my mind, she has brought me to this point—regardless of her absence in this room, indifferent to the truism that oceans separate us now. I want her here nowadays. To put her under a hot light. To examine each pore of her amplitude. To find her perennially uncelebrated. Discovering that which is hidden.

I cut her off pulling in for gas. She is so very tall. All in black stretching fabric. Lycra, Spandex, polyester. Not of my fashion, but certainly of that which is in. Her cathedral column legs, the concave and convex of her ass. So at ease, resting. Wide panty line shining through. She bends to open the fuel tank, letting my gaze in. She holds the gas nozzle with both long hands and begins to pump, swaying, frustrated. Her ass, the varying shapes and even textures. Her chest appears, but further details null. Unimportant against those legs, those extensions of her feminine grasp. Furthering what really matters, the limbs that lead beyond the universe. To the truthful beauty and the beautiful truth. The place of cliché. The residence of anti-Kitsch. A so pristine locale. She bends and rocks, maneuvering the steel and plastic nozzle into the fighting hole. She watches the gallons count up, solicitously. The metrics of time. The surveillance of action. The countdown to countdown. Waiting, speeding. She fumbles withdrawing, spilling on the cement. The fluid runs underfoot. With a paper towel she wipes her fingertips. She shakes and pumps her ass, adjusting the panties which ride her crack. From behind one can see the tag from the undergarments, untucked, exposed. She retrieves her change and leaves.

Astonished beyond words. An excessive wonder might overpower my learning of a strange fantastical fatigue. Sure, this makes a great excuse.

A French cut. No maintenance on her channels. Some kind of slavery chic. Unbearable in all of its manifestations.

The fear of the naked woman; the fear of the Dominant Paradigm; the fear of her lips (all, in their entirety) and her walk. Go ahead and drop me, but don't break me.

I experience a stifled ability to find appropriate words for this gruesome ennui which penetrates me constantly, unrelentingly. Of course, I do not expect any major changes in mood or character of the remaining friends—yet stagnation is always a serious matter. Sickness and pseudo-Leftism. An infinite sense for suffering. All I need is some good intercourse. Let's not talk about such calamities…rather (as always) it seems much more rewarding to turn our attention to more luscious objects that surround us, waiting to be embraced by our senses…*women!* One has to try and turn the hearing sense off…after all those *geez* and *you know*s and *I was…oh my God* and *squad goals* in these particular voices. One or the other erection will certainly lose its virility. And I can't even.

Not even the simplest pornographic mind could avoid a full-breast load of association while being visually penetrated by those objects. America was the clitoris that Columbus discovered, steering his Santa Maria right into it.

Mad laughter.

The importance of cleaning, this voluntary self-abuse continues, not admitting a certain anxious prospect of this delicious domain proportionately between skirts' length and temperature—at times mathematics can be so seductive. Lusciously exposed skin beside me. This is strictly a personal matter of taste. And we know that some of us can be quite deviant from time to time…Baroque women and all.

Real love? Who can tell these days.

It is, though, dismal to see our sacred last bastions of post-modern lifestyle tradition obliterated.

Accents™: for the Natural-Looking Bustline you've always wanted!

Her torso does not move when she walks…it glides horizontally, hurriedly, with legs at full pace, head straight, as if she wouldn't dare share a glance with me…there is only so much one can do in a day…she used a pink/purple handkerchief as a belt…she is the domain of an entire subculture…I watch her watch me and as she walks away she doesn't look back or turn around…when the circus came to town…like a good dog, I will do what I'm told…she is self-indulgent, sheltering herself behind the guise of a thousand self-inflicted *fantasias*…I want to take it out of its imprisonment within the confines of bourgeois domesticity, to a modern sexual culture, to spawn a fever dream of debauchery…victims of a demagogic thwarted press, unite…she liked to steal very souls of men—like any mortal, I…

Solace in the thought that all this will result in more lovers and stupefaction.

At times, it looks as if reality takes the fast lane and passes that sacred realm of oblivious imagination, all before it is known. Be sure of the jealousy. So please forgive the banality of the profane things stated, which intrude upon the sacred time which is best devoted to the research of the female attraction that draws all on.

And then she told me: *Male and female genital parts are the same in function and underlying structure, though their appearance may be different. All external genitalia develop from the same set of fetal precursors. All fetuses start out with female morphology; if they are hit by androgens, they masculinize—outer labia descend and fuse into scrotum, inner-labia elongate and fuse into a penile shaft, the clitoris remains as a penile head and the clitoris' head as foreskin.*

Pearls of salty water on their bronzed skin. Shredding her hymen into oblivion well before hitting adolescence. A seeker of the muse to kiss the lyrical inspiration. Her father has an apartment in Berlin. The other in Paris. Just one step to Ultimate Blonde. And it goes like this: We are having lunch in the same restaurant, yet not seated together. We have never met. The waitress takes my order, then walks away. I see you looking at me. You smile and continue to eat. You are wearing a black spaghetti-strap camisole. Leather spectator T-strap with a patent polyurethane toe and adjustable strap shoes. Your nipples are visible through the fabric. Under the table, I see you are wearing a charcoal silk taffeta dress, lined with velvet. A slight breeze pushes at the dress confessing to the fact that you are commando. My waitress returns with plate in hand. She leaves and I see you gone. Across the street you vanish into a taxi. I rise and hurriedly hail a cab of my own. The driver follows you. Block by block we pursue. Your taxi runs a red light, leaving us waiting behind the crosswalk. I see your taxi stop and you emerge, to enter the building where you live. I jump out and reach the door as it is closing. I am too late and the door locks. I buzz all the buttons on the directory. I hear a click of the door and I let myself in. I climb two flights of stairs without finding you. I reach the fourth floor, the top floor, and see at the end of the hall a piece of fabric. I approach, discreetly, to discover a lavish lace underwire-cupped bra with the removable push-up pads removed. Apartment 418. I knock. I place my ear against the door. There is an unfavorable calmness to the quietude. I wait to hear footsteps. I anticipate. Linger. Nothing. I lift the bra to my face and put it to my nose. I smell your skin. Your precious skin. Your visible nipples. You.

From: caliph8@sharia4ever.org

With the intention of diverting attention away from itself, the US has flooded the world with poverty and tyranny. This is not fake news, it is no joke. It all starts with economic dominance and exploitation disguised as "globalization" which trickles down in the form of support for so-called Muslim tyrants who serve as puppets. It is all over the Arab media but everyone in the west likes to think we are paranoid assholes. And you ask why all the hostility? #inshallah

Full, sensual lips have long been considered an aesthetic ideal. Perhaps the most covetable of all features with benefits that include improved appearance and heightened self-confidence. Plump lips are a subconscious biological sign of youth and fertility, and are a symbol that transcends cultural fads. They also make you look more relaxed and inviting to kiss, the first step in mate selection. But as we age estrogen levels decrease, the lips lose their volume and appear progressively thinner over time.

Applying lipsticks and glosses is often counter-productive, resulting in "lipstick lines" caused by creasing along the lip border. The nasolabial folds, those nagging vertical lines above the top and bottom lips, causing shrinkage of lip tissue.
The only way to a permanent lip job is through using the dermal filler Artecoll, a very heavy substance that would normally show as white through thinner lips but in your case you are naturally full. The puffed up ness will eliminate the smoker lines and wrinkles. As will the laughter crow's feet. We will avoid at all costs annoying any lingering nodules and small lumps. Then we will target problem areas with an ablative treatment of Fraxel laser light, to kick start your skin's natural rejuvenation process. This will smooth the creases and pockets that are causing the wrinkles. These results are focused and effective. For ongoing maintenance we will go the topical route by irritating the skin with applications of Capsaicin, an ingredient that swells everything it touches, and when time allows, suction pumps to vacuum increased blood pressure in each lip...you see, to pull them out a bit. We have instruments to properly adjust lip length. We will avoid overfilled lips.
You will have that desired Charlize Theron trout pout. Your two weeks of recovery will entail: redness, swelling, itching, bleeding, unevenness, bruising, and a very possible recurrence of herpes simplex lesions. Any questions?

If I were a woman I'd lower my moist lips and circle your erect throbbing member with the wettest tongue you could ever imagine in your wettest dreams. I would slowly rise up and down against your chest with my moist pubic *hair, and after a slight of your lips against mine, I'd rise just enough to urinate hot piss onto your hairy chest as I spasm my own cum onto you—all the while watching you eat it, like the hungry man you are. I'd lick my cum off and snowball it right into your welcome mouth…and then with that champagne bottle that we managed to finish off, I would raise your legs high and wide and with my saliva and juice as a lubricant, would shove the neck of the bottle where it would hurt and rapidly retreat and attack it into your virgin asshole…and then, you know that candle that was burning, I would take that and pour the wet wax all over your freshly-shaven balls. Then I would pull out the glim lamp and all the electronics that I previously attached to your genitalia and give you an electrocuting orgasm. That would be the easiest thing to do. But, of course, that is not really an option. No. I would force you to remove my black stockings. Once they were off I would bind you and wrap your head with my dirty g-string. Then, like the nasty and hateful person I am, I would drown and douse your torso with the piss-colored liquid commonly known as petrol. The erotic sight of lighting you on fire would send me into uncontrollable chasms of spasms and send the aural senses highly pitched, an uncontrolled sound of ecstasy and then…*BOOM, BANG, BANG*!!! You have been done in…but was it not worth every minute of debauchery…*

It wasn't until the hangover passed that I realized the idea wasn't brilliant. The idea of me asking her if she loved me as much as I loved her. Those three words. They can be just *words* to me. To her these words are taken to heart as sentiments of profundity and sincerity. I thought maybe that would be the best way for me to get the upper-hand in the relationship. Instead, now, I choose to do it with ultimatums. I choose to work with fallacies. The false dilemma fallacy. Either or. This or that. All or nothing. My way or your way. No compromising because I am a man of standards, of very high standards, and I will not lower myself.

Visibly Revitalizing Solution.

So when she called I was still in bed, unmotivated. I put on some coffee, went to a window, opened it, and lit a cigarette. She asked if I remembered anything from the previous night. I lied and said yes. She asked me if I meant what I said and I replied: "I always mean what I say, drink or no drink."

Maybe we should commit or finalize, I told her.

Silence.

Finalize, is that what you want? I asked.

I could hear a faint whimper of a *no*.

Then, *damn it*, we are going to have ourselves one hell of a relationship, because God knows, I'm the best man around, I told her.

"I know," she said. "I know."

Later that day, we met up and went for a walk along a dock. She wore a black crocodile embossed leather single breasted jacket.

Everything I've heard about her is true.

Under starlight at the windmill upon the mountain.

The humiliation in the never recovery.

Hi baby,

Finally you write me. Thank you. You are secretive all the time. You never tell me anything. Why? I want to know what's in your mind. Unfortunately I can't tell you anything of interest. I was at the gym today and I wanted to kill myself because I realized that getting a hard body won't make my breasts any larger. Today I met up with the guy I told you about. The one I had sex with. Oh, God, when I think about that*! Well, I am totally obsessed with him. I have noticed that I think about him all the time, every time I am going somewhere. I always think he'll be there. Crazy. Especially when he doesn't want me, and when he has a girlfriend. I have to stop this and find some other guy to fancy. But who? I am getting lonely here. I really, really, really wish I could come and visit you this Spring. I even considered the possibility today, but time and money. I know we would have a lot of fun though. By the way, since I know you like this information, I am wearing seamless microfiber panties.*

Love...

From: caliph8@sharia4ever.org

Perhaps I can best explain this through an imaginary parallel. Imagine if you will the Ku Klux Klan has obtained total control of the state of Texas, of all of its oil revenues, and having done so, uses this money to establish a network of well-endowed schools, peddling their peculiar brand of Christianity. This on the surface is not so bad as in the USA there are functioning public schools systems, but in the Arab world we do not have public schools, so we need the funding to support the Wahhabi-sponsored schools. Really it is the only hope for an education. The Wahhabis have to carry the message to everyone and everywhere. You see, they control the word. One ruler, one authority. The USA tries to take all oil money everywhere they can in order to cut off the funds to the Wahhabis. Does this sound like a fair fight I ask? Pics soon or I'm gonna start thinking you're not real! LOL #inshallah

I presuppose it depends on how I think and perform my craft. I surmise I could play it off by saying I am a professional. But then I would need the proper equipment (i.e., imposing lens, light meters), not a disposable camera. I could say that the photo is for a friend in the hospital. I could say it's for a class project at the local junior college. I could say that I am a casting agent and that my equipment was stolen but that I think that she would be perfect for the part that I had in mind. I could tell her that I'm not a pervert and that I promise not to masturbate to the photos when I get them developed. I could tell her the truth: *that I find you totally beautiful and I would like to have a photograph to remind me of your lovely good looks.*

Could work, possibly not. Play into the urge. Feed the beast.

Oh, the craziness of one-way passion! The humor to the fact that they don't see and acknowledge me.

(I am overcome by concerns with contamination—dirt, germs, chemicals, radiation—and/or acquiring a serious illness.)

I must strive for it. I must take what it takes to get things rolling, implement the strategy of my own destiny. If I don't, who will?

For the world to take notice, we've got to take the initiative ourselves.

________: *This is not a poem, this is not an apocalyptic letter—this is simply an explanation of how I feel. I thought that everything might be more lucid if I put pen to paper instead of blurting out random statements which, for the most part, are inaccurate. Firstly, I apologize for lashing out at you physically—that kind of behavior repulses me and I'm sorry you witnessed that.*

However, I probably reacted so violently because this anger is inside me. I know I need to see somebody, a counselor or therapist about it. Secondly, I want to put my past behind me so desperately—you know how painful it is for me. He *is a part of my past and a reminder of the way I used to degrade myself. You changed all that for the better and I thank you for that. Throwing his name at me is only putting a match to my anger—the* ONLY *reason I saw and see him is because I want to remain friends with her. I told her the trouble it's causing between you and I and she suggested that maybe the four of us go out for dinner or whatever. He likes you and respects you so that would be an option. By the way, I realize how crudely this letter is written, but my thoughts are pretty raw right now and I don't have the patience to put them into prose.*

Anyway, back to us. Firstly and lastly I LOVE YOU MADLY. *It is the first time I have experienced this strong type of emotion—sometimes it's just too much. Picture this: Girl gets badly hurt* several *times and naturally begins to build a wall around herself to protect herself from the past and the present. She learns to fend for herself. She becomes truly independent. Enter _______...This whole wall crumbles to leave her exposed, vulnerable and scared out of her wits. Not a very comfortable situation to find herself in. She lashes out in any way she can—hence this morning's episode. All I can say is that we both have problems to deal with and unless we start helping* each other *we'll never progress, develop and become the complete, whole individuals that we are destined to be. Yes we* ARE *different, but we can enhance each other's personalities in a positive way. That will take time. Our living situation is crazy, but I'm so used to waking up beside you that I can't imagine the morning when you're not there. We will work it out as long as you remember how much you have changed my world—all I need to do is focus the lens so that this adjusted world appears clear to me. Please respect my declaration of love and don't question it or me, or my past. I don't have the answer. I'm still searching, so bear with me if you can.*

Anyway, that's all for now. Love...

Then I realized she was kissing me. Deeply. Penetrating the back of my mouth with an erect tongue. I was being attacked. She didn't back off. No, she persisted, eager, starved, gluttonously hungry. The wonderment of her actions and ways of going about things.

I am overly concerned with keeping objects—clothing, shoes, groceries, tools, receipts—in perfectly arranged order.

I did not know this woman. She smiled to me and flirted with facial expressions from afar. It was in a badly-lit room, people everywhere and cigarette smoke rising. She looked at me unceasingly, until the moment and point when she approached me. She wore a black fur-trimmed, embossed-leather pantsuit. She did not say a thing, she just stood there. Quite tall, we were eye to eye.

Where are you from? I asked.

That was all it took. She did not understand me. It was enough for me to invite her in. We shared stares to the lips. Flashing our retinas from eye to lip, lips to eyes. The buildup erupted with her grabbing my shoulders and pulling me to her. She kissed me, deeply.

Now we stand, groin to groin, her tongue buried in my mouth. She reaches up from my shoulders to my hair and pulls on it with both hands, clenching. I feel the skin of my face pull back. I grab tighter onto her waist. I slide my right hand down her backside and embrace a full cheek of her ass and feel it in my hand. My other hand I slide up and under her loose blouse to feel a bare, full and luscious breast. I play and tickle the nipple between two fingers. She penetrates deeper into my mouth with her tongue. I begin to gag. She takes this as a demonstration of my own excitement. The sound of heavy breathing is silenced when she seals my ear shut, entirely. I look beyond her, to her friends, and see their laughter to this particular act by my lovely.

I slide my hands into the back pockets of her black jeans and push her back a bit and whisper into her ear. It doesn't matter what I was saying, she took my hand into hers and guided me through the crowd of people to meet her friends. Then she hands me her pint of cider and says *please*.

A few feet away, a girl says: *At the end of the day, the last thing you want to feel is your makeup*.

She laughs to herself. We groove, moving in sync to the beat of sampled music. She tells me that she only wants to be with me and all the time.

She tends to render other women obsolete.

New Feel Perfecte.

It transcends words, communication.

An incalculable chaos.

Dearest_____!

Thank you for your card.

I'm not in the best mood right now, because I'm very ill. The inflammation has not gone away with yet, and is now threatening to spread to the brain. I will have a tomography done tomorrow and the results will tell about what kind of surgery is necessary. I will probably get hospitalized soon, but there is also a slight chance that I won't. The whole infection unfortunately did interfere with my studies for several tests I was not able to take. As well I did have to quit my adventurous way of life for a while. Most of the time, actually all of my time, I spend in bed. I need a great deal of rest and sleep. My apartment I leave very seldom because it is too exhausting and the bright sunlight would be a strain on my eyes. Furthermore the medicine has a weakening effect on my body. Admittedly, all of this sounds as if I'm facing death, but on the other hand there is no reason to deal with the situation thoughtlessly. Lying in bed all day long and doing nothing (physically) makes me ruminate about too many things which sometimes ends up in a "Sinnkrise" (untranslatable). Sex does not exist for me right now and I know that this is the worst thing about all that, but I'm sure as soon as I recover and regain my health, sexual desire will return. Of course I will let you know immediately. I'm sure it would be nice to have you here sitting near my bed, holding my hand, feeding me or just entertaining me. I'm sure that would help me up. There is nothing more to relate, since nothing happens. I need to quit now because my neighbor will get this letter to the post office for me. If there are any mistakes as far as my English, please correct me and let me know. I would really appreciate that. What are you doing all day long? Tell me. When are you coming to ____? I think of you. Many hot kisses (luckily the medical fever has dropped).

She walks by every once in a while and my heart skips a few beats. Unequivocally, I find myself thoughtless, unstrung, grabbing onto a delirium, a vertigo of red. I wonder if she knows what she does to me—or if simply she is aware at all? I often pass by the place where she works. A little ten table bistro. Looking into the window, hoping for some contact. Usually I get it. Sending me back to that nervous state which I painfully desire. I ask myself, *why*? Because it is so torturous, the teasing.

I successfully balance play and work—I evenly shift between business attire, athleisure and slight nudity.

Today she passed by, hurriedly, on her way to work. I came to know that she lives up the street, not down the street. I came to know that she starts work at 4:30 p.m.

She carried a new-sprung red backpack. She wore a red cashmere sleeveless shell and a lambskin skirt.

It is all too much. *Yes, really!* When we make eye contact, I am filled with nothingness—yet one illustrious question regarding her interest in me remains. If she knows what she is doing to me, why does she do it? Does she like that thought in anticipation? Does she merely enjoy the aspect of perpetual teasing, a never-ending session of erotic foreplay? Does she ponder and build up a consummation of sorts? Or does she simply enjoy the fact that she moves men, shaking them up inside?

If sublimation could be verbalized, we could answer the eternal enigma of her.

The veneration of the quintessentially exoticized American woman is not of the decades of old fashion and anecdotes. It is of now and here. It is the means for which one can escape one's own time and space and culture. It is a rich alternative to what could easily be described as mythology or history or classical allegory. Basically: she offers a venue for my dreams and fantasies. She transcends the Gypsy girl in Spain, the Moor in Northern Africa, the white trash girl in the trailer park.

An exercise in form with no soul.
Consumer Literacy Consortium.
Coital Alignment Technique.
Aging is a fact of life, looking your age is not.

Before I was to surreptitiously meet her on the stairs next to her room, I attempted to recall exactly how she looked. I remembered her face from the lobby, but I have come to accept that my memory does play tricks on me.

After I told her my room number, she surprisingly called within an hour. She explained her dilemma, why she couldn't meet with me under normal circumstances: I am sharing my room with two of my girl cousins and we are on a road-trip with my grandparents. The grandparents were staying in a motorhome in the parking lot.

She declined the invitation to my room, saying that she likes the adventure of the outside and that alone with me in the room would not be a good idea. Meanwhile, I was recalling exactly how her face looks. She was brunette, with the hair past her shoulders; she did have fresh, youthful eyes; her lips were well-shaped and her teeth were well-maintained. She reminded me of someone, at least her general charm.

I finished off the bottle of gin, pouring it into my cold coffee. I finished off a plastic bottle of gel, slicking back my hair, and sprayed extra cologne onto my neck and wrists, stomach and crotch, failing to empty the small, white glass bottle.

I got to the stairs early and found that she had yet to arrive. Breathing in fresh sea air, I pulled a cigarette from my jacket and lit it.

"You smoke," she said from over my shoulder.

I saw a smile as I turned. She flashed a pack of cigarettes.

"I'm happy you smoke too," she said.

I offered her a light and she inhaled deeply. We sat comfortably close on the steps of the stairs. She turned to me and I turned her way. She smiled. I was silent, and she quickly pecked my lips with hers. We giggled. I couldn't think of anything to say, so I offered: you are very beautiful and when I saw you I was completely enamored by you and your sexiness.

"Enamored, huh?"

"Yes, you know, that rarely happens to me."

"Well, I quite fancied you myself."

"You must," I say, changing the topic, "be enjoying yourself, vacationing with your grandparents and all?"

She laughed.

I first kissed her lips, then moved down to her neck, then up to the ears, and back to her mouth, heavily. We continued kissing for a while. She opened her shirt for me and placed my hand on her bare breasts. She massaged me between the legs. I began undoing her pants, then she slowly and politely stopped me.

"Not yet," she said.

She went down on me and sucked me off, swallowing. When it was done with, we smoked a couple of cigarettes.

"I'm sorry I didn't let you screw me, but—"

"What do you mean?" I said, with feigned disbelief.

"Well, I have to be careful, if you know what I mean."

Impermanent silence.

"I really wanted you," she said. "You made me *so* wet, I'm gonna need to clean myself before I go to bed tonight."

"Tell me about your parents, are they alive?" I asked.

"My parents, ah, yes very much so. In fact they met like this, at a hotel."

"Really?"

"A bit different though—my father was a bellhop delivering bags to my mother's room," she said, pausing to put out her cigarette. "And when my grandparents were away, my mother called down to have my father sent up. When he got there he found the door open, went in and saw my mother completely nude on the bed. Needless to say, they did it."

A passing hush.

"My mother said they did it mostly from behind, doggy-style, as that is my father's favorite position. They said I was even conceived that way."

I offer her another cigarette and she takes it, stroking my hand.

"I like doggy too," she tells me, matter-of-factly. "But you know why I like it?"

"Why is that?" I ask her.

"Because it's not about the pleasure I get—the actual pleasure the woman gets is very little—it's about the pleasure that the man gets—I know, because my father told me so."

"Is that so?" I ask her.

"Yes, he says that he likes the power of it, the angle of the penetration, having the woman on all fours while he's up top on his knees, the shape of the woman's ass, all that flesh, the width of the hips coming off of a thin waist. Do you think I have a nice waist?"

I tell her yes, very much so.

"That's nice because I realize that hips and waist are so essential to the femininity of a woman—"

"Not to mention her breasts," I add.

"Oh, the breasts are the quintessential feature, rather, *features*, of a woman."

"No denying that," I say, nodding.

"When my mother was younger, she had incredible breasts—you know, the kind that hang from their large weight, only to curve upward and outward by the ends of the nipples."

"Bs or Cs?" I ask, piqued by the thought of her mother.

"Ds, 36Ds," she informs me.

"My God!" I exclaim.

"Yes, 36Ds—do you think I'll get there?" she asks me, revealing her breasts once again.

I tell her that she should and not to worry if she didn't, that her breasts were already very beautiful and that she should be proud of them and never to be embarrassed to show them to anyone.

Off in the distance a police car's siren begins its outcry. Moments pass and a car alarm in the parking lot below lights up. Unfelt wind above blows a cloud on its course—revealing a cluster of nighttime stars. I place her flowing hand off my knee and begin to rise.

"I told you I didn't want to go to your room," she tells me.

I know, I know, I tell her.

We begin walking the length of the corridor. We reach her room and I kiss her on the forehead. I tell her that I find her very charming. She promises me that she will stop by my room in the morning, before leaving, to get my telephone number.

Be outside by looking inside.

It is apparent she knows her worth.

(I leave before she wakes.)

From: caliph8@sharia4ever.org

I miss you friend. Been busy. But you know I am very frustrated with our efforts being described as fundamentalist, our movements being deemed extremist by the fake news. These terms are unfortunate for a number of reasons. Fundamentalism is originally an American Protestant term. Now it is tied to Jihad! It was originally used to designate certain Protestant churches that differed from the mainstream. There was liberal theology and biblical criticism. Liberal theology is no problem in Islam, but what is a problem is criticism of the Qur'an. The literal divinity of our Book is the most basic dogma of Islam. It is a confirmation of what was revealed before and an explanation of the scripture. It is from the Lord of all the Worlds. If there is anything I can teach you friend, it is that key point. Talk soon, got to jam out of here! #inshallah

It was her profile. Or her hair. Perhaps a combination of both: how her bangs fell over the sides of her face. At least that's how things began. Right there in that clothing store. Right there in an anonymous French suburb.

I looked at her first, admiring. Then she at me. Aptly, she wore a gray plaid viscose-and-wool suit with nylon faux-fur collar and cuffs. She did not stop looking. No smile, nor frown—just a stare, a nervous stare.

(She has the perfection of foundation; she puffs and sponges on effortlessly; she goes from daytime to dinner flawlessly.)

She paid for her things (two bras, one pair of panties, facial cream, Q-tips) and left the strip mall. I followed her to her car. I said nothing and got in the passenger seat. She drove an expensive white Peugeot. The warm leather seats were welcome against my stiff body. She did not speak. She started the car and drove and we drove for nearly an hour until I realized we were headed for Paris. She smoked half a pack of cigarettes (the only clue to her intentions). Getting to Paris, we drove to the Moulin Rouge.

We stopped to pick up prostitutes.

She broke the silence by gesticulating: "You choose three."

Bewildered, I did as told. The girls had seen better days. The first of my choices was one with little makeup and a subtle behind. The second was heavy-chested with full lips. The third took longer to choose, but she ended up being the Euro woman of the times: Slavic, tall, thin, precise curves.

Wearing a Diabolo Louis Cartier watch.

Headed for superstardom.

Together we drove to the countryside. We ended at a large mansion. We went in. A North African servant started a fire. We mostly were in awe, unable to take in the reality.

Next came the commands. Although in French, it wasn't too difficult to understand. We were to shower. Once we were in the large bathroom, I realized we were to do it together. We showered, gently playing and teasing. The girls kissed each other, as was commanded. I began masturbating, but the one with the large breasts got down on her knees and sucked on me. We finished the shower and came out into the living space to find large plush towels, bottles of champagne and whiskey. I poured a whiskey, dried and dressed in a robe that hung on a door—a door that led to another unknown room. Together we moved to the room with the fireplace. The four women conversed in French. The beautiful one came to me and offered me a lit cigarette. We flirted through the eye contact and it was apparent that she was enjoying this trick. The other women made small talk and I savored their presence, languidly drinking into a spirited state. The commanding lady kept a continual eye on me, allowing herself the occasional smile and wink.

We were ordered to all make love together, while the commanding lady watched and got off. At the end of the three hours, she came to us and asked me to eat her out. It only lasted moments, as the buildup must have been unbearable. The girls poured champagne on each other and licked it off, drop by drop.

When things were finished and complete and everyone was exhausted, we were guided to a room with a large bed with many pillows. On the bed we played some more, until I was the last to sleep, well into the morning. When I woke I was alone.

Enchantment might be appropriate to describe the benign vibes that haunt me since yesterday. A day that I realized the cold fog penetrates one's sense for the essential. Having been absently drunk from a haze of work, I went out for a bite to eat. Suddenly, my eyes, wandering along the blue linoleum floor, caught tender legs of naked skin in luscious motion. The sublime struck me. And this is when I recall what Lyotard once said: *the only question worth asking of today is the question concerning the sublime.* She was the type of beauty to leave one numb and wordless. (It was not a particular body part, or signature movement; or that intimate sway of her skirted hips, when she walked in front of me.) I hope I will see her later, then I will give her the camera.

To hear her speak my name, resulting in aural climax.

Continuous postponed messages.

Like science in sync with nature.

Simply, *it is a new element of desire.*

By the comfort of your sweet reply.

And the soft hair of your mane.

And everything we struggle to not explain.

Beautiful girls pervade while sanity fades. Into the night, dark and darker, revealing the plight…for attention and redemption, from this hideous temptation. Beautiful girls ubiquitously placed for our pleasures. Now you are some seconds older. Always steal from the best. A postmodern character artist. In every woman there's a little girl. Would there be anything better than owning a flower shop?

Her seduction begins each morning in the bath. Women like to roam, like hungry animals. For whatever that is worth. Cinema provides a passing escape.

Maquimat Ultra Natural.

Then again, every once in a while, I attempt at being a nonproductive member of society.

A satin pajama inspired by a menswear classic.

I transcend her thoughts. I will listen very carefully, hoping and longing and craving for that faint whisper of your thought to fight its way through the wetness and into my awaiting ear.

I could fan her fire with my lips.

And burn with each turn.

Idyll in neutrals.

LipZone: Anti-Feathering Complex Under*ware*™: every day, every sexy way.

Personal style is a state of mind.

We smiled and shared a laugh, but never consummated a thing. I thought about it, just for a sneer.

Certainly, if she arrives wearing the red velvet bias-cut dress.

Feels better than the hair you were born with.

So I went up—balls in hand—to the most gorgeous woman in the establishment. She grabbed onto me and we started kissing—macking right there in the middle of the bar. She wore a black jersey dress with crinoline. It turns out that she is a model. So I am there thinking to myself that life cannot get any better. I spent the rest of the night lounging with her, then came home to listen to jealous hate talk on the answering machine (I did record the messages to myself, I admit).

How old is beautiful?

Things were not possible with this woman at this time, otherwise I would be having lunch with her right now. I find solace in the fact that she found me attractive. She looked like a Stephanie Seymour, but more beautiful and with the hardest and tightest body (not to mention large natural breasts). This place I went to goes off quite well. When there, I can't help but think of myself as some decadent eighteenth century king.

Nothing can stifle me...except myself.

I am reminded of an Indian fable about a bird who was kept in a cage by a man. The man was going off to the jungle and asked the bird if he could send a message to the other birds. The bird replied: tell them that I am kept in a cage all day and night. The man goes to the jungle and tells a tree full of birds about his kept bird. One bird, on the top, suddenly falls over and drops out of the tree, dead. The man goes back home and relates the story to his own kept bird. When his account of what happened is finished, his own bird drops over, dead. The man panics and sadness overcomes him. He picks up his dead bird and sets him on the window's ledge. The man walks away. He turns back and sees the bird standing up, ready for flight. The bird tells him, "All this time, I was the prisoner *and* the guard."

I ask her: what do women want?

She replies: we want to be *delicious*.

The smell of sex permeates the five senses and from this corner I see three. Relief, sweet relief. She is a threat to my complacency. I long for the perennial sadness which accompanies all attraction and distraction. They are so innocent, yet very woman-like. I guess they could be from America. I did hear from a German friend that American women give the best blow-jobs and that the reason for their large breasts is not implants but homogenized milk.

A gracefully insolent hiatus: that intricate skin, waiting at the stoplight of my lechery.

A riding crop and a rosary cross.

Enjoy the view from above.

All the people with their top secret blueprints. A some kind of essence of imagination.

Forgive me for being blatant…shock effect may work in our postmodern times, yet girls will have to be lured out of the pervasive realm of oblivion. Having taken the first step, I am doing fine...the impeccable beauty abounds. Now it comes to the seduction, which, in my definition and for our sole purpose, must include the sense of eroticism. Seduction can occur when, say, one lights a new cigarette—a medium in that respect. One is too vulnerable to outer and artificial forces, dragging one into believing that there are certain things that one is missing.

Eroticism occurs when: ratio and the body merge, Apollo and Dionysus in conspiracy, one longing for the ultimate balance and unity of thought and body, the other the epitome of debauchery.

Theatrical High Altitude Defense.

Quantitative Risk Assessment.

All you have to be is you.

Pure desire…the invisible lift and support you need under your lowest necklines.

Then there is the mask, the dark realm behind the dubious veil.

The TV experience, perhaps.

The GF experience, maybe.

A letter to *Quilters' World*:

Dear Editor, Your recent article regarding patriotism and quilting was most timely. I have often the problem of deciding between an American flag, which would be considered federal, and my home state's flag, which would be considered, well, stately. See, where I come from (Ohio), the state flag involves five colors. Now, that would not necessarily pose a problem, but when I think about our national flag consisting of only three, I have to wonder if I am willing to spend that extra three dollars and change on more yarn to cover the added colors.

Now, I love *America. I think this is the best damn country in the world and if I had to do anything for it, I would. I mean that. America is the land of the free. It symbolizes freedom that Russia and the Asians just don't have. And your article was just on the money when the reporter said that the country's flag should come first over the individual's state flag. When I read that I immediately turned to my husband, Bob, who was watching television at the time, and told him how impressed I was by this here writing.*

Well, that pretty much sums things up here in Ohio. I have decided that my next quilt will be of the American flag, all that red, white and blue. Glorious, ain't it? As for Ohio's flag, that will just have to wait. Hey, I've only got two hands!

Maybe when I finish the quilt of the flag I can get Bob naked and have him shit one of those diarrhea farts right into the center of it. Then I could take a picture of it and send it into you for publication. I think your readers would like Bob, he's a good man.

I hope you keep up the good work and to all of your readers: Happy quilting!

We are driving in a sedan I rented with false identification. We are on a lengthy drive into far-distanced and deserted mountainous locales. She looks warm in a black gabardine zip-front jacket. I told her, last week, when we first met, that I was a location scout up from Hollywood, and that before I could have any pleasure, I would need to take care of some business, and if she would like to come, she was more than welcome. I would be scouting locations for a thriller about an obsessed husband who hunts down his estranged wife and eventually kills her. I know, I know, it sounds awful, I told her. But, hey, what can I do?

The region was used each fall for car commercials. The ubiquitous green grass was now brown, resulting in a somber, yet volatile mood. The dry grass would be very flammable. I looked in the rearview mirror. I took a final drag on my cigarette and flicked it out of the window. Watching the spreading embers in the mirror, I drove on and advanced in time.

"This is crazy," I pause, "but I never did ask what you did."

"It *is* crazy, you never did ask."

Silence.

"Well, what is it?"

"I'm not telling," she says, defiantly.

We continue driving. No particular destination in mind and the thought of actually arriving anywhere specific feels awkward. Time passes. Time makes age, while age causes time. It *is* a vicious circle. But without there would be no progression, no betterment and no upgrading. Humanity advances at its own pace. The most profound and everlasting breakthroughs in technology and information have occurred in the last century. Imagine that the earth was once flat and the sky was once unapproachable. Intellectual masturbation—leading one to no particular conclusion except noisy joy and a smile on the face.

(Open your eyes; what is most important is right in front of you.)

Here we are in the car. Surpassing coming seconds and moments and contemplation and introspection. Here we are with absolutely no shared past whatsoever, a present which might as well not exist, and a future which is completely and blatantly random. I look at her, at my side, and see the profile of her chest—two well-rounded and suspended orbs, better enhanced by the seatbelt strap. I imagine and predict that if one thing is for unfailing, it is that when we get wherever it is that we are going I will kiss her (and she will like it) and then at this time tomorrow, when we are driving back to wherever it was we came from, that I will be more than welcome and invited to reach over to her and to touch her breasts, free to fondle and titillate.

There are some aspects of certitude to chance.

Now your skin doesn't have to act its age.

The beautiful on, beautiful under Sweet Nothings® Savvy™ Bra from Maidenform.

(What's your lingerie doing for you?)

Otherwise, she was impeccable. No justified reason to complain. Just a simple girl with a similarly simple way to approach—rather than reproach—the external world. Uncomplicated comes to mind with the sight of her. Once said: simplify, *simplify*. She knew this was all too satisfactory. With her, less is truly more.

When she dresses, she would always be found in jeans, sandals and a T-shirt. No makeup, no socks, no brassiere (she doesn't really need one), no rings, no earrings, no bracelets, no tattoos, no scabs (maybe a scar or two), no belt, no watch, no wallet (instead loose cash and one piece of identification), and, most pleasantly no panties.

Her simplification is sublime in its splendor. She is like a small souvenir from a nonexistent country. She likes to tell me that the story ends with her. I ask: what story might that be? She replies, you know, *the* story.

Simplification has its prize.

I lose her in the enormous night club, under the pounding black light fluorescence, thumping and siphoning tribal noise, amid the flaming protoplasm of women, sweat and dampness against cotton and nylon, the delirium of release and discharge, and I find myself unwinding. What is left to discover when looking for some action. I could wait for a lifetime, or come upon corruption happening now and involve myself. I slip, in passing, on the floor. Pass the unisex bathrooms, peering in to see bodies engaged in situations. There is no civilization here, just postponement for perfection.

I escape to a darkened room, void of toxic flair and character, and sit in a deep, soiled sofa. I sip on whiskey and watch the skirts as they pass by at eye level. Victimization and its rewards and failures. She may be treated like a queen. It could be the best day of her life. Flooded with luxury and corruption. A dance to the waltz and a certain anonymous meeting at the center of the dance floor.

I am nauseous.

With withered energy I rise and return to the central room. I watch a woman—dressed in tight light pastel colors—dance alone on a throbbing speaker. She flashes the unconscious crowd her silhouette, a map to find the way. Shining, guiding the procedure. She is approached from behind by a male, who, unknown to her, gyrates off beat behind her. She eyes another girl, who is similar to her look, just down from the way. They share a glance and eventually join each other. They hold hands, innocently.

They peck small kisses. Then embrace and slide the other's contour.

Having set the standard for such symptoms, I finish the whiskey and find my way out. A cab is hailed by a homeless man and I make my way home. The magazine I pull from my jacket details the following: humiliation, trampling, heavy spanking, please masturbate with me, I'm a sex kitten that needs her pussy fucked, lesbian couples need men for intimate pleasures, I need big stiff cocks in my throbbing pussy (day and night), talk or just listen, I'm barely legal, toll-free tongue action, fuck me in my virgin ass. The battery-powered reading lamp flickers and I switch it off.

From: caliph8@sharia4ever.org

The basis of the existence of imperialism in the lands of Islam is these non-believer rulers and their western interpretations of our beliefs and global power policies. It is our duty to concentrate on our Islamic cause, and that is the establishment first of all of Allah's laws in our own country and causing His word to prevail through Sharia. There is no doubt that the first battlefield of the jihad is the eradication of these infidel leaderships and their replacement by a most perfect Islamic order, and from this will come the release of our energies. The Caliphate has come home to roost baby! Do you feel me friend? #inshallah

The aesthetics of porn, and the fundamental idea and philosophy or thought behind it. It is the actual way it looks, the dimensions, the colors and the flesh. The off-white. It can be perceived as an addiction, an affliction, a disorder, a sickness. Moreover, there are groups that confront this craze. Twelve step programs. Detoxification resorts, shelters from the dissemination and ubiquity. It *is* better than, say, gambling or drinking alcohol. It is very exclusive and self-seeking.

Objects carved as phalluses, widely found in Upper Paleolithic art, have been incompetently interpreted as spear supporters or batons, but these batons fall within the size range of dildos. It seems disingenuous to avoid the most obvious explanations.

It breaks down to aesthetics—when actual consummation, with graceless wholesale display, takes it all away.

Across the glass dining table, she continued on:

"The female vagina is the gateway of life and it is this meaning that is symbolized in ancient Goddess images around the world. The Goddess is the source of all. The Domina may allow the submissive to gaze upon her panty-covered vagina. The very color of her lacy panties may be symbolic to the event. Example: purple is the color associated with the Crown Chakra that expresses a connection with all of humanity and the Goddess Spirit. The panty crotch symbolizes the veil to the feminine mystery."

I had a sublime time. The smoke ascends, never descends.

Lots of things transpire and most is lost in oblivion. Amnesia…one should slow down, breathe, stretch, smell the women. One would have been fortunate to have been paralyzed, to become numb. I would never have imagined or believed all the beauty there, showing everything, spinning like Sufi mystics, being in a never-ending state of ecstasy. I saw this sign in the delirium, it said: *show your tits*. Although I could not see the backlash, every now and then, I could see that pleased smile on her face.

I have succeeded in getting the latest Euro-interest to become more of an exhibitionist. I am a voyeur, and I like the reaction of other men when they see exquisite femme. She likes to tease men—especially with her long brown legs.

At the modern art museum. A grated catwalk connects the separated top floors. She wears a blouse and a short black and red plaid skirt. Thigh-high socks and Mary Janes. Under the skirt are floral-patterned white panties. She takes the elevator to the top floor and I wait below, on the ground floor. I look upward and allow the attention of other onlookers to be drawn. Two men approach me and ask what I am looking at. I tell them that this young lady just walked across the catwalk and has flashed me her panty-covered crotch. They ask if she would return. I tell them it is to be determined.

We stand idle in forlorn wonderment. She returns and languidly walks out onto the catwalk. I whisper to the men: *that is her*. She walks to the center and casually parts her legs. She then reaches under the dress and pulls the white panties to the side of her womanhood—fully exposing her sable fleece. She laughs girlishly, vexing a provocation. One of the men, under his breath, says that he would something or other to that piece. She quickly closes her legs, smiles modestly, and returns to the waiting elevator. The onlookers are awestruck, dazzled. I linger transiently as she emerges before us. She walks to me, eyes locked onto mine, grins and wraps her arm around my torso. The atrium's lights dim, the closing hour arrives. The elderly guard locks the main entrance from the inside. We exit through the emergency door.

I retrieved her prematurely. She had yet to ready herself, but I told her that it was okay, that she wouldn't be clothed for too much longer. She wore an off-the-shoulder nylon-triacetate dress with crinoline. We went immediately to my apartment. Before arriving I informed her that there had been a power outage in my building and the electricity had yet to be restored. In the apartment, my attempt to turn on the entranceway lamp fails, deliberately. Beforehand I turned the telephone off and now the Bose plays a European pop album rather loudly. I light three white candles as I roam through the darkened space. She asks how the stereo is working and I proclaim to her that some circuits function.

The mood was befitting and all that remained was sex. Sex everywhere—on each countertop, on each arm of each chair, against each wall, in front of every mirror, on the sill of all the windows, in all the positions of all the books ever written, against each fiber of every rug, with every pillow another prop, and all things tangible potential devices.

Sex saturated and scalding and shriveling.

I disrobe her, then myself. We are naked before I can conceive time. We verge upon the intercourse unwaveringly. We begin in the living room on the floor. She squats over my manhood, faces forward, toward me, and lowers herself onto me. She moves downward and upward, accordingly the penetration is shallow. I beam and gently pinch her left nipple between my teeth. She shakes aloft and bottom ward, detaining the infiltration at inconsequential echelons. I am wading in her pool and she has brimming reign. I want to bathe in the deep end, tread water past the floating line. I want to evade the watchful eye and slight panic from the wallop and outplay. But I am not in my jurisdiction now.

She moves perpendicularly and then descends, headlong, captivated, ensorcelled. The explicit invasion waiting, wading.

Uprightly, downwardly. She then goes deep.

We move to the coconut-and-resin sofa. She is sprawled on her back and I am upright on widespread knees. I lift her pelvis and enfold her legs about my hips. The incision is absorbing, although this is not the cardinal constituent of these circumstances. It is the placement of my member against her vaginal wall.

After she comes, I stand her up and we cross the room, abutting the window. My back is against the wall, she faces me. I lace and lock my fingers around her backside. I reach further below and feel her pappy fleece from the backside. She grasps my neck and I hoist her, permitting her legs to drown my torso. She is suspended and her feet are bare against the tapestry of the wall. She fails at attempts to rise, crashing down upon me with each undertaking.

I come inside of her and set her down. She shepherds me to the bedroom and we lay on clean black sheets. On her back, she assumes a semi spread-eagle pose. I situate myself atop of her. I slide into her moist loins and compress against her clitoris. With my torso hovering on her padded chest, my arms are afforded a cessation from the weight. She envelops her legs around mine, her cold feet resting on my calves. We aimlessly undulate and oscillate, tediously, sidelong and crabwise, obliquely. Our frames thoroughly contiguous and compelling, demanding and entangled. Her clitoris is pulped nonstop. This persists for just over an hour.

Aggrieving protons and neutrons decamp from my body, the layers of connective tissue conceding exhaustion to overcome me. Our perspiration homogenizes, intermixing, producing the same warm cocktail, an interchangeable woo potion. The fluids emanate and overflow, unrefined, crude and raw. Our odors commingle to incorporate an ethereal mélange of perfume of blossoms and honeyed scents.

I must finish. I am consumed. We have validated and upheld the junctures of orgasm. The zeniths of our joyance. We are sideways, on our right sides. Her silky hair is dry in my mouth. I am facing her backside once more. She naps without delay. I raise her left leg and arrange my left leg between hers. Entering her laterally, my thigh squeezes severely against the clitoris—intuitively, by gravity's decree.

As she sleeps, I tenderly slip and glide within and without, into and out of consciousness.

From: caliph8@sharia4ever.org

Some people say I have extreme views but let it be known to you my friend that a Muslim who insults the Prophet must be executed. Who can be more wicked than one who can invent a lie against Allah? We must prepare the doom of the disdained and dispense with the formalities of arraignment and trial and go straight to conviction and a quick and fierce slaughter. Allah said "If anyone insults me, then any Muslim who hears this must kill him immediately." This my friend is not murder, it is Sharia law and it is the just and right thing to do. #inshallah

Dear Interested Customer: Thank you for inquiring about the vacuum pump. Individuals have been using vacuum devices for penis and scrotum enlargement for centuries. Yes, your penis can be enlarged, because two-thirds of your penis is made up of muscle tissue known as corpus convernosum. This space is expansive due to the lacumar spaces. Unlike conventional hand pumps, the MegaVac Electric Vacuum System is more efficient because it creates a continuous and even flow of vacuum pressure. In addition, the system is personally gratifying, "feels great" and it's ideal for masturbation due to the variable-pulsation feature only available with the electric pump. No other system can beat the MegaVac Electric Pump System for self-stimulation and intensifying orgasms. The MegaVac unit is quiet, lightweight and dependable. For permanent increase in penis length, penis girth, scrotal enlargement and masturbation; this is the most serious and most aggressive enlargement system for men. Also, take advantage of our Nipple Enlargement System and Foreskin Suction Unit. This device includes a cone-shaped cylinder and acrylic ball. It is designed to strengthen and lengthen existing foreskin. For those in the latter stages of foreskin restoration programs this device is ideal for gaining maximum results. (Special prices are available to students, disabled individuals, military veterans, unemployed persons, or other people of financial hardship.) Thank you for your interest in the vacuum pump. I trust you will find the vacuum pump sexually stimulating and a source for personal growth and confidence.

I deprive myself of the deserving things, emphatically. Procuring gratification in the forfeiture.

Restraining from all sweetness; refraining from the indulgence of cigarettes. Then, once away from the office, there is no stopping me.

I withhold from myself her essence. It is ambitious and I locate myself amid a laborious cycle. I require her. I lack her. My lifeblood, the plasma of my verve. She coats my interiors, painting lustrous and grand works of art, unutterable treasures and showpieces, yet vacancy apprehends me. I am forsaken by my own invention of lackluster fraud.

Mother nature never smelled this good.

Through the gamut there is nothing more liked *and despised* as an absolutely grand woman. On a frivolous and superficial level, she can be a social butterfly and know half of the town directly, the other half circuitously. She can be ogled by luckless men that are afforded only dreams and fantasies of such women, rendered impotent by a passing glance. She can be viewed down upon, called a whore and a slut and a half-wit by resentful women who daydream of attaining a remote semblance to her all-encompassing, drawing-in and enticing looks. For this, and other deductions, she is truthfully a melancholic figure—for her God-given qualities are both a favorite confidant and a wanton nemesis.

As if full-on fellatio weren't enough, she segued her way into an aural exposé which involved the usual visual delights of certain lingerie, the privy reserved by the foremost of champagne, and the projection of exaltation, full tilt. As I sipped on the sweat of her inner-thigh, she kindly asked me to go on down. I obliged her with my rendering of an aristocratic performance, the least of a myriad of contributions booked for her. Compelled, she did her part by relinquishing a small water flow. Then the image of her symmetrical head dancing atop my manhood, the small brown curls of brushed hair tormenting my hips and stomach, entangled with that of my own. She always looked so bourgeoisie like that.

An affliction for the raw, I further saw to it that she got what she wanted.

Alike to a span of inadequacy.

Discover the luxurious touch of longing and a cosmic confluence now.

The supraorbital ridge better known as the brow ridge is not very prominent in human women. The frontal bone and supercilliary arch located above the eye sockets are more pronounced on male primates. The margins of the orbit outpace that of the eye. The imbalance of the face and the neurocranium, along with the anterior displacement of the face relative to the brain, combined with the morphological variation in torus size, and the load ration of the craniofacial angle cover the spectrum from the proto-Mongoloid to Nicole Kidman. The pneumatization or expansion of the frontal sinus cavity creates the prominence of the brow. This is bone stretching due to underlying air expansion. The brow bone bossing is genetic and cannot be modified by external pressure, only through surgery. This requires an osteoplastic setback technique, removing the anterior table of bone from the frontal sinus. For the best reduction effect the brow bones should only be reduced to the point of leaving some bone break to best feminize the forehead. To get a less hyper-masculinized look, a bicoronal incision near the top of the head will be made. There lies the watershed area of the frontal sensory nerves. This yields optimal exposure and clear access to perform the bone bossing. We will setback the anterior wall of the sinus and preserve the membrane as a barrier for the setback area. This delicate process will require extensive craniofacial precision in order to allow for the bone shaving along the periphery of the frontal sinus. The shaving will smooth the edges of the setback area setting up for the use of a micro titanium sheet for reinforcement of the newly contoured forehead. The sheet and screws are biocompatible and are guaranteed for life. Finally we will apply the synthetic bone substance (calcium hydroxyapatite) to cover the entire new defect to join the surrounding bone, ensuring the perfect integrity and most beautiful shape of your new forehead. Shall we begin?

I taste the necessity to embrace slowness once again. I locate myself in a sped-up pace, assailing to gain…to secure what is masked under a dubious guise as singularly tangible *slowness*. Hinder and retard down. It will all come around. She will come around. Vigor will come around. And if I grasp it, recognize it, I will undergo gravity anew.

Idleness. A shrewd pace to things. Passive, waiting for it to transpire. Longing to attain. Soaking, bathing and lulling, in the here and now. Simplification for an extended interval. Dress in slacks. Walk with just enough cash. Shave closely, using extra soap when lathering. Eat essentially. Stand with a tight stomach and a straight posture. Discard the loose notes and cumbersome consumer goods which surround me. Drink hot tea. Accelerate production. Defecate liberal quantities. Wipe meticulously. Trim erroneous pubic hair. Rinse the teapot immediately after use, and prep for the next brew. Bask in the glory and rejuvenating powers and forces of the sun as a little color never hurt anyone. Read the morning newspapers quickly, preferably before ten, and efficiently stack them systematically in the recycle bin. Read and scan and look at subscribed magazines, cover to cover. When finished, place them in the magazine rack for when there's company. Keep all shoes polished all of the time. The necessity of a seldom-used pair may arise. Follow necessary actions in such an occurrence. Keep all buttoned shirts ironed, all sweaters folded. At least ten forever stamps always available.

All files should remain in their designated folders, until further notification. All compact discs will be stacked on top of one another—aligned as to compensate a semblance of equilibrium. Plastic cases will be discarded, while text and covers are to be kept for reference in the accordingly designated folder.

Computerized files are saved onto flash drives; all drives are updated weekly. E-mails received obtain a rapid response, then are immediately deleted. White letter-size paper is continually placed in the printer tray (an ever-useful standard operation). The utilities program will self-check the computer, maximizing, defragmenting, and optimizing all files. This will be done with each use of the system.

Reserves—in the form of bottles, jars, tubes and boxes—of toiletries will be stored in the event of a shortage, or other emergencies. A bonafide bathroom bug out bag. In the case of a bad odor or unattractive smell, *all* rooms will be aerated. If the foulness lingers, incense will be burned or air freshener will be sprayed (whichever is more convenient and/or appealing).

Otherwise, two proper showers daily. Two teeth-brushing sessions (morning with regular whitening paste, evening with baking soda and hydrogen peroxide). A balanced diet of fruits and vegetables. A minimum of two liters of tap water. Three vitamins.

Finger nails will be filed as necessity dictates.

Contemplate, as illustration, her.

Individuality of expression is the beginning and end of her. Beyond that, it defines the human character. Perhaps even the core of nature. A phenomenon of disposition. When she wears that stretch rubber top.

Feels indulgent, yet vital in the relief of dryness.

Her eyes blink, pensively.

Brevity is the soul of lingerie.

Visible results invisible feel.

From: caliph8@sharia4ever.org

I have been ordered to fight against the infidels until they testify that no one has the right to be worshipped but Allah and that Muhammad is Allah's Prophet, and to offer prayers and give obligatory charity, so if they perform they then can be saved. You see, there is no God but Allah. He is the one God. No more than one, no two, no three. Only Allah alone is worthy of worship. Sorry friend, how are you? How is that lady friend you speak of? Seems you make a lovely couple, I would hate for her to find out about us. Talk soon, k bye. #inshallah

I will mend if I just give in. It is regulating me. I tried to limit, even stop what I have been doing out of guilt for this sort of behavior. I resort to it to vent and fly away, because I cannot cope nor relieve the anxiety. I am despondent and downcast following. Liability frequently overcomes me. Circumstances are more compulsive. It has interfered with my relationships. I resort to the images. Urgency defeats me when she offers. I find that I have various lovers. When the right one comes along, that is when I will stop this insatiable behavior, this promiscuity of one, this anti-selective demeanor. I need her deeply and miserably. When I pursue it, I find I act nonspecifically and nonchalantly to things. I lose my concentration and potency, my ambition and incentive. I even miss work at times. My standards fail me and I find myself in strange environments. Recurrently, I must leave her there, laying in want. Love may be killed by lust. Attachment strangled by exploitation. Each stride of surrender nearer to the edge of amnesia, the brim of sensibleness, the border of derangement.

This incessant and ceaseless debauchery of the mind.

My frustration now mightier than any fear.

I attempt, prudently, gradually, to scent the calm within. To learn of that certain ethereal substance which I fathom I must retain but cannot find. It surely does exist, this invention of the mind. This brainchild of the intellect. This placid and unruffled tranquility has come before. Unfailingly, this peace will surface anew. Perhaps this is what everyone is righteously looking for. Not for money, not for sex, not for power, nor prestige. Rather, the *objects* that will bring this quiet rest. Superimposed into the mind, into the intellect, leaving human beings with material and aesthetic standards which will only appease when obtained.

Nebulously obscured this subduing comes and, like any vice, wears down the tolerance and the endurance against its first effects. One is left with desires for more and even more still. The addiction embodies ample proportions. One remains with much immunity to the object(s) which draws one on. All of this and the original appetite were for the unruffled placidity.

Like praying for a gift that one will never receive, the pain reasserts itself—the psychic pain—revealing this promised omnipotence as a simple illusion. Originally, the purpose of the image of the flesh was to simply numb the psychic pain. But, like most image worship, when the future has past, nothing lingers.

One can become enraged with the cognizance that sexuality is not *all* encompassing. Any evidence can set this off. A microphone in the stilled frame. A passing shadow on the sound stage. An audio glitch. One may see the world as being pornographic. That the spectators are justly too tired to partake in the truth. When the hard facts of porn's fictional nature begin to surface, one destroys this reality: *for one has only pornography and nothing else*. Resulting in a longing for that delirium of smooth and sensual surfaces. One is victimized by the entropy, by the fall of exciting forgetfulness, by the betrayal of off-white exteriors.

In the end, this attraction is unwavering for so many. With this understanding, one must ask: *is it then not natural*? But, then again, there are those who have denied themselves, who, in a sense, have recovered. And they did not die. *Did you die?*

An oppression of thought is the command.

The cycle is fueled to start again.

Bring to light what you've been missing. Profusely intense color saturated with moisture. She gives you the pathos and the pity that made you want her in the first place. But now you can love the way she feels on your mouth. In twelve delicious shades, from chocolate mousse to cherries jubilee.

Just so I can funnel that energy. Just for a swim in your sublime resplendence. To disrobe the striped rayon suit, fluidly, from your body. As she utters: *have I got news for you*…maintaining her rag doll look, the unsullied attention to her every detail…her misconceptions…her belief that looking so cheap made her surroundings seem so much more expensive…the large bag-shape outline of her two breasts confined by a tight bootlick bra...the sweater puppies brought together to appear as one large entity…the timing of a fine machine, the precision of a primed engine…the attitude of God, and that elderly fragility I have come to count on for her ascendance.

The streets full of cars burning with the sky covered in smoke, and my face against your fluids soaking in the tropical dreams that we aspire chasing the cargo in the lightning night. We survive our saviors and the flavors of our enthralled undoing…the ensuing penetration, emancipation, infatuation of the hotel corridors and your objects of oblivion...when I can part your seas with my long face, and have a hard time breathing with your impatient fingers down to part yourself, to provide more real estate against the whole of my mouth.

When did we lose yesterday's dreams?

And tomorrow's longing promises?

See what's possible in the traditional madness, in establishing the absurdness. I fly from reality. Consisting chiefly of behavior and thought. It may be contemplation, rather than judgements and dispositions of nature. These are my views, my perceptions of encumbrances and paraphernalia.

Echoing introspection, aural hallucinations in the third person, flippancy and senselessness; dreadful mirages, catatonia, stolidity and stupor—all of the aforementioned plus particulars. None of it is outside of me at this junction in lastingness.

A lenient clarification: *the obvious never intrigued me.*

She is showering. I am awake. I spy her jewelry on the night stand. The 1,400 thread count sheets are on the floor, tangled. Her pillow is against my head. On it is her remaining makeup, a gesture of her attendance. I ruminate on the night's passing whimsicality. Her hips, her waist, her lower back, her chest, belly and ass. Bouncing soft hair, strong legs. Inner-thighs bulging at my head. The water from the shower is loud as I hear her drop the razor. The morning light elucidates the strapless corset dress just beyond the sheets, on the floor. And the slimming control slip. The sound of the falling water ceases. She enters the room wearing a bloodless looped cotton terry Kimono robe. I gaze up during her approach, and view the completed nipples of her breasts and the towel that she wraps, languidly, turban-style, about her hair. I welcome this fugitive pleasure as she takes a seat next to me.

A delicious festivity research: the road is so hot that the heat rises to block my view, driving faster and swifter to the destination, further and more distant from a breakdown of patience and a longing for peace; *hey, I'll let her do it once more and again*—she turned me upside down, now it's my contingency plan.

She goes down on me, delicately.

Deep in conversation with a girl in a brief leather skirt. I have consumed one bottle of champagne and it has affected me throughout the crotch region, rendering my junk numb. I watch her tell me a story about this wild and demented experience she had with a friend when she was on a swingers cruise some time ago. I glance at my watch and see that it has been eleven minutes and forty seconds since she went into the ladies room. Panic overcomes me and I light a cigarette, curbing the anxiety.

Her legs are sensuously plump. The nylons are dark, yet light enough, yielding the hue of shaven (perhaps lasered), inviting flesh. The shoes are not the most appropriate, but will do for the theme that she pursues. She could exist in one of my many fantasies, being the classification she is. Then again, there is never a general, stereotypical type to occupy my mind. Rather, the simple fuel for the circumstantial jiffy. Hip-long, her legs appear petite in comparison to her entire body, taken in whole. Her silhouette juts outward, leaving most everything to the imagination. I take pleasure in the stimulation of the tautness, finding solace in the *no risk element*.

How can I turn away?

She is still in there, yet to return to me. I ponder entering the ladies room and taking her from behind over some smelly urinal, but I remember that ladies rooms do not have urinals. She is adorned with a simple radiance, but, hard still, I would not want to be with her. Aesthetically, she is optimum. But she misses the essential flaws of beauty. The scar, the straying eye. The slight limp, the broad shoulders. The speech impediment, the large nose. The pointy ears, the small breasts. The well-covered ass, the unnecessary modesty. The unambiguous humility.

She emerges from the ladies room and I hastily discontinue my conversation with the exquisite one, cutting her off with a dispassionate *I must be going*. I take her by the arm and we enter the elevator, descend eleven floors and exit to a badly-lighted parking garage. We approach the car and she asks me to open the door for her. I oblige and follow her around the rented black Alfa Romeo. As we approach the passenger door, she sensuously slides her medium-cut dress up her thighs, just past the brim of the black stockings. She doesn't look me in the eye. Rather, she bends forward into the car as I open the door. She pauses with her ass in the air and refrains from movement. This is when I push her dress up further, stretching the expanding fabrics around her broadening rear. I see she has wet her panties. The soft cotton is now damp.

Triumphant moments pass.

I continue my advances. She opens her evening purse and empties the contents onto the leather seat. I touch myself and move closer to her backside. She welcomes my progression. Among the contents from her purse is a photograph of me. She delicately props the image between her fingers. She views my face, studying it. The snapshot falls from her fingers when I enter her from behind.

I hope that now the worst is over.

I remember touching your backside. I remember each detail. I remember wanting such movements. I remember telling you how much I loved you. I remember hearing your voice on a telephone. I remember you so very clean after those long hot showers. I remember the taste of your food on my tongue, the taste behind your ears. I remember the alkaline taste of your pussy. The taste stays with me. I remember the way that light captivates you. I remember the finest of all things with you.

I remember you.

Turn on the stereo, switch off the light…what you feel and who you know and what you have…women, they will eternally move on…the fusion of poetry and architecture…do you have any dreams for lease?

Pay attention to the obvious…the tapestries and the textures and the hues of you…I've only got two hands…I failed to mention my intention…she burned me down to the ground…sun worship, female worship…while the earth moves as designed, a passing infatuation, enlivened, affirmed…the three components: passion, commitment and intimacy…feebly attempting to stifle these ever-shifting sides…an erosion of sorts…novelty's sense of lost and found…leading into the commonplace…I do wish to end this vicarious sexuality…jumpstart your lust and daydream.

I was left to moon over the nameless woman, the woman I knew I'd never ever see again…a blank screen onto which I project so much. Search the recesses of her mouth…maintain eye contact and disrobe slowly…stay-up stockings, pointed toe pumps…stop, make a joke…laugh before continuing where you left off…no need to act it out—the revelation itself is everything…vary your touch…restlessness hounds me…make like the prey and not the predator…a whole new soiree circuit…I want to want to be alone…under the spell of her milky ways…feather me silly.

Supposing it is not the ennui that drives me to such musings, then it is the complacency I am afforded.

Live better electrically. Touched by her tropicalismo…and non-navigable undying sublimity…escaping surveillance for the time being, the finite indifference and Kitschitecture…Foreskin Restoration Movement…a pair of pumps with elasticized, crisscross straps…Visualize Plants Here…enslave Tibet…mystico-feminine…she told me it was there purely for trash-art value…allow the mystery…erotomania…a stretch lace bodysuit (purple)…slide sandals in full grain leather and topstitched…better yet: a platform espadrille sandal…pendulous breasts…unladylike fantasy scenarios…slightly less mysterious than chemistry, unmercifully…Breast Man; a subtle glimpse of cleavage…the quick flash of panty…a vista of stretch marks.

The stuff of operas and Greek tragedies…she liked to play peekaboob…do you sleep next to an open window…lots of lace and mesh and fishnet…will she ignite a trend…so refreshing how she allows her imperfections…her tone was steeped in doubt…a strange relationship with time…ignore fly-by-night fashion trends…one's perfume should benefit everyone involved…carry a magnifying mirror…make time for morning runs…shed old skin with a nonpartisan sea sponge…necessity, not preference, dictates action…think it over during a massage.

I was all alone in this, taking her into outer-space…other memorable events that shaped my needs: 24 snapshots over the threshold of her eyes (and the craziest is the location of the return).

Tomorrow's fortune will reign my destiny.

Scarves are my choice gifts for her. Because she utilizes them so well. From tying them up and folding them into clever placement, to nighttime shawls and stunning halters; covering stained chairs and decorating pillows tainted with cum and other secretions.

Various sagacious maxims come to awareness when I see her in under-clothing. A demi bra offering a décolleté shape without padding, adjustable straps and stretch satin in back. Lovely things come in lovely wrappings. Leaving it undone is often for the best. The actual travel to the destination can be better than the arrival. The delicate things she wears underneath. Closest to her body. Against her skin. When she is so exposed, yet not fully nude. The proclivity in the unhurried act of disrobing, of disentangling each hook one by one. Of rendering useless each button, while the appropriate textile falls to the floor. A bustier with a shirred loop trim. Driven mad with the appetizing exploration of her privy locations. Cognizant of the exposing capabilities in my hands. Abandoning the act unfinished. Permitting further lunacy. Immersed in the delirium of derangement. Consuming more water while drowning. Embracing the hallucination. Relinquishing the ability of separation.

In abandoned hopelessness. She is a celebration of the senses. A bud waiting to be opened, taut and appetizing.

She radiates as if in suspended congress.

That is how I see it.

It is a look defined by her. She draws me in—like any good woman—so much so that the lustful energy reverses, resulting in her directly piercing into my bloodstream, leaving my heart pounding. I believe she is unaware of it. When I see her, there is that curious unseen dance unfolding between our eyes. We share a smile and in a split second I ponder saying something. But it is all over too soon.

Excuse me, I'm...

I'm sorry to bother you, but...

You are just so *beautiful, I had to...*

After she walks on, I am all too overjoyed with myself for not speaking up. The silence only perpetuates the eroticism. She can only say to me things which will hurt—things like: *I've got a lover* or *you're not my type, sorry*. But, again, she could counter my introduction with coy flirtations. That just might do me in!

Tomorrow's horoscope reads: *Tonight: create a fantasy.*

From: caliph8@sharia4ever.org

For the new style jihadis the slaughter of innocent and uninvolved civilians is not collateral damage but it is instead the prime objective. The blurring of distinctions is immensely useful in our propaganda. You see, because of the rapid development of social media our attacks are not aimed at specific objectives but at world opinion. Our purpose is not to weaken the police or the military but to gain free publicity and to invoke widespread fear and panic through amplification. We want the psychological victory and to traumatize all corners. Look at the old school terrorists in ETA in Spain, the PLO, the Irish...they were so good at it! And that was before the facebook and twitter! We make the shock then let them make the awe! #inshallah

I am watching the front of the shop. It is tiny and discreet. Four velvet bras adorn the window display. Those passing by do not turn their heads. Yet, this is where they go, any hour of the day—assisted by an intense and fascinating, even intoxicating mental cinema—to buy underclothes for their mistresses. It is that ritual, that culture of desire which I have come to know.

Most men share the inner scenery of imagined and remembered erotic fragments that now crowd my mind, visuals and sediments stirred up from the bottom—a kinship ruled and branded with lust, regardless of our sensitivity or politics. A gilded spank bank of nervous torment.

I wait, rendered blind and fidgety and completely incapable of making a rational decision as to where I should walk. A tall and thin model with straight red hair and luscious pimento lips enters. I beg her for help. She shows me the purple slip with the lace top she has come to choose.

"Go ahead, touch it. It won't bite. See, it's biascut silk. I lounge around in this all day."

She heads to the dressing room. Through the curtain I spy freckles and long sheer legs. I am distraught and frenzied, enacting not to play the fool.

She emerges wearing a purple top and bottoms made up of a single string in the back and a mere lace frill in the front. I feel so intimate with her, like we are time-sharing our privates on the tabletop.

I am subdued with the ambition of buying wind for my lover's hair, heated sand for her toes, and a prairie night through which she might carry a lit candelabra to my bed: *what I have come into this store to buy is not for sale.*

I am enchanted to stay and continue the scientific research, but some are suspicious from my breathing, and my Dictaphone recorder just clicked off.

Left vacant and barren, at a loss for words, passionless and aloof. Yet my mind and body tingle from the remaining waltzing electrons and protons of her sensation.

Austere when nothing around you is sublime. When the sneaking look of seduction dripping from the eyes of the shop girl does not do it for you any longer.

Am I insatiable? Am I deprived? Am I depraved? Am I debauched? Am I blasé? Am I decadent?

Was it not good enough? Was I not a gentleman? Did I not show you enough? Were you not satisfied? Did I scare you? Did I not promise you everything? Were you not promised green-eyed children?

Simply put: *it's another day without you*. And to be quite virtuous: my exhaustion has nearly reached a greater point than my love for you.

Realize that late-stage capitalism has undermined my romantic endeavors, I must thank you for your style. And instilling it into me. I thank you for the standards that you live by. And allowing me to acquire what I did. I thank you for everything you have shown me, everything you have exposed me to. I thank you for the love we made. I thank you for the meals you prepared. I thank you for your touch and all the kisses. I thank you for pulling me through all of this. Dropping me into myself, setting the course for directions I did not know. I have embarked and returned more of a man. But, most of all, I thank you for your love.

Just the other day, I thought we would be together. Now you are gone. You have left and have different plans. I wish I was strong enough to not distress, not to care. But, I cannot do that. No, painstakingly true—I wish I could kill these images of you. But, I sit and replay each smile on your face, over and over again. I am not the last one you have loved.

Is it not all a simple guise? Is it not a distorted semblance of some fiction, some falsity? Would it not all just be better if I thought less about you? Would it be healthier if I thought more about the now and the here? And not about certain possible outcomes. Can I be concerned about the future, so much so that the present seems to cease to exist? May I permit my misgivings to guide me to sad locations, to territories with doomed dimensions? Should I indulge myself such musings for the lucid title of martyr? How much longer should I allow this to continue? How much longer is too long? At what point does it all become too much? When will we say good-bye, or hello? When will we embrace and my tender lips touch your face? When will I be over you? When will the memories rest at a far distance? When will our genitals dance in an unending harmony of pure love once again?

Through you I am completed.

I go into the room and cross it to touch her. She does not respond at first. A rapid instant passes and she takes my hand, cautiously. She then places it on her exposed thigh, just below the Worsted-wool jersey (lace-and-nylon embroidered) skirt.

She then directs me.

First, pressing my palm against her hairless skin, casually pulling my hand upward and inward, coming to a stop when I make first contact with whatever pubic hair remains. She lets me know, without words, that actual penetration is the only means for which she is satisfied. So I place my middle finger into her moistness and rhythmically probe it in and out, in…and…out. This goes on for a few fleeting moments. Her excitement overcomes me and I further involve myself. She is now against the wall, against a hanging calendar, the month is December.

Facing away from me, her face turned against the hard surface. Her skirt is above her waist and I have penetrated her. She suppresses repeated moans while the temperature intensifies. My arms now are wrapped around her torso, my hands cupping her breasts. I feel her nipples between my fingers. My mouth is tasting the perfume of her hair. Burberry. She reaches behind me and pulls me in, deeper. She begins her shaking and quivering. I do not let up, and she subsequently orgasms against me. I stop, refraining before my time. I step back. I look at her there, taking in all of the femininity. I view the leather high heels. I pause. She remains there, glowing. I go to her and enter her once again. During this interval I complete things, relieving myself in her. She smiles and shines completeness. I withdraw and step back. I look at her again. Her legs remain slightly spread. The skirt disheveled and lingering on her hips. It was at this moment that my discharge, dripping from within her, hit the wood floor.

(I infer the feasibility of getting stimulated by a woman smoking a cigarette. I assume I could get aroused by lesser forms of amputation. I surmise sexual curiosities could emanate from mere fantasies of such things. But, facing the particulars, I find that the simplest of visuals will always do it for me. A wink, a certain speech pattern, an over-voluptuous ass, even the overflow of a fat breast in a small brassiere.)

I was standing on a corner when I saw a girl that looked like you. She was so very beautiful like you. She dressed like you. She walked like you and moved like you. In skin tight black stretch pants, an oversized turtleneck, fine leather shoes. She was merely walking by when this happened, but she shared your grace, your style.

I was drawn to her. Something about her, something about you. Her hair was curled, though. The timing in her walk lacked event. The bounce with each step vibrated somewhat less. I came to realize that she was not you. That you are the only one. The semblance of your essence and your intimacy still linger in my mind, deeply.

(The average woman, in her lifetime, will use 7,488 tampons. She will spend over seven years menstruating.)

I hang onto the surfaces, only touching upon the interiors. I know what I need to do, and I have the utensils and capacities for the execution. I just don't know how to get it. I pilot my musing away from her, away from the havoc and refusal. I attempt this return to the vortex of the distress that she has procured. I do not want to stop thinking of her, but I must. Leaving it all behind me is the only brightness for upgrade.

Proceeding commands enclosed in sealed envelopes…infinite variations of the same game…the sublime is now…second skin satin bra and panties…she says that she thinks of me as a brother and I respond: then, *let's commit some incest*…a small high-tech photo-camera…only a stolen sight is exciting at this point…a reluctant assassin of sorts…presented for entertainment and novel purposes only, a photo series of centerfolds, much like aerosol cheese and blow up dolls.

An iconoclastic pervert. Ankle-wrapped sandals with slim straps that lace the foot and tie up the ankle. Healthier hitherto—a jacquard robe in rich satin weave. I was in a large department store which possessed a trans-friendly dressing room. I went in there with a bundle of clothing in hand. Into the stall, much your typical stall, the one nearest the common mirror. I failed to fully close the cloth curtain. I was rendered an outward view. I did not change my clothing, rather I waited for a certain woman. She came into the stall directly opposite me. Her curtain did not fully close. I was afforded a view into her space. I saw her disrobe. Exposing fully her chest and pubic region. A tall buxom brunette. She bent at the waist every once in a while. Her curves were gratifying. Her softness was appreciated. Her femininity admired unknowingly, from afar. She changed a few times, full commando. A Piqué knit bodysuit. A re-embroidered lace camisole. I watched each time, intently, doggedly.

As my presence goes unknown, I pass on the mere peep while they slip in and out of tight clothing. I should *imagine* that they would be embarrassed and ashamed if they knew I was here, but this is not fact. A heavy mental exercise. Yet, hard still, the idea of seeing movies and stills of exposed females and their genitalia, shot by other people on other continents, provides for me a thrill like no other.

Voyeurism technique can be charging.

Regarding communication, women love to talk about fashion, even underwear fashion. Never be a victim to silence. Pay a compliment. Say it with respect and sincerity. Comment on the bra you have discovered under her blouse. Tell her about the panties you like, the ones you prefer, and even the ones you dislike. Ask her opinion regarding the bikini in the shop window. The stockings in the fashion magazine.

This act is not in any way as exciting as pure voyeurism, but it is a means to *share one's tastes with others*. To appreciate the sensibilities of the generic female. She may even be willing to show off the very panties that she wears. The purpose is to convey that the voyeur is not a sad and morbid pervert, but rather a man with aesthetic taste, sympathy, refinement and a vulnerability to female seductions.

Soon it will be known.

I was only interested in her when she sat down. Her skirt hiked upward, exposing the top fringe of the black stockings. Impetus was further complicated by the plausible revelation of more. She never was a sexual object to me. Until this moment. Now she is in every way that and more. Her ass is rather large, with widened hips and a generously-spread crotch. The buttock cheeks shape downward and outward, falling with willowy overflow. She has no tits, rather mere accentuated nipples. I imagine the areolas as dark brown and withered. She wears her femaleness well. A fat upper-lip ceaselessly tinted with sober solar hues of red. Long black hair continually positioned atop the head contrarily. She rarely finishes a sentence. Looks dumbfounded by the remarks of others. She has nothing going for her except that ass. I often imagine her bending over—I have actually seen this—protruding outward those two ass cheeks, that thigh gap. So endowed, so voluminous and awash. So womanly. So much the center of my pornographic attention and intention, and that of life and a place for which we are born. I want to bend her over, position her with a concave backside, legs spread invitingly and enticingly, and touch the exposed pouch of black pubic hair and, possibly, unveiled red lips. To see it in the light. In all its display and dazzle. To note its perfections and imperfections. To better understand her physical breakdown from behind, from where it matters, with an unpretentious, objective and unbiased regard. A point of view for which many eyes have shared, but for which I will see with new and unconventional vision, a renewed fervor if you will. To see that elegant area where the flesh parts ways, where womanliness takes its definition, form and cut. Does the black hair obscure the fleshy mound? Or does the hair instinctively part ways? To wipe clean whatever juices and mucus may linger, to mildly touch the lips like so, better aiding them in their state of rest. I want to see the size of her clitoris. If it is immense, white, pink, dwarfed, slight, full-blown, life-size and/or vivid. Are the inner-folds of skin wrinkled, smooth or untouched? Does she become ecstatic and aflame from soft contact? Or does deep penetration provide for her only relief? Is she pleased internally or externally? Does she like to be licked there, or does she prefer to be kissed on the mouth, heavily, while being penetrated? Does she like to touch herself in the presence of a man, or does she not do that kind of thing? I would leave her wet with perspiration, smelling of blossoms in springtime, refreshed as a moonlit summer breeze. Then again, she would be bending and it would be dark. I would only know from the sounds and the smells of the scene. Leaving more to the intellectual figment.

Photosynthesis as I recline in the park. The sun's heat is challenged only by the inelastic air. The people move and proceed. Melancholy (a pleasant one) is present, inside of me and outside of me. I ruminate about last night. The Hefe Weizen, the lemons, the merlot. Her lips on the glass. The way she took the burning cigarette from my hand. The laughs. The nonsense. The numbing effects of it all. The language that we used. The language that we invented. I would stroke her arm with my fingertips. She'd grasp my hand, steadily. Cheers to your hands, she'd say. And to your *belleza*, I would add. Did I mention what she wore? A sweetheart tank dress with an empire waist, back zipper, kick pleat. (Over a demi bra with scalloped underwire cups.) Shoes: X-strap sandals in matte polyurethane. In essence, she was an aesthetic anesthetic. Evading categories all the while. I haven't seen her today, but I do know what she is wearing. Her attractiveness transcends such things, yet: a yellow cotton/linen tunic with a rayon satin-checked cutaway hem and shell buttons.

Cutting loose on an endless spree…a sonic thunderclap…drain daily…at times her pace was superhuman…automated photo enforcement…an information-processing mind-set…she doesn't even know her real name…you call the shots, lay off the psychobabble…I appreciate her attempts at femininity…our nights could be untold, but I do know what I want I will get…that woman of my fantasies will appear and apprehend me…I will make her mine and she will be overtly gladdened…just the right alchemy and geometry of the trick…domination through all things feminine…a higher headcount drives me on…she behaved like a hyper-promiscuous chimpanzee…I was the outside admirer of her charisma…she was proficient at leaving well alone…between us was a ribbon of energy…we all long for a pure form of physical awareness…a data love glove.

Her mouth was saying: *every day I have the most difficult time trying to park when I arrive home*…and her eyes were saying: *my only remaining sexual longing is for you.*

Is symmetry the answer.

Can I take you away from all of this.

What shall we do after we make love.

Various shades and hues of blue overlapping one another, wind blowing and water crashing. To be truthful, all I wanted was to see the palm trees. Shaped with whimsical curves, abandoned to the wind. Disfigured driftwood, magnified footprints, shapes of hearts drawn into the wet sand trapped under a hot sun, beaten by the afternoon rain. Ships passing on the horizon, clouds transient overhead. The people jamming, together.

The young woman in her prime. Gifted and beautiful. The image of the naked lady. My want for more illusion than reality. She is beyond price, sensitively soothing and temperate. Like divine contact. A wake in cosmic current. A ticket to her inaccessible cave. Finding imperfect peace. Those poor immortals. Her small mountains of flesh. Dazzling radiance blazing with radiation. For me and this…the first pilgrimage. Liberated from the confines of physical bondage, infatuation's prodigal child, painlessly still.

All that is truly necessary for experience is an urge to have some.

All the rest is left to simple immersion, us together, enjoying simultaneously the heat.

I want to know what it is like to taste your mouth, to lick the folds and the crevices of your stately and bounteous body. A subversive edge…remarkably, eminently, distinctively…a sarong-style skort with side ties…a relaxed silhouette, that is what she was reduced to…that alone…I preferred her in a square-neck dress, or a cotton sweater with ribbing…something to amplify the breasts, just a tad more…I do admit to looking forward to the sight of her in that rayon georgette tank dress…daringly sinuous but not brazen…her simple touch is beloved and when I see you, each time, I am suddenly amazed.

The salty taste of oblivion…that certain forever quality to speaking with her…an entrance that could never be emulated…she confesses of how she relishes the thought of being completely shackled and bound, blindfolded and left alone in a room…as I view her topless from a third floor balcony…or through half-drawn shades, her silhouette through stained glass…or her front-side through the reflection on the lingerie shop's storefront…the best revelation of any kind…in her eyes, a skyscape filled with stars, boundless, illuminated beyond all conventional light…the luxuries are here for us…the facilities for alteration.

When will you again wear that maxi dress in rayon moss crepe? Or the hot pants and the continuous underwire halter bra?

A play of proportions.

Her shoe collection: 6" spike heel platforms (zebra, leopard, baby pink), closed toe platforms, open toe platforms, double strap pumps, spike heel platforms (cow print), knee-high lace glitter boots, 5" over-the-knee pull-on boots (silver), over-the-knee side zipper boots (royal blue), spike heel granny lace-up mid-platforms (yellow), and 5" buckle 8-strap boots.

Imagine: zebra-print cotton/Lycra® spandex leggings. Suppose, here and now, her French blue oversized V-neck tunic. Assume, regardless of what you know, the jungle jaguar dress, made with suede nylon. Picture her laying there, a flash before nudity, wrapped only in the snake-embossed bonded leather belt with a gold-tone oblong buckle. Disregard the imagery of the cotton knit jumpsuit with the white zip-front bodice and flared-leg pants.

A love of line.

Triple-pleated pants with a ten-button front and a bandless waist with belt loops. A one-button blazer with a welt chest pocket and two besom pockets, a natural flax with flecks and slubs. Finally: a symmetrical button-front dress in a batik-like rayon challis print.

Candidly: *her style is the gesture.*

I was not prepared for what she was about to say:

"Since shaving, my periods are much easier to deal with. I used to get my pubic hair all clotted with menstrual blood, and sometimes, over a course of a few hours in a maxipad, the blood would coat my hair and then dry so I'd have to pry off the clots to get my labia apart before I could even pee."

I retrieve a black Mont Blanc fountain pen from the nightstand drawer and begin to write on a Hilton Hotels pad of stationery:

I want to hear it, I want to hear it—I want to hear your voice…two glances which together we rejoice…I love you, I love you—what more is there to say…except for that it's stronger with each passing day…I place my hand between your thighs, look at your body with my eyes…your heart is greater than that of fire, and within you I see my heart's desire.

As I note that she has stopped speaking, I whisper:

"I want to be enveloped by you. I want to wake to find that it had not been a decoy."

These images are stops of my mind. In limbo between two certainties. With her I simply engineer a different landscape—it's better this way.

As she looks at me puzzled, I continue:

"I drank our one year lost in sunshine instead of honey from the seasons of your tongue."

I kiss her leisurely. The sublime act of her rising as her shorts dropped to the floor. Her body of a twenty-year old. The experience of twice that. That tigress face, those protruding cheekbones. The proof is in the final state. To be left numb, unloved. I was relieved when she left the door open when peeing. She talked of the time she had three fingers in her. And how now she is ready for an entire fist. Her submission to reality. I would love to give her oral sex. Even in full menstrual heat. To pull her hips off the bed. Observing time stand still. While she may touch her lower lip, there is nothing I can do. Her black lashes still wet and matted. Postponing bliss, as we burn. Hands on her hips, hair swept to the side, the bounds of rapture. Those thighs wrapped so tightly around my neck. That wet slit of wrinkled skin, encompassed by soft hair. In my mouth, between my teeth. Her affliction for affection. An inclination for indecency. The inhalation of her hot breath. Her words which blister by electrocution. Such figures of desire. Her intentions overheard. Conjuring the memory of her tonic spilt in my hands. Her underdone proposals. These are the obvious things.

I hear her say: tonight I want you…I want to taste your flesh in my mouth…feel you deep inside me…deep in my pussy…feel you shoot your hot juice into me…and bring you up again so that I can suck your hot cock and savor your pearly essence…*I want to fuck you madly!* The phone sex recording interrupts to request authorization. More payout. Click.

Sagging upper eyelid skin? Wrinkles and folds around the eyes? Puffy pockets of fat? Aging, stress, heredity and exposure to the elements can make your eyes look older. Do you want to look rested and refreshed? Bright and open eyes are characteristics of youth and attractiveness. The aesthetic modification is fairly simple. Performed with excision, our goal is the removal of excess tissue and adipocyte fat, combined with a precision shedding of the reinforcement of tendon tissues while resolving the cosmetic problems of the periorbita using a carbon dioxide laser.

The endgame is the restoration and resecting and eventual re-draping of the excess fat of the retroseptal in order to produce a smoother anatomically transition from lower eyelid to the cheek. This operation is what some Asians have done to look less Asian. We are trying to minimize the periosteum covering which comprises a two-layer connective cover that connects tissues with blood and blood vessels along with a deep layer of collagenous bundles, composed mostly of spindle-shaped cells and a network of thin, elastic fibers.

****Three hours later****

Initial swelling and bruising. Light sensitivity and double vision.

Post-op canthopexy stitches placed near the outer corner of the lower eyelid (these will dissolve in four to six weeks).

Midface elevation will be required to rejuvenate the lower eyelid-cheek complex.

Worse case scenarios: dry-eye syndrome; palpebral skin laxity; malpositioning; eyeball prominence; protrusion of the eyeball to the malar complex; ectropian (lower lid inversion); hematoma; thyroid eye disease; under correction; chest pain.

Her fantasy involves her being bedridden. It involves myself, or any capable—or culpable—male, for that matter. I am to dress as an orderly and come into her room unannounced. There I will find that she has relieved her bladder and bowels on the sheets. I am to struggle with her while trying to clean up the mess. At this point she becomes violent, thrashing the soiled sheets, pulling my hair, so on. I am to threaten her with sedatives that will render her unconscious. She tells me to fuck off and that is when I inject her with the drug. Fulfilling her fantasy, I am to make love with her unconscious body. I am to take my time, and to be sensual. This should last however long I desire. She is to wake hours later with my semen spilling out of her vagina, onto the filth of the bed. Furthermore, she is to be startled and scared. She will call the police from her bed. I will arrive dressed as a detective, with a badge on a lanyard around my neck. She will go over all of the details, as I write it all into my notepad. After her rundown of events, I will ask her if she wants to press charges and she will say no. That in fact it was not all too unpleasant after all. She will then ask me, the detective, if I wouldn't mind having my way with her. I am to concede, reluctantly, explaining that I am still on duty, and all. She offers me oral sex, sparing me from contact with the soiled sheets. When it is over, I am to threaten to have her arrested if she ever tells anyone about what happened. She begins to cry and mumble about how she is a victim and she cannot trust anybody. She says that if she weren't confined to a hospital bed, it would all be easier, but that in this state she is sitting prey, helpless. I am to button up my pants and leave. She will call the orderly and I am to return, dressed in the orderly uniform. She will tell me exactly what happened and I will tell her she is delirious, that maybe some sedatives and sleep will help. I find the vein near her elbow and inject her. I move her on the bed, away from the polluted center. She is lumped over the end of the bed. I enter her from behind. She wakes hours later and calls the detective.

Coming in with inspiration, going away with the ability to fulfill. The cost to look cheap. Will they ever absorb me as much as I do them? Like the bafflement of intimate magic. The confines of thought. Copyrighting the name Jesus©. Stand by. If women were good for you, they would not be sublime. A confidential situation.

The line between what fantasy promises and reality dictates…time is limited and all of this beckons to be acted out with a sense of urgency…she claims that I looted her gold but left the artwork…her acts of haute-hedonism…those super-petite breasts which poke and stare upward, saturated and ripe, tight under her chest's skin…a lust for bust…she cannot let it end like this…upon apocalyptic rumination, I promised her that I'd believe in her so long as she supplied the goods…like I say, I am okay with it…with the pursuit…with the indictment…with going down…and the role of lingerie…have faith in me, I will help you become someone…the rebirth of my collapse…with the smell of all the bouquets of the world…the liaison of the outcome…it may be a strange notion to you…and the denial the prize…the silhouette is the reason…the scandal the token of her love…a little lower please…right there, that's it…if only every day could be like this.

I asked her if it was free and she replied: *In this country nothing's free, baby—except for the 800 numbers.*

The glimmer's off-take.

You walking idle in your own glow.

The heat a mirage off her bare stomach. Rising to sink in my loins. Her breasts hanging to the sides in that white tank. The dark nipples creeping through. She inches the skirt further upward. Provocatively exposing enhanced stomach flesh, closer to revealing the entire breast area. No nonsense. Time spent at the beach. The forwardness of fake eyelashes. Gridlock. Focus. Scandalous is an understatement. She told me of her Dutch sexpot friend's arrival. The kiss in the vegetable section. The article about postmodern virginity. The other day imagery. The one that was ultra-fine. The one who drew the line between romantic and jaded. Grounded yet glamorous. An infatuation for real love. A tense promise. She was deep in more than her muse. Those so very long brown legs. And that arched back. A licking invitation. Anything involving the teeth. Clothed, she appeared waif-like. Nude, magnetic. Her style was of the briefcase-toting power suitor. She douched regularly. A conundrum of desire and shame. Sparse makeup. Her friend, the neo-go-go Bolshevik warrior nymph type. C cup. Plenty of breast/bra overflow. Arched eyebrows, unplucked. Wide smile, feminine laugh. *Am I embarrassing you yet?*, she'd ask. *Because I mean to be*, she'd add.

Energetically she told me of her partiality for spanking, her secret activity as frotteur—biting, pinching, scratching and giving hickeys to married men. Also of the apparatus known as the Angry Vagina. About the way she womanscapes. With a well-placed middle finger down the center, shaving strokes outward. Her dislike of the word *poontang*. Her preference for the word *snapper*. I have this beast within me, she'd say. The baby doll. The post-jail bait li'l missy. A star quality floozy. Her passing righteousness kept the glamour in the girl. She liked the look on strangers' faces when she would ask if they'd like to eat her biscuit. With that good-enough-to-munch flavor. Knock one dead for the hot shit, she'd claim. The dream peach sex kitten. That extra oomph in the night. The display when the lights are off. Members of the lunatic fringe.

For these lingering days.

Which drift by, bleeding into this continuum.

I run wild with your luxury. And trip as I enter your ill-lighted room. Sliding in your silver lining. Inside you I smell all the flowers. The lush sound of her breath. She preserves each moment somehow. Her need for consistent lighting. As she pulls her bra off through her sleeve, she taxis down the runway of my affliction. As if she needed ulterior motives, her movements are quite enticing. Everything of hers is a secret weapon. With the slightest nuance she vouches for all of humanity. She destroys my sleep. I kiss her small breasts with the wounds of nipples.

She is of the last reel, the last show. This, the autumn of her luminescence. She gives me more light. I watch her from the shuttered window. Her elegance elusive but worth the odyssey.

I sense the updraft of where we once walked, which is now a tomb. The perfect red buildings crumbled, olive ivy grown over time. I recall when we made love standing against the brick wall, she held her skirt up and I cupped my hands, protectively, around her ass. She got so hot like that, she'd say. Her faultless facades would go down and she would want people to watch. Her desire was to be viewed, to be cast in a dirty light. The porno queen, the alleyway whore. The exploited sex kitten. She asked me to regard her anonymously. She arrived unsolicited and she will leave unsolicited. I could think of more anti-erotic places. The non-there there. The porno aesthetics: off-white shag carpet, gas fireplace and tall blue vases of peacock tail feathers. Details I will not need cataloged in my mind.

She is so gratifyingly notorious. What she proposes during daylight and what goes down when night falls. An influx of her pressings and demands (both sexual and emotional). Her charms and assets watched by a flotilla of eyes. Exhilarated by the fact that women have sixteen square feet of skin. A look at flammability. Camel toes. Coin tricks with her vaginal lips. Her body is a sea where I act upon regular mutiny. I want to swim with the jellyfish in her waterways. Her, the one at the other end of the umbilical cord. Women like this are from the lot of the original fabricators, infiltrating the specter of my bad conscience.

For her, sex was a transaction. At last count she had seven sexual personae. Clouds for which I cannot scatter, she said. Adding, the only acts for which concern me are those that are non-instinctual. Otherwise, continue. I hear the moans she makes and the air she takes. Her baroque nuances, from deprived to depraved. Uneasy and shaken, a technicolor in fast-forward, shooting through your mind. Images of corrupt acts, of innocent girls doing guilty things. Of female beauty portrayed in medical and gynecological manners. Of eroticism turned upside down, spilling onto the floor. Of bright lights and loud sounds. Of rapidity and entertainment, set reeling through my mind's organ of sight. Brushing against the fringe of derangement. Mingling at the cocktail party of mania. Defiled and spoiled. The bad taste lingering like alkaline. My choice destination down the annals of my undoing. The power of the small of her back. The width of those hips. The line from undergarments. The jingle of bracelets on each wrist. The batting of her eyes. The raising of her legs. The high heels. The way she held her dress above the knees. This majestic gesture better outlining the contour of the silhouette. The flaw in her stockings. The streamline of her brassiere and that see-through cream blouse.

Detained only by lastingness and oblivion. Grander with each gesture. She took another, now she'll take me. Two a.m. as I look down the blue neon gaze of the boulevard. The inaudible angels that once touched the ground. Jump-starting the magic warmth. The smooth rhythm of modern travel. 2:01 a.m. California time.

From: caliph8@sharia4ever.org

I bring my unrequited love to God, not to women. Do you not stand in awe of Him? The ornaments of Eve, for He made the world beautiful for you, and allowed you to obtain Paradise never aging nor greying. The Prophet said, "Whoever kills himself will not receive torment in Hell, but will be greeted with magnificence on the day of resurrection." That's what I'm talking about baby! #inshallah

The forms and shapes taking place about her. The distinctions, crystalline and explicit. Of the decorating she underwent each time she dressed. Of the landscape she crossed with each aspiration. That unaffected exactitude calling out to the silences of the world—to the hum of the clutter, to the small reflections of the sun. All episodes which go unmarked. All so prosaic and frequent. So blatant to the point of absurdity. She did wear her clothes well—a systematic flow of fabric and accessories, all equally synched so as to neither draw observation nor repel it. That soft, high-pitched voice. A chirping bird or a young girl. Those colorful moods—when she wanted to argue or when she wanted to role play. As varying as the weather of an Indian summer. The way, when cooking, she would pull from her brassiere one breast and place whatever sauce she was preparing on the nipple, inviting removal. Or when she would come to you and pull up her skirt to reveal no panties and squat on your lap and proceed to make love. These are the going-ons which allow me to slip and fall down my own slide of cataclysm.

She would be the dawn of something new.

Unabashed, reasoning absolute.

Beach wildlife, paradise found.

She leads me with authority. Our movements so very synchronized. Her infectious light rhythms. Her legs hanging uncontrollably from the bed. Each finger, each toe, each nail. Liquid semi frozen. I hold her tightly. Nothing complicated. A simple kiss, stroking. Yearning for that focus and concentration. No more feast, I want the hunger. She could attract a following. She surely had one. I don't care for the way she paints her eyebrows on. I do like her suggestive ways. How in the elevator she informed me that she lived alone. Of her inability to look me in the eye; quick darts of her retinas taking the form of bashful flirtations. She was thin, perhaps too much so. A small chest, twiggish legs. Voluminous lips and cheeks. Large eyes, thick pulled-back brown hair. The palatial vastness of her mystery pushing the card a little with each glance. The turmoil setting in. Beset by trifling moves and avoidance. Evasion and scheme. The artifice of her conspiracy. The deference to one's own desire. The alchemy going down. Her felicitations to my propositions. The extrasensory love consummating. Unseen charges tripping the rays of light. Pulses registering the blood flow. Accelerated mind waves crashing against the charlatan of my complacency.

The female intrusion. The empowerment from her sex flower. The questions become incessant. Not wasting time from the devotion to femme. The threat thereafter of becoming insane is quite alert. Exquisite cuisine on the run. Within the seeds of unavoidable psychosis, the phrases, tainted in blurred outlines of pseudo-ironic self-reference. The circle avoids completion, contaminated by the virus of loss. Cultivation or animal conduct: *like orgies*. The tongue is in jeopardy. I drew a line and turned toward the thing of imminent regard: that which makes the waves sparkle.

Of the cult of the new, pornography as the exact opposite of a fanatical and seditious artistic practice. Devoted to distinguished and first-rate modes of manners. When the intention is to make pornography, the end product is not porno. Porn is the calming and tranquilizing recurrence of a small exhibit hall of everyday images. The superlative and foremost of the human psyche.

In those beige riding pants, she bends at the knee. Then, lowering, extends the widening buttocks upward. Meanwhile sliding stretching fabric over swollen hips. Then the narrow panties from within the soft cheeks. The black elastic lingers, entangled. Her lower-back now concave. Shoulders pulled back, the shape of wings near flight. Each cheek with lines of red from the textile's mark. The riding pants restraining her knees. The muscles strained. Her head down, hair overflowing onto the table. Lips dampening. Her sex protruding from between the legs. Those thighs so wide. Her cheeks like pillows, inviting lasting handprints. The pores glistening. Deeper breath and flesh color changes. Quick movements and strained advancement. Her concept, the spirit of such surrender, willingness and want. The lips buried in the patch of hair. The trembling muscles and the ultra-feminine shapes she exudes, effortlessly, unknowingly.

That evangelist shine.

The glimmer of an exhausted messenger. The fatigue of a worn traveler and the luster of each freckle. The proof of purpose. Reason for permanence. To straddle, to succumb. To stretch the expectations and concerns far beyond fair play. At the fringe, at the nowhere between two worlds divorced by a transient range. Her topographic qualifications. The snapshot of her gaze. The outlet retrieved in the image of human definition. Attracting me merely because it was a name. Devoid of reference. An absence of history. Replacing taste and smell with the sheer excitement of numbers and figures and statistics. This perpetual advertisement. Never failing to make one feel good about it. Stripped of her every attribution, those things that may have disturbed the viral simulation. The true bearing of the greatest threat of all—*the checklist.*

I find myself in the belly of her beast. Those upward-set brown eyes. Her uncharted waters. The magical surrounding me. A continual and unrelenting state of delirium and forgetfulness. On the mezzanine of my life. Having to make due with a fluctuating obsession. Something that at moments does not exist and at other times dwarfs everything else out of actuality. To be consumed by the practical and menial task at hand, to abruptly cross a street as she passes, with her curves expanding and the flesh affecting, her sway giving way—each specialty is pronounced, each detail spotlighted. A certain unattainable consumption and consummation of the mind and senses and logic. To lose a total sense of who you are, of convinced advancement aspired, whatever focus, all shattered, gone in a flee(t)ing exodus. Leaving you captivated and perplexed beyond design and thought. Uprooted and frayed. Drowning willingly. Walking into a burning house out of pure curiosity. Leaping off the top floor for the unobstructed view. This is where it drops you off. Knocking at your door unannounced. Taking with it a little more sobriety, a little more coherence, leaving in its wake: you spent and the mere semblance of an outcome.

The slow length of my urge. The slow length of my demise. The transfusion of her fixation. The long legs in black tights. The short skirt wrapping those thighs. The nuance of that hand. Those indifferent eyes. The only non-frivolous thought is that of the woman. The free fall of all hesitance and the future of leisure. The destination somewhere inside the location of my elation. The tunnel of my anticipation. I saw the fear when she caught me staring. Her slip slid to the knees. The outward wash of her trailing wake. The convenience of fantasy. The legend of herself. Along the rooftops of our ferment. The break in smell. Engulfing, absorbing and drowning. Those female curves. Slowly coming undone. Those distressing gestures and sways. That calmness when applying makeup. That ignorance of her own sublimation and glory. The subject of arousing discourse. Her atrophied demeanor, and that cacophony of sound.

Ominous in its languishing as she gesticulates her dreams beyond this bilious existence. The internal polarization, the libidinous and poseur ways. Her upheaval, sangfroid and hybrid. The intrepid speculum of her unmasked sex, the center of the circus. A spasmodic passage to one's dyspepsia and longing, sketching fantasies to be between those thighs. It was all very innocuous. Unaware of the anguish she causes when passing by.

Alive beyond the absence of the there. And the now of here. What is left of the in-between. The air of temptation for which we inhale. The glowing haze she drowns you with. All before the appearance of words. My capacity to perceive the auricular pleasures previously cited, endangered by the reign of graphic photographic fixation. I watch them walk by. The American walk. The goal to achieve, to eat to get thinner. The mechanical tumbling strut. Juxtaposed with the gliding and swinging hips, movements of a true femme. With a stunning mastery over gravity. The absence of equating for a waiting cameraman.

Refinement in time and space.

Only the movement is debauchery for the real connoisseur.

Breaking through the standoff of the thought.

Your remedies beneath my hands and your fingers in my hair.

The shelf of your lower back.

The shelf life of your ingredients.

Hovering between notions of the uncanny. Strange fuses blowing out the hoax of the pyramids. Amid the realities masked as mazes. The outside labyrinth world we once thought that we had successfully negated. Chains of quotations beyond reference. Decide yourself. The embodiment of p.m. life. The junk of her valley. The American countenance. Deciphering the noise. Theoretical stimulation. Stuck in these voids: *friendly, personal and unhurried—hometown girls with their skirts up, their panties down; these* coeds, secretaries *and* nurses *show it all and do it all just for you; let's talk head to head and experience pain/pleasure.*

One's need to learn all there is to know about one's fears. It facilitates the overcoming of them. A woman's rage, those kinds of threats. To know they are idle, temporary. The enormity of space and all its intricacies. Inconceivable urge. Great sin, feminine attraction and mercurial appetite. Twisted fantasy, elaborate, preposterous. Love, death and commitment. Violence and consumerism. To know these things is to walk beyond.

From: caliph8@sharia4ever.org

When we attack I am not concerned with the cops or the military response. The FBI is not ready to wage war at our level. Look at Beirut, the morale was so low that they left within 48 hours of attack. Their hearts are just not in it. It is funny how the leader of the New World Order will run in shameful defeat. God is on our side and this jihad is righteous! Are you with the losers or the eternal winners amid all the pussy in Paradise. What will it be boo? #inshallah

To watch her is like standing at the scene of an automobile accident: the fascination overrides the not wanting to see carnage and broken glass…the ultimate in quintessential…oh, *please*, give me something juicy, something to obsess over…an offer I cannot deny, tomorrow, yesterday…one needs fantasy…tall and skinny…making me run hot…hiding behind soft lies…hooking through the vertical shadows of my mirage thoroughfare and the credit scroll…the pores of her breasts…her charisma and anti-anorexia…my libido's confidant, her vulnerability threatens…staring unflinchingly into the face of the apocalypse, full knowing the rapture is not too far behind…as time moves differently, like the devil's last cigarette…everything is speculation…do those things of infinite truth still really exist…we are left to enhance chance…with each passing femme in and out of the realm, the mastery becomes more unavailable…now it seems this is not true, having left the breeze-penetrated sparkle for the endless grids of anesthetics (things have started to take on circular shapes)…life here is forced to adhere to the tyranny of perennial change…only the refreshments promise refreshment…refrained from much human interaction…we were just friends…very little future in this, I resolve to reconcile…the stairwells of our lives…I believe you are due for another examination…I will not take my hands off you…something about the skyline, the prologue to the downfall…every day of exile…I'll be with you soon…so well-equipped…you affect me so…how far is enough…a love for science and diagnosis…her hygiene, a bomb unexploded…those flush cheeks and high brows…that poise and pout…I am happy about those that I have never met…the way she feels so good from soft strokes, the whimpered moaning, the embassy of my abandon…her casino elegance…progress impaired…in part the impossibility…a high-speed motorcycle chase into my crotch…high decibel engine noise and exhaust, a tunnel now and there…those jungle lips and the smell of Laundromats…stiletto rooftops and the insatiable commencing during rush hour…her manners were fugitive, outlaw…she told me about how she did it in a taxi, with the driver…who was married and Arab…she only let him go down on her…he wanted reciprocation, but she told him how the idea of an uncircumcised dick made her sick…I always believed she was of a dying breed…so lovely and intense, a made-up-my-mind quality…physical body of the typical Jew…and somewhere between girl and woman…I think I'd like a test drive…I promised that I'd love her all night.

The autumn of my satisfaction…I can taste her intentions to exploit, to further the push beyond all integrity and patterns…she wants to be bad, so very sinister…she needs depraved and lubricious behavior to compensate for what she feels has been deprived her…lost time, what she never got…all those stories of legend she has been told…the photos she's seen…all that is happening this moment, perennially in occurrence…all of which in no part she plays…she wants participation and when partaking she wants the guilt of the indulgence…she wants regret for what she's done, she wants her hands in all of it…she wants to be regarded badly, thought of in the most degrading ways…she wants strangers to be drawn in by their own fear and panic…she will wait in the concourse of her own descent, blinded by the gleam of new experience…to taste the spiced cuisine and drink from potent concoctions…adrift in perfumed waterways, amid the ambiance of ornate deterioration, careening through the flood of withdrawal with the cool and pristine of neoclassical architecture…plagued by a heat for sanctity, she is at her zenith, the horizon of her being.

Ambition resulting in celebrity…unbeknownst to her…to tango barefoot…naked but for the lipstick…a perfect Silent Red lipstick…a pacifist anarchism to her…when one wishes upon an asterisk…I like my tea to steep…the requisite ness to ply to the fickleness of women…this woman that I will never compromise…Girl Scouts can tie knots too…giving a female flowers that another female gave me…don't touch a thing…she could stop traffic...at an airport…her instinct the enemy of humanities…miracles cross religious denominations, too…a sweep of light penetrates the night…it is about timing…critical…misjudge and damage can be done…just a smattering of sex thrown in…I woke from where the women could shave without looking…solicit them to be as blatant as men…in my dream: a wooden sculpture of a lusciously curvy woman's torso, with the varnish on the breasts worn away…I will conquer Spain someday…a nebulous expectancy that the demoiselle across the lobby shows up in a foreign metropolis…the same goes for the molding of desires…the nicest, bourgeois sadist in the world…an exhibitionist's dream of walking naked around the city's streets…this will be my plan zed…like a thief or looter in the night…please be tender when you cut me down…a method to an end, beyond the sullen and abstruse clouds…an incomprehensible tumble in endless and continuous liaisons, cosmic pleasures existing merely in hidden realms of mutual enjoyment—and, at times, this realm is reluctant to step out of the infinite possibilities of anticipation and juicy discourses…to neglect the dull and prosaic reality...feel thirst and the way she combs her hair, ethereally…a dispatch to her.

Under the archways of our end…a break from this awashed perpetuity…nothing more, nothing less…the thrill of peering up skirts and the obscurity that you may find…the web of my condition…her parasitic behavior, which I grew to like—eventually to fulfill me…she simply belonged to me and I could luxuriate at my free will, any time, any place…I got off on observation, venerated by her aesthetics…which weigh more than consummation…there is no label for this plight…there is no femme for such seclusion…a concern for her discern, a cryptic passage into the house of detention…super sexy quiver device, her genital enterprises bottlenecked…she brought with her plenty of new material…under the guise of her long thighs…she wanted to make a distinction…*hush*, I say…walk with me through the emergency exit…in the cross-passage we can talk about it…I just want to be there when it happens, thankfully.

Her shadow in transit, verisimilitude…the apparition of a nymph from a lost epoch…salutary for the mind's glasshouse, the paucity of defects and flaws…Draconian in its excess and unrelenting distinctions…her inattention insouciantly…she is nubile and I only know, that walk, that caress, that polish—truly inimitable…her womanhood turgid, boastful, egotistic…rapacious in the truth that she's the only one to hold the code…she will be my paramour, eventually, unknowingly, unaware, unacquainted…yet willing, in the face of my overture…to walk with me… cavorting in playful undress.

The act of fellatio is a symbol of the highest trust…think: one is placing one's high-priced possession [besides the testicles] *into a woman's mouth.*

He said: *would you be interested in receiving one of my special, all problem solving, cervical massages*…her wide eyes, thin lips, round face, aloof stare…walk of grace, melting eyes, deafened cries…her invisible electricity, depending on what she does, depending on what she remarks…depending where it is she falls…I have heard the carnal calls…blithe in her way…standstill to look, one might see…stolen promises with one peep of her eye…cut me and watch me bleed…burn me and watch me melt…she got Toxic-Shock from forgetting a tampon inside of her vagina well after the onslaught of menstruation…the lightlessness which may be felt…the wind passes over a flower on the field…the battering waves, tidal surges, ocean storm wages within…a symbol of the libido's wild waters…a spotted castle on the horizon, a notion of life after death…outside is glittering paradise—a lifetime of wandering…eat drink and be gay…this demi-utopia, on solitary way, matter of engrossment, life of trekking, nomadic…the ubiquitous virgins in the garden of wisdom, under ordinary skies while the blissful sleep…at play beyond the powerhouse, under space infinite, and all that endures are whores and their houses—the magnificent are called to the penthouse…and you: munching scones and sampling gin in your tea house…suppose there's a rose and it would transpose into champagne and pantyhose.

She is worn by the vexation…the chasm mid desire and pedantic execrations…beginning as an intelligible surmise, ending as her private slang…the means of respite and hiatus, she had become the cognoscenti of facetious shenanigans…her sojourns as a way to calm the unfathomable and illustrious fantasies…so very blanched on the surface…so very venerable in their supplications to her self-satisfaction…she was robbed, mugged, unrequited for all the favors she had done…the paranoia and xenophobia setting in—a belief in dark conspiracies beyond all omnipotence…the preference of airbrushed photography, the reaffirmation that society prefers fantasy…silence itself as scheme…she wants me to touch her all…simple, sincere and haunting…elaborate refinement, reality, delusions…fluid in my hands…she kept her lips wet…secret knocks when she came over…sexuality on a compass…wind blowing gently over the hot sand…an impaired amulet, she hangs around my neck…I keep looking for the wedding ring…my blood awakens and kindles…the stir of it in her gaze…I eat from her cleavage a freshly cut fruit…after the initial kiss, a long series of kisses followed, all distinct, all interchanging…from the minute I made this resolution, I knew I would execute it.

There was the one time we made love in her dry marble bathtub…she was in the midst of full menstrual discharge…the tub left splattered with blood, clots and cum…she instigated that it take place in the tub, an alternative to ruining the sheets of the bed…she straddled me and her blood would squirt from the orifice with each thrust and small withdrawal from her…blood got everywhere…after a while, it didn't matter…it was in our hair, on our mouths, blanketing our hot flesh…it was stunning the amount she bled…she later told me that the orgasm was much more intense as she was pushing through the blood shortage…my bones ached against the hard marble…but, a peacefulness overcame me: a woman surrounded me, engulfed me…her blood splattered the scene, warming, comforting, consoling…the erotic was a result of the alchemy of sex and a crime scene from a non-murder…it was as if we both had been shot and our throes of passion were really gasps for life.

A brief rundown of assets: a whetted edge, an often desired angst, a deafness and blindness to bullshit, purchased happiness, a dozen reasons, trembling self-confessions, instances of attraction, a jammed gaydar, over-the-counter poisons, germs, bacteria, madness, a virgin to sacrifice atop a jungle pyramid, a kindled fire by the time she leaves, an overwhelmed liveliness, high voltage calmness, several internal organs, superconsciousness, a need for sleep, dream sequences of suspended animation, affinity for eternity itself, preposterous expectations, dire fears, disobedient thoughts, a wondrous story, vast spaces, midnight enlightenment, anterior and inferior astuteness and intuition, a luminous joy, the underbrush zone, a bathtub sea, an abrupt departure, opposing wishes, sometime shining tears, an inward flow, a panoramic gaze, the effect and cause, endless shores, a swelling glory and balanced abyss, daily routines, sheer morning light, a role amid an aloof world, a threefold nature, vast vistas, an intense craving, an elusive still, powers of seduction, an Eden within, active hours, subtle direction and other minor details.

The *philias*, the *isms*, the *otics* (some past, some present): *acrotomophilia* (deprivation of oxygen during sex); *algolagnia* (painful sensations which turn into sexual pleasure: hickeys, scratches, love bites, pinches, spanking, whipping, slapping); *encratism* (deliberate abstinence from sex for a period of time in order to build up sexual energy so strong it magnetically attracts others); *hyphepheilia* (love of hair, fur, furry things); *chlamydia* (presently erased from my system); *frottage* (the occasional getting of sexual pleasure from rubbing one's body against something); *infantilism* (urge to wear diapers, and be put to bed); *klismaphilia* (love of enemas); *feuille de rose* (analingus); *incontinence* (lack of restraint regarding impulse); *libertine* (lecher); *mutuality*; *narrotophilia* (erotic literature); *orality*; and *satyriasis* (the Don Juan syndrome).

A brief rundown of assets on loan from women: a pair of black wedge heels, white sandals with a buckled strap, an ankle tie thong sandal in black, a brown toe loop sandal with ankle strap, and a red slender T-strap buckled ankle sandal; a French blue bodysuit with snap bottom, a white cotton/spandex bodysuit with soutach swirls on mesh (slightly soiled), a black seamless convertible bra (34 B), a worn-thin cami-bra bustier with gentle boning and laced cincher back (34 C), a white deep-plunge cradle bra (36 B), a beige veil lace bra with built-up comfort straps (32 A), and a tulip cup bra, light and airy, yet holds well (34 D), three "large" thongs (2 black, 1 red), an expired black AmEx (male name).

From: caliph8@sharia4ever.org

Hi friend. It has been a hot minute. How are you? You asked for my thoughts on the American way of life. Well, so much of what we are led to believe are good things are actually crimes and sins. Look at the liberation of women...so debaucherous and the vile use of women to sell commercial products! Free elections just means when we elect rulers we are the ones that will suffer for their misdeeds, we will be held accountable not them! The separation of Church and State! Rather than rule by Sharia we choose to invent our own laws, and this contradicts the pure nature which affirms Absolute Authority to the Lord and your Creator. The Christian ethos is that of moral decadence, with the promotion of pornography and sexy women, of abortion and homo living...so much the hypocrisy of the moral Christian. How can your church allow the gays to marry? How can your society allow women to make more money than men? The

USA is perhaps the biggest FAIL witnessed by the history of mankind. Write soon or pics, k? #inshallah

I believe in numbers and scientific fact…in ideals regarding freedom and such…in technology and its advancement…progress and betterment…of the moving effects of art…mostly, though, I believe in removing stockings with my teeth.

I was the only one to see her trip and fall from the curbside…it must have been the high heels…the only injury was a wound to the hand…a fairly deep gash which bled generously…I offered her a paper napkin to control the bleeding…she held it tightly against the cut, then handed it back to me, soaked, a dark cherry red…I held it momentarily and then, in passing, placed it in my coat pocket…she thanked me, while scanning her legs for additional impairments…I looked down then rested my eyes upon her breasts, then mouth…she smiled and giggled uncomfortably and awkwardly…I failed to find something to say…we stood there and listened to the hum of the enclosing noise…I reached into my coat pocket and felt her blood…she took my hand from within the coat…my fingers were wet…she brought my hand to her mouth and sucked the blood from my fingertips…then I tried to kiss her, but she wouldn't let me…she excused herself by saying that she didn't know me well enough…that a kiss to her is too special and too intimate to give away to an outsider…but I am not an outsider…and besides it could be a little audacious and defiant…even electrifying…she wasn't listening at this point…this was apparent…any form of furtherance would not occur…I watched her continue down the street…as she sashayed more remotely from me, her blood languidly stained within my coat.

She liked to play out rape scenes—grabbing her by the hair, throwing her against the wall and her begging me to fuck her in the ass…I refused to have any part in it…she claimed to be a hard-core feminist before the first ass-fucking she received…never assume habitual silence equals ignorance….brutalize me, circumcise me, desecrate me, she would say…hypnotize me, satisfy me, suck and stroke me…I'd just stand there on the corner, watching all the asses go by…wobbles and shakes, her jolts causing wakes elsewhere.

When it happens I hope that she will be riding her bicycle uncontrollably down a hill in a park and come crashing into me. We succumb to gravity and the end result is her collapsed on top of me. There will be new problems to approach, new institutions…proof positive that its circumvention is already in place…she liked to go fast…and keep her lips wet…she was left with a limp…each pathetic stride, as if her hips would collapse…discreetly I stroked her cheek, inhaling the fragrance of an unfamiliar perfume…I entered this world under a lucky star, now realizing that the outcome of all of this is inconsequential and what she wants and what she gets are two contrary entities…and they have nothing to do with me…I will manhandle her with infrequent patience…I can compass her everything…and the hypothesis: there is nothing more dangerous than when she is the only one we've got…the slander when speaking to me…if you feel you have reached this number in error.

She is 4k television: she doesn't degrade the further you get from the screen…she was the picture of splendid…plagued by the desire for…the sigh of the woman is the finest praise that can be offered…time stands still as she blinks…I fail to believe that her face has escaped my memory until now…and in the same breath, I told her, I feel the dark and empty loneliness of my future…she touches her lower lip, I am paralyzed…if she would shed tears I would kiss them away faster than their formation…her black eyelashes are matted, heavily…postponing bliss as we burn with longing superfluously.

Relentlessly dark, rain drums onto my windshield, blurred red taillights, residual emotion emerging with an infinitely unfinished future and dreary imagery…nevertheless, her inaction takes its toll and is causing serious disturbances—there is so much left, so much to expect…is this what one calls excitement…allow myself to be embraced by the morbid beauty of the peculiar sky…the dark and sinister seem to creep back up to their inevitable climax…after which, the covering of the worshipped view…feeling preservation is always linked to images…will do my best…the more one is occupied with incurable contemplation—standing between now and then and before—one loses one's congenial aesthetic playground: *WOMEN*…their moods and bodies, the way their schoolgirl outfits lift up when they lean forward…and that is the reason for which one ought remember what is *essential*—because time is limited and research is necessary…the polarity of man and woman will lead her back to me…I just caught a glimpse of her…hoping her storms won't sink my ships…managing to get by, with the mad dogs still barking, a tailspin plunge into chaos…to order call now…makeshift envy and spite…curiosity can appear to be semi-frivolous…a human race driven to sabotage…she is a relic of a bygone era, an infinitesimal longing, a sigh of satisfaction…the highest prize in the world is not the approval of others, it is the being desired by her…what's your dharma…beyond your wildest dreams…defies her age…driving one to rewrite history…we drank Chandon Carneros Blanc de Noirs (187 ml.).

Always rapture, rapture forever.

All I want is to kiss your lips again…there is no more left of her which wants to give in to her appetites…faith is limited to what is realized and experienced by immediate generations, past and present…each ingredient within her is of the finest attainable…while each one of us waits for gratification, it is already hers…relieved of the cumbersome vicious reality of simple fantasies. there is no return from that particular state…*emballe-moi*, *cherchez la femme*…she told me: I've changed men many times, but never my drink…attempt to resist the hypnotist…a personal apocalypse coming down to simple erotic tension…after all the fun has been had, the check will eventually arrive…she wanted me to be her golden boy of the Valois dynasty…a personal renaissance…*morgan de toi*…left insatiable, like a starving city so hungry that it must eat the zoo…enrapture me, *supergarce*.

She would say: in your eyes I see the derangement…beyond the little white fence lies fields of black decadence and ominous retrogression…the priests are all jokers, the doctors all thieves…the setting: some spilt nail polish, a broken dinner plate and a torn piece of an aged strip club voucher which reads *escort for professionals only*…menstrual blood-stained sheets, butterfly motif teacups, cold instant decaffeinated coffee…the city night intoxicates me into a befuddled frenzy of neon, smoke and crosswalks…a distinctive gloating flavor with each elongation of every intrinsic part of her…all I ask is that someone fill this void, a perpetual and unending adoration…disregard the sun, adhere to the moon…crank calls in the dark for abundant repentance…one need not be a physician for this type of exam…she does what she wants—for that is what she is told…the masquerade of her…a reversed negative photograph of a semi-nude woman…a soundtrack to rape…little girls are kitsch, not women…she had on a Rouge Sublime Mat…even when you weren't with me, when you spent all your time running lost, tall and above under my foot, they were here, stand-ins, fluffers, doubles, if you will…I just saw a wounded pigeon take flight.

An infrared-vision scope, indispensable in taking voyeurism to another level…she moved as if guided by irrational voices…the note read: IKNOWWHOYOUARE…Don Juan was a fag…remember your first blow-job…how did it taste…my mind was in other people's panties…she wore makeup like a dirty metro Parisien whore, was a direct descendent of the Druids…I'd like to check your soul, while blindfolding you…filthy young nomads begging for something to drink…for whom she still holds the romance…television, a thief robbing of all good intentions…words are unfinished conduct…not this cattle baron and not today…she wore white pearls from the sea and nothing else…and that's when she said: *suck enough dicks and you'll get what you want*…she has a way of manifesting herself in unexpected ways…an orgy of sorts…I wore the bad guise, a trinity of the sex-death-object thing…honeychild, that was mighty spiffy…malice will replace age…development, advancement descending from her lips…the land of the solitary vice…an avant-garde stage performance, a post-porn-modernist…a Caucasian massage parlor prostitute…she was fond of reminiscing the story of when she got caught shoplifting and blew the security guard…and then she added: *do fuck off and peel off your inhibitions*.

What is it that would leave you satisfied…she despised the idea of looking down at men, but she couldn't resist wearing her high heels…what shade is nude…the coloration of you…a tenacious and convinced way about her which makes a man remember…the silent and quiescent trauma…blame it on the taboos, every last one of them…all the fervor of all the fantasy abduction and rape scenes played out in the minds of true crime America…she is slightly more concealed than that innocuous moment before declaring one's love…home is where your pimp is…the laughing gas man…auto-erotic fatalities…a full-blown amputee fetishist…picture this: *a woman with an amputated foot using the stump as a prosthetic penis*…not by my loins alone, she would declare, laughing, drunk…I whispered to her face: I am attracted to you even if you wear a padded brassiere…it's an entity in your ways, your bitchy, pouting ways…she causes eyebrows to raise, thumbs to twiddle…that's what you ceaselessly say…motel art on my mind…a playful diversion party…we're talking about the *dark side*…she is forever a guilty pleasure…as she joked: eat me out and sleep in the corner…according to her, no one is worthy of her sacred portal…she has an aura of command…to fall upon the thorns of vipers…what is impossible for most women is possible for her…a very jaded child…I caught her cooking the books…her ass cheeks spread like knuckles on a clenched fist, legs wide and high like fingers of a peace sign…all in the name of bloodsport…a bag of toys and a mellow night…this will also work if she is wearing a skirt, or if she is down to her underwear…a kind of flirtation, in a darkened room, in secret solidarity, exploring fantasies…the flicker of a film…what is at the heart of her matter…her lips stiflingly large, a zone and territory undefined…her legs relaxing and hanging, lending to the kneeling position…inviting, enticing, engaging…a sexual zealot of equal lengths…her bronzed arm extends just enough forward, allowing for the opening through her sleeve—freeing a view to the outside of her side boob…a subjective take on transcendence fused with dim red lights and glowing billboards…the shirt's thin blue horizontal stripes wrap around each breast like latitude lines on a globe…elevated overtones, pure inflection…please place your seats in the upright position, we have been cleared for landing.

I was turned off by the stretch briefs she wore…telling me that she preferred them because they don't crawl up or bind…hands on her hips, just above bloated and irrational thighs…shoulder-length olive-drab hair, swept to the side, in a ponytail…rare and solitary magnificence, feral and untamed face…protruding mid-level cheekbones…she stood unmoving as her briefs fell to the floor…a submission reality, giving my fantasy to the dominant…she could use it her way, to her advantage or hindrance…her hair gets in my mouth…in her navel I find white lint while her nails dig waterways in my back…what did other men do to her…a cure for neurosis like slow poison from her maniacal tongue.

I followed the scent through the countryside to end in finding her sun-dripped thighs…there, I watched the way her tapestries hung…I let her work her magic on me…humanity's ultimate artifact, the object for which its genius is most intensely displayed.

From: caliph8@sharia4ever.org

The unbelievers are always looking for a miracle. They pretend to doubt that God would not help them out of their dire situations, or lift them up from mediocre social standing. There is nothing for Mohammed to do but to try and convince the skeptics that the Qur'an itself is the miracle testifying to his veracity. The Qur'an is a phenomenon unprecedented. Its verses are not inventions of the Prophet, rather they are the heavenly prototype of the Mother of all Books. Mohammed cannot add or omit a single word. Confirmation from the Lord of the Worlds, the bearer of this exalted message and the last mouthpiece of revelation sent forth by the Lord, it is beyond the comprehension of mortal men. You see friend, there is no explanation why and we don't need to question anything at all. #inshallah

In the midst of the garden, I want to eat your apple…see me, detect me, grope me, handle me…those were her words…doctrine and dogma claiming absolute power and infinite knowledge…a universal spanning entity which is deeply concerned with my sex life…the frontier of exhilaration, like smut…adulteries are to be forgiven, sexual misgivings to be pardoned…when they find they are naked, they will succumb…distress is someone devastated by mutation and transition, not disaster or fate…take all of this away and one is left with a perpetual nightmare involving deprivation in many manifestations.

When the panic is gone, only I will remain…I am the watchman and the watched…as she laid on the bed, in the white sheets, naked, but for a knit sweater…with the glide, stealing through the smells unseen, beckoning me over and I cannot but heed her call to the kindred woman who cannot keep from exposing herself…gently throbbing, sparkling to my heart…her name is…it was all just a simple convergence of ideas, random associations of images, with a few words now and then dropping from the sky out of somewhere, out of nowhere…the idea of the black box…her very small breasts…the mere reasoning for the bra is to hide her extremely large nipples…I noticed that her overall, that which she was growing out of, fitted tightly on her over-thin shoulders and showing how their line was spoilt by the deep dip of the clavicle…why that imperfection should make her more real to me than she had been when I had thought her wholly beautiful.

This body is for you…I can feel your tongue on mine…wet and smooth, an expensive booze…I'll live with this tortured memory because that is all I will have left of you and me…light shines through years of time, your face in everyday, each place I go—*no one will ever supersede you*…discontented melancholy—worldly desires pulled to the shallow surface of truth's realities by painful gravity…I have walked under a thousand moonless nights, wandered shamelessly, aimlessly, swallowed sour and bitter pride, while you…were a mystery to me.

A total work of art…the sun could be looked at with a steadier eye…habit is second nature…the taste of authenticity in the eating and sucking…lust, calenture, degeneration: specifics of madness, yet not enumerated among diseases…daze me, amaze me, brutalize me, enliven me…the most succulent song to be heard is the whisper of the feminine spirit on her lips…the sensuous joy of her…an unceasing attempt at pubescent fornication…unfeasible and totally impractical while the crisis actors are in the streets.

The key to the game is to take it to just the befitting level in the madness—a point of return, yet dangerously close to falling. Just act crazy—*it will come.* As the hunger crawls into you, from somewhere near the sound's location, it creeps into you asking for your hand, asking for a framework of automation.

She declined the charge but I still offered the payment…just a bit of my contribution to the ethereal cosmic cash flow…we then set up the floodlights and sifted through her wreckage…the real figures may be higher…if it ever is withdrawn…a cut up consumer-oriented approach…driving toward the outside clinical applications…it is not as odd as she would have us believe…contrary to the predictions, she is far from finished…her behavior, that of a terrified castaway, shriveled in a wet corner, famished and unloved…the entire populace aware of her myth and her platinum rule: *tenacity*…when told no she would then follow through…the open space and suggestive dissension…in closing she added: *I hope you had the time of your life*…come in, have you seen my castle…the bizarre times of her emerald eyes, pacing down the aisle of my torment…the measurement of her smoothness…in her garden I will stand for quite some time…actual suction is the only solution…at times, one must lay one's own tracks.

There is a time for some women, and a time for all women; a time for great women, and a time for small women…I watch her watch me as she walks away…she never looks back…an undeniable woman always has her revenge ready…the riddle of a woman's mind, the ornament of her sex…actions do not happen alone, she made a virtue of necessity…(men and) women are most apt to believe what they least comprehend…interpretations are pauses the mind makes between doubts, and there will always be questions…I recognize I am part of each and all that I have met…beyond time everything will be condensed to the mere countenance of a simple plot, a story, an anthology, surfaces of words…she slips to her requisite end…my wages of sin, languishing…a man's valuation determined by his female company…necessity has no law…we are never so happy nor so unhappy as we suppose…to live without her is to live horribly.

It was your face I looked into unflinchingly each time…it was the soul which offered me your everything…your sapphire eyes…as if I were losing you again, as if again you had offered yourself to me and again I had let you go…a denial that was hard, and harder still—it was for a whole lifetime…alone, in the vortex of a vertigo of one thousand suns, burning with love…no companion body in bed, nor in the sand…longing for the coming of you into my nameless kingdom once again…and at the end of space-time: *the eternal coitus.*

She walks like a vamp in pointy, laced-to-the-ankle boots; slick patent leather gives these boots a racy bent…I read: *Wanted-slaves of both genders and all sizes*; *fellow lovers of lingerie*; *white girls with fat asses (PAWGs)*; *albinos*…her haute kitsch method was to wear enough makeup for two faces and then wipe that which overruns and smears onto her C or B cup bra (the size depends upon the cycle and the mood)…a fondness for douches, urine, boots…a sexual desire for pregnant women…thigh-high tights, stockings…nothing else obligatory, meritorious of the deference…my thirst and my sorrow…the tip of her tongue peeking through the gap of her teeth always revealed her eagerness and ardency for whatever it was that she was doing…I refuse to quarrel over such petty and lesser matters…the most peculiar and outlandish of things…hovering above an atmosphere of languor and unrest…overplay, overuse and depletion on her face will remain implanted on my mind for a very long time…her desolate abode was passé by the animosity of what she called *the disparate gaucherie of the cathartics*…the requiem to her fantasias was that of pious worship, passing hyperbole and distortion, nothing of gluttony and demand…cowed into doing things by her subaltern zeal for an invisible paramour, that maniacal cipher was just that: free of worth or influence, complacent exhuming the conundrum of her prurient chutzpah…in the end, staid with the simplicity of her quixotic onanism.

It's your black market love that massacres and heals.
It's your festival of strut and switch and shake.
The heaven in the soft parts of your thigh.
I long to be the last king to drown in your floods.

A balanced, proportionate face can be divided into three equal parts: the distance between the hairline to the mid-brow, the mid-brow to the base of the nose, and the base of the nose to the chin. Individuals who have an exaggerated and high forehead tend to be more self-conscious and look older than they really are. But with our double board-certified surgeon you can look years younger and feel more confident now! Our surgical practice is entirely devoted to hair! We perform traditional hair restoration and advanced Follicular Unit Extraction Techniques, as well as scar and plug revisions! Your safety and well-

being are our primary responsibility! A good result means far more than having good hair on your head! Hairline lowering is all the rage! Enhance your feminine appearance! Scalp advancement allows you to have your hairline advanced whatever distance your scalp laxity allows, and it is customized to meet your goals. The ideal female hairline is 5.5 cm above the point between the eyebrows at the top of the nose. This is the most natural and aesthetically pleasing look.
The one stage forehead reduction surgery will begin the moment the intravenous cocktail sedation kicks in. We will mark the anticipated postoperative hairline. It will be drawn wavy to mimic a natural line, and will be just in front of the eventual hairline scar. The scalp will be separated from the skull going back almost to the neck, incising the galea which allows the scalp to stretch. Mind you, we will not be using a scalp expander which is what sets us apart from other surgeons. This will eliminate the need for fat grafting in the temporal area. Implantable devices and sutures are used to secure the scalp to the bone at its new forward location, closing the wound with two layers of surgical clips. Finishing with several targeted steroid injections. This final look will be subtle and not overly pulled, rather the results will highlight your eyes and a new smooth forehead.
Post-op: If there are cowlicks and/or shock loss the scar will be visible but only temporarily, this can be covered up with your basic foundations; possible nerve damage; infections are rare, but you will still take antibiotics; loose stools; glue in hair.

Foolish with outburst, carnality, lubricity…that for which I cannot act upon, pushing the insanity card off the table…extinguish the undergo…lunacy in the rehabilitation…convalescence means lock up…incarceration means time for productivity…efficiency results in accomplishment…attainment carries a heavy price…value can vary from precious to bargain…being righteous isn't always easy…being sinister isn't always jolly…at least that is how she put it…with all facts noted, her English wasn't perfect…her use of bizarre words, taken out of context in her language…she frequently created and assembled terms that escape me now…I let them pass and drown with the verbosity of her speech…but she was very delicate and choice, equivalent to a child's eyes: unexposed, unmade…it was much better allowing her to ramble and go on without end to the satisfaction that she was fully able and competent to speak to me in my language and not hers…with and within her we have many surrenders to partake.

She asked for a care package…so long as it contained contraband, mainly sexual paraphernalia…actual firsthand adventure of her is rare, but opinions are in ready supply…slow reels of tango escapades…I begin this anecdote by attempting to elucidate a small interval of time which, more precisely, exists on a plane involving space…more perfectly, this meantime dwells between moments of surfacing urges and emerging cravings…solicitations for human contact, fornication and infidelity…the considerations in between allow for pure rumination, untangled pondering of that for which applies to the everyday, the mundane and the commonplace.

Her unfettered religion of libido, far more than what most could ever seemingly imagine amid the framework of my sexual reference…she wouldn't stop at anything in her efforts to refashion the exterior or enhance the subterfuge of her persuasions…she has developed unforgiving formats of quick nuance and erotic subtleties which require intense concentration to be grasped…between the buried and the roads, we make love for the benefit of making love…the art of dissection, a manipulated balance of logic and delicacy…more importantly, the ability to conceptualize…*big fish do not swim in small pools*…an enticement to relapse…on paper she sounds like dry and balmy stylization, but it is reality which views her wetness…her soft washes of colors and depletions, abundant to fulfill the hype, adequate to stifle the murmur…she smothers the conflagration with a single operative aphorism, summing to result in an end that resembles many stories sewn into a seamless narrative…the real charms occluded by inert textiles and varying shades of red…the sight is of hypnotic power…how she lights up when in the dark…the usual incoherence of such imagery…her instruments of percussion beating hard in the night and the disparate fragrance when she enters the room, her notoriety wafting about the air…elegant and perverse, a radical aromatized pleasure…to possess and then to mingle beyond the unmasked confines of that for which resonates so true…her love of performance, ever exerting for the moments which exclude thoughts of sex, death and money…she appeared through a wall of light, knocking down the hereafter…evacuation procedures culminating, interrogating the complacency of my days…she takes the concept of new anatomy to the next level.

Each time we lay down it's a palatable and appetizing occasion…something else in an ordinary world would be less spectacular…I refute all past macabre declarations, summoned to her flowered throne, drafted into her garnished concubine…her physical skills and attributes have made a mockery of other women's attempts to stifle the memory of desire and reconcile that which truly breathes between the sexes…as she laid an unforgiving ambush on me…the scene of supermarkets and department stores, the deepening murk and anxiety for more as the practical ramifications of *not possessing it* sink in…whatever progression and profits in getting nearer to her may have forthwith evaporated…my endearment for her will never dim…she has taken it upon herself to demand sexual autocracy, allowing her and her partner to have sex where and when and however they should seek…she advocates all of it, without fail…this is what she wants: unconditional, unreserved and unlimited promiscuity…those who inanely deny her saunter away vilified and unsatisfied…one could never be ashamed of what she espouses…her competitiveness and guile reveal when she enters a room to find other women…anything to keep me subsequently hanging on…corollary with hearing *I've heard so much about you* and feeling flattered…since the (unspeakable) accident, we make love with the lights on, the lampshades covered with thin silk shawls and shrines of tall burning candles…not a good idea, I insisted…she replied that it is my duty to cause the friction for the flame.

Poolside aqua green, the hum of chlorine pumps…the flush from dry torridity, the deep and glistening sun, the sprinklers alive—while my identity floats, levitating between sex fantasy and gravity, nudity in the sun and abstruse womanhood on my face…a light meter's dream, intensity, burdensome, wet…I am marauding as someone else, not the me me, but a fantasy man who does fantasy things…one body once removed…the celluloid set reeling: casually going down on a large pussy…squirting endlessly the cum onto the hot concrete, poolside…basic savagery without consequence, executed with unparalleled grace…nothing left to separate screen life from real life…a continual performance of exalted hedonism and friction…a hiatus from the dream realm, from the id's mirror ether, the there over there…where everything the tongue touches tastes of saccharine and honey…where completion and fulfillment meet the sky…an interlude with candy-coated quintessence…the weight of her breast on the face, the shape of her lips against the skin…the pliant breeze penetrating each pore, the veins pulsing in clamorous repercussion…pushing on until the far end of the trail resembles a mere semblance of that which is so familiar…certain advancement dictated by plan…doing the unbelievable, manifesting the unheard of, plotting refined greatness, achieving commonness…disregard this as illusion.

She will show the way to mitigate the ravages of deprivation and hard-line libido…afloat far in her petal-covered hinterlands I mapped her unmolested frequency…a slow dance to something uncertain…an alchemist's dream of unbridled fervor, ardency and abandonment…how she takes in instructions so offhandedly, appearing as immaculate and that of unalloyed intuition…moreover, the sound of satisfaction and the resonance of inclination…the glitter and gleam in her eyes—swimming pools of sparkling blue…the outward hang of the oblong pear-shaped breasts as her bony and upright shoulders move inward, together, her body folding forward from laughter, the bending knees, the small waves of cashmere, the modest orbs suspended by a reliable and comforting brassiere…that hell world called moderation and the rule of outcalls only.

Decadence has its price…booze makes a good man better, she read on a wall…I wrote her: I am a man without a sovereign state and unable to walk on water…the bride capture, the everywoman…she is merely required to be the exact opposite and inverse of man…for her to possess the feminine things: laden, head-sized breasts, broad hips, engaging curves and a vagina…I tell her that I will make it, but then I run into the dim night and I believe that I'll be there as the wind blows and the clouds follow the silenced sarcasm, tonight…and the reality I behold is that I am not coming home…she isn't required to satisfy me physically, I prefer her to feed my essence (physical satisfaction couldn't hurt)…she is a very deep and profound girl, as claimed, her own private impressive canyon on the inside…the enlarged and amplified inflammation of her breast nipple—leaving the aureole wide like a small plate, pink like salmon—a typical symptom of *thelitis*, she told me…in her liquor cabinet I found mostly gins and vodkas, some nearly empty bottles of rum and whiskey, three liqueurs and one anisette…and the largest red dildo…strategically situated behind the tallest bottle (which it towered), hidden to be found…surely molded from a horse, or a baby whale…she played it off by saying that all her girlfriends had one, some even two…she offered me a chance to hold it and I politely declined…archaic figurines, endlessly asleep, getting together in the night with all the lights on…the morning would come and she'd have a cup of tea and lose her panties and lay on her stomach, with her legs spread…slumbered with the bright light penetrating the shade-covered glass…bringing her grapefruit and a magazine as she acted as if she were sleeping…mumbling aloud the shrouded truths for which she could not normally ventilate to me.

Turn off the lights and lock the door…voluntarily, do not be so masochistic, exercise the uncertainty of free will…she retorted: that is unequivocally who I am…when art itself turns pale, buy me something I wouldn't buy myself…she prefers production to consumption, dedication to resignation…in my mind she will reign forever, weightless and serene, a collector of the new millennial kitsch…the avant-garde in technologies of reproduction, facsimiles, manifolds and carbon…an overthrow of the accepted order…I am afraid I do not comprehend the question…she is so predictable that you must wonder what is under her overcoat.

She sipped her G & Ts and smoked her five cigarettes a day with style…I am so undomesticated—*if you only knew*…as we rode bareback (naked) into the moonlit winter night we were left with honeymooner's burn…and all things visible slipped away…remember when you were mine and we engaged each other with all the lights on…and we swam where the tide took us…we will walk along these feelings until the day comes…do not despair, leave all your sex on.

In her deep loveseat chair I will sit and from here I will watch…she knew her outfits and instruments well…her streaking was not a means of political protest, nor the result of a simple dare, rather it was a form of indulgence which she often looked forward to and planned for properly.

Up to the sky with flowering glow, stretched like a teal ocean, widespread, out of sight—the analogy of time's end…gazing upon the glittering sea below…nude women swimming, weightless on their backs; the breasts as small islands, unbridled to and fro…the sapphire lagoons and whalebone shorelines filled with these imposingly sly creatures…the broad moon rose while the heated waves splashed...regarding the lips drawing near and clinging into a kiss, a deep dragging and prolonged kiss, of gullibility and eagerness, of corruption and ill-usage…into the misguided direction of that which is above, where such kisses and significance belong, in the shadow and in the sentiments…blood as hot as lava, pulses scampering, hastened, left in disarray…the shackles having faded…with each osculation awakening the dead…where the strength of the kiss is judged by its length.

Consolation in that there are no two women alike in this world…no more than two breasts…two aureoles…two pair of cheeks…two sets of hands…the measureless variations and takes on fingernails and necks and asses and taints…the diversity and innovation of nature…presenting us with a large faculty for entertaining ourselves when all alone…often calling us to these precious reserves…teaching us to realize that we are owned partly to society, but chiefly to ourselves…and the notion that that which needs to be proved cannot be worth very much…a man in love will submit to and relinquish all things…in revenge and in love we find women the most barbarous, learning how to hate in proportion to their forgetting of how to charm…when she departs she will leave behind the small black right hand glove she will drop unknowingly.

The shadow of her presence hangs overhead, as she hides all loneliness and detachment with a kiss…beyond the eyes and features fall her hair, the small conduct, slow and refined…unable to come to grips and terms, go forth, kiss her lips…shielded and sheltered from disease, take it for granted…close to a decayed psyche and mortified flesh…the altar where she now resides, all remaining in the tearful eye.

Faked orgasms have nothing on lackluster fellatio…she seemed to be inexhaustible for hours…a technique borrowed from nipple stimulation…mango fruit sucking…there I go again, worshipping her essence…*my brutha*…a supermodel's dirty g-string…about as busy as a child with a box of band aids…in the dream there was a pornographic motif dungeon up in the sky, an endless loop of moaning and panting…feeds of sequential themes and scenes which propagate the faith, beyond all the replicas and bargain fare…an institutional hoarse voice told me so: *you're so slick, baby*…groovy and hip…sleep with me…kiss me with your wet lipstick…let me play with your tits…dance like you're impaired, as if you went mad…walk around nude more often…claim you are the living God…lose the umbilical cord tied around your neck…castrate yourself, if you've still got it…shoot up for a day…wet your bed…ride naked through the streets on a white horse…believe that this is heaven to no one else but you.

From: caliph8@sharia4ever.org

Praise be to God for the religion of Islam, for who so embraces shall be successful, rightly guided, and who so upholds shall be saved! It is for this that nations are craving and souls are longing. It is the living light and the crossing to the eternal abode of perfect happiness in which there is no grief nor illusion. God is indeed to be praised and blessed, and there is no end to his Kingdom, and nobody can change His words. He is the Benefactor and the Wise who has revealed the truth and enlightened It. Our duty is to visit those in doubt to call them to eternal victory and the shining light! Can you get with me bro fam? #inshallah

I thought about her thrice…her colors were dazzling…as I listen to the weather reports and traffic updates…another police emergency, another commuter pileup…she tantalizes me so, with the rush and outburst of honeymoon assault…misuse as a backlash to itself…I have not chosen any of this…nature has imposed it entirely upon me, the interpreting powers that be…*your body does not belong to you*…I find myself lost in her labyrinth…as she breathes through the smoke of my hopeful excitement…she is the scrupulous innuendo of the cosmos with her boudoir energies.

Her lashes were immeasurable…dovetail with her loveliness, her indications quite the complimentary, her traces so favorably designed…I have a vision of waking in her hotbed of promiscuous activity…*when will I be told not to*…talk of her just finishes me off completely, the time-warp of my discretion…the lingerie section of my mind…she is the difference between indefinite and infinite…her preference of milder months, her genre never seeming to exhaust…she spoke of Hamburg and the rivers and the cafés…I got drunk until I made sense…I forgot Ramadan…chomping down on the face of creation…her outlaw logic…a terrible bliss.

It was her who initiated the looting, then the coup and the crackdown…as the champagne flowed, she took it to the streets…in a spiral of retroaction which was manifested through and fueled by insatiability…amid the atmospheric emerald haze of bent thighs and the full spectrum of nipple color…reality is her foil for inventiveness…*to be unfeigned*…having long ago conquered all realms of such opulence and eminence, her unfettered viewpoint thus detached and disjoined…seamless transitory moments, one after the antecedent other…the whole of modernity in a classification of borrowing from the other, of taking the thrill and titillation from another, and then vicariously ejaculating…apathy breeds apathy...belief in theological seduction and the aristocrat/gypsy fantasy, mild to wild.

An automated slow-motion fall into her chasm…there is insight to the rear of her smile…an infrared vision scope peering through the unlit colonnades of her forbidding appeal…I am afraid you will have to experiment a little…she wore the dress like spilt champagne from a flute…only her watch was unnecessary…the extremes society contains and the extravagance nature allows…femininity in a myriad of radical guises, reality under no obligation of being simple…a little anticipation before the invasion…this could be our reality momentarily, a dangerous place to put a zipper, a one woman show-and-tell…peeling off your inhibitions.

My desire to go down on her…to taste it in my mouth…to know what she is like there…her cleanliness, her shape, her design, her mutilation…to feel her soft hair against my face…to smell her from within…I want her vacuum wrapped around me, clinging…all her strength engulfing, her fleshy sweet synthetics on my tongue…her excitement and thrill in the discharge…her breasts firm and upright, her brown hair with slight curls…her bottom full and wide, soft and voluminous…skin warm and inviting, lips full and red…we never shared an introduction and I do not know her name…the scent, with the softness of morning light, the sight, nebulous as wet fog…everything she possesses and all that she doesn't…that luminous sight, something to behold for a lifetime…all that exists behind that skin, the cavernous vaults…her essence creeping out, through the portholes of her anima…she belongs just above the depraved, just below the high priests…her dancing, those serpentine moves…I savor her flavor and that imposing spectacle…graphically: *I ate her discharge and secretions*…nothing more than hard cream, curdled…dull, sour, odd…I am not repulsed, yet surprised by my sudden unsubtle action and friendly gesture…she revels in it all…consumed by her own rapture, unaware of the motions, of the process…she presses her pelvis hard into my face…bone against resilient bone…my tongue penetrating further…her thighs tighter against my head…my ears sealed shut…her right hand in my hair, pulling, pushing me harder against her…she wanted rougher…I backed off…in her frustration she came with her own chaotic fingers.

In order to capture her prey, her hunted, she would use all her endowments of lure, all her might of corruption…thermal expansion through the mind, fusion with postmodern shades, shadows of the avant-garde…attempts at time, space and film…the more open I make her, the more closed she becomes…an elongated perpetuity to it all…a vision of osmosis…roundness encircling a smaller brown island of skin…are you not the one who told me: an insult is like a roofied drink: it only affects you if it is accepted.

Appearances can be deceiving, you can trust that she doesn't own a single pair of panties…her womanhood is wet and dark and deep...I have fantasies to keep and kilometers to travel before I sleep…love gives one the feeling that survival past total annihilation is possible…that that which does not portray itself as obvious is blatant to the eye and what is dubious is unclear to the blatant…I am tender, she must be delicate.

The downfall of contemporary civilization: the confused shopper.

I would even venture so far as to remove her stockings with flame…another rationalization to celebrate similarity…I always got nervous and unstrung when she would cuss me out in her native language…I searched for and pursued her in each café…her flawlessness in itself was a flaw…perfect control around the unashamed curves, she has contours and outlines and arches in her body that repeat themselves in her eyebrows…the most liberating and disengaging aspect was all the violating going on…living made elementary, life for the girls across the corridor.

She finds good pornography empowering…she says that her own fantasy would be to take on several men at once, *a train if you will*…she claims to possess the ability and emotion to handle it…to go to whatever extreme or frontier is required…to be occupied and done completely…she knows she couldn't satisfy all the guests, but that is not her concern…she plans to wear a leopard-print blouse and string panties…eventually the blouse will be removed to reveal her bare breasts, but the panties should not come off—she finds it too pleasing optically…nevertheless, such talk is not expected from such a woman…she is far too exquisite, too elegant, educated, refined, proper and conservative…I am almost disgusted, but I am captivated by her…these ideas are unsettling, but they drag me in.

She possessed the magically alluring formula…she would surface and feel like chilled water in my spine…she came through in closed caption…the Renaissance ideal: a kept body lingering in a paler side of blue…the idea of this is cruel, inexorable…do absolve me…per her orders, she would wear stockings of Ethiopian blackness…all of that unambiguous sexual signaling…the provocation of a half-naked thigh is devastating…I want to be so deeply inside of her that I feel all twenty-seven feet of her intestines…prosthetic vagina look-alikes…a high and omnipotent capable bosom…the in-between of the vaginal gap…surrounded by mail-in rebate consumerism and red shopping cart crashes, I was rendered impotent—left with a diseased disposition and an absence of merriment…later, amid the clefts, cleavage and nuances, I at last saw her come hither face…she whispered in my ear: *I want you to bite off your lover's eyelashes*…overlook that…in another life I was a decorated chief in a large non-Asian concubine…there I was, sitting on a velvet throne in the back of the burgeoning unripe garden…imagine beyond the fray that this is our last night.

The setting: elegant and overrated restaurant, mid-evening, she and I are seated toward the back of a large room. She wears a rayon skirt (chestnut brown) and a cotton crepe sweater (pale pink)—a sophisticated edge—with a side slit of silky texture and nude hose for evening. I wear a gray wool suit, new leather shoe-boots and a scarf of cerulean shades. We drink the whiskey and cokes that she ordered. An appetizer of carrot soup is served and we begin to eat. Our conversation drifts and sifts through a paltry and scattered discourse of nonsense. She stops everything, saying she's had enough, that now she will say whatever may come to mind.

She begins with: "When you spank me you need to know that the sweet spot is basically the two areas of the ass that are closest to, and on either side of, the genitals. Imagine, if you will, that each cheek is divided into quadrants—the bottom right-hand side of the left cheek, and the bottom left-hand side of the right cheek—shaping the comprised sweet spot."

The main course of prawns and rice is served while she further elucidates:

"When I shave down there I am careful. It is for you. I soak in a hot bath, use a fresh razor and *take my time*. I have to shave every day."

She paused until we were served the small dessert of truffles to enlighten further:

"Off the topic, but similarly intriguing, when you lick my nipple, the nipple moves slightly back and forth under your tongue, and some sensation is lost. To slow this, spread your index and middle finger apart and place them on either side of my nipple. Spread them even further apart. The nipple is noticeably bulging out when this is done. The nipple is exposed, immobile. No sensation is lost. Apply your tongue and note the difference."

The most taboo of taboo words, in order: motherfucker, cocksucker, fuck, pussy, cunt, prick, cock, bastard, son of a bitch, asshole, suck, nigger, tits, whore, shit, bitch, piss, slut, queer, bullshit, ass, spic, blow, damn, hell and pig.

You can take the child out of the treacherous desire, but you can't take the anxiety for treachery out of the boy…and you do it again and again until you cannot restrain it anymore…I want you to take me to the faraway places that I visit in my fantasies…just take care of business, I need some love baby…I had another profuse and gourmet dream last night…I want to be the towel that dries her off after a hot shower…quitting now greatly reduces serious risk to your mental well-being...on her glass coffee table: an unloaded automatic pistol, a tape recorder, a dead butterfly and a blond wig…such evil frivolity, conjecturing how far to go when one thinks one has gone too far…as I watch the girls walk by, surveying how she smokes a cigarette…an act of provocation in and of itself.

Down the hookers' avenue…that jungle swagger with small titties and a large ass…and she's *white*…I suppose she decided to get a real job…those freaky lips, so plenteous and overgrown…so full and moist and wet and anticipating and sweet and innocent, so virgin-like…she had a limp, and something wrong with her crotch…she always said the money was good…I surmise that low-income superstores don't pay too well…172 billion human souls have lived on this planet: sages, wisemen, cowards, lovers, dwarfs, witch doctors, popes, prostitutes, paupers, Egyptian inventors...a mystical alliance, a bloc for the supernatural occurrences she would invoke…repent or perish—judgment day is coming…evolution will surely bring us Whoredom.

Names women have called me: flesh peddler, hard mack, maggot, bitch…The Man Who Gained the World but Lost his Soul…this fact: there is a high percentage of women who have become amorous toward their doctors…"victims of rape or incest are sexually more promiscuous"…they live in a hothouse world of daydreams, movies, novels and fantasies that is no more twisted, in its own way, than their parents' world of suburban fortresses…their attempts to find something real and thrilling in life has delivered them into the unreal and surreal—nowhere so gloriously realized as now…nothing she hates more than catching the eyes of the person she had just slept with staring at her as she struggles into her pantyhose.

From: caliph8@sharia4ever.org
Some say the universe was created by the "big bang." But the Qur'an asks: "Do the unbelievers not see the heavens and Earth were joined together as one before we tore them apart?" (21:30). This profound scientific truth emerged from the deserts of Arabia 1,400 years ago...and they call us dumb? My friend, how are you? Sorry I get so wrapped up in this and want to get my thoughts out that I forget my manners. Do you miss me bro? LMFAO #inshallah

I want to conquer her unsullied nature and run impulsively through her pristine wilderness, feed off her regime, be outdone by her tributary profits…the conundrum of this sequestered individual, and to think of all the love being made at this moment, knowing fully and complacently that I have no part in any of it…a temporary directional loss of my genital energies…once the taboo is formed and calculated, the intrigue and complicity set in…the finest innovation is that I have not been properly invited in…we all need our own revolutions.

Whereabouts of gainsaying, the spark of manipulated memories: blurry, nebulous images of smiles and laughter and a vertigo of flashes of society and the things of what constituted the consequence of luck and calibration and matters of time…it computes and sums to the mere repercussion and sequences of illusion…and the aftermath and misfortunes of passing distant reminiscence…new musings and encounters launching and catapulting out the former and forgotten, vacating space for the future, for the cliché of the unknown…play that picture again in my mind, that introspection, those very pleasant reflections…simplicity and duplicity, monotony and invariability…the way our enchanted encumbrances were—but, most magisterially, how things will come about and acceptably unfold…into the aftertime which will be missed, and the bygone that will be adored.

All of the elaborating epiphanies around me…she is not a likely unfeigned outcome, merely a thought experiment…simply touching and caressing her—in any form or format—can be regarded as one of the highest human acts…to future illuminative escapades, to my preferred erotic welfare…unique, unequaled, unmatched…it is true, I admit, I didn't read it: *I scanned it for the dirty passages*…a wretched victim to an unruly libidinous begging…that chronic perpetual female sensation, waiting fretfully until the epoch when beauty will become the task and labor for every new day's mission…glimpsing across the faint threshold of a mere instant, the one thing sustaining my vitality is the hope of her prompt return…her apt exquisiteness enlarges my whetted potentiality and lessens my fatigued validity.

Her fragility and delicacy drive me on…I observe my blood kindle as I kiss the brown tip of her breast, seeing the stir and uproar in her vacant gaze…gently stroking her cheek, fondling her bends and creases, inhaling a foreign fragrance of perfume…understanding that I entered this world under a lucky star, on the white washed coattails of future kings…eating from her cleavage a freshly-cut fruit…the initial kiss then a series of kisses, closing in a whirlpool of overlapping folds of wet flesh, tender teeth, inflamed gums and aroused breath…each kiss and each mouth unlike…manifold and multifold…from a doomed juncture I made this resolution…the alright love erudite…knowing I would execute it, fulfilling the covenant I had made with all those femmes…to find how we ever fared without the other.

It is all just an eternal chain of exalted and pompous loveliness…I can feel the torment then savor the afterglow…her eyes of ember left translucent, lustrous…she went silent, while her manner and bearing did all the moaning, a variation on the porno refugee…the only advice was to keep on one's guard toward her cleverness and inventiveness…but, then again, those were second- and third-hand rumors, I may entertain them as conceivably delusive hearsay…inducing then disposing her there can prove to be one of the most arduous and wearisome tasks…come on, don't bite your lip…everything else was a shoddy detour, a victimizing obstacle.

The same stale light that is cast upon her is the same hardened light which has cast me into the act…slightly drunk, city cabs, a late hour, subtle rainfall…all the superficial fun passing me by…the fear of missing out, the playful scene taking place under the white linen-covered table…she considered most conversations to be variations on static and unmoving sound…she described it to be somewhat between walkie-talkie static and the rumbling from a projectionist's booth…the only way she would take things was by de-poetizing them first: a nebulous erotic image reduced to obvious and clamorous pornography;

glorious and gratifying sunlight to harsh and common humidity; a wild and reckless impulsive voyage to the simplest of simplex transit…don't tell her I told you so.

All this unavailing time which surpasses…the remaining particles and dust of the masses…and if you are inclined to venture to remember I didn't promise anything…you may exit with a grin…for all there is to ever apprehend and appreciate after the research is complete…she will possess nothing but you to exhibit…she chose to speak in that militaristic sort of dialogue, insisted that she is never fervent when faced with tricky predicaments, rather poised and nonchalant, willing to overcome and conquer any affront or dare…I put her to the test…urinate on me…on my chest, first…yes, there…now into my mouth…accommodating reluctantly…drain your bladder…only stop when there is no more left…that's it…now stay there, straddle me, thighs apart…finger yourself…expose that agog clit from that massive plot of black hair…bring yourself to orgasm…don't forget that I am right here…watching…witnessing every shaking and slipping moment…I want to see your ejaculation project itself, falling onto the floor…(her pace is steady, unrelenting)…*you are not afraid*…I feel the heated, acidic liquid in my hair…her clit swells to a size near that of the accompanying index finger…the lips part by their own accord…she discharges heavily, solidly…her moistened hands tremble…the knees slightly buckling…her facial features shut…the skin flushed…she is complete.

She seemed to always think that it was upright to be depraved…she will corrupt your soul, I was forewarned…and if not your soul, your behavior and conduct…she asked me if I was interested in being there when we made love…I know I cannot help her sense and reason, but I can place my lips upon her…just as long as I leave her as I found her…I deliberately arise and dream of wanting to fly and aviate away…there is no purpose in me demonstrating, she proclaimed…my own justification and apology are severely confidential things…I don't think there is anyone that can perform like that…after dinner she joked: *we can kiss like cousins and have ourselves a mighty fine good time*…one is never too close for leisure…her claim was that she could suck the chrome off a trailer hitch...proceeding through one's existence without an exclusive idea or opinion…undergoing life-changing, mind-blowing affairs and episodes…never retaining any of it, not allowing them to assist me on the later scaffolds of life…to help in character development and expansion…self-advancement, self-reliance, self-peculiarity.

The meaning and intent in her reflection…I struggle to believe that she likes to perform these bedroom acts…her broken surrender beckons me alongside the foremost…she moved as if to calypso music, the polished dance floor is waiting, the glories of her scenery, the intoxicating panoramic gaze I am afforded…help me, spare me from exposure to that which I cannot have…I don't want to know about it, moreover I don't want to know it exists…the miracle of her is eternal…I snorkel through her coral reefs…the sunlight becomes a prism when reflecting off of her…in the mainstream of your overflow…those unrequited, non-verbal gestures…so eloquent in their intricacies and sincerity…whatever meaning there may be behind her walls of secrecy…the long torturous strokes of her hand, languidly manipulating the surface of all she touches…in search of the element which pulls you in…to the hum of the traffic, muffled by the noise of our sex…the ancient equation, the placing of the fitted puzzle piece…I inside of her…she made love purely for the aftermath.

The close proximity she offers when talking to strangers…the intimacy, as if she were about to begin kissing them…the way she hides her full and voluminous breasts behind the facade of loose white clothing…she does not want you to know what is going on with her…what she is made of, what she is about, even her next intention…her blatant disregard for your curiosity…that visual spectacle flirting to the voyeur world, saying: *this is what I've got and you can't have any*…bordering on ludicrous, tapping into the perpetual, the ongoing, the eternal deprivation of such things…she could be labeled evil for such distressing trappings or even called selfish for not indulging some lucky and envied soul…surely she could lay blame on anybody and anything but herself…she is a victim ensnarled in such an exquisite encasing, a prisoner to the burden of such pleasing.

The arrival of and to, the on-the-verge state, as she spills the sticky soda down her chest…I choose how my hours are filled…I need a deep breath at her oxygen bar…she quickens the tempo of my confessions…I rarely feel such clarity…the fragrance of her potpourri as I sink into her sea-salt bath…the dawn of my high times, an unbalanced viewpoint of her sex and all its accessories…I have noticed her tired bewilderment of time and surroundings, neglect and other worthy qualities…with each fresh emission…twice without withdrawing…my reason is powerless to such aesthetics…this level of excess can be harmful…in taintless agony of bliss…under her skirt I feel the dampness, even a well-turned fold…she gave me the signal for retiring to the bedroom…she said she could not elucidate how she gave pleasure so…I kiss her thigh just above the stocking…the quiver of her lips and the rosy-tipped nipples of her breasts can be seen and best distinguished when they rise and fall in heaving thumps against their feeble concealment…the shapes of her thighs and legs, the mass of curly hair that overhangs their lusciousness…I stood there motionless and entranced, gazed upon her fairy-like qualities…she asked me to be her companion for the night, with those lustrous and luxurious eyes…she banished her modesty, replacing any leftover docility with the most lascivious abandon…her amorous spot, her fond locale, the little cleft at the bottom of her belly…to the utmost, she spread her thighs in receipt of me…she threw her legs across my back, prepared for this delicious combat…then in her mouth she palated me with her tongue…this was how my inamorata did things…I reveled and basked in her most hedonistic charms…unparalleled non-machinelike suction on the folds of her precision cylinder.

Supposing for a moment this was a dream…you are a whore, I am the customer…you are very curvaceous…I am sitting in the corner…it is dark…you are being observed…I suppress certain jealousies for something that you possess…as well, for having not known about this until now…for the roaming nature of the wind…and the laughter…the flowers that don't belong…your tattered and frayed undergarments…your incessant sensuality…the branches of your replication…the absence of light…this wonderful and pleasing examination…my inculpable foolishness…chasing you about, all around…in circles…in the periphery I see you smiling. The room was heavily curtained…hanging textiles of dense and pressed vermilion velvet and gilded rope…it had more to do with lust than with connection…her totemic imputations were the tourniquets against the wall, organized and arranged by individual dissimilar format…hers was a minimum of artifice, the bottom of deception…coming down to this: *the inevitability was arranged when names were given to these nameless things*…acrobatics in the TV room…a streamlined emergence, shining lustrously on the way home…the suggestion in the shadow of her crawl…across the poorly lit room…she hands me a tube of white lubrication, an ultra-thin condom, then winks…the idea that it was planned as betrayal should make it easier.

The tonality of the accent from her lips, a weathered whore at closing time…her smell like daisy blossoms freshly cut…waves across the skin like a stone and the pond's ripples…nipples rough and uneven, basecamp before the first snowfall…falling round eyes like portholes to the open sea…she is bubbles floating in the air…there, part your legs…the frowning lips on a small child…whirl your lower-back concave like a pink lawn flamingo on one leg…the innocence of your rhythm and stroke.

Against a backdrop ablaze.
Your meteor body that cuts through the air.
And your empress shadow splendor.
Your lowland fires that burn downward.
Your electric crescent shape.
Your soft skin valley nape.
Tomorrow it will not matter what we did tonight.

From: caliph8@sharia4ever.org

All praise is for God, the Lord of the Universe. We seek His help and His forgiveness for all our sins, and we submit our regret and repentance before Him. We seek

His protection from the malice of our hearts and from all evils that we have committed. Those who are guided by God to the right path cannot be led astray, and those who are denied guidance by God cannot be guided to the path of truth. #inshallah

Begging, she wanted me to taste her hair…so I swirled and twisted it slowly and brought it to my nose, all the aromas surfacing…I inhaled deeply, pausing for an instant, then tasted it…I secured a secondary whiff and soon afterward the aftertaste…in the altogether it was resplendent and floral…such glossy indiscretion, her amorous weightlessness and unadulterated levity…sunshine's forefront innovation is so wonderful, she'd say…her reactive shades of ivory and creamy-white…laughing: take me impeccably through an invisible safeguard, where hour after feeble hour furnishes it all to you free of charge…soothing and refreshing even to the most susceptible skin…the flickering images in a darkened street-level room…inflexible and ever-unwavering, she is free of bona fide synthetic flavor…challenging the burden of passive thinking and motionless cognition…you will find this only in the West…the discovery of convenient longing…she might have been the vanguard, but she wasn't the maiden…while constricting emptiness and depravity opens wide space for this balmy and senseless mind, late at night and on the floor.

A debased humanity, its awareness and hospitality of inevitable death, the one of erotic fulfillment and discreet secretion…a sensorial blue light special…the murderess and perilous woman embodying the artist's erogenous fantasies…do away with these nonsensical taboos and insipid prohibitions, finally, for once, for me—

por favor…and in a non-catastrophic manner I was abandoned with myself by a solitary kiss.

A tremendous optical distraction…residing in her withdrawn and lemon-scented catacombs, the underground of and for all her byproducts and casualties of foregone infelicitous preventable catastrophe…confined to her strict and despotic bourgeoisie methods and well-bred procedures…we all are swimming amid the murky refuge water, navigating the sharp and sudden turns of the precariously flooded hallways…the beating sounds of flogging and evening jungle, the agitated pulsating rhythm, then and now…the redolent sundown perfume, the plastic flower trees…the flaming sun, blinding, burning and the loss of certain unfailing morals…the hedonism propelled and impelled further, the depravity elongated, augmented to an extremity and the continual rush entailed…the risk of one-way transport and an unattended place in one's own decadence…just beyond the wall, with no return in sight…the cobwebs over the mind's window pane…the way she relates without forgiveness, her disregard for reservation and the seduction as sham: deep breathing and an undone zipper fly.

I beg you to believe that in the pleasure I promise myself, I count for a great deal the reward I expect from you…it ends with thrashing passion in a bargain motel room reeking of others' sex, unchanged sheets, ashtrays and empty pizza boxes…illuminated by inlaid mental gargoyles and her gothic grandeur, an eclectic wealth of decorations on avenues and in exhibitions…her too-hot-to-touch skin, understanding that she is yours…her tan-lined hips swayed in a most compulsive manner and my actions constituted senselessness from being unlearned…yes, impending small attempts at innocence…I listen for the toilet flush…just a smattering of penetration thrown in…I want to go where the women can shave without looking…the non-erotic condition of crotch less fishnet pantyhose…I will have none of that and the same goes for the molding of desire…please be well-disposed when you cut me down…gladly received subversion to my consumed complacency, from a little sprinkle to a huge flood, as the hours melt down to habitual instances.

Expectation is tension, belief is unease…the nightlife was kicking amid the frenzy of her vertigo: *spinning breasts, legs, thighs, ass, nipples, necks, lips, breasts*…your chambermaid eyes amid mass fornication…tonight is your night, but tomorrow you do me…that which before long must take place…the wayward details everywhere, a new premise mounting in the imagination of the passerby…succumbing to the temptation rather than mortal logic…she is a blend of the real and the surreal, provable and disputable…her smile slipped a little each time she caught my eye and that is when she told me: *life is too short for softcore porn.*

It was all about the possibility of getting caught in the act…lost in the process, the female side of life…she found a certain sense of immunity in shaving…her lips were their own color…accessible with instructions…her layers formatted…the shine from gold, glamour and allure…the shape of a princess…what we have is not conventional decadence…the more we do, the more performance possibility…I am touching upon insanity, when she and I reach harmony…while the sum of all of this is nothing, taking me nowhere…I don't want to leave there again…when I asked her why she did it, she told me: it was as if my entire life had flashed before me, and it wasn't worth watching.

In this prairie of abandoned neon…and together we will share this smile…an act of furtherance…I rejoice in the thought of you…she can be quite candid…amid an atmosphere of relative calm…one of the last truisms: *nostalgia's luxury*…she asked me to emulate selfless paragons of oral virtue…the hair swept up and back in a thick tail, the eyes dull and sullen with the overhang of high brows…the mouth projected outward, pulling concave wide cheeks and enduring lip flesh…the breasts large and widespread in a Satin Fantasy full-figure underwire bra…matching rosewood control briefs…she is a symmetrical study of triangles, ninety degree turns and spheres…until I lose interest in myself.

You are an absolutely fabulous person with some very intriguing qualities…at any rate, she was the one screaming in silence…I was treading through her mind, without comprehending, then again, I was in a bind…I'll take it in just for you…the smell of her filled the air…the first thing for us to do when we meet is to dirty the sheet…some kind of sexual zealot…and all I ever wanted was that for which I did have…running toward the trifling, returning to the pre-excitement hue…a utopian fantasy to fulfill in play, and she said: *one never graduates from women*…transformational invariance…waking up dead in a place called aesthetica.

Baring one's impotence for the sake of mystery, she thought herself sublime…I am struggling; I can't take it any longer…those brown leggings removed to reveal the sea of blue from her lace-up boy-shorts…she asks me to log on…requiring more circumstance…she calms me with her technique, then she does it again…the ability of earthquake sensitivity, of some kind of return, cross the bottom and swim through the outset…the eternal agonizing search for unrealizable moments lost in time…I demand revisits…save up your creativity…new ridiculous methods…approaching the mutual target…forgotten corners in this simultaneous state of uncontrollable beauty and horror.

The absurd scene of her descending the spiral staircase in that vulgar pair of gold-enameled panties…the cleavage could be felt in the air…all the hands on all the hips…the polished concavity of her back, so unapologetically a matter of perfect symmetry…she exists amid the static of light, surfacing for the short-lived display, the show-and-tell, and then returning to that other place…only in her offering does she live among the viewer and the more she reveals and discards, the better off she is and the closer she is to circumspection...prime time attention for her unsettling commercial of what *could be yours*…combing her hair in a different light…beyond the bounds of moral authority, beyond time's ability to tell, beyond tomorrow's savagery…that offered precision in her dream realm—the perfect picture feature, theater-quality sound and widescreen format…the visual/aural reproduction of voluptuous young women being molested by their own defiling intentions.

Exerting to underscore her rapprochement, I am bemused by her one flaw…that she is too willing…that she organizes her wants, and their subsequent fulfillment, by and through syndicates—with an upsurge in fleeing sentiments and downtime with ardent policies and the thereafter…exquisite in the way she wears tone-on-tone hues, so simple the shapes and the depth of the soft textures…her anticipation apparent in a silk v-neck, under a faux suede jacket…as she comes through in 4k, she systematically, in a robust manner, transgresses the system…her broadcast in a new analog…what she calls ocular by-play…the visual alchemy, the distribution of pixels…the etched super-real qualities in the shallow aftermath of such displays, she is laughing at the world.

Her purity of heart, the simplicity and naiveté of her own nature, all of this she wears on her nipples…pre-pubescent, gentle, salmon, unexplored or out of danger…deaf to a man's suckling, not yet indulged by the love of an infant…in the beams of sunlight from the glass ceiling, bolting a white silhouette up between her covered legs with each beating step…overindulgence will get you nowhere…the gypsy made me do it…I am a part of each and all for which I have pressed my lips against…staring at her while she struggles and squirms into her pantyhose…then again, that is her sphere of duty…I am in search of my feminine counterpart…she will be of my persuasion: cute with her fixations, deviations, insecurities and manias…try it sometime…a solution to this absolution…I could tell you the truth but you'd probably lose interest…this is the best that it will get, just allow it to hang out, it could all be dismissed as theater…a certain something for her soiled linen.

A post-everything state of affairs…the transpiration of red hot Mecca…the invisible hope of the alluring girl at the next table showing up in a strange city…she enters and exits, passing frames on the screen, longing for a long vanished epoch, or a season when all was radiant…greetings to my grooving stranger, a languid sojourn into the posterior chambers of the mind…she is the only authentic motive force in the world, nothing to do with what I have done…it is what I am going to do…welcome toxins spill, light flows, her panties are in the wash, on spin cycle…phenomenon in place, proper technicalities in motion, I hear her say: *kiss me boo, bye.*

Immaterial and trifling efforts at reflection of who I was…what I possessed and owed…who I shared, and did not share, all of it with…of the personalities and the qualities…makeup, undergarments, products and accessories…of all the women I once called friends…the lovers and paramours I tasted, the tears and lamentations of exultation…all escaping me for now…the old and the new moon, by the same flamboyant design, lying and dying and never meeting those who pull the strings…let's find the location of her rose garden…actions don't happen by their own accord…the best proof of her cleverness is in the catalyst of her carnality and obligations…discard the map, you have reached your manifestation.

She demonstrates that she likes to drive fast while taking off her bra through the sleeves of her blouse…strip down to your panties and reveal your deepest thoughts…the solidarity of this vice, a fickle and crotchety attitude…her lithesome upper-lip shaped so extraordinarily…fleshy, plump, saturated, overgrown…a wretched tenure as her lover…locked into a ruthless stupefaction of such ideal and incomparability: that is when the wheels began to fall off...she occupied an opposite charge…the essence of animation and antimatter…only she could produce such an outpouring, disappearing in a clang of vehement diffusion…a frenzy of cancellation…of massive stars from a long forgotten transformative epoch…more technology and discipline…her cut-off jeans and pulled-back hair…those ostentatious sunglasses and attenuated legs…those heavy thighs and brown skin…that complicated chest, her maze of corridors, a labyrinth of sensation and sympathy…be still these defective apparitions, there is more from where that came.

Taking relief in her aesthetic values, for their flagrant merits and openly scandalous entitlements…more so than tangible carnal endeavors…she submits a visual thrill, while absolute consummation would be methodology toward cessation…the end of the erotic, the closure of licentiousness…longing to have the dew on her skin sucked with a lapping tongue, to have her skin peeled to the sides, flayed back, exposing her insides, the adulthood…the young bud of her flowered loveliness…the fragrance she emits, the smell of coral and palm, of guava blossoms and bouquets in humidity…she asks to have her fruit eaten, to have it bitten and nibbled on…sucked of its juice, then swallowed…she quivers with each word, hanging onto the sensations projected…she will rinse her skin beforehand, in preparation, yet careful to stay succulent…the small hair of her skin will rise, her soft lips will turn the color of rose…her curves will take shape and swell…she will assume her role as something edible and become fulfilled when completely devoured.

Turning off the Global Positioning System for a while…she is the state of art, so unsanitary…loose blue jeans, plucked eyebrows…her ass up sideways, toward the firmament, while the creases and the folds fall into place…a natural woman…at home in the badlands…the lingering taste of a powdered mistress on the teeth…these small attempts at innocence amid clean sheets and depletion from stillness, altogether still…footsteps in the covered way, the mezzanine of our minds…the phantom floating that they manifest…the dreams of yesterday are the lies of now...the destination in everywhere…passing by in furlough dress…from the deceived to the deceiver…she litters my mind…if you squeeze, it will please…exhume the complacent ghosts…the acoustic perfection linked to her moans and laughter…when she says: *now we will rest and refresh ourselves*, or, when she demands: *kneel down and kiss me there, and thank me.*

A grand faculty for self-entertainment—we owe ourselves partly to society, but chiefly to ourselves…exigency has no law, all lovely women are as perplexing as they are rare…now and then the candle would flicker, lighting up the girl's hair…what with her splendor and all, I was puzzled and flustered…we were getting on well…*kiss her*…waiting for the unavoidable flash when the sun burns out…I only wanted to keep staring at her face…I was full of inner-noise.

Let me start with an experience…there is no room for optimism, but a necessity for hope…with the advice: *one should think about death all the time because it could come at any moment*…this fear is future-oriented…in your desperate eyes I see the blameless skin, the perspicuity, the immaculate, the hasty losing…all right now…oh radiant and angelic woman…*you outlaw*…allow me to interlude with a thought: her narrow face is the first attraction, the detailed small features, the primped lips and the small eyes; the pinched cheek bones and swept-back hair, dressed in a tight black business suit, brown Fendi bag…she stands tall and the pants tighten around her hard ass…such an unexpected ass…it appears she is commando…the essence and root of the secretary coming undone myth, giving in to her desire to fuck the one in charge…in all positions on a desk…she perpetuates and condenses the plots of the porn industry…in her wake, with the smell of sweet perfume, she leaves each man with another scenario, another motion of pictures to be played out, another reel of torment…of her undressing, bending, spreading out her legs on a desk, thrashing paperwork to the floor, undoing her blouse to reveal that secret cleavage, pulling down her skirt to show that garter belt (responding to your shock, she says: *I can't imagine dressing any other way*), letting her hair fall to the side…merely unraveling the ambient artifice.

The ether is occupied…this apocalyptic escapade…it comes down by the sides…she is crazy-loca…the germ of her is everywhere…the smell of freon, the buzz of electricity…she is the stuff of legend and gossip, a zeitgeist intermission waiting for the slightest touch…depth, creation, impoverishment and an absence of narrative existence…the excitement of these role games, romance products and empty words…completing agreed-upon circles…gazing down the sunny streets…indulging in observation: *the stimulus is everywhere*…she initiates my daydreams, then vacates, leaving the fantasy to my approach and mechanism.

The spark of manipulated non-recuperating memories, blurry, nebulous images of grins and laughter…her refulgent mausoleum of abstract misdeeds on display…when all that is left is to push on through the madness and the reliance…surfacing with the canvass pristine, enamored by the hostess's pleasantries of hot tea and cakes…the visions of light particles escaping from her womanhood and a vertigo of flashes from society and the things of what constituted the consequence of luck and timing and matters of time…it all adds up to upskirts, upshots and passing recollections…then pushing out the old and confirming room for more…clichés and naïveté…play that picture again in my mind, those thoughts, those very pleasant thoughts…simplicity, duplicity, despondency…the way things were and how they will be…the future passing away.

She tastes of lingering champagne…I just listened to her pee and flush…it saved me, allowing me to partake in something so privy…the sounds set reeling the projector of her pomp, of her brown thighs on the porcelain, the tissue wedged into the pink cleft…the panties around the knees, the toes pointed inward…her eyes gazed upward, the last twinkle of tinkle…the expanding cloud of yellow in the bowl…standing, she tugs the undergarments around her waist, the elastic cling and the closure in the flush.

Better libido. Increased energy. More lean muscle. Decreased body fat. Increased collagen production. Tightening of the skin. Improved mood and memory.
You have nothing to lose and all to gain.
You control the levels, you control how you feel.
Initial dosing will involve estrogen and progestogens. Introducing these into the body will have an impact on every level. The goal in the somatic treatment is a more satisfying body congruent with your identity.
We dose low then gradually increase.
Estrogen is what causes breasts, wide hips and feminine patterns of fat distribution.
Estradiol is the most predominant natural estrogen in women; this cocktailed with congated equine estrogens administered first by patch transdermally, then by implant. GnRH will stimulate the pituitary gland which will then produce the luteinizing hormone in turn causing the gonads to produce the sex steroids. This works by over stimulating the pituitary gland then rapidly desensitizing it to safer levels. This also results in a smaller prostate.

For the biggest effect we will administer progestogen, even though it is mostly involved in menstrual cycles and pregnancy. This will aid in breast development and smoother skin and hair. Better sleep and less anxiety. We will watch for enlarging areolas, much like that of a pregnant woman, overall mammary structure and shape. We will try and get you to stage IV of the Tanner scale. You will have an increased appetite. You will have healthier bones and some bone building by osteoblasts. Softening and thinning of the skin. Decreased body hair growth and density. Decreased muscle mass and strength. Decreased adult acne, skin oiliness, body odor. Decreased size of the penis, scrotum, testicles. Suppressed or abolished spermatogenesis and fertility. Decreased semen ejaculate volume. Changes in mood, emotionality and behavior. Decreased sex drive and less incidences of spontaneous erections.

Shoulder width and size of the rib cage can play a role in the perceivable size of the breasts, causing the breasts to appear proportionally smaller than they really are. Breast ducts and the Cooper's ligaments develop under the influence of estrogen. Progesterone causes the milk sacs to develop, and with proper stimuli you may lactate. Nipples will be more sensitive to stimulation, and may be itchy.

The stratum corneum, the uppermost layer of skin, will become thinner and more translucent. Spider veins will be more noticeable as a result. As collagen decreases tactile sensations will increase. As the skin becomes softer it will become more susceptible to tearing and irritation from scratching or shaving, and will become slightly lighter in color because of the decrease in melanin.

Sebaceous gland activity lessens, reducing oil production of the skin and scalp. Lotions will become necessary as part of your daily regimen. Pores become smaller, many sweat glands will become inactive as body odor decreases, and remaining body odors will become less metallic, sharp or acrid, becoming sweeter and musky.

Dimpling cellulite becomes more apparent on the thighs and buttocks as subcutaneous fat accumulates. Stretch marks may appear on the skin in these areas.

Susceptibility to sunburn increases as the skin is less pigmented. Arm and perianal hair is reduced but may not turn to vellus hair. Underarm hair changes slightly in texture and length, while pubic hair becomes more typically female in pattern. Lower leg hair becomes less dense. Head hair will change in texture, curl and color.

Eyebrows will not be affected as they are not androgenic. The lens of the eye changes in curvature. The meibomian glands produce less oil, preventing tear film from evaporating, causing dry eyes.

Fat on the hips, thighs and buttocks has a higher concentration of omega-3 fatty acids and is stored for lactation. The body begins to burn old adipose tissue in the waist, shoulders, and back, making those areas smaller.

Subcutaneous fat increases in the cheeks and lips, making the face appear rounder with slightly less emphasis on the jaw as the lower portion of the cheeks fill in.

A general reduction in muscle mass and distribution toward female proportions. Hips will begin to rotate slightly forward because of changes in the tendons. Hip discomfort is not uncommon. The slow movement of pelvic ossification and the pelvic outlet and inlet slightly open. Resulting in a widening of the femora and wider hips.

Mood changes including depression are common, however significant euphoria is common as well. Dopamine levels are affected so deep depression is a possibility.
A significant reduction in libido will be treated with microdosing of testosterone.
But you may want to put your sex life on hold. Morning erections will likely stop. Voluntary erections may not be possible. A reduction in brain volume toward female proportions will alter your perceptions of emotion, social interaction and how you process feelings and experiences.
Potential side effects: breast cancer, thrombosis, embolism, macroprolactinoma, liver disease, kidney disease, heart disease, stroke, high cholesterol, gallbladder disease, circulation or clotting problems, peripheral vascular disease, sickle-cell anemia, protein C deficiency, paroxysmal nocturnal hemoglobinuria, and hypertension.

She liked to be watched from behind on all fours—as if she were cleaning. She liked the idea of her lover getting off on her while disregarding her own satisfaction. Her data is compiled. Her womanly excitement, the cul-de-sacs of her craving and the flirtations. I ask to be forgiven in advance.

She sucked me off with eagerness. That is, *avidly*. I pressed her heavy breasts together and lapped my tongue over both nipples. She moaned and slid her tongue in and out of my ear. I ran the length of my hand between her open legs, between two large wet lips. I grabbed a handful of ass-cheek, squeezing, groping. Expanding her gap wider. She just got wetter. Eventually to leave juices everywhere she moved. She stroked me with one hand. The other cupped on my balls. She laid on her back and pulled me on top of her, into a mounted/straddled position. My hard dick on her chest. She pressed her breasts firmly together, engulfing my cock. She licked and sucked the tip. I pumped slowly in and out of her mouth. I pushed half my fingers inside of her. Inserting them quickly until she came into my palm. I came on her chest. She licked the cum off her nipples. I sucked the juice out of her pussy. She rolled over and spread her legs wide. I entered her from behind. She reached for my hand and guided my fingers to her ass, where she inserted them into herself. She gyrated her own hips. I was left with no part in any of it. She arched her ass, widening her hips. This went on until she came again. She stroked me until I was on the edge of ejaculation. At that moment, she slid my dick into her ass, where I came.

From: caliph8@sharia4ever.org
Hi fam! How you been? Today I am all about spreading the message that Islam is a total way of living, not just a religion. Islam regulates every aspect of life, to the point that cultures, religion and politics all bleed into one and are inseparable. And Allah! There is no God but Him. The Living, the Self-Sufficient, the Infinitely Enduring. Slumber or sleep never reaches Him. All things are His, in the heavens and the earth. He knows everything that happens. His throne extends over the heavens and over the earth, and He does not tire in guarding and preserving them. He is the Most High, the Supreme in Glory. Is it not wonderful friend to know He has your back through all things? Write soon. #inshallah

She started dancing for me, her belly undulating, her jeweled navel languidly wrecking, her hips gyrating—I was transfixed by her veiled loveliness…she weaved her way toward me and before my spread-eagled legs she began teasing my flesh…my dick rose like a viper, and with hypnotic movements of her hands, she made it sway with the serpentine wriggle of an entranced cobra under the spell of a flute…I had become a slave to her sorcery…she masturbated me slowly with one hand then when I was about to explode she unveiled her lovely breasts and replaced them with her hands until I came all over her chest…her nippled melons were a drip with cum, still she leaned over and pulled her hair back, forcing my mouth open...she stood above me fully naked and pushed her wet slit against my face…she ground her womanhood into the bridge of my nose, her hot juices scolded my face…her heat was stifling and I was suffocating…with my last breath she became rigid with a tense tremor…she snapped in sexual cataclysm…this only changed the pitch of her sexual wantonness—for she reversed her position and took my dick and balls into her mouth where I readily came in aching torment…as she led me to the bed I noticed through her clothing the lush breasts outlined, her soft curves and succulent ass…she stripped naked to her perfection…her breasts, engineered by a master architect…I closed my eyes and abandoned myself to her voluptuous pleasuring…she explored every fold and outpost of my body…she delivered her breasts to my lips (I took each hot, stiff nipple into my mouth, one at a time)…my throbbing dick was firmly up against her gash…her whole body worked on me…I opened my eyes and saw—in delicious delirium—a wild-eyed lioness devouring me in a feline fuck, unyielding in her carnality…she carefully sat herself on the head of my penis…*beg me for it*, she demanded…she collapsed herself and swallowed me whole…she squeezed me with her vaginal sphincter and locked my prick in a strangled embrace—she teased me by gently rocking up and down…an excruciating heaven…I wanted to remain inside her eternally…finally, this psycho-dramatic rape of me had spontaneously combusted…we laid still as not to break our blissful state…suddenly the sublime was cracked when her roommate entered the room…she was half naked and I could see the juices that moistened her fleece—she asked if she could join, while the flush of fuck was on our bare skin.

Paused on by the neon and bright lights, I cross the sidewalk and enter the shop with the most signs…it promises LIVE NUDE GIRLS, a no-drink minimum, a two-girl sex show, women with two and three clits…the motif: filth, nude velvet art and the glow of cigarette machines…outdated film posters and small profane graffiti…*and then you take it like this…and then you suck her off like this…watch Nikki go down hard…if you're hot for fresh twat*…in the meantime, the video rolls: two guys take on one girl in one hole at once…with a tissue I change the channel, pausing at one girl on one girl…it is coarse, erratic and gratuitous…the video stops…I am assaulted by a shotgun blast of Technicolor ads:

DOUBLE YOUR PLEASURE
KINKY SLUTS, STICKY CUM
SOAPMYASS
SEX ITALIAN STYLE, MARIA
STROKE IT FOR YOUR MISTRESS
LACTATING HE-SHEs
HUMILIATION WITH BOOTSIE

Spent, impotent, inept, disturbed…I rise and leave the booth…to the street, the fog against my face…the urban perfume, the gusto of its dwellers…never more, never again, in the wake of such displays...my profoundest sympathies.

In my reverie I am left on the outskirts after dusk…making it through the promiscuity of our realization, on the horizon of our fruition and the zenith of expectation…the skyline of our demeanor, the seeking out of greatness…the car chase of fame…our abandonment to wayward concerns…the obedience to transgression…the trespasser of decay…our thankfulness for that which we do not possess…the omission of that which is ours…our donation to progress and the role in betterment.

Inelegant constellations shine through urban chemical mist. The air nauseous with blue hues melting to red clouds front lit by chemtrails. *In case of evacuation.* Awaiting intermittent downpours. The soft breeze to a demon's sneeze. Mutation in the ether. Swallowing the daylight. Oxygen voided and sunlight discounted. That which is cyclic takes place no longer. The birds have stopped chirping, leaving the vagabonds in charge. The remaining imprisonment for the most part. The jailer the jailed, the Samaritan the sinner. Hygiene obsolete. The banker the debtor. The cripples the athletes.

We welcome the ill-fated into the enfold of America.

Captivated by the boisterous night completed by solitude in a vast park of women full of life—as night falls…I am a luckless pioneer with malaria resurrected from my vanities…learned proverbial ineptitude…profound silence under mysterious air, I swim in the darkness of the enchanted lake and learn that what I do is not in vain…found within is the highest road to the holy shrine, a runaway from the helpless mountains and the cosmic compulsions fighting their way through the crowded lane to the closed door…simple words for a life-long obsession—she took my hand and led me to the chalet within the jungle clearing…the nuclear center…an outward gaze turned inward…once more, the sheets of the lake become motionless—waiting for the lotuses.

Operating under a scavenger's imperative, besieged by ecstasy in every direction, left to eat or be eaten, penetrate or be penetrated…all remaining mysteries have been sanitized, from her genitals to her whole person, she was architecturally muddled…possibly to attain selfhood one day…her, the sexual exile, searching the earth for that lucky despotic ruler who would control and manipulate her as best he could…the abyss of sexual lewdness…an orgasm for a thought…failure to conceptualize fully the mirage at hand…variations of sexual mania, and patronage of items, collectibles, devices and visuals…she asked me in to view her private collection.

The narrative of shopping lists…sexually bound, my reassessment of past images (blurry at times) is complex…it is improbable to recapture the full context of the moment, of the sensory and the discharged delivery…what we imagine and fantasize, and the resulting skewed and misled truth…there is no denying what exists out there, what pure rush of ferment and tingle may turn the forthcoming corner…but substance has set and further fancy is limited to the reels of the mind…innovation the only remaining tool…she can bend, she can kneel forward…her breasts can hang, unrestrained, full, heavy…an expanded ass, large, massive…the ever-fluctuating molds of lewdness…the yielding to will's wants, wanton or cautious, thrilling or discriminating…across the last night, we sleep in a field of wooden sculptures of naked women. Our backs against the same wall. In the midst of a fool's errand. Something in primitive floral. Tripping down the passageways of our significance, we watch the scene unfold. Pornography is insanity, the madness and disease. We must wake ourselves from the fascination of lust and take the necessary measures for correction. Among our pure thoughts and mild sense for deprivation, this cleansing will call upon all our wills. I am untrained toward the stainless and the immaculate. My method is to yield to carnal fascination.

The satisfaction before the need.
The quench before the thirst.
The feast before the appetite.
The attainment before the craving.
The release before the urge.

Nearing the drawbridge of our incarnations. Afloat in the water taxiways of our concession. We are all technological artifacts. The exit is the opening that we might find. *No means yes all the same.* This slow boat will reach the shore one day and I will wash my hands of all of this.

Under such stars we are born, prepared to drive real far, avid for these real dreams, tonight. The more intriguing, the more we like. And what is next to be said. In a car all alone. Under the waterfall of subliminal enrollment to find the way. The engine of our undoing. The mirror of the soul's widow. The stars will shine and rotate...we'll think of each other. The consequence of the outcome, the outgrowth of the sequence. At least we see. Et cetera. Et al.

So little done. So much yet to do. Are you going to miss me when I am not there?

A lot is happening right now.

Someday I will tell you about it.

From: caliph8@sharia4ever.org

We are the ones with the exclusive character of self-assertion. It is us with the mettle to seek ourselves within and to be the Awakened Ones. In the West we are imprisoned within a narrow cell and the more hostile the guards the bigger the fight we will bring. It is Allah who will grant the victory to the believers. The hypocrites and the deceivers will meet on Judgement Day. Whoever desires the conquest of the West will nourish the righteous guidance through Allah. The non-believers may colonize the hearts of the media and the weak men and women, but our methodical approach to the most spiritual of wars will be their ultimate loss and the final collapse. You see my friend, we are on the good and just side. Miss you boo! #inshallah

Guilty as charged—I saw the end and stopped time. Addicted to you, unable to waver, surf the dream, live through it holding hands, sense the spiritual. Remember the rendezvous, asleep, being watched, regarded in the same breath. Shaken, trembling, never feeling more alive, nor aloof and complacent to the realization that in the end there is no end, but an eternity, an infinity, a very long siesta. Hollow as an empty well, dwell on the denial of such repossessions. Walk to the flame and reach out for the burn to find the warmth and charge, the electric, the static. Go ahead, don't be afraid. It won't bite.

Put me on the do-not-call list, disconnect the phone because I don't answer it anyway, unplug me, abandon me, leave me here in the parking lot of my own depravity, give me peace or give me war, remove the parasites from my backside, the narcissist image of recreation and organic groceries, SUVs, big screen televisions, boastful nothings of a false life, an empty well in the throes of a spiritual drought, borrowed time, borrowed money, self-love, self-hatred, a skeleton in the mirror, a key that unlocks no door, a car alarm that won't stop when the battery is disconnected. It's a long way up…if you're gonna make it out.

The constellations around our hearts, the colonies of our attention and concentration, confuse me, break me, break in and burglarize the maze, spank me, hurt me, boost my ego, stroke my fantasies, cut me down…navigating the labyrinth of desire and fire and water and earth and wind…contaminated by your soft breath, the contours of the melodies of your voice and conviction, the innocent insertion into your warm folds, the ingratitude, the initiation of infection…what a system of errors, and comedy, and drama, and bio-pic, the rom-com, the thriller, cops and robbers, action, mystery, courtroom…made-for-tv…erase 10 years of age, the laugh lines, the laugh tracks, the bags and sacks, lose the memories, lose the moments, put down the gun, step back, on your knees, nylon against linoleum, does the carpet still match the drapes?

An obstacle to your obsession and nonchalant extravagance, improve your memory, attain atonement, ride the light shining through the crevasses of body limbs, a category 5, evacuate, landfall is soon, not guilty, Allah Akbar…do you have what it takes to beat these incredible odds? Are you with me for life? Will you stand in the doorways of the Pantheon and burn my skin with the stare of your gypsy eyes…abandon the repetition, search the dictator's quarters, lie down in the emperor's bed…sleep the deep sleep, after a long soak and a rub and tug, a pull on some Jesus juice—the essential manifestations of high resolution settings, fixated on our every move, the nuances, the objection, the watch that has stopped…now you know, now you care…your tourist visa license to live has been reinstated, most notable for your illegal ways, when you pick the orchids at the botanical gardens, when you feed the animals at the zoo and when you pass gas in the crowded train.

Well aware of the isolation and disdain for the bourgeois ways of neckerchiefs, of polo shirts and chinos, of caviar socialism, of caste system efforts, of the permanence of the anti-poverty, the hand-me-down country villa...the median price of a good time. Location, location, location…the next wave, the next fad, the next must-have…ripe for her definition, the reverse traverse cowgirl, in spite of the interior volumes, and the volume of the sounds that permeate and deviate from the norms and the flexibility…the soft lump, the round bump, the tight cotton wrapping around the circular brown skin, the icon on the horizon, the peak in profile, lionized and feared at the same time, in the same time zone, same continent, same language, same ways, strange ways, without you in my life, in my dreams, not along for the ride, but for the strife, for the aperitif before the main course, before the dessert in the desert, in the Atlas mountains, the Berber fires, the totalitarian state of mind, the elusive superpower, wind power, hydrogen power, life power, vitamin power, forget the fundamentals, be fun, go mental, stray into the disarray, order another side of some disorder…the anarchy of swimming atoms, wild with light, pulled back and forth by mercurial rises of non-importance…the refugees fleeing the homeland, the security, the exposure and insurance—a Diaspora of the mind, wandering and wondering what if only if?

Can your psyche and neurosis come out to play?

An end to this insidious half-life, or life light, a diet life…asleep in the unmade bed in my head and in your veins a virtual playground, a rundown mansion in bad need of repair, of renovation and/or restoration—new carpet and paint, curb appeal, sugar coated. A very special place to reside. *If you lived here you would be home by now.* The department store mannequin provocation, the detachable limb, a gangrene-free amputation, the fetish-free fetish, a lack of cleavage, conventional or butt…the currency of reconstruction, a repositioning of assets, evidence of progress, skin tape pulled tight, the pains of beauty, an endless segregation of two halves, one half reflected back in a mirror, for your own good, a split screen, dual tuner, dual disc, dual cup sizes, dual folds of lips lacking lipstick…*come on, get your lips on.*

The irresistible seductions of duty free and the boundaries of nudity. Stop making sense of the delirium and incoherence brought on by too much war paint, by sticky ice cubes, glycerin skin, stampeding bulls, fund raising, awkward moments (aren't they all?), silicone valleys and Botox, black boxes, enlargements and reductions, pectoral implants, hair plugs, liposuction, no more authenticity, only trickery of mirrors and smoke. If you love me you will take the pain for me. When god sees your eyes and the cosmic cosmetic action, body love, body glow, memory, RAM, society and all the black associated with a white room. Connect the dots and you will find the most peaceful insults, an enabling for the masses, registering the squeezing of the member, the fattening of the girth, the light strokes, the rush of blood and mixed signals, the surfacing of fundamental intentions, of evolutionary senselessness, well-traveled drugs and drugged to the breaking point of depletion. The audacity to not look, to not stare at the car crash which envelopes you, the van melting in flames, on the freeway shoulder, igniting dry brush. Drop the act, drop the addiction, drop the tits you support hopelessly with a bra that no longer fits, a bra that hurts, the metal pushing throughout, leaving red lines and indentations for the sake of beauty and support. Disembark from this gene therapy, abandon the construction site, cancel the upgrade, shutdown during installation, for it does not matter in the end. A gull force breeze of hurricane proportions from the tornado of your false hopes and forewarnings...unwarranted dismay for what you think you are and what you will never become.

Close your eyes and imagine a tropical island, the breeze is warm, the air is scented with indigenous effects like fruit and flowers, you are barefoot, the soles of your feet are massaged by each and every warm grain of sand, your toes tingle from the primal retreat of being barefoot, your body clock slows to the rhythmical percussion of softly crashing small waves, of water which has eternally been at sea, hitting land for the first and last time, you are not alone, you are searching, you have lost direction, you breathe deep, deeper yet still, hold it in for a moment, count to four, exhale for eight, you have lost control of all you have believed in.

The worst case scenario is not the only scenario. Of infectious diseases it meets all the expectations and vibrations. The shantytowns, the body cavity searches, the slashing of your car's tires, nightmares of Ebola and spelunking…*relax brotha.* Your fingerprints are gone. There is no trace back to you. The moment you feared. You have taken a bite off, now chew. You wanted the bike now ride it. Stand tall and thrive in your resolve.

From: caliph8@sharia4ever.org

Qu'ran (4.170): O Mankind! Surely, the Messenger (Muhammad) has come to you in truth from your Lord: Believe in Him: It is best for you (to believe in him). But if you reject Faith, to Allah belongs all things in the heavens and on earth: And Allah is forever All Knowing, All Wise. Stand out firmly for justice, as witness to Allah even against yourselves, and your own beliefs. Allah protects you much better. So follow not your desires (of your heart), and do not decline to do justice. Allah is Well Acquainted with all you do. #inshallah

The sheen upon your butt cleavage leaves little to the fixation and the transgression of your transmission. My days are often dark but my mind is bright. Why did we have to part? We will see each other again in the fields where freedom lies. We will be delivered from the wilted leaves of life's autumn afternoon, the twilight, the void time between day and night. Dance with me. The dark thoughts are unwelcome. *Bienvenido* to the sweet dreams of pleasant thoughts, of warm ideas, of completion and finality. The house no longer standing. We start the sinning, full knowing that this is it.

Photos of successful terrorist nightclub bombings on far away Asian islands, the token Australian national killed.

The coupons that come in the snail mail.

The truth in love.

The absolution in virginity. The truth in your eyes. The truth in the heat of the sun on your face. The truth in your weak knees. Every bourgeois has a run-down apartment inside them. The truth in incoherent enlightenment. The truth in bikini waxes and over-plucked eyebrows, the tween who has over tweezed. The truth in natural disasters, tsunamis, hurricanes and earthquakes. The truth in videotaped police beatings. The truth in arrogant indifference. The truth in limousine liberalism. The truth in what your ancestors could not destroy, but for what we can and will. The truth in an overgrown abandoned garden, the entropy, the ruin by design. The truth in wiped out past civilizations, their pyramid remains, their rituals no longer observed. The truth in a soft landing. The truth in multi-tasking. The truth in downsizing and synergy and outsourcing and being a player for the team. The truth in leakage. The truth in your lady friend. The truth in thinking outside the box, in leverage, in paradigm shifts. Your call is important to us…irregardless of your 365/12/24/7 preexisting random thought circuitry, a circus of un-caged wild animals fueled by the chemical imbalance in your brain. Per our discussion, furthermore, at this point in time, at this juncture, in actuality, it really is a non-issue.

I would like a venti, extra hot triple cappuccino half caffeinated soy latte with an extra shot of decaf espresso, no foam, with a double sleeve please.

The truth in compassionate conservatism. The truth in ballroom dancing. The truth in your boredom. The truth in business banking and online access. The truth in guesstimates. Do not even go there. I am sorry but I think of you as a friend. We haven't touched base in a while. Tag, you're it. This is the last time I will get your voicemail. Another whimsical binge on anti-inflammatory over-the-counter 400mg dosage tabs cocktailed with adult vitamins. Try to wrap it all into meaning, try to wrap your mind around this pre-packaged bulk item, available only at Costco.com. The truth in time in rotation. It's simple really. It is not you, it's me. Time is incoherent. Time is superhuman. Time is a super hero. Time is concurrent with other scattered realities. It bends like you want it. Mold it, fold it, rotate it. Surround it. Give it 5 stars on yelp. The truth in medicine as myth. The truth in myth as medicine. The truth in facial recognition. You do look familiar now. The truth in your own reflection. The truth in deflection, the reverse magnet, a force field around you. Cancel my subscriptions. Throw out my prescriptions. The quiet hum of indifference, come back into my arms. Contribute yourself for the sake of party atmosphere and recreational drug use. Your life scored with electronica pop music in the background...upbeat, colorful, aurally stimulating, much unlike your personality, against reality, contrived and manipulated, as real as reality TV, authenticated with commercial breaks and shaky cinematography.

The sexually transmitted disease that has lain dormant for the last dozen years incubating before deciding now is a good time to surface, to flare up, a bloody rash, a messy Dijon sheen, this does not look good. The girl with the extra thick calves who against her doctor's orders only wears high heels, the kind with long leather shoe string-type straps which she wraps around and around and up to her knees, drawing even more attention to her cankles, determined to dominate, focused on letting you know just how proud she is of her lower guns, at least she shaves on the nightly, in the bath, with a double or triple razor, an expensive razor, the blades disposable but not the handle, a product she got turned onto when she was mailed a free sample handle with one trial blade, with the coupon too tempting she never turned back.

But I digress.

Did I move inside your mouth? Did you come into contact with every follicle? Was that a whimper I heard? I watched it all closely from the side of the room. I took it in—with difficulty, with indifference, with a hint of decadence, acting like it wasn't really happening, with close-up zoom abandon, uneasy with the thought, nervous with the imagery, frightened by the ability. Spyware, terrorism, Netflix. Do not fret. Stop drifting off in vacant thought. If you think I am stalking you take a good look in the mirror my friend. Conspiracies abound. I don't want to know your name. This conversation never happened. Your influence can be life threatening at times. Will you come over tonight? The luxury around, the opulence abound, the surround sound of soft hues and faux leathers and velvet. 100 years ago, no radio transmissions, no satellite signals, no cellular towers, no sport utility vehicles, no e-mail, no http://, no J, no exfoliating rub, no vanilla flavor candles, no aromatherapy, no feng-shui, no Brazilian wax jobs, no mp3 players, no TIVO, no hardcore porn, no Hollywood, no Las Vegas, no Amazon, no jet travel. We, the lucky ones in this world of light and conduction. Now with no blues to sing. No cracking leather palms. No dirty underpants. No bad hygiene. No campground stories. No government handouts.

From: caliph8@sharia4ever.org

I believe that when I die my physical body may be shattered but my ego will transcend and survive into that wonderful abode. Yes I am young and yes I love life. I know I sound like a cranky old man sometimes LMFAO. My annihilation will be delivered with trembling hands of terror. I will be happy because I will be enforcing my will. I will have climbed the scaffold and lept off without a net. The windows will be wide open and with the fresh air will come the vigor, and the views will be splendid! You will see my friend! #inshallah

Let us not forget the violence. The gang rapes, the drunken assaults, the speeding car races—when all the love is gone there is nothing left of the great blue dream, why not just end it all and start anew. The domestic violence, the international violence, state sponsored terrorism, home grown terrorism, sexual torture, non-sexual torture, electrocution, drowning, sleep deprivation, amputation. Intimidation, car bombings, paradise. On a scale of 1 to 10 please rate the pain. This horror sophistication has been lost on earlier generations. When will it all be over? The crusades, the revolutions, the fatwa, the orders handed down, the deception and our own decapitation. More and more dependent on the chemicals to counter balance the imbalances, to deliver us to that final waterfront property destination, another day crossed off the calendar, another day closer to the end, so vast and inexhaustible, free of history and safety, free of language and solitude, free of the bourgeoisie and non-sophistication, free of the caviar socialists, free of the talking heads, free of the hypocrites that roam and rule, only playgrounds and soft light.

Wait.

Get in.

Don't say anything.

Not a word.

No gunpoint pressure.

Free to leave at any time.

No traces of your DNA.

The clean abduction.

You begin to feel bad, to feel sorry and pity for your loser self when you realize that the mountain you thought you stood on is so insignificant, the size of a grain of sand…nothing, like your own nothingness. You are sad and abused. Tainted and confused. Bruised. Defeated, but liberated in your own thoughts, and mind games, at home in the struggles of everyday life. Take pleasure in doing a load of laundry or washing the dishes by hand. The broken down machine. The hurt device. The one place of no entry, where no one is permitted, where the fantasy resides, where I am spiritual, where I answer to nobody but my God and angels. They love me, they really do. I find strength in them. All part of the ongoing struggle, the machination of humiliation.

So long—I slip into my liquid soul, sold to the higher bidder. There is no safety net. Your regret is so unfocused. Your gardens so unmanicured. Your pubic hair so overgrown. Your disease with no cure. Your dysfunction as function. There is no hope or consolation for your position. All pleasure is the same just gauged by its proximity to pain. Take me to the far spectrums, the outer rings of this pendulum, give me the choice or give me nothing. Save my soul from fear. My future disappears into an evaporating white light, an atomic explosion of sudden enlightenment, of a sudden escape, the freed and his freedom. Magical thoughts, a city by the sea, soft skin, a perpetual tan, regular bowel movements, a simple diet of water and fruit, a wardrobe of athleisure, an unlocked front door, unkempt hair, temporary health. A tide and flow rhythm, alert and awake.

The long drawn out daylight to midnight moments.

The passion to loneliness, the fluttering to falling.

The comfort my soul knows from hindsight.

My heart's failing insight to fill these voided chambers and blow wind into the face of this old skin.

From: caliph8@sharia4ever.org

And remember the Favor of Allah on you, and His Promise, which He confirmed with you, when you said: "We hear and we obey." And fear Allah, because Allah is All Knowing of the secrets of your hearts. You see my friend, we are fundamentally and inalienably spiritual whereas your American counterparts are purely materialistic, and that means our spirituality possesses all skills and we will be well, and in the end we will win. Are you ready for all the winning that is about to take place? #inshallah

In houses and apartments and commercial buildings all around town right now there are people on their deathbeds, there are people fucking, there are kids sucking each other off, there are people sad to be alive, there is absolute loneliness, there is devastation on large scales, there are the people left behind, there is mass hopelessness, there is emotional and sexual confusion, there is despair and anguish, bulk melancholy, prescription drug induced euphoria, medicinal marijuana highs, crystal methamphetamine binging, people drunk, stoned, blasé to the pain, a collective numbing, teenagers choking themselves with belts and their daddy's ties, hanging from a door knob, taking it to the edge of consciousness before they free themselves, they will be found with their clothes on, ruling out sexual fetish, there is assisted suicide, overdoses of morphine; there is ghetto abortion, there is white trash abortion, there is late term abortion, there is self-cutting, there is purging, bulimia, anorexia, *thin is in*, there is Down Syndrome sex, uncontrollable urges, there is amateur porn being made, there is bum sex, there is pimping, and there are girls who do unspeakable things to men they are repulsed by, over and over again, destroying their privates in the process, often damaging it down there beyond any repair, ravages against time, aided entropy, they will contract disease which may or may not lay dormant, diseases that are theirs for eternity, diseases they cannot pass on, there are girls getting their periods for the first time, some are delighted, some are scared to death, there are young boys who notice for the first time some hair down there, there is molestation, from a family member or a stranger, there is a future victim meeting her friend for the first time in a chat room, there is another abduction, there is another head on collision, there is another house fire, there is another abandoned baby, there is another conviction, another one let free, another miscarriage, another rape, anal penetration for the first and last time, another lie, another smile, another lone tear, another forgotten moment in a hastened day, the hours and images blurring into a warped non-reality of what you think it is about and realizing that your life is quite dull.

Slide into preciously jeweled territories, of silence except for the heart beats, the knowing that you won't ever lose what you have, that this will not end, that this is eternal, eternally...no hunting and no killing, no disease, no hunger, no loneliness, no hopelessness, no happenstance, no blues, only innocent and incoherent tributes to introduction and initiation. A place where you cannot stop until every drop is drained. Of having very little. Of already having what you want. Of needing only love, and love abounds. Entranced in sucking motion, your eyes locked with mine, no empty space between us, the **lust** underlined and in bold. You know what comes next in this dream world. There is no surprise, only expectation. It is always easier where you are from. You are so wild. You and your companions. Your satisfaction won't last for long. You are so well trimmed. I know it is not natural but *oh how it seems right.* Your sprawled fragments of bad judgment and stardust gentle kindness, abused and confused. You see the loaded gun on the table? If it was there right now I might use it on myself. Maybe on you first. I always imagine an overdose of pills. Downed with a lot of water, maybe some alcohol thrown in, for that final taste on my lips. But not a gun. It is not the pain, but the mess. I know it would no longer matter to me, but still it would be hard for those left behind and it would be a real mess for whoever had to clean it up. Whereas pills would cause a slowly sliding lapse of consciousness, an unhurried fall into eternal sleep, an uninterrupted sinking, the dreamscape tunnel of final thoughts, final sorting, final eroticism, final blinks, final pain and discomfort, final worries, financial and otherwise, final breaths, final beats of a weakening heart, failing organs, the sound of church pipes and angels, a polluted blood system, a deadened nervous system, the quick deathbed. Then the shine, so high, the increasing volume of the love sounds, the floating feeling of no more pain, the memories erased, welcome to a time without end. You belong, you are wanted, you are not judged, you will fit in nicely. It is because of this you should not worry. Death is nearest to us in the midst of life, in the moments when we feel most alive we need to remember that death is always near, always very close by, and waiting, arms wide open, always just on the other side. They can see us but we cannot see them. If we could and if we knew how it is we would all be dead.

We are meeting today to customize your surgical plan and aesthetic goals. Just like your lifestyle, no two surgeries are alike. We have a keen eye, the eye of the artist, if you will, with a deep appreciation of facial aesthetic harmony. The hallmark of our practice is creating a natural appearance, avoiding an "operated on" look of pulled skin and exaggerated features.
Step one is successive radiographs of the mandible and wrist bones to make sure that all facial bone growth has stopped.
Eye socket recontouring is suggested.
Brow bossing, including the suborbital rims, for less indentation at the temples and some hollowing at the frontal sinus.
Female eye sockets tend to be smaller, located higher on the face. This is called the intercanthal distance. We can make the eye "box" smaller through coronal incision into the lateral orbital rim.
When the female mouth is open and relaxed the upper incisors are exposed by a few millimeters. This is why we will remove the small of skin just below the base of your nose. This will lift your top lip. Your lips will look fuller.
The sliding genioplasty will leave the jaw reshaped through reduction surgery, done through the mouth, removing some of the chewing muscles to make the jaw

appear narrower. The dramatic correction will be most notable in the silhouette of your face.
Blepharoplasty will correct the eye bags and sagging eyelids, restoring the aesthetics of your eye region.
Hydroxyapatite bone cement can smooth out any visible missteps.
Freeing the SMAS (superficial muscular aponeurotic system) layer that lies below the skin and fat will improve overall appearance.
If none of this works then we will proceed with a full blown cranioplasty, where the glabella bone is taken apart, thinned and re-shaped. It is then reassembled in the newer feminine position with small titanium wires and an orthopedic plate and screws.

The very conception of the concept of ambivalence. The side effects of Ambien and over-the-counter sleep aids. In an earlier time you would have been hanged for this behavior. Now they always know where you are, and what you do, sometimes where you will go and your brain-dead intentions. The slow urination. The corporate death structure. The slight gasp when you come. The shock and the taste. The religious oppression. Pay attention please. There are others, other than the intruders. Other than the ones afraid to pull the trigger. I am talking about the gangsters, the real motherfuckers, the dogs of battle, armed, dodgy, ready to roll. There is a quivering motion behind the gentle curve of her spine. Here's a bag with all your belongings. I waited for you there never sinking under while floating in and out of perception. Things begin to come under wraps, the test results in, the revelations that from here on out it will not be the same. The indeterminate flow of information and sounds and feedback and bad thoughts and energy and synergy you never asked for. Blind me. Take away my hearing. I want immunity. I am a refugee seeking asylum from my identity, my name, my face, my world, my view, my reputation, my status, my bank account. My experiences are not unique. Take me into custody. I am a bad, bad man. I didn't know it but she was there the whole time. And the definition had its own circular logic, its own uncommon sense. What do you think those muscles are going to do for you? There is absolution behind the violence. But there is no justification for your abuse. Your lips burn like a setting horizon sun into the expanse of a blue sea. Indeed this is contagious. Sorry you didn't know that the documents were fakes. I'll be sure to clue you into the secret next time we circumnavigate naked the passage of humanity. The truth, the desire incarnate, the paranoia, the suspicion, the terror, the proof, the guarantees, the handicap accessibility. You will know when you get there. You will not need to ask. You will see it with closed eyes. You will feel it. The solace and relief. The ADA compliance. The flowers after the flood.

These hallucinations are not life-threatening. I know you wished they were. Your enthusiasm is infectious. Trim your wings. Shorten the leash. Nobody is listening—your audience has gone home. Reign in your dreams. To dream is to fail. Stop talking for a moment and listen. Close your legs. Look me in the eye. Shut your mouth. A little less vulgarity before you are called home. I would come around more but this is too undeserved. It is not you I love, it is your silhouette. It is the pretense of my counterfeit thoughts of who you are and what you mean to me. I focus on the thrill and the familiar touch and laughter, no memories of the bad, the dread, the unhappiness and discomfort. The yelling, the rage, the let downs, the fear, the loss of hope, of love, of care. You are on the pedestal, full of broken judgment, stained, ruined, damaged, someone else. I am the same. Insane and inane. You will not let me down. You cannot hurt me for I feel no pain. I do not hurt, I do not injure so easily anymore. I see it all differently. I have paid for what I have done. Now I am just trying to get back.

I imagine that your insides are as clean and sleek and as attractive as your outside shell. The curves, the soft skin, your hair, your coloring, your texture, the smells, the sounds. Your healthy gym look. If one could just open you for an examination, what would they find? The sheen of the adrenal glands, a thriving appendix, a well-shaped bladder, a chemically-balanced brain, a functioning duodenum, a pink gallbladder, a pear-shaped heart, tightly arranged intestines, a running kidney and liver, unsoiled lungs, ripe ovaries, a thriving pancreas, an unaffected parathyroid gland, an untouched pituitary gland, a shining spleen, a small stomach, a shrunken thymus gland, an unflawed thyroid, a waiting womb. The perfection of your insides, efficient, hygienic, exquisite and scenic. The labia, the left majorum, the right majorum, the left minorum, the right minorum, all modest. The cervix, clitoral hood, Bartholin's gland, G-spot, hymen, urethra, uterus, vulva, Fallopian tubes, the Gartner's duct, rete ovarii, Skene's gland, bladder and epoophoron. The anus, the anal canal, free of trimming, no recent waxing, no pre-anal cancer, abscesses, warts, fistula, bleaching, fissures, itching, hemorrhoids, birth defects like stenosis and imperforation, anal stretching, residual sodomy proof, flatulence tears, cloaca, pinworms, sex toy damage, extreme piercing, ancient medieval mutilations; the shared wall between rectum and vagina, OB-GYN exam tools put to the test, foreign objects, domestic objects, fruit, real and plastic, leftover home improvement materials, fingering, fisting, double fisting, up to the elbow, gloved, no glove, the ease with lubrication, KY jelly, saliva, body lotion, butter, menstrual blood, bareback, girlfriend experience, nothing, au natural, dry, very dry, peristaltic waves, toilet paper and bidets. Just an observation. A side thought.

Another watchful scrutiny, the female breast in profile. The hanging then the curve, upward, away, culminating in the dark tip, the small mound on the larger hillside. The important parts, the mammary glands, the axillary tail, the lobules, Cooper's ligaments, the areola, the nipple, the T4 dermatome, the pectoralis major muscle, the 2nd to the 6th rib anteriorly, the superior lateral quadrant, the mammary tissue, the clavicle, the arterial blood supply, the thoracoacrominal artery, posterior intercostals arteries, the venous drainage, innervated, puberty development, hormones, estrogen, lymphatic drainage, milk production and lactation, basic everyday functions; no female mammal other than human has breast of comparable size when not lactating suggesting that the external form is connected to factors other than lactation, dimorphic, or in plain talk, secondary sex characteristics, the frontal counterpart to that of the buttock, allowing for frontal copulation not just from behind, an increase in size brought on by premenstrual water retention, swelling from side effects of taking the pill, the misconception that there is a correlation between breast size and the ability to breastfeed, boob jobs, nipple reconstruction, breast reductions, mastectomies, virginal breast hypertrophy, excessive breast growth during puberty, hypoplasi, when one breast fails to develop properly. Tits, cans, rack, hooters, knockers, headlights, funbags, milk duds, milk wagons, melons, cantaloupes, coconuts, grapefruits, globes, fun cushions, jugs, bazookas, bazoomies, berthas, big berthas, blouse bunnies, twin mounds, top buttocks, the twins, woofers boulders, buffers, chubbies, coconuts, double lotus peaks, droppers, knockers, puppies, ski slopes, ta-tas, thirty-eights. On the smaller side, bee bites, chi-chis, dumplings, knobs, muffins, tweeters. Think Ishtar with multiple breasts.

From: caliph8@sharia4ever.org
The Great Book (5.105): O you who believe! Guard your own souls: If you follow righteous guidance, no pain nor sorrow can come to you from those who have lost their way. The return for all of you is Allah: It is He who will show you the truth of all that you do. Miss you fam. Send more selfies plz! #inshallah

There is blood on the dashboard. There is a lone brunette pubic hair on the steering column. We will soon be there. What is your question for me? If I wanted to hide, you wouldn't know it. I would be emotionless, empty of thoughts, nerveless. I am an artist, I am her lover, I am a criminal, I am a groom, I am her prince, I am a skeleton. The pain is inexplicable. All her kisses permanently burned images in my mind. One by one. An endless loop projected in the theater of my thoughts. Does your seat need readjusting? We can stop at the next station if you would like something to eat or drink. I understand. You have the most delicate eyes. Again, I am sorry I had to remove that bracelet but I will give it back later. It's okay to look away, I realize you weren't expecting any of this today. You are more courageous if you don't try to flee. I won't harm you. Your shoulders are so tense. Try to take in a deep breath, hold to three then exhale. It works for me when I get a little nervous. But, really, there is nothing for you to be nervous about. That blood? That is mine from when I cut myself yesterday opening a can of tuna. Here, look at my hand. I took off the band-aid after the blood had dried but I guess it cracked and may have dripped a little. Have you been working at the mall for long? I had never seen you at the gym before last week? Where did you work out before there? And don't tell me you didn't—you are way too toned. Sculpted by the gods really. Let me guess, seven percent body fat. *Amirite?* See, I know my female bodies. I thought of being a personal trainer once. I hear they make a lot of lady friends, if you know what I mean. Don't tremble. I said I wouldn't hurt you. Do you have a boyfriend? A roommate? Someone who may notice you didn't make it home to that cute condo. It seemed like you lived alone, but I have only a week's worth of surveillance. Did your parents buy you that place? The complex is too new to allow anything other than homeownership. The "waiting for tow" sign on your dash should buy 24 hours with mall security. Usually I have longer surveillance to work off of. It helps to view it all with a wider scope, to work out the minor glitches of everyday life, the fluky breaks to one's daily routine. I am sure you don't care about these things. I am sorry if I am boring you. Nonetheless, you will be home soon if you are a good girl and behave yourself. Please don't judge me until you get a chance to know me. The rose bud will never bloom if you don't let in a little sun. I know all of this is awkward but if you just let this happen you will get to know me and you will like what you get to know. That is what I liked about you at that shop. You are always so nice to strangers, you treat everybody the same charming way, that divine smile. It is a very special quality you possess. We are all just regular people inside. Wanting, needing, craving love and affection, hungry for the same things. Be careful with that smile. It could get you in trouble one day. Someone is going to get their heart broken and it's not going to be me if I can help it. Wow, you really are a looker. I only do this because I think it will be fun. Tell me if you don't like it, it won't hurt my feelings. I can handle rejection, at least in small doses. My ex would tell you the contrary but you shouldn't believe a word she says. There is a reason we are no longer together. But let's not talk about her. I always hate it when people are out together and one of them insists on talking about their past relationships. About the time their ex made them so mad, the time their ex was such a gentleman and did this or that, bought flowers and a card, or when they lived together and went on that trip to Mexico, or how he used to be abusive, mostly verbal abuse but sometimes physical. I am not like that. I don't need to know about who you were with, what he looked like, how he was so nice to his mother, how he was in bed. I don't want you to think that I don't care, because I do, I just don't want you to talk about those things until you are ready, okay? Well, with that said and that cleared up, what about you? What are you, like twenty three, twenty four, max? Do you have brothers, sisters? An only child? You deserve to be the only one. Your daddy must have been so proud, so jealous when you got older. I bet your mom is a knockout. If you get your looks from her then I cannot wait to meet her. She is probably one of those moms that looks like the older sister, aging slowly and gracefully. *Amirite?* You know, I thought that you had on lipstick but now that I have been looking at you so long it seems like you aren't wearing any and I find it amazing that your natural lip color is so rich, so flush, so brilliant. Are you wearing eyeliner? Tell me yes because I cannot fathom such natural beauty. Don't you just hate the pressure that all the fashion mags put on you girls these days. It's like, hey, sorry, but it's not normal to be so skinny, and besides, the only way to be so skinny is to smoke and guess what, I don't like smoking. I find it really refreshing that you don't buy into that. All that loose clothing, the huge hoop earrings, exposed thong whaletail, open bisexuality. Tell me what I'm missing. Don't tell me you have been with a woman. I mean, it's okay if you have, actually I like the thought just so long as you are discreet and that you are doing it because you really do like it and it turns you on, not just because it is the thing to do, the latest fad, a way to turn on your boyfriend, a favor to your girlfriend in order to surprise her man. Tell me you really like it and I can't oppose. I mean, yes, I do find that thing to be very exciting. Who wouldn't. The thought of two women together, sharing their desire, touching each other like only they know how. Stroking in the right places, pressing just so hard, caressing ever so lightly. In and out with light fondling. And those lashes? You know what they say about long lashes. Do you have any tattoos or prominent scars? Any recent piercings? Is your dentist local? Do you always answer your cell phone? Is it not unlike you to return calls until the next day?

When calling 911 your number and address may be displayed on a viewing screen regardless of whether or not you have an unlisted number or Caller ID Blocking. This enables the emergency agency to locate you if the call is *interrupted. If you do not wish to have the telephone number and address from which you are calling displayed, call the appropriate 7-digit emergency number. However, be aware that if you do, your number may be revealed to the emergency agency. To avoid this, you need to have Caller ID "Complete Blocking" or press *67 to block transmission of your number.*

The tiny start embedded in your soul's eye, the sacrifice, the pleasure, the love. I knew you weren't finished. How silly of me. You never cease to amaze me. No, I don't think I need a menu. I will be having the usual. I will wait for the fall and collapse when the taste changes for the worse, something fishy, saltier, a little charred. I told you I cannot be objective. Daybreak will bring a different dance and with the morning swim a new chance at sparkle and form. I don't want you to feel you need to be the preponderance of the evidence. A verdict beyond reasonable doubt. You have to be, for the sake of clarity, something more joyous. You have to be, for the unity of experience, something absolute.

Let's go find a rainbow.

Be content with less.

Permanent measures can be taken. You may have been brainwashed by the ghost nurses. An outbreak of maladies of the mind. You are a time bomb waiting to be detonated. Nobody able or willing to dismantle you, break down your DNA and start from scratch. The epidemiology of fear and aversion to disaster. The safety in perception, the fascism in liberation. The security in knowledge. Be sure to stay tuned as we bring you the latest on this developing story. The vagina as metaphor. The slow walk through a desert wasteland. The thousand-year wait.

You blew my mind. The failure of science. The facelessness of your dreams. Underfed, underweight, underfoot. The detoxification when I hear your voice. The sobriety when I see you smile. I get drunk again from your femme juice. The dampness when I cross the threshold. The sanctuary between your legs, the sun, the stars, the moon. Spinning, taking on speed, this ship is no longer on autopilot, take your seat please and fasten your seatbelts. Do you remember the solitude? The slow motion one-man dance? Are you all grown up under that gown? Is there really an adequate substitute? Have we been in love this whole time? There is space for it all within the outline and shadows and resistance. The delirium before the dementia sets in. The research before the debilitating pain. A man has to make a living. The parallel spinning within this curved space and your private oasis of limitations and lost dossiers. The crusade beliefs of self-revolution and sexual preservation, the dichotomy of woman and girl, the forbidden and the allowed. The unripe fruit and the fallen crop. The underdeveloped and the overbuilt. The unsullied, the spoiled and soiled. The moist and the dry, the firm and the drooping.

The special language of escape. Wrist cutting, overdose, poisoning, choking, jumping, the single pistol shot. The momentum in self-propelling. The copycat, the tragic hero. The sadness arriving with autumn. You know I need you. Act as if this isn't happening. This is the last time. How spectacular it would be. Your staggering iconic beauty. I want such looks to be among the last things that I see. Your drama enriched in its own folklore, a legendary magnificence, a celebrated work of timeless art. Remove me from the flock, be my shepherd and lead me into your enigma of infamy and discretion. I do not want to end in the arms of the collective void. I want to re-circulate through the portals of my faith and my design. I don't want to be discovered. I don't want them to find my body. I want it to seem as if I vanished, traceless. Leaving them to their imaginations and false hopes that one day later I might just walk right through that door.

From: caliph8@sharia4ever.org

You see my friend, He has the power to send serious harm to you from above you or from under your feet, or to cover you with confusion or conflict. Or give you a taste of the mutual evil so that you suffer a bit and you may better understand. My friend, I know my e-mails of late have been downers and grouchy. Sorry boo, I hope you are still reading them. It is just that I need to convey to you the message of our movement. Why is it that we are so angry and how are we going to make things better. Hope you are well, hit reply some time! #inshallah

The metastasizing desire. The spreading flames of longing and distraction. An exercise in self-restraint. An implement in the battle for love and fondness. An impediment on the road to explanation and illumination. The rage in the form of teargas canisters. The ire in the backlit fire. The indignation in the mood-setting smoke-filled streets. *We live in a beautiful world.* The radiance in vandalism. No plan B, no net below the trick flip. To exist along the violent fringe. A throwback political chic concept of rising up against the Man, the establishment, the institutions, the banks, the schools, the administration. Excuse me, the line starts back there. Your reputation was one of the first casualties. A united front behind the slogan. Resentment in the blight. The alienation, the rage, the fade of memories, the end of funding, the sense of abandonment, the heart of the conflict zone. Your heart, my heart. I will always be waiting for you. To come, to arrive, to misrepresent, to represent, to share, to be kind, to be nice, to offer help in dire times of need, to restore the cracked lining of my heart, to be tender, to not change. As the ghetto inside burns, the flames spreading from building to building, car to car, failed attempts at extinguishment, the inferno a bonfire of fear set loose, a manifestation of the angry ghosts, the demons realized and exercised. I am engulfed in your neglect. The festering resentment in who you are, what you have become, your behavior unbecoming, your flavored expansions, your profound self-importance, your working class savoir de vivre, your telling implications of reality versus non-reality. Did you really come or was it part of the act? The influx of your illiteracy, your immigrant demands, your native abandonment, your evacuation, your colonial occupation, your refusal to obey orders, the salvation in your commands, the low-income in your high-rise, the government aid in your rewards, the concentration camps in your warehouses, the fear in your dark skin, the limits and the difficulties, the inadequacies and truncated taboos in your once secular heart. Blend into better hues. Complete the integration. Dream of lesser frustration, a better fundamental operation. An invisible rebellion, irreversible and marginalized. Excluded, expelled, disbarred. The grey walls and the wasteland. Your hopelessness as sexual kerosene. Dismiss me. Frisk me. Free me. Blame me. Don't treat me the same.

A strategy for the underneath. Dehumanize me and launch the righteous uprising. You are indebted to the excuses, inebriated by the veil blocking the view of the other side, the room behind the curtain, the body below the cloak, the eyes behind the glass and the head below the crown.

You are all the same in the end.

Classified information.

The results not expected for another week.

The DNA matches maybe sooner.

Because you're worth it.

Night blindness. The end of an empire. The rise up and the burning trash cans. The lock on the bathroom door. The shite and the Shiite, the stumbling down from the high up you once were. The forever alteration after the downfall and the restructuring. The view of you sideways and the constant quiet hum. Your flame pinned beneath, your kitty lounging in the dark. When you fled you never returned the same. I see you watch yourself, a self-admiration, a self-love. We are wrapped into one another, hibernating for the duration, lost inside the space between...warm, moist, slippery, furry. I am found in your dissolution and the technological advancements of feminine hygiene products. The old school versus the new school. This call may be monitored. Take me off the grid. As the colonial subjects rise up to their empires, a full circle completion to sophistication versus barbarism, enlightenment versus backwardness, science versus witchcraft, white versus black...the children, the criminals, the blaze across the horizon. You may live here but you do not belong. The underneath, the underside, the under belly of the beast and her wants. The subject peoples, it is them that you see when you look in the mirror, the same insect stare, the stench, the taste. Blank looks for a better dreamscape. Rancor and bitterness, vent about your life, start a war, speak in obscenities, you are marginalized, isolated, trapped in your skin, shaken to your core, the mayhem has become you, gang warfare, the worn away plastic memories, the short final strokes, the product in your hair, the lost sheen, the days of dirtiness, the contrived chic in your filthy look. I watch you make love to me. The false insecurities and the charade desire. Lay your love out before me. The humidity doesn't lie. Your treasure parted, divided on its own terms. A brand new look. Glam yet retro.

The laugh lines around a certain other smile. A guide to the seduction. A better fitted brassiere. Comfort in the small things. The details adding up to profound differences, changes for the better, changes for the worse, differences in your fake age, in your real age, in your real name. The carbon dating does not lie. It's time for you to come out. You are surrounded. Don't let this opportunity go to waste. Bend over a little more, arch your lower backside, push it out proud, lift it up for display, let me have a look. Expand your hips. Slither and sway. Don't hide that womanliness. It is because of this that I am. You are magnetic there. A captivating washbasin, an enchanting entrance into darkened contentment and bliss, a gate into the unfamiliar. An alien entryway into the nameless, the faceless, the unidentified The foreign perfection, the uncut, the wrinkles, the rim, the unbeveled contours, the unleveled light and shadows. The future in the folds. How could we never take a chance? A promenade of wander and wonderment down an unlit alleyway of completion and cessation. All the things that you keep cherished. The treasure in your awe and bewilderment. How much longer now? I would like to stop, pause and still frame all of this as is, permanently, lastingly and bring to an end all time and movement.

From: caliph8@sharia4ever.org

Hello friend. Do you wonder why these messages from the Lord have come to you through a man of your own people via electronic mails? These messages are to warn you of the impending doom. To make you realize your chance at receiving His Mercy. You see, with Him are the keys of the Unseen, the treasures that no one knows but He. Not a single leaf falls without His knowledge. I am just a messenger bro. Do not hate the player, LOL. #inshallah

The next day, away from the commotion and mayhem of last night, you make plans to take things to the streets, at late night hours, in your car, anonymous, nameless, unknown, a search out and witch hunt for new experiences and new individuals. Unattended gas stations, the cashier behind bulletproof glass, a sliding drawer for transactions. You ask for the restroom key, it is passed to you attached to an infinity-shaped coat hanger. Behind the dumpster, away from the flood-lit parking lot, the door knob is wet, the key barely fits. You cannot find the light switch. A glaring glow emits through the transom window, illuminating the ceiling, the overflowing wattage enough to get started. You had hoped to bait someone to this location, but you have not been followed. It may be better that way, you think. A dry run, the initial experiment of such indecent behavior, the unbecoming forthcoming actions. Your hands have touched the coat hanger, the door knob, the walls, the sink. You proceed without washing them, you slide your hand down the front side of your pleated skirt, you part and rub, massaging circular motions, the loosening and warming, the dampening, the revelation, an expanding universe in your hand. Your eyes stay fixed on the door, awaiting an unsuspected visitor that will not come. You think about the Iranian cashier, you wonder if he owns the station or if the owner is his uncle, you think he must be wondering how long you will take, your car is still in front of the gas pump, you haven't purchased gas yet. You feel a rush knowing that the bacteria of the room is in direct contact with your crotch, it is being deep-seated into the folds, applied and lathered universally, generously, you know that you will have to wash later. You are extremely wet, it will not be much longer now, the door is unlocked, anybody could enter, a bum, a pervert, a child. You are bracing yourself against the sink now, bent forward, propping yourself against the stained porcelain, your free hand grabbing the empty soap dispenser. You find yourself locked in gape at the seat-less toilet, the dissolving mess inside...when snapping out of it you look up, you stare at yourself in the warped and scratched sheet metal mirror, the slight reflection of a distorted visage and contorting body, your pale blue leisure suit blocking the sightline of the door. You think you look like a john doing a whore from behind, you imagine: this is what it must look like, from the backside, up on top of it, hitting it, tapping that, her ass the sink, in control, living large and taking charge, overpowering, self-determining. You hear soft footsteps outside, perhaps it is the sound of blowing litter. You slow your hand. You listen in the silence. You pull your fingertips away from the throbbing and clamminess. You continue for a brief moment and come hard into your cupped hand. You wipe your hand onto your pubic area, into the small rug of trimmed hair, and onto the skin below your belly button. You think of leaving a message on the wall, maybe a time to meet at this location, but you don't have a pen and you realize the thought is foolish and perhaps more dangerous than you are ready for at this point, even entrapping should there be a sting. You recover and grab the keychain coat hanger, running your hand the entire length of the bent wire, over the key itself. For theatrics you flush the toilet, you are flush and scarlet in the face, it is night and chilly and poorly lit. You leave the restroom and return the key to the cashier through the drawer, he barely looks at you, you go to your car, license plate ZVU-678.

You left all four doors unlocked, a standing invitation. You see the backseat is empty. You remember an email you need to send in the morning, an online coupon code that soon expires, and that you still need gas, a box of tampons, and to feed the cats when you get back. Replete, exhausted and spent, you head for your apartment, a minor detour, a distraction on the map, on the way you will cruise the wide alleyway behind the shopping center, along the loading docks, an obstacle course of empty pallets, shopping carts and dumpsters, employees in the dark, smoke breaks, on cell phones, a couple in a car making out, makeshift homeless camp outs. The surveillance noted, you know who, when and where for future ventures.

You come across the ad about donating x amount in order to fund 20 meals at a local soup kitchen. You write down the name of the organization and their address. You will drive by there after work. It's in a bad part of town, all the good ones are. The vacant lots with overgrown weeds and abandoned mattresses, your mind drifts to daylight sex fantasies, with multiple lovers, a train of indigent and impoverished men who would prefer a quickie over a meal. You regain your focus and find the warehouse soup kitchen. The only entrance crowded by bums in filthy clothes with dirty hair, their worldly belongings bound to shopping carts with bungee cords, their dogs leashed with nylon rope. More men than women. As you park in the distance you begin to feel out of place, unwelcome. You decide to watch and then return at a later date, on a weekend or holiday, dressed more appropriately, more into character, method. Pass yourself off as down-and-out, make new friends, bring along a roll of twenties, money to buy them off with pints of booze, go back to their tent city. See if there is anyone to protect you, see if there is anyone that can complete the fantasy. Become someone's bitch, a prisoner of street-level jungle warfare, someone you could always get to a YMCA and get cleaned up, closer to a societally acceptable level, but never letting on your real self, your daytime self, your comforts of home, your bank accounts, your access to credit, your financed car, your two cats.

Be savage and primal, sullied and soiled.

You think of cruising high school parking lots but realize that they must be well monitored and that it's possibly illegal. Further rumination of coming onto teenage boys working in fast food, retarded guys cleaning the office, recently released prisoners, soon to be released prisoners, conjugal visits, swinger bars, lesbian rallies, porno shops, the guys all hot and bothered...blank stares at random strangers in parking lots, at older dads with young children playing at the park, frequent military hangouts, sports bars, used car dealerships, go on test drives, community colleges, home improvement stores, ob-gyns and male nurses, highly frequented rest stops, truck stops like the lot lizard you really are, calling repairmen, ordering pizza delivery.

From: caliph8@sharia4ever.org

*Hi fam! Been thinking about you lately. I wanted to write but got so busy with the movement. I am back with a message you can get behind. Do the infidels see nothing in the dominion of the heavens and the earth—all things that Allah has created? Do they not see that it may really be that their time's coming to an end? What message will they believe? You see, it is a FACT that you will not survive your own death. But if you die a martyr you will go to an especially wonderful paradise where you will enjoy seventy-two virgins. Spare a good thought for these virgins as they do not know what a beautiful man is coming for them! *LOL* The heretics, blasphemers and apostates should simply just be killed. There is no salvation awaiting them you see. Why prolong the inevitable? Talk soon, bye. #inshallah*

Nocturnal stillness. A self-probe. On fire your crotch burns with urine salting the small scrapes and breaking skin. Smoldering, the fluid settles into the small cleft cuts, paper cuts nearly invisible to the naked eye but nonetheless susceptible to the agonizing torture. There is no blood, flesh wound nor menstrual. You need a break, a time out, a pause to let the abrasions heal. A chance for the skin to get back, to fuse together, for the lips to soften and glisten once again—rejuvenated, anew, far from the pain, rested, more capable and replenished...all to commence again. A return to childhood body form, an innocence, pure and incorruptible. This may help you get over your own false porn stardom. Your fictitious thoughts that you are indestructible down there, immune to disease, durable to the abuse, resistant to the pain, impervious to the sting. You never should react the way you did. Maybe now is a good time for self-reflection and pause. Allow your body to retract and get back to a semblance of its former self, much like a woman after child birth, the tightening return of the skin, the closing of the curtain, drapes pulled tight, the velvet crumpled, crushed and soft. A bendable flexibility and pliability like moldable plastic or super hot liquid bronze, you make the shape, you spread the wings, they maintain their position momentarily, then a thought or desire, and they shift inward, folding onto themselves. An instinctual self-protecting mechanism. A wilted flower petal arching within. The door is closed, the shield raised, a rock over the cave door.

You, standing there, the intimate epic film shot angle, backlit and restrained, we embrace. We kiss, slightly at first, exploratory, then deeply, my tongue wide into your mouth, then your tongue overlapping mine. Your hands are in my hair, your fingers parting and tugging, holding my face tight against yours. I reach further down and from your backside I feel the wet spot between your legs. Your free hand slides down and holds tight my manhood. Squeezing, sliding slightly more and more over. You try to speak but nothing comes out, you have nothing to say. I reach up and with pinching finger tips tug on your nipples, using both hands, hard and throbbing, swollen, pulsating, red. I pull from your mouth and kneel down and begin to suckle them simultaneously, your breasts pushed together, pinched and pried, forming a fjord of pressured soft skin. They fill my mouth, their terrain rugged and harsh. You push forward but you know you are not ready for the penetration. Not tonight, maybe never. Your flesh against my flesh, full body length, the ultimate intimacies. You taste like perfume smells, your panting and heavy breaths leisure to my soul. You quiver and tremble and are enjoying this. I am weakened at the knees and push forward as if to lay you down on the mattress, but you won't move. We continue upright. A faster pace. A stronger hold. A hurried fervor. A tighter grip. Deeper tongue plunging. Oral spelunking. The lust and its release. The buildup and the detonation. Our bodies jigsaw puzzle pieces finding the other missing piece fitted by design. I run my hands down your outer hips, over the stretched skin against tight pelvic bone, the feminine shape and outline, the true essence of womanly intention and invention. My cupping hands a guiding force for which you yield, submitting now to my commands. I push you forward to the sofa. You lean back, seated now and open your legs as I part your unstable knees. Your glazed eyes are locked with mine. No question of control, only mutual acquiescence to the same aspiration and end. I find truth with my face pressed up against your perilous essence. I part your forest with my tongue. Then the forbidden doorway, pliable, relenting, surrendered. My hands glide self-guided to your nipples which I slightly pinch. The throbbing in the small capillaries and the blood rush. Your fake nails graze my scalp and I tingle. You taste like hard candy that takes a moment to hit the taste buds. The taste does not wane. A breaching dam of unregulated juice flowing a sinuous small river of appetite and demise. The flavor varying but a constant tang of dignity. You swell and spread out, the feast mounting, the buffet incessant, your abandonment indefatigable and pounding. You suffer so well. I pull away to breathe perfumed recovery, cold air on my damp face, I pan your jiggling inner thighs, soft, remarkably smooth, flawless, cellulite free. I run my wide tongue lengthwise from your cavern doors to your knees and slowly back. A break from your flavor, a respite from the taste, more robust with each homecoming. Look at what I have put you through. You are brittle and delicate, close to an end. There is wonder in your tenderness. You pull me in by the hair. I take you between my teeth, nibbling, suckling. Your hood and its shattered inhabitant pinched and held through to completion, you draw to a close slowly, a restrained brutality, a bloodshed within. Flowing at swift rates, your raw aches tell me to stop. With a wink in one eye, I continue through the thundering rhythm. You shine bright before me, in the dark, out of sight. My eyes closed and held shut by your pelvic floor. I hold my breath through the finale...not much longer now. Your whimpers turn to soft squeals, animal-like, feral and wild. Your final movements an orchestra of collisions and contusion, until a shuttered final revolt, then the calm, the lifelessness, sated and still.

"I used Fenugreek as part of my enlargement program and I increased a full cup size in about 6 weeks. No side effects. I even added wild yam to the progesterone cream. I was worried about breast acne but nothing happened. I did breast massages twice daily and drank Bustea like a maniac. No complaints from my bf, gurl!"
The ideal cocktail is a mixture of estrogen, progesterone, growth hormone, and IGF-1 (insulin-like growth factor). This will simulate puberty and by default the development of the breasts. If we do not plateau with hypogonadism

then the results will likely be just slightly smaller than one cup size of an adult cisgender female.

We will test you for Laron syndrome, a rare disease that keeps the brain's pituitary gland from producing growth hormones. If positive this will slow the process.

We will combine GH and transdermal estrogen to decrease IGF-1 levels and bypass the liver to induce activation of the androgen receptor (AR).

Your diet needs to change. Low protein intake and intermittent fasting. Consume whole milk. Avoid vitamin D as it inhibits breast growth via activation of the vitamin D receptor. Try creative visualization. Buy hypnosis CDs online or record your own guided visualization. In your recordings, encourage yourself to feel warmth pulsing through your breasts, to merge the pulsing with your heartbeat and to feel each heartbeat sending energy into your breasts. Practice this once a day. Look for results in 12 weeks.

Exercise will also increase GH levels.

All of these are downstream actions of increased activation of the preostaglandin receptors. Deep within the mammary gland tissues we will see results in the potent induction of the amphiregulin expression, a critical growth factor in women with complete androgen insensitivity syndrome (CAIS), capable of mediating significant breast development, with breast sizes in fact larger than those of non-CAIS women. Overexpression in mammary gland tissue produces hyperplasia that potentially results in a self-perpetuating cycle of growth amplification. This is the goal.

On rare occasions there is the perfect storm of excessive growth resulting in two cup sizes with a ski slope profile, which is very natural looking as well very hot right now.

Items to avoid: aspirin, ibuprofen, naproxen paracetamol, celecoxib.
Side effects: mild nausea, vomiting, bleeding, cramps, breast pain, loss of scalp hair, discharge, breakthrough bleeding.

Trailer park hotness. You wonder what the aliens think. Downed power lines. Bomb threats. Road rage. A white trash brush fire. Your titty nipple bleeding from an overly ambitious bite or failed piercing. My thoughts that spin in perfect 101010 circles of the same command, lost in a void of misdirection, beyond ctrl-alt-delete. The only option is to reboot. The fixated misgivings, the circuitry alit, afire the chemical tunnels and viaducts of my mind and nervous system. What am I supposed to be without your reflection. You love me but I can't stay. I stop functioning in certain departments. Everything that contributed to my depravity, to my drive, my daily ambitions, my kowtowing to the ways of my wants, my ability to deny myself, to block out bad thoughts, to hijack my own undoing and keep the ship bearing straight, to the horizon, toward further suffering and certain death, allowing only partial denial of the sureness to creep in enough to remain sane. Imagine a place without denial. We would all be mad. The endless cycle of origin and demise, the passion and refusal. An Eden in your eyes I attempt to escape, gone missing in your dreamland undertones of soft whispers, casual disregards, a feather tongue in the ear and saccharine promises of late night wanderings, in the dimness of the shadows of your backlit silhouette. Another universe, at a place like home, but still a false address, vacant and un-rented. The anti-rundown and self-restoration in the throes of restitution.

I have been here before but it was a long time ago. Next time I want to be on top. A money grab for dirty thoughts and mental film reels. Fast-forward to the good parts, slow-motion the best scenes. You set the location, the ideal locale of tropical inspirations, sounds, smells and temperature. A modern room furnished with contemporary beige and off-white furniture, floor to ceiling windows, palm foliage in each corner. A brown fur throw strewn about the extra-long sofa. She enters the room, dressed for success, smart in business suit attire. She leaves on her black sunglasses as she crosses the room. You don't know if she has noticed you. She sits at the edge of an ottoman. She undoes the buckle atop the high heel of her left foot, then her right foot, then kicks them off. While rising she undoes the black leather belt, then unzips the fly, her pants drop with the weight of the leather and buckle. Classic white cotton bikini panties. Nothing fancy, nothing vulgar. She turns away from me and bends forward to adjust the throw. Her hips widen, her package grows and swings into a better, more exposed position. She stands upright again and peels away her dress jacket to reveal a proud and bountiful chest, held tight and firm by a full form fitting brassiere. She pulls over her head the silk blouse that remains. You see the sheer girth of each tit, and the strength of her hard nipples, attempting to escape the confines of the polyester restraints. Her boobs bulging out from all sides. You get the picture. She is chic hot. Ready or not. I will stop there. Fading into the lies and false advertising. An atmosphere of skepticism. I want you held on unrelated charges.

From: caliph8@sharia4ever.org

Hi friend. Can you feel it yet? The tremor and the thrill in your heart when the Name of Allah is mentioned...when you see His signs are everywhere, when your faith is becoming stronger, when all of your trust is in the Lord. My friend, the GLORY! It is almost too much to witness sometimes. He is the Mighty and our Salvation. Shout out to our Big Guy! Hope all is well, reply some time "bro fam"! LOL #inshallah

I am closer to knowing less as more is revealed. A leak in her sublimation of jiggling tits, red fingernails, mass confusion, the drum beats that follow her wake. You, there, halfway across the room. Looking away from the gaze of my eye, and the revelation of my wants. Cowering, you crouch enough to act afraid, like a cornered animal, enough panic and trepidation that you think I will be concerned and stop. Enough to cause me to pause. I will not give in and buy your pathos act. The sunrise is coming up and the room is getting lighter. We see more. We see more of each other. I admire your tears and swollen eyes. Tell me now why the fear. Why the apprehension and change of heart. I am not hear to take more than what you need. Break the cycle of artwork imagery, backlit angles, puffed-up lips, enlarged and swollen genitalia. A new name, new wants and desires, new tastes and dislikes. A place where the colors better bleed into one another. I wish it were different. I continue to pray. There is still a diminutive hope. An emergency exit across the white room, no windows to kick out, nothing flammable to set ablaze, there is always at least one way out. My broken heart in check, the veil of grief wrapped around me like a blanket over my shoulders, pulled tight with my cold hands on a winter night.

Comforting and troubling. Passing semblances of relief amidst all the sorrow. Hopefulness in the chemical imbalances. I have collected my things. I am ready to leave. The stigmata will remain eternal. Another point of no return. Since I fled the first time I will never be the same.

The sad reality among the glad handler yes people and latter day saints. Perhaps we should take the stairs next time. Alive at the edge of *raison d'être*, the motivation becomes clearer, the wants similar, the desire levels the same, the debate close to its end. You turn, hurrying, confused. Your appearance shook. A spook of voodoo logic in the dark corners of incentive. The morning mist, a cold shoulder, a missive submissive miss, she is on the scene, bliss incarnate. As skilled as an assassin, her solvency a matter of temperament. Her judgment not based on income. Nobody knows what will happen. Aggressive and determined, she argues her point to abandon. She acts like the schoolgirl, or the playground thing, the naughty girl caught in a compromising position, lost, exploitable, ready for the blackmail. She thinks that by mouthing hard words she understands hard things. When she gets smitten, she stays smut. Good people come to wisdom through failure. Be everywhere, do everything, and never fail to astonish the customer. She doesn't mind a little praise.

There is no sweeter sound than the crumbling of her dirty mind. To know her thoughts…all the rest is just details. A reward for the new law breakers. My toughest fight was after my first three-way. Her undefined problem has an infinite number of solutions. Her determination is the willingness to kill and be killed for trivial reasons. While onto another whooping, sorry, that is Congolese for *love stroke.* With each chance you put forth you invite more disconnect and future foes. The circumference of this island called life. No beginning, no end, no roof, no walls, no corners. Whimsical yet ever chic, like a geisha in wait.

I salivate along the in between of your silk lined sidewalls.

The mellow aggregate of a melted determination for prefabricated lust and devilish behavior. The coordinates are just in. Another improper response, another indecent suggestion. Exponentially you have potential. Your decomposing crotch does not warrant such diva behavior. The archetypical tint of a well-lit accident. There are always funnier things. You never know until you are in them, until you are in her, until you give way to the deluge. Lose yourself in the inaction. Wither in despair as you stand helplessly by. There is little accuracy in your explanations. Contrite, shallow, petty. The barometer is failing as your abandon is no longer traceable.

Consistency is the last refuge of the unimaginative.

When women go wrong, men go right after them.

No fire retardant protection from the hiss of your hot skin against mine. You, the handmaiden of try anything. On a cloud, in the sky, a bedlam of female voices, whispering, multi-lingual, the stratosphere an assimilation of pillaging and consensual semi-rape. Her buttocks a vase. Nocturnal daydreams. Breath in, breath out. I can vouch for you if need be. The parallels abound. You are dissonant and a dissident. The specter of your bust line and frame, a land grab, a gold rush, prime buxom landscape, the rarest of real estate.

Visitors only.

Wherever you see her she is there.

Fresh off the boat. Your vanilla ways and means committee. Techniques and the gifts you give me. Stampeding wild buffaloes off the edge of a cliff into certain peril. Speculation of the ride on your saddle, straddled and enduring. I am a pacifist only to a certain extent. Your life of crime and robbery, a new perspective, your pear-shaped backside, a three dimensional model, a DNA map. The beautiful dark person with Tahitian features. The unopened letters, the traffic on the street, small embarrassing moments of humility. The lust quietly building to a slow overflowing eruption, squeezing, easing. This robbery of underpinning wants. Friends with benefits. Your insides intact and the flavor of your wetted cleft. Something partially non-consensual by definition. Bite marks, red, swollen, lingering.

The heart of the man and the quiver of woman. The face of beauty. Do you believe in the extraordinary? The anxiety everywhere, all over my body, tight in my muscles. The only relief a combination of Vicodin and Xanax with my meal tonight. It will take seven minutes to completely flood my blood stream. It will seek out the tension, the knotting muscle mass, the pinched deep layers of tissue skin, onion-layered, deep and deeper still. The anxiety in my mind will fade when I begin to think of distracting scenes of sex, relaxing sensations like warm breezes, tanned skin, a full stomach. The sex scenes will be wild composite women comprised of those I have seen recently, in the street, on TV, in a magazine. Or something really wild and out there like sucking on a breastfeeding mom's nipples.

Netflix and chill. She is upright on a sofa, I am laying down with my head in her lap. I have lost track of the movie, my attention directed to her massive breast just behind my head. I shift my head from time to time, pushing against the immense bags, trying to gauge for a response. There is a fire burning. The room is lightly lit by the flicker of the TV set. She rests one hand on my shoulder. I turn my head to look up at her. She pauses before she looks down. One breast now is warmly up against my cheek. She is ready as I turn my face into her chest. She takes my head in her cuddling hands, very motherly, her fingernail tips scraping my scalp, erotically...the message well received. She pulls up her shirt to reveal a rather large dark and rough nipple, split, uneven, abused, bumpy. My mouth goes to it like a suckling animal kingdom instinct power move. The milk breaks the skin the instant my lips encase the tip, my tongue dragging along the surface. The taste is odd and bitter but not disgusting. I close my eyes like a newborn falling asleep. Her grunts and muffled flutters the proof of her thrill. She is getting hot from it, her skin is throbbing in abandon, there is a wet spot through the lycra, I slide my hand down under the elastic of her yoga pants, I touch her there and she nearly explodes as I slither my index finger between the floppy folds. I run my fingertips over the swollen hood of her defeat. She whispers *continue*. I suck at a hardening pace until her right breast runs dry. She pulls her nipple from my mouth and better adjusts my head and pulls out her left breast and I continue to indulge, my mouth never drying, the stream of milk constant. She may blow me to completion, letting me cum in her mouth, the full girlfriend experience, not letting me out of her mouth until I am way past limp, or I may lay my bloated dick between her swollen tits which I just drained with my mouth, she will prop them up and squeeze me between, her strokes becoming my strokes, the tip entering her mouth every other pass, and I cum on her neck. Or she will position herself over the backend of the sofa and I will do her from behind. She will leave her panties on and I will slide into her with them pulled to the side. They are damp and should be washed. She is sopping wet so it is very slippery and loose but gratifying. Her ass cheeks vast with a certain cartoonish heart shape. Her lower back narrow, refined, gracefully curving outward into a mass of my ruination. My hands hold tight, pressing down, imprinting her flesh; she is held by me, I control her next move, I don't allow her to shift. She will come several times before me. Then the Vicodin and Xanax take hold and I no longer feel my body. I lay myself out flat and try to feel my feet, then my legs, then my stomach area, then my neck and head and everything is at peace and nothing hurts. It is then that I sleep. And I may fantasize in my dreams something strange or wild, or have random opioid nightmares that I forget when I wake.

From: caliph8@sharia4ever.org

From The Great Book (35.13): He merges the night into day and He merges the day into night and He has forced the sun and moon (to His law) each goes on their course for a fixed period of time. Such is Allah! Your Lord: to Him belongs all of the Kingdom. And those, whom you invoke other than Him do not even own a tiniest skin of anything. Do you have skin in the game? No one here gets out alive said the Lizard King. My Lord has guided me, and you, on the Straight Path. The other option is with the losers. And we repeat: You alone we worship, You alone we ask for help. Say that 17 times a day! Love it, and love you! #nohomo #inshallah

If you pay close attention you can almost hear her whisper: *I am over here.* They are finished interviewing the friends and acquaintances that were at the party. Nobody actually saw her leave. But when they found her cell phone in the gravel they knew that it was bad. This will not turn out well. It never turns out well. The first three hours are critical and it has now been an entire night. And it was cold nonetheless. She only had on that cocktail dress, probably not even a pair of underwear, nor stockings. The lead detective writes into his notebook the undisputed fact that she was wearing Versace perfume. The scent followed her everywhere, a signature, a wake of Eros, the essence of woman. She was so bubbly. She didn't have a single enemy. Her friends called her ______, even though her real name was ______. She didn't gamble. She didn't hang out with anyone *undesirable.* She could be extremely posh with a European sophistication and still be the humble American girl that she was. She wasn't currently dating. She wasn't loose or overtly sexual. Rumors didn't follow her like some of the other girls she knew. She was flirtatious, that is for certain, but she was not a one-night-stand type, nor one that would do anything on a first date. She drank but never got so drunk that she wasn't able to sober up with a cup of coffee. She never fooled around with other women. Girls these days would do that, sometimes to satisfy a boyfriend they would have a girlfriend over and kiss and fool around letting the boyfriend watch, he may then get involved with both of them, but usually would either beat off or just quickly do his girlfriend while her friend watched, maybe satisfying herself at the same time. The more involved it would get the worse the outcome later, usually everything crumbling. But apparently from her closest friends she was not like that. Her parents lived on the other side of the country and nobody was sure if it was both her parents or if one was a step parent, if one of her biological parents was dead or just out of the picture. She didn't have a full time job. She worked a couple times a week as a yoga instructor, then she volunteered with a senior center where she taught the old people how to use their iPads. She didn't need to work as she received living expenses from a trust fund started by her grandfather. The terms stated that as long as she was enrolled in nine or more units of higher education she would receive the money. Most of those being interviewed she had met at the community college. A high school with ashtrays, one called it. She had a drama class that was for certain, and most thought she had a creative writing class, but no one could think of what would be the third class. Modern jazz? Spanish? She had a crush on the creative writing teacher. He was close to their age. Handsome, rustic, poetic. But she would not do something like that. Cross that line between student and teacher. She did mention a few times that her landlord was a bit creepy and that it always made her nervous that he had the keys to her apartment, and that sometimes he would come around unannounced, just to ask if anything needed to be repaired. He would make small talk through the cracked door and she would always be as polite as she was raised to be, but she would never just ask him in, to sit down, if he wanted to drink something. He was an older guy, married, lots of kids, lots of rundown real estate, a slum lord really, but with her apartment he seemed to be more than happy to fix even the slightest problem. He even told her that he would change a light bulb should it burn out. That's okay she said, I am a big girl. She said she regretted saying that, that the imagery of the girl as woman metaphor may have got the better of him. She said he was disturbing and that in the beginning she was certain that he had hidden cameras strategically placed about the apartment. A control room in the basement of the building where he could switch the channels and watch her on different monitors as she walked from room to room. She said that she used to look throughout the apartment for small lenses. When she couldn't find any she would still keep a robe on while she walked around, while she dried her hair, while she removed her makeup before going to bed. Even on really hot nights when she wanted to sleep in the nude she would still wear panties and a bra and stay under at least a thin cotton sheet in the event he had a camera above the bed and even though it was dark she was concerned with night vision lighting. She would envision herself rolling around in fetal positions on the bed, being watched in green light, like a military experiment. She also liked to swim at the college's indoor pool. She said that she didn't like to do it, but she would shower before and after in the locker room. Depending on the time of the day there would be either just a couple of older ladies changing or the showers would be full with a girls soccer team cleaning up after practice. She said that there were always a small amount of women who would seem interested and had a wandering eye while changing. She got used to it, but was adamant about not looking their way. She did have an ex-boyfriend, if you can call it that. He was a guy she dated for a couple of months but it ended abruptly, and badly, when she confronted him about not answering his cell phone for an entire evening when she was trying to reach him to make plans for the coming weekend. He told her that the phone wasn't working that day. When he went to a store to buy a bottle of wine he left the phone behind and she looked up the call log and found that he was on the phone several times the night in question. She confronted him and he exploded and raised a hand like he was going to hit her but didn't. The damage was already done, she had seen enough to know she didn't want to stay with him. She made him leave and after a few days of him coming over and knocking on the door and calling at late hours he seemed to go away. She never mentioned anything disturbing about her upbringing, like an uncle who touched her inappropriately, or verbal abuse which made her feel bad about herself. She seemed okay in that regard. But she was beautiful so she could have easily been a target, at least more so than most women. Who wouldn't want a piece of that, one of her male friends said. She had that particular charm about her, like an up and coming star, vibrant, fresh, alive. Everything was fun, everything was exciting, so upbeat and reassuring. Where in the world could she be? What could have happened? Who would want to harm her? It's usually a stranger, one said. Someone who doesn't know her, someone who has not been charmed by her ways. She could have met up with a guy online, started fooling around, things got kinky, she liked it, it progressed, she wanted him to stop, and so on. Or she was wilder than she ever let on. Maybe she did unimaginable things with unimaginable people. Maybe she cruised gas station restrooms late at night. Or trolled the dark shadows under overpasses. Maybe she went to swinger bars and fell into the wrong crowd. Maybe she liked older men and one became a little too obsessed with her. Maybe she had something going on with her landlord, and she just played it like he disgusted her. Maybe she was into alternative activities, if you know what I mean, one said. Whips, chains, candle wax on the nipples, spankings, paddles, bondage, leather, cutting, toys, role-playing, wigs, so on. The fetish lifestyle I believe they call it. Has anyone actually ever seen her naked? Any tattoos or piercings? Did anyone ever see abnormal bruising, handprints, cuts? A full bush of hair or smooth as linoleum? Do you know if she had a dentist? Who was her general practitioner? Who is her healthcare provider? Did she have an OB-GYN? Did she belong to a gym? Any other friends of interest that you can think of? Any off hand comments about strange occurrences, other than her landlord? Do you know his name by the way? Does he live on-site? She did mention recently about a really cute realtor she met. She was interested, I mean *is* interested, I can't believe I am referring to her in the past tense, she may not be gone, anyway, she *is* interested in trying to buy a condo. And she found this one realtor online. She liked his dazzling good looks so she emailed him and they met up at a café. She said he did show her one unit that was vacant, but that they were going to do an open house tour on some Sunday. She mentioned that she found it erotic to be in an empty place with a handsome stranger, and that if she were just a bit wilder and less inhibited she would maybe have done something. Anyway, she didn't mention anything else about the guy except that he is supposedly a hot shot in the condo market and that he is also a broker, whatever that means, and that he put her in touch with a loan guy and that guy had pre-approved her over the phone for $___,___. I think she was looking forward to previewing places with him because she said that she felt like she had finally arrived. She did mention that he didn't have a wedding band and that when he picked her up in his Audi she could tell he was a bachelor, with a gym bag and racquetball racket in the back seat, some men's magazines with the last Sunday paper scattered on the floor, he did mention they were there to protect the floor carpet, that he was anal about keeping the carpet clean, that the car had that new car smell, his cell phone rang several times with her but he never once answered it, not even looking at who was calling, she thought that that was very polite, or that perhaps he knew who was calling, like a jealous or stalking girlfriend. She did have a crown done on a molar last month. I remember that because she wanted to make sure I could pick her up at the dentist office after in case it required a root canal and then she would have been tired and all that. Yeah, the dentist office is in that new medical/dental office building on the corner of ____ and ____. You could probably find their address or name in her bills. I know she was really particular with her bills and paperwork in general.

From: caliph8@sharia4ever.org

You see my friend, no bearer of burdens shall bear another person's burdens. And if one person is carrying a heavy burden their only option for relief is to reach out to the Prophet! But again, you can only warn those who fear Our Lord. You see, it is for the benefit of our souls. The non-believers have already been led to damnation. I know it is early in the day and this is a bit strong, but I needed to get it to you! Please understand that my messages arrive with love and determination! When you need to talk I am here. When you need to off load I am waiting! #inshallah

The ghetto chic look thrills only in short sustained intervals. The boob tat, the lip gloss and lip liner. The big hoops, the crusty overdone hair. The exaggerated booty in the high heels and tight jeans. The exposed thong. You seem so dirty down there. Prove me wrong. You will do what your man asks you to do. A blow job with no reciprocation. To tell you sweet lies, like I will go down on you next time or give you a massage by candlelight with champagne and chocolate-dipped strawberries this weekend. Just as long as you let me hit that shit from behind. Girl, you know that booty needs smashing. Damn, your onion backside, peeling away the layers you got me crying. I know you don't play it like that but I got to get me some of that. I get you all lubed up with some margarine or a stick of real butter, get it all melted and shit right up in your crevices. Damn sista, you are hot. You know I don't like to eat tacos but if that is what it's gonna take bring it on. I know you like it when I talk like a black man. Your white chocolate lover. Getting all freaky and shit. I don't hate you. I am not bothered by those stretch marks all up in your business, on your tits and love handles. No girl, it's cool. All the real sistas have that shit. Or worse. So I ain't mad atcha. Besides I know you know wassup. I know I can take it or leave it. But someone is gonna be happy to hit this shit. Treat you like a real woman, like the queen you are. Show you things you could only imagine before. Take you places you never been. Places you were never going to anyway. Yeah, that's right. I want to get freaky witcha. Don't hate the player hate the game. I ain't mad atcha. I just hope I represent. I bring it all to the table. I don't leave nothing behind. I take care of you mama.

Soft-core sequences rolling, a bowling ball build up, your skin so supple. I twist and turn and burn inside. Catch the next ride, this was not supposed to cause anyone trouble. Really, you don't suppose. The dichotomies of being and the crimes of societal norms.

Drunk girl on a bed. Consensual. Spread eagled. The ebb and flow of desire and misfired missiles at what it is that you want and what it is you fantasize about being one and the same with slight variations on the same theme, the same thread of undoing, the same shades of untanned skin, elastic line imprints of too small panties, sitting in the same position for too long, unattended to wild hair growth, ingrown hair and stubble from the last shave, just before you started to wax, the peach fuzz, smooth is how I see you evolving, the picture and ideal of body hair at this juncture in history and there really is no option now, you cannot just let it go, you cannot just give in and be natural down there, yes it is still not too awful but with the zeitgeist proliferated, there is a certain élan of shame in association to anything but smooth as hardwood floors, you really are not left with much of a choice, now are you? There will be a time again when it is en vogue to have a bush. The thicker the better, long, untamed, uncombed. Something to disguise. Something to provide for cover and hide the smile behind. This is eroticism and discovery only when you have passed the point of no return. A parting of the forest, a taming of the mane, the wild animal domesticated if only for a moment. Fleeting and hurried, you cannot see what you are up against. The pinks and the reds muted and diluted with the dark foliage, cover in the storm, protection from infection. Cro-Magnon at times, a break from the perfections of bikini waxes, of close shaving, of the technology of triple and quadruple blade tightness. The released endorphins in a carnal assault on the subconscious ability that is pulled down to its most basic purpose. Whether you like it or not you are drawn in. The muff takes over, you find yourself unabashedly wanting more, perplexed by the medieval, that which is so non-modern. Crazy and wild you scream inside, what beauty before me. You press your face up against the flowering shrub, never wanting to leave, blinded by curly hair pressed hard against your closed eyelids, just what you need, your tongue parts ways, finding flesh, warm and moist and salty, you come upon the smile and part the folds with an erect tongue, your lips assisting in the plight of so much hair in such a small area, you drag your tongue from top to bottom, a sensual probe for dimensions and scale, a blueprint for your mind that is now out of control...where am I, what am I doing. I am right here right now and I wish I could stop time, hit the pause button, create a remote control where I could jump to the scene over and over again and return to here and now at my pleasing, when I am lonely, when I am cold, when I am sad or confused or have a million thoughts charging through my mind and I cannot slow down or stop them, this grounds me and the peace allotted to the act, the defiance in the half face, the visage without eyes or a nose, just the lips of a mouth that cannot speak. The neighbor below that lets off a slight smell of processed functions, of waste and lithe lingering side effects of the last trip to the toilet.

The broken smile, the loitering for a while. I love you there. I knock on the door with the tip of my tongue. I feel the abrasions of my taste buds dragging slowly along the door frame. I wouldn't mind spending everyday starting like this so that you would get off with a smirk and a wink or a dirty thought. Damp, trained for the morning licking, tickling, taming of the beast. I could catch you every time. I would call this a drizzle but I eagerly await a downpour. Bring it on. Gush, flush it out, release your bodily fluids for a transfer. I slide my nose between the folds and push into a slow insertion, a burial if you will...I continue to breathe through my mouth which I have pulled back, but I now press down to kiss her there, the brown spot, the forbidden orifice. I rim her with my swollen and aching tongue. The alkaline taste comes and goes as I am overdosing on bodily functions, secretions and aromas. Her bouquet is vintage. And an advantage in this world of perfection. She becomes nervous. I can tell by the pinching of the doorway around my nose. I refrain momentarily for her to settle in and realize that there is nothing to worry about. Sit back and submit.

The whole purpose of the procedure is to alter the pitch of the voice to sound more feminine. This is measured by fundamental frequency (FO). Optimal pitch is between 100 and 105. This is done by shortening the vocal folds, decreasing the whole mass of the folds, and increasing the tension of the folds. Increase the pitch range and by default we remove access to lower frequency ranges in the voice. We bring the cricoid cartilage closer to the thyroid cartilage with sutures and metal plates. The cricoid cartilage is shifted backward and upward and the thyroid cartilage is moved forward and downward. This will mimic ongoing cricothyroid muscle contractions that tense and elongate the vocal folds which cause the pitch to increase. This procedure will lead to a more authentic sounding female voice. Voice therapy may still be needed. You will need to practice Diaphragmatic Breathing Patterns, and stable posture. Resting your voice for long periods of time is important. Relaxation exercises will include tension releasing techniques for the jaw, tongue, shoulders, neck and overall laryngeal area. You will have to start talking like a woman. So much of it will be non-verbal communication. There is a congruence between a person's visual and auditory gender presentation which contributes to perceived authenticity. Fake it 'til you make it. More smiling. More open facial expressions. More side to side head movement. More expressions with finger movements. Touch people more. You are selling the whole package. Negative effects include reduced voice quality, reduced vocal loudness, difficulty swallowing and/or breathing, sore throat, infections and scarring.

The stage set by dull lighting to hide the flaws, to bare the glistening, set the mood of decadence and nonchalance for this or for that, for her or for all of them in the same room, at the same time, naked, hungry. Spin the reels, feel the blood flow. A break from the constant friction and glitter. They wear wigs as if to disguise. I make a late entrance, after the party has started. They are warm to the idea and in limbo, unknowing. There is low laughter, giggles, mischievous smiles, small hands covering their wide mouths, like geishas or Arab princesses. Nobody deserves sympathy here. Perfection in a room with walls of colorful tapestry, bowls of fruit, candles and incense burning. The first hand I take into mine trembles. It is weak and delicate. I feel her heartbeat with my eyes. Nothing needs to be averted within sight. They all want the gaze, the look of approval. The appearance of care. All are ready and eager, or so the fantasy goes. Primed and willing. They are from all walks of life, friends of a friend, someone who wanted to be invited or someone who had done this before. In all of the nudity it is difficult to discern who is who, who comes from where, what they do or do not do. I was told in advance that there would be a homeless woman present and I must admit this is quite thrilling. I am eager to try and discover her identity but then again I need to stay in the moment and not get too caught up in the intellectual ideas and dynamics at work, only the carnal craving and sedation to the appetites, and the charisma to keep alive the dream. The eyes are elevated and scanning like cats lingering on a porch, bored, hungry, looking to be entertained. Who is the vagabond. The dirty look of famine and bad posture and rosacea. This canvas is ready to be painted. Sundown was the code word. Nothing is forsaken here tonight. Nobody will be left with nothing. The light will break through. We will see through each other's eyes. There will be praise and thanks, but the expressions will be non-verbal. The gratitude will not be read aloud. The space between will cease to exist and this will be a moment we will not be able to escape...if all goes as planned. Imperfections will be set aside and there will be no comparison or competitive studies here. No contests or assessments. Each body part with its own unique charms. A passing embrace of dragging warm skin against skin, fingertips against erect nipples, a pinch, a tease. I close my eyes in fleeting moments. A slowdown, a calm down, a meltdown of the beating, the throbbing and the subduing. The desire maintains and lingers and paces its best speed, the verve of swarming bees in flight. I work the rooms like the guest of honor, a nod here, a nod there, a smile across the way, a silent acknowledgement, a political wink of the eye, *yeah, I remember you baby*. This is the worst of things to aspire to, a wild honey moment, glowing in the dark, the radiation reaching dangerous levels. I am brought to the knees in my mind, a clear expression of self-doubt and a sudden drop of atmospheric pressure. I stop trying to be someone that I am not. The conversations are unimportant, the lighting only secondary, blindness not so bad after all. She takes my hand and places it down there, wet, un-denied and undefined. The source for all inspiration and ambition. I feel the force shine upon me. Take me, abuse me and use me. Reach out to me and I will respond. I want to slide on your dance floor, falling I will yell out my approval ratings.

You are genuine.

At play in the room similar to children after school, the exhaustion everywhere but nothing to stop the party or stifle the panting. The task is close at hand. The finality and finale imminent. I stop time again. The adoration in the scene is flattering, the fervor baffling. Some have become shriveled and spent and return to the underground for a respite. The serendipity of good fortune I do not forget even in idle moments of lost trains of thought, of confused ships at sea in thick fog, no beacons of hope, no promise that this will end and tomorrow will start anew. I cannot stand it anymore. I follow this feeling like a lost dog. I could walk away from it all, leaving them to their own procedures but I would not do that to them, for my own sake, not just theirs. I want to be their friend, their lover, their toy thing, their brother, their cousin, their landlord, their boss, their servant, their fuck boy. If I could find the time. I want to sing out that I am sufficient enough for them, that I have the destination and the map, that yes there is enough time at the end of the day, that I have been all over and all around, that I am bound to be here and now and I will be at that other place tomorrow or whenever they decide to call. I promote for this colony of a bygone era of concubine splendor, of kept women, of Roman orgies, of publicly acknowledged infidelity and travel to that other place. No further obligations...*just be sure to spread the word.* Your work is done. This book is out of print. You have been called home. Whoever else is left is invited to stay, incited to frivolous rioting at daybreak without leaving the bed. It is as if I am living someone else's dream. Seeing colors that have never been seen and sensations undiscovered. A new fruit on a new tree, blooming in the backyard. Her backside and the valleys of sin and skin. Glistened with her own saliva which she will remove again with a slow tongue or her new friend's tongue. Someone will take care of the mess. I rewind what has played out then replay each angle, a director wanting another take, what if we placed the camera over there, what if we she moved her leg more to the left next time, what if we lit up the room just enough to better reveal and divulge more of her lady package, so on. Scenes are replayed and re-interpreted, altered, paused, forgotten, rearranged. Too much on this night to process. My mind is far from idle status. I ask the girls for assistance with new positions, new inclines and tilts. I want to arrange my dolls as in my mind while I still have the thoughts alive. You go over there and look busy, you stay here and get comfortable, you be patient and wait for your cue. Bend over like so. Close your eyes and open your mouth. Spread your cheeks like this. Do that thing with your tongue. Cup her breast gently. Keep on keepin' on.

From: caliph8@sharia4ever.org

We have set our fixed number at 19 guardian angels. This is of course a trial for non-believers who will ask why 19? Well, Allah set the number and He does not wonder whom He is to please with answers to these petty questions. We have a term for the non-believers, it is "kafir" and it is a very serious insult. But the 19 angels for us the "saved," well it is a warning to mankind. And it is not open to mainstream interpretation. But I believe we are being warned of the distance between the East and the West, and the premise of how opposing we are, and our non-coinciding value systems. The social and moral stage is so disparate that our agreeing is not possible. As we cannot occupy lands like the foreign oppressors, we must bring the battle to a town near you. We must demonstrate our capability, and contribute to the further progress of mankind. Be it through united information and a propaganda apparatus. Be it through blood and explosives. Be it through terror and chaos. Be it through calculations and consequence. Do you see my friend where I am coming from? Do you feel comfort in the mission and the guidance of the 19 guardian angels? Talk soon, k bye. #inshallah

The assumption of the certainty behind all things you, the particular mystery in your reflection and riddle in your rhythm. You are so fresh. A springtime freshness. A just-sliced guava. Newly picked and moist. Spread open, ready and willing to be devoured, to be eaten savagely, to drip out all over your face and down onto your chest. To be sticky. To be sugary. To be hard to wipe off. To want to linger, to penetrate the small pores, to stain the flesh with discoloration.

The way her breasts parted and hung outward, suspended full-grown pears, bouncy, ripe, adult, alive. Something out of the Garden of Eden. So pure and innocent and full of life-force. The shapes and molds behind the curtain of a crimson cashmere sweater. Confined by tight polyester and other rigid synthetic fabrics, refrained by a manmade brassiere wire-lined symmetry. The imagery of them bare, of them cold, revealed and timid, and the dangle of your proud brunette nipples and you there pushing them up and together, forming a wicked and eye-popping cleavage, your nipples peeking through your pressing fingers, as if to whisper, *let me out*, then you smile and close your eyes to expose the aqua blue eye shadow and playfully bite your lower chapped swollen lip, a love valley of despondency, running wild thoughts of a Russian or Spanish release, *una cubana*, not a pearl necklace, but you swallowing it whole while I come quick, no evidence to speak of, no stains, nothing to photograph, no abandoned crime scene. I promise not to get any in your hair. We will keep your hills clean. No trace of my existence. No remnant of my undoing.

The parallels in the sublimation and the not so subliminal forms. The crescent of the moon reflective in the bow of your black matted eyelashes, regarded in back light splendor. The curve of your hips reproduced in your shoulders and knees. The buckling of your toes and fingers, the folding of your knuckles, repeated in the cellulite bumps and ingrown pubic and non-pubic hair, amplified up close. The way your knees buckle in the shower when taken from behind. The profile of your nipples, alert and on guard—smaller versions of your breasts regarded in whole. The outward curve of your eyes behind their lids, the clit revealed below the hood. The pursed lips of your bung hole, clenched tight like a fist or a pouting mouth. Your dangling earlobes strikingly akin to the hang of your vulva in silhouetted daylight. The soft skin behind your knees wrinkled with life and love lines like your armpits. The smell of them, the smell between your legs. Exact and on point, the correlation between the areola coloring and/or texture and those of your mouth lips and pussy lips. The link between your natural eyebrow growth and the natural stretched carpet spread of your tamed, and sometimes tanned, bush. The thickness and darkness eerily the same. Quixotic. All before the manicuring and lawn maintenance.

From: caliph8@sharia4ever.org

Hello friend. Do you not see that Allah has subjected to your use whatsoever is in the heavens and whatsoever is on earth, and has in a large part made His gifts come to you both as being seen and unseen? Even then there are the haters who will dispute Allah...you see, they are without His guidance and His Book to show the light to them. They hate us because they ain't us. Does this not make you feel special? You are part of something so much bigger than yourself. Can you feel it? Ok enough for today, sorry for all the emails, just wanted to share the joy with you LOL. #inshallah

Tijuana International Airport.

Cairo food riot.

Satellite of Charles De Gaulle.

Masquerades and silhouettes.

The unintelligible yearning, the nothingness, the nothing to attain to, the void in the calm and the soft in the wet spots. There exists no substitute. She was backlit in an explosion of shadows. She fled in the afternoon and never returned the same. It is no longer a question of rational behavior. It is something more, and at the same time something less. It is all about the struggle. Nothing to do with attachment, more about the half moments, the in and out of it all. *Start here now.* Later when we are awake and weaker we can stop. This existence at times so unexpected. Thank you for spending this time with me. You sweat hard like melting butter, you look half there, a sideways film splice, distorted and feeble. This moment, lying in wait. The engines of this lubrication machine. She comes back across the room, across the waves, across the sea. There is no turning back. Stripped away and naked against the moon. An enemy against the campaign. Moments of freedom, moments of virtue as the walls begin to collapse. I no longer remember her name. Her nationality. Her tastes, her likes, her wants. Dreams in the afternoon siesta. The ground quiet beneath her limbs. I want to be your underwear.

The transitions and juxtaposition of shades and reflections. The colors lost in dismal longing, affections for the unattainable, desires for the unlit fires and watered down misgivings of a forgone yesterday. It is all memories. Even the future, futile in its hope and *esperanza.* No room for prediction in the superunknown, just you, there, in the darkened corner...lost, perturbed, confused, ignorant of the situation. A time capsule of sorts. A remnant for a lost time. A souvenir of wanted aching and pains. A long and dry harvest. A cut down rain forest, the animals and their flight of exodus. In the span of minutes all lost, abandoned to the halls of the mind. Another draw at time and a reorganization of sorts, sorting out a new frame, a new perspective, a new formulation of the contours and an assault on the avant-garde. 36Ds. 36 double Ds. Everything else is left to stand and remain between the brush strokes and the lines of dimness. Reflections and manifestations, a matter of perception, these are all pathways to the same place, to the same end, to the same warmth at the same dusk.

Traffic and weather straight ahead. I'll see you just outside of customs. Mixing with the gods. America, the accomplished coexisting with the idiotic. Where there is darkness there is light. To the extent of neurotic depravity. Maybe a Polish porn flick for dessert. An after dinner mint. A blowjob front lit by fireplace light. Some farewell gin and tonic madness. *Partouz* stories while you are cooking. Eat my beaver you slut.

You need not look too far, often only past the nose hair.

The sculpture of her form, the slight bite from the flame, a forest fire out of control, raging inside, the mistake in the doing, the lingering you long for, the makeshift pandemonium that my Jezebel produces. I only read from the index *Librorum Prohibiorum.* What the French would say, *incartade*, for my breaks in thought, split, divided, voided and avoided. Aback she takes me with her pronounced thighs. *Omne ignotum pro magnifico*—everything unknown is thought to be splendid. Remember, come up for air. Her chaste origin breeds proper deviance. I continue the endless stimulation of these depraved souls, the smell of Mediterranean aphrodisiac. Golden access to the corporate accounts. There is duty then there is simultaneous longing for the endless array of swinging ass. But still…there is something better. I almost cannot take it anymore. As I scan through radiant mainlands, I skim over luscious landscapes. From time to time I receive the coordinates from a failing GPS device. The *messagerie electronique.* On the way I got a taste for the big beats and a perennial protrusion into esoteric realms.

Embellished, embezzled, embarrassed.

All the famous architecture, all the grand museums, all the street-lit storefronts, the mannequins dressed up, ready to go, ready to entertain, still, quiet and immobile. A villa overlooking the rolling sunbaked hills of Tuscany. Something essential is still missing. All the grandeur of culture and history and civilization, all of the Michelangelos and Rafaels, their traces flew by like something through the windows of a speeding car. The blur. And I realized it was the scent of the feminine. Sitting next to you in a train car. Standing against the door in a metro. Across the lobby of a three star hotel. A body of resonance to grasp what others have coined beautiful, and also as a shield protecting against amnesiac slipperiness, her salty skin a mnemonic device. And proof of proximity to the sea. All this time devoid of libidinous laissez-faire. A sanity I apprehended. Amidst all the enchantment I could barely stand still. *Eurotophobia*—contrary to the thought that it has something to do with Europe, it is the insect-in-your-face subtext subject of *any fear of female genitalia.* A topic that may require a small serving of Chianti. Just enough to ease you in...it is not in the cut rather in the spread. The moveable feast, the tasteful but inedible. A molten lava flow of tinted hues of magnificence, abundant with life-force, vitality, juice and friction-danger. Another night train headed south.

Her superiority complex, at times, the narcissism. The Freudian term taken from the Greek mythology.

Narcissus' rejection of the nymph Echo. Then banished to fall in love with his own reflection in a pond. She could be like that. And at other times she is like a wounded bird, or drying flower. In need of help, in need of being wetted again. In need of attention, to the details, to the everyday things that she takes for granted and leaves to neglect. Like properly shaving, like eating healthy portions. She says she needs to warm her throat, and there is only one that can do it properly. She says she will not elaborate. Her cracked lips a remnant to her earlier neglect. But she had turned on herself. She has no one to blame but herself. She needs to learn to trust others. You cannot blame her for the reluctance after a decade of burning imperialism. All that has fallen prior. Her shelf life shortened by an ever increasingly improved product. That is not hers. That is not her.

From the whispers, from the blinking LEDs, from the tremble in her weakened knees. Or the clutter in the garment bag. Her mouth is burned and it hurts to swallow. The day turns to night and the hum from the machines gets louder. The origin is somewhere in the moonlit seascape. Are you tonight wounded and thinking of me? She murmurs in hushed tones. This will all be forgotten one day and given to the dark recesses of the mind. There are of course other options. The favors and the flavors, when the learning never stops. The menstrual cycles and the transcendence and the resistance. There is no common ground. An utter lack of lucidity. When we drink, you inevitably spill unto yourself, the watermark stain a slight blemish to an otherwise semi-perfect veneer.

I want to drown in her.

I want to night swim in her warm waters.

I want to be the breath that fills her mouth.

The night patrols have increased and the perimeter lighting is on all night. They have begun to pay for information. It is all about the scenery and the condition of your lips. Homesick for the intrigue, and homeless bandits in a forlorn night. The contentious visual intensity. You see it only in your sleep. It comes around when nobody's looking. Her manicured lawns have gone past neglect. She has stopped bleeding there. Another sign that all is not okay. Her eyes a distant entrance to a vacationing soul. For moments she is discrete and her charms resurface fleetingly like a seventh wave pounding the shore. Her walk unchanged, a walk without end. I do not blame you if you believe in gravity. The glory in the orbit and splendor in your orbs.

Aside from the shivering, things are on schedule.

Please do not look away.

Her kiss was smooth but without a return tasting. She looked best when descending a staircase, suspended with my gaze upward, her visage a towering pinnacle to an otherwise flawless form of vertical femme dressed to disfigure and disarm. Her bosom, a heaving forward balancing act. Her hair backlit by chandelier glow. Her legs pinched under stocking wrapping. Her heels dangerously close to the edge of the step. A tragic, perhaps paralyzing, accident waiting to occur. She rolls her tongue, a hint of ennui. Her mouth agape, an upgraded resurgence to the frustration of being between here and now. Her legs widen with each step. Her skirt rising and riding upward along her diamond hips. The more she reveals the more she buries. The concepts of what she keeps to herself oozing out like a secreting pore, an injured soldier in the last battle. Another hour, that is all I ask. Can you feel the pain, can you taste the anguish. We are all just detainees here. Hostages to our own destruction. Prisoners to our own avarice. No more beliefs toward self-preservation. No more thought to self-perpetuation. Nothing to uphold, nothing to surrender. If only we could have been born in a different time, a different place, a different state of mind. She says she only feels it when she is pinched there. Like an adaptation of a classic she barters her goods, a little of this for that, a little wink here for a future favor. Almost as pure as things can become, she comes in committed strides of consistency.

Her eyes were closed as she arrived upon the child of god. His soul unwashed, huddled and shaking. You cannot have the both of us. You will know when you are ready to go, ready to calm down. The path is muddy and wet, a sign of things to come. The comfort of the warm water in the womb, or the wet spot on the sheets, slow stains on the mattress underneath. A trace and a memory. Everything else comes later. This fairy tale of loss and gain. Inhale the insecurities, a drug you crave, they overtake you. Your greed is blindness. The mainline an option. You are on my mind. Here it comes. Get ready. Yes, just…now…any second. Is this really what you wanted. What you get is what you debt.

From: caliph8@sharia4ever.org

Hi friend. It has been a minute. How's things? I want to share with you this: The disbelievers spend their wealth to keep men away from the Path of Allah, and so they will keep on spending. But in the end they will have regrets and sighs, at the end they will be defeated, and the disbelievers will be brought together in Hell. And for those who are rebels and are wicked, their homes will be set afire. And every time they want to get away they will be forced back into the home, and it will be said to them: "You taste the penalty of the fire, which you rejected as a lie." You see friend the metaphor? If you deny His existence, if you choose material living over spirituality, then you are doomed. Our path is the righteous one. Can you feel it bro? #inshallah

The chemicals spoke directly to her, into her, a direct line, a land line, a two-way radio, loud and clear. Do you copy? Roger, out. Telltale signs open to interpretation, bilingual, trilingual, a cunning linguist, subliminal, criminal, integral, sublime. Overanalyzed, redirected, shunned, ignored, deprived. All in a word it was: *cavernous*. It comes through in surround sound. At time 5.1 or better. The petals are soft and round and colorful. The trajectory of her shapes and sizes. The disintegration was immediate and profound in later regard, after the fact, after the intel was gathered. Different depths of breath, sideways, always, every which way.

Knowing what I know now doesn't ease the pain any more, for the better, for the worse, for the sake of conversation or lack thereof. The pain is the same just clearer and heavier felt. More objective and better suited to be scrutinized and investigated. It is there to blow the mind or blow your wad. Numb it with a large charge on your credit card. Concentrate when you breathe. Go deeper with more focus, more ambition to fill your failing lungs. Hold in for three counts, exhale slowly. Let your face feel flush. The capillaries under your adult acne need the oxygen. That is what the oil is trying to tell you. The sight of a big spread extra-large ass in front of me, in a forest, parting two ferns, the fern leaves against her skin, the slight breeze, the litter off in the distance, an abandoned homeless camp, the thrilling thought that a jogger, or a hiker or a rapist could come upon us at any moment. The flesh of her womanliness hot to the touch; it would steam apparent if it were any colder out now. Come on, not much longer now. There are small branch twigs and pollen trapped in her curly hair, fallen from the springtime trees. Her skin is pale and angelic white. Then there are the thin blue lines of her healthy veins, spidering like a river delta across her back, dissolving at the outer edges, disappearing under deeper layers of skin. A grid to zero in on while getting your rocks off. A delay to the inevitable. She clenches me, holding me tightly with her inverted elephant trunk, a sign of love and commitment and devotion even if we do not know each other's name.

If there was ever a more appropriate moment for gloves. Slowly pull them on. Make sure they are tight and difficult to get on, clinging around each finger, around the orbit of your fist. Imagine what your bare palms and fingertips would feel against her flesh. The warmth, the unevenness, the texture. The compressed skin, a body bag wrapped tight around its victim. Or a condom enveloping a swollen member. Secured as can be.

Hatched from fate remember: there is a woman under that skin. She can see beyond the rough edges, and disseminate her beauty each time she freshens her scent. Her female scent, like motifs of blue and escape. Paranoia is good for the senses, a throwback to everything we learned before and everything we do not know now. As the incense burned the water torture continued. This is a smash and grab job for anyone’s undertaking. Resist her lips just one more time. We are all Cezanne lovers under a cloudless moon-filled night. No need for a menu—we will have the usual. I can remember what we did but I can no longer remember how we felt. Nor the afterglow. Her breath was always so fresh. That will forever stay in the distance of my memory. Never to be edited or reframed or shredded. I remember clearly her long hair covering her face, like parted curtains on a stage, the anticipation of a performance. There was an entire conversation in the stare from her sullen face. She transforms you with that intent look. You have to wonder what is going on back stage. Her lips look like they were washed ashore, with the warm sand, with the curves of driftwood.

Her arched brow the underside of yesterday. She claims to have not eaten in days, her survival is in the tap water. Can you hear her quiet hum in the darkened corridors and the faint bouncing of the failing light bulb. The cries of the hummingbird. It is safer this way. You will not be held accountable. You are witness to the follicles of dead skin upon her neck and her lovely hair. Upon closer examination, flaws to her faultlessness. But you overlook these and see the larger picture—her perfection, aptness and the *ne plus ultra*. The roar off in the distance. The echoes from the far side of your thoughts and memories. Perplexing places to visit but not safe places to stay. Her vacant expressions. The misrepresentations of a less than guarded soul—crying and screaming, *let me out*. She will be alright. She will reply appropriately. If it is appropriate.

The movements lack full motion. The smoke signals spread confusion. *There must be a better way.* Inhale and you might jeopardize your own safety. These brief moments of authenticity. Do you see yourself in the reflection, enshrined in the comfort. The proliferation of choices, the relief in the pain, the danger in the wrong ending. Her attempts to avoid eye contact fail as she walks the path of old age alone, in despair, confused yet liberated. This night will shine.

The gravitational pull of your sorrow, of your heartache, of your undoing. The demise is the end prize. You, drugged and blind in all the convenient ways. A victim to modernity, a casualty to consumption, an injured party to abuse, a scapegoat to the non-virtue. A new journey now—a way to break through, a new labyrinth, a new maze, new tools of navigation, a new star, a new moon, a new west. You must deaden your senses, attempt to exist between the now and the immediate then. A safer type of vacation. No passport required. The plane will never leave the ground. You fill the need of your insides. That void that grows bigger with each passing unfulfilled moment. It is primal and it is real. It is a place you have never been, each moment a new adventure in discovery. Another unconfirmed sighting. These doses of illusion tangled in the webs of nihilism and apathy. Come on, give in a little. You have become unrecognizable in your imperfections and actions. Your portrait in baroque illusions, in rococo romanticism, in overdone restraint.

Surplus in the corruption.

From: caliph8@sharia4ever.org

Allah is not limited by the laws of nature. He makes them and he can change them or suspend them, if he so chooses. The Qu'ran has revealed to us that our Prophet may lead mankind from the depths of darkness into light if He so chooses. He is the One worthy of all praise and the Most Exalted in power. Do you feel the comfort in this knowledge friend? It is all in His hands. Grief to the disbelievers who will suffer a terrible penalty for their lack of faith. I miss you bro fam. Write soon k bye. #inshallah

Please do not disturb. In all the confusion she has left in a rush. It was like this earlier, before she arrived and now it is again like it was before—the void. A lack thereof. Just the smell of her wafting perfume. Fainter with each passing hour. The fading scales of memory, of the images of her—blurred at the edges, losing the Technicolor and their tone. Imagine her lingering in the corner, staying behind in the room, blending in with the shadows, tidying up the memoirs, recalling the reminiscences. She is a sovereign nation landlocked, embodied by the burden of her body, the onus of her essence. Behind the door there are subtle adaptations and innuendo, rituals wrapped in different souls, flamenco, salsa, rumba, tango. Different glows of soft blues, and even softer greens. The circumference of the invisible electricity—in the walls, in the bulbs, between us in the air. The dehydration setting in. I am weakened further at the knees, in the shoulders, my vision blurs. The profile of her backside serpentine. The flow of her long hair, the sparkle in her eyes cosmic. I am no longer concerned that there in fact is no perfect viewing angle. Just a series of one-off perches to partake the sights. All of the quasi truisms, the semi legitimacy, the partial fidelities. For sacrifice, for pleasure, for love. She was always playful when dressed in black and satin. When pushed to the extremes she would suspend judgment and postpone sentencing. If not this then what. If you don't get it someone else will. You will know when it is your time. You will know when the stars shine for you. Our hearts beat in synch pinned beneath bones that one day will return to dust. Our moments merge into one, we free flow in timeless fashion, victims to nothing, warriors for the good cause. As the simplest of truths unfold, these are the words, they are all we have—and the girl. Through the peephole to reality. An undercut and undercurrent to the lust, to the covetousness and itch. Perennial and everlasting. The permanence in the impermanence. Before the diagnosis, before the knowledge of the disease. If you are not struggling then you are not living. Come over here. I behold you in transition, through narration and soft tones. Beyond the notion of self and space. The experience was so raw, the evidence so damning. You suppress the urge to run, the impulse to escape. There must be a better way, you tell yourself with tepid reassurance. The storm of your love swirls about me, over me, against me. Clenched tight like a scared child frightened by the thunder. Do not search it out—let it come to you. And become you. Behold you. Beckon you—to the forefront, to the vanguard, through the shadows, under the eclipse, against the terror.

The men were still back there. She hadn't seen or heard them for a
while, but she knew they were there. Even dressed in their heavy assault
gear, they wouldn't give up. The moment the X Squad had arrived, sirens
screaming, lights flashing, she set out across the field behind the house. Over the fence a tangled thicket dropped off into the woods that eventually gave way to the dew-covered meadow. That's where she was now, fighting her way through the field. The men were not far behind.

I should have taken their cue. And not been so compulsive, so determined and focused—so one track minded, obsessed and fanatical. My infatuation bordered on the obscene—I started to visually imagine her not as she really was, but a better facsimile: hotter, sexier, prettier, way less flawed than she really was. That is what the mind will do for you. Call it survival techniques—it will not let you dwell on the bad stuff. A healthy mind will not permit the shit, it will tweak the reality for a better fantasy. The tunnel of her seemed to have no end. All I knew to do was stay on the track and keep going in the same directions. Little did I know the further I traveled the more lost I became. Looking at her backside, the shapes, the curves, the contours, the concave and the convex. She brings me to my own prison. In spite of myself, in spite of herself. Unknowing and unwilling. An audience member to her psychodrama. A prisoner at her art show debut. Kneeling on the brink, a tear in my eye, acquiescent to my end, the outcome imminent. By now they must know. All of them. Everyone and every last judgement. You get what you give. Requirement is the mother of forgery.

The tempers scented in the wind...the atheists will be damned...go to heaven for the climate and to hell for the company...you will not get over the hill if you stay in the valley...a sorrow out of reason, a famine in fall...strike while the others are preoccupied, while the getting is good...be in it to win it...the torture from a child's love, the fidelity you must not forget...the clouds have passed from my mind...ever since the night before last...she smiled to me through the stained glass window. She saw me steal a glance. It is just the same. In folly or vanity I go along. I blow the bubbles back her way. The struggle is over. The violent gesticulating talks of hurt and anger. Have you ever experienced such bitterness.

Derailed and full of messianic hyperbole and dogmatic ifs ands or buts. The grandniece of the second cousin was directly linked to Casanova. I believe her name was Claudia. She is hard to forget, that pawnshop brushfire of a woman. The wind balances her silky sea-roving hair, the thorny edges of her self-possession dwindled, melting like a pot of gold, honey dripping on flesh. Bankrupted and ruptured by the bourgeoisie falsity and cavern warmth of night. Her petals bear the velvety crush of a provincial smutty face, a necklace of pearls, a coat of silver fleece and five hundred euros. Her skin a plain to traverse gently like new snow, like a first dance lesson, like drying off sex toys. Yes, it is rare and wonderful indeed. She did not know that I already caught a glimpse of her stomach, and the edge of her underwear. When she itched herself there. I wanted a closer view, I wanted within range to smell it. To smell something. Anything. Like the previous visit. What do you say. Can we give it a go. You are: *marvelous*; *perfect*; *flawless*; *staggering*—all with an exclamation point behind. Behold your misty dew top mountain peak melons. Firm, hard and erect all the while defying gravity and age. The deeper the valley the steeper the peaks. I am here to claim the long forgotten gold, the family jewels, the harps of angels and the spilling goblets. The fur of your womanhood, a warm blanket on a shivering night, a life preserver from a capsized boat at sea. The light blue and pale green outlines of her eye makeup, buoying afloat in limbo. Nobody remembers those nights, and especially the mornings. All of this before the delirium, the dementia and debilitating pain. The numbness is what we seek out. The void of the shouting and the arrival of the soft smells. The aroma arisen from her creases and crevices. The character study in her seduction. The information is out. The pieces fall together, the progress better visualized, the quick and rapid movements less suspicious, the lingering doubt. A product of her own atmosphere. I cannot take any more in my eyes. She wears it so well on her face, the scorn, the ridicule, the magic and lure. She is the difference in preparation and duration. A prelude to the groundwork and failure, the breakdown in telecommunications and wartime paranoia.

She blurs the seams of horizontal light.

Walk toward me. Mesmerize me. Simplify me. Coexist with me. Me inside you and vice versa. She wears the hint of shame with pride and gratification. A war medal, or coat of arms of discernment. And here I am with no flame for the fire. Just calmer now, breathless, a heartbeat stiller. Shallow. Swallow. Follow her to the magic waters. A hesitant kiss, this could be called love. As I come upon her smoldering backside, the remains of the release, the lingering of discharge. The in between moments, the dead time, the static. Wait for me in the calm. Distracted from the task—the rebuilding, the reconstruction, the effort, the remaking. Drunk and disorderly, a nuisance, an indoctrination. There are strengths in her moral fortitude and distant relegated memories left to recall. A place where you can take a morning swim.

Why a different glow to your skin. Why the gleam in your eye. An indeterminate flow of infatuation and ardor. She pays the price for the hubris of her past. She whimpers behind a smile, *kiss me*. I am yours and you are mine. Parallel glaciers melting at sea. Do you feel the pull. Do you feel the warmth. The world is here for your own formation. As she busies herself with candle rituals. It is all a new beginning but with an older end. New-age technology dressed in Turkish fabric. Memories lit by techno soundtracks. You forget the smells, you forget the pain. The lions only fight over pride. When she pulls me forward there is no friction. No chafing. No abrasion. Only sublimation and equanimity. Composed we enter the end of the era. A new kind of new awaits. Something glimmering and shimmering. A newer kind of white. She is so ripe—that is what all the singing is about. The abundance, the radiance. A counter to the counterpoint measures, a qualitative gauge to the solemn solitude. The telltale day dreams of her soft winter gaze, her dragging fingertips, her long unkempt nails, she spins her body in slow motion, an unconscious blur, her hands now clasped behind her back. She vibrates with the rhythm of the drums. The jungle cadence. The wild woman pulse. I behold her womanly garden by firelight...it is so well trimmed. The nervous laughter, the late hours, the moral crimes, the emotional heist. I roll my tongue along her bottom edge. And it tastes like guava excretion. My head begins to hum, a continental picture of unrequited love. There is no hope. An unbridled squeal and a sudden death grip. Grab, hold on, and swing. This moment will pass and the age will be long forgotten. Statuesque in her own revolution. We walk on unafraid, forward heading into our every days, on a walk without end. It all could add to post-apocalyptic horror or sublimation. You decide. No need to protest—the resolution will give way to the truth. As we walk on toward unwarranted condemnation, self-oppression and self-tyranny, a paved road of domination and masochism. The assumption of genuineness. A veracity to that which is bona fide. The cast of the window shade shadows along her naked back, a barcode of allure. She is jettisoned in my mind to her own exile, an island where only I am permitted to visit, only I can bring her food. The curve of her hips a new coastline for my private undoing. I will drown there and like it. I am tired of the war, cold from the elements, lost from the artifice and deception.

Shall we begin the empirical investigation.

She is the figurehead, the cult of personality, the face for the public square. The relevance in the piece, integrity in the dissatisfaction, nourishment in the shivers. We shall remain entrusted to the naïve truths and ancient human longings, we shall hold this secret society knowledge as self-evident. The paranoid exposure could be a call to the wild. The proof an instrument to de-clutter the muse. Since that one afternoon she never returned the same. She is less chemical and more rational. She grows supple with each flirtatious pinch of her bottom, *oh, those lovely cheeks, fat, full and firm*. There is no path to take, no whispered curse to warn. The official version has yet to be developed. My gentle caresses of her are habitual motion, instinctual, paternal. Did she come for something more. Is there a reason she took an earlier flight. Will I ever find that slip of paper. That note that might shed some insight. Limited to an internal investigation. The methodical police work. Slow hands, big lips. Something for the avant-garde. I do not call for help as I drown inside you. The water fills my nose and mouth. I inhale. The small bubbles surround. I convulse back and forth. I give in and things turn dark.

From: caliph8@sharia4ever.org

The existence of the universe is because of Allah. The absolute cause of all things is Allah. The reason for the existence of all things is Allah. The reason itself is Allah. He is the Most Perfect Possible Being. Oh Prophet, prepare the unbelievers for battle. If we are only twenty men we will defeat a thousand unbelievers because they do not have the understanding. Allah has made our task easy for we are the enlightened ones! The call to arms is near my friend. You are looking good! BTW send more pics. Nudes even...JK, no homo. #inshallah

She will certainly run from this. She might hide out in the foreign language syntax of her own confusion. Curving like her own lines into a comfort zone, driving down, sinking deep, deeper still. I can smell the heat of her exhaust, the dreamlike dissipation of the clouds, the running of the bulls. Are you still coming over tonight. The taste of zinc and oxide. The conversation could turn dark at any moment. The simple colors looped, regained—*jazzed*. Her frame lifeless and transparent through the filters. Storm clouds in the distance again. You could only see the sunlight behind the mist. She threatens to throw herself into the sea for the mystery of the tides, for the martyrdom, for the attention and longing. Unwavering, undeterred, she continues her way through the effervescent plain. I told you I could not be objective. Her kiss was smooth; it made me wonder who I was really kissing. Was it a memory. Was it a fantasy. Was she real. There was nothing left to taste. As if her well was dry.

You float, you drift, you transcend in slow motion. In and out of consciousness, in and out of wellbeing. We walked on in the wake of a stripped bare revolution of sorts. Sincerity has its moments. She danced and I watched. She put on a show. Her female parts varying shades of opium den red in jungle satin. It was our moment of eternity now and forever. Rendered in the abstract we paused for the feel. The origin of somewhere. Relegated to the moonlight seascape, nothing is withdrawn from the periphery. We close in on brief thoughts of self-preservation. These truths are sound and we hold them to be absolute and self-evident. Even this experience is not given as authentic. There are depths to be divided into and caves to spelunk. We forgot what we were fighting for. Self-interest has fed upon itself. We waste our insight on sleep and loathing. She cries out for the pain and for the guilt, a victim of the future, her guile catapulted into nether regions, upon neither religions nor vice. We are all just strangers here. Visiting for the long haul. I follow her shadow along the stucco wall. It is so accessible and retrievable. I drank from her empty cup, and then tried to fly. Everyone seemed to be touching her. If not for the technology then for what?

A smooth urban and urbane sophistication, something lost on earlier and present generations. Ruffled, the distant entrance in her eyes. Small discrete moments, translucent, transparent. There are no seams, she is geometrically perfect. Eliminates then redefines the path, skillful and artful she must change yet remain the same. In my dreams we are in love. In a span of moments she can close the books of time and clear the horizon of debris. Love, the continuing vortex, the heartache, the source of pain that for which they all fought. But it is more complicated than that. It always is. The penchant for an easier summation. For better friends. For fewer enemies. She is now carefully robed, a prophet of discipline.

Unaccustomed to the seasons I waited in hibernation. For what seemed an eternity. I was a terribly sick man. I rode the train alone in the rain and came to realize that functionality outweighed imperfection. Her flaws, the brushstrokes of god, subjected to an unintelligible yearning, she came to me in a moment then she was gone. A different impulse, a different venue. Apropos of nothing and nothing lost. Only a newly acquired disease to speak of. A souvenir not too soon to forget. There was an explosion of shadows, I could see her through the distance over loss. The mixed fortitude in the gratitude. She says she had been descending the staircase for hours when suddenly there was no floor to speak of. No trust, no wings to fly. Just empty closets and bare walls. A poorly built series of not so stable illusions. More evidence for the propaganda campaign. Once it had been so good. Under these particular circumstance the silence is simply indicative. Re-tune and try to love—bring back together the fringes of the wind. Who is sorry now. For all the ritual and revelation the structure of time and discovery is now. The timing never better. Take a deeper breath. Bewildered she sits in the chill of yesterday, far from the sample shock of tomorrow. A notion nevertheless, there is something in all of that. The pitches, the chirping, the timbre. Syrupy and feminine—*oh, so very feminine.* She loses me in conversation, a victim of primal etiquette and rustic decorum.

Where does your heart go when it is not in the room. She recalls vaguely the course of events, the moments of emptiness and despondence and desolation. The slight differences and variations and the lighter shades of blue. The indigo and pastel cobalt. I wish I had known you then. I wish that person had known you as you are now. The half memories and frayed remnants of scattered ash and unspeakable untruths. Pull me forward, draw me near. Hold the back of my head, my hair between your fingers, and press my face against you there. I will learn how to breathe. Relax. I love you. Dance with me. She whispers close to my ear, *there is no clock in the room.* Her flavor consumed me. The low fog sets a somber tone but the fake documents in my overnight bag give me needed hope. If you walk without stopping no one should suspect you. I follow her naked body as she climbs out into the distilled light. There is hesitance, but what could be next is more jarring. Or it could be nothing. Reality drips in and dissipates. Is this the end. The clouds over the rain, the crystallized chill, the forgotten thrill. Her unused and un-abused skin exposed to the elements, faded dashboard postcards to distorted memories. Today is about yesteryear yore and tribal folklore. Before the chemtrails, a time when the sun burned brighter in the sky and we were wetter from the rain. I want to fight my way underneath her cool shivering. Get in there and warm her up, from the inside, grassroots, organically. The love I prefer from her is unrequited and unreturned. Forgotten in the trailing haze of her own self-importance, her own shielded abundance of substance and fortified exile. I have heard all the voices and late night commands. I have doused all the flames. The forecast is looking promising.

Do not lose your trust…in the design, in the continuity, in the spirit, in the progressions. You have to get away, and get outside of it, free to roam. No more wars to fight. No battle left inside. Straight to the underground, a better existence. Off the radar maps. Off the infrastructural grids. As if we could remember the end of the serenade. When she collapsed on the worn out rug. The resurrection of sorts. The awakening of the sleeping exquisiteness. She whispered to me her portrait, a façade of the woman she had been, with a glimmer of prospect for the woman she was to become. I calculated her symmetry before I got lost in the curvature, at the wheel of a runaway car I did not know how to drive, disoriented and bemused.

We try to walk hand in hand through the distortion and the shadow of recovery. Smile, she said, overcome the recognizability of surprise and attack, the conceptual reality scattered at the edge, invisible yet extremely felt.

I watch her watch me make love to her. In the reflection of the stained relic mirror. Fuzzy yet remarkably accurate. Slow strokes in and out. Over and over again, with only the slightest of deviations. Methodical in our approach, logical in our delivery. She envelops me in a harmonious melody, holding tight my love comfortably and warmer still, like a new designer purse with its contents top secret. In the old days it would have been more chaotic and seemingly displaced, but now we arrive in silence. The naked embrace speaking volumes, the purity outweighing the tampering.

The zero grid of transparent space between dots, the legroom between pixels. The melting candle wax takes shape like a recessive gene, easily manipulated but with a mind of its own. The brilliance had outdone itself. Realism is the new crime. She was never on time and that seemed to validate her claims. As if her torso was wrapped in heavy explosives. Those eyes, on these sheets, no need for redaction. Do you smell the light—wafting across your hot skin, waving like an oasis in the distance. No basis for this theory, she probes and formulates for questions and answers when necessary. I clamor for her style. I pull the urge into her, the restraint from chic and the absence of polish. Lovely none the same. The intense frailty of perfection, of flawlessness cast in a different light. She takes on more of a continuation stylized in a different medium. I do not doubt her professed humanity. In a haze I circumnavigate her body, holding her outline in regard, wandering into nighttime spots of arousal, places where the limbs meet, locales that could use a cleaning. Standing here in the depths of time, a prisoner to her perfect time transport. She can take me anywhere and this pleases me immensely. I have forgotten the beginning and the end is unscripted. Unknown and potentially sorrowful. With her I can come full circle, like a tightrope walker, determined, focused, on task. I sensed my way through the invisible openings in her sides, pathways in her edges, a place for the search party to pause. The backlog underground all that remains, a veneer of forgotten fantasies, lost images in the back of the mind, cuddled in the folds of corner darkness. Crowded in the overflow, waiting for the collapse...the burn of the predominant paradigm. She speaks truth as dissonance, the inequity enumerated in equality. The silky segments and transitional moments defined by tire worn aging. The aesthetics or the outcome, a so called leap of faith binding the truth with the justification. A hard candor released with a soft voice through intensified moments, quadrated in pulsing rhythms, a target of wrongful aggression in a virtual sea of life. I was not sure if all of this would ever blow over, or if it was simply a dream state wonderment of cinematic screenplay proportions. I survey her cracks and fat folds, like a topographer at work, in the field, from the air, my feet in the dirt, boots on the ground. The surroundings, the drop down valleys, the rises in flesh and fat, the fullness and the flatlands. She murmurs in her sleep in hushed tones of forgotten dissolution. A better place at a better price. The competition is there, but her product is always superior, universal in any language, written to be forgotten. She shields her sight from the black light I scan across her naked body in the moonlit darkness of this autumn night. I taste the sea salt moisture under her arms, against her neck and between her legs. There is history here. It is in the corners, on the ceiling, watching over us, closely, intently. I craft sanctuary out of her place. I carve a low spot in her bed of flesh. A place to hibernate until I am stronger. A place to hide away until the coast is clear. She is clean for the ritual. I prepare to dive toward the ultimate depth. I will conquer nothing and replace her virtue with ease. We pause through the gentle steps, take shelter from the rain, resigned to our own humiliation. The aftertaste pushed forward, isometric and encoded, another burning sensation. A steep step back in time, a motion behind the curtain, a flair to the temperate curve of her spine. We can speed past our own mortality or lay down with feral animals and let nature take its course. We are better prepared, a campaign against the fall of modernity, against never wanting for nothing, against the cold lines of enlightened progress. This too shall pass, but not before I partake a bit more. I need memories of this and I will need them for some time to come. Quiet like moratorium splendor her moisture permeates in silence, her bliss apparent only to me, her clothing down around her ankles. I now remember the solitude, and the loneliness. It was not better then. I do not mention how we got here. She does not need to know. And I will explain the burns later.

We are almost done here. No one should ever have to respond to that particular aspiration. What proceeds is the virtue of love. Love as a remnant of deconstruction. Love as the undercurrent, below the abyss, through the nihilism, after the fall, the phoenix from the flavor. The sublime. I hung the sound of her on my wall. Through the prompts you arrive at the release. When you hear the doctor call out your name. I would try to entice her out to play. Sometimes I would just pull on her hair. The sounds of the machines in the low hums behind her. Clank, clank, clank, the slow dragging sound of her higher than high heels against the faux Brazilian cherry flooring. Call it a genre choice—the overdevelopment of a one person arena. She tells me that this is why I am like this. And I really should be trying harder. Be assertive, do not hesitate.

Reaction, cause and effect—affected by your culture of climate change and deranged sorting of misinformation. Are we not all just bystanders to the circumstance of location, location, location. Let's start from the beginning. Rewind, let me play this thing out again in my mind. Is this all because she is ovulating. "*I'll be nibbling on your cock in my dreams for fun*," she says to me. So thematically aware, non-dismissive to the ethereal and missive. Such distinctive forms of desire. Are you wanting for anything. Do we start near the end to get to the beginning. She sometimes gets by from being heavily medicated, her illusions a structured protection from the loss—the one emotion she is forced to feel. There is no escaping it. There is no exit door. You are trapped.

In particular I think of the tan lines, the varying and differing shades of brown to sunburnt red and the final dissolution of illusion and makeup. This is how I see you. I know how you see me, all of the blank and echoing statements that are best untold. Aside from her quivering, things appear on schedule. She tells me that the men in her dreams and dirty thoughts are all faceless. She is uncertain how they find their way to her but they are good with their hands as they are all legally blind. It is their bodies that matter most. Of course these are the fantasy men, not the men that she would really be with on practical terms. In her throes of self-delivered orgasm she pauses to reflect—a life lived fast, blurry nights in Tangier, sex with other women, the taste of pussy, the smell of cock, recreational drug abuse, the mind games, the psychodramas, the visits to the hospitals. It is not all bad, nor bad girl behavior, she reminds me. Her bare stomach glistening in the sun like prime waterfront property, the low angled pitch from her belly to her crotch, the crest fallen terrain of her jutting hip bones to the center of gravity, the end of public access, the invisible badlands borderline just above her tightly manicured pubic line. Beads of sweat and opened pores, tiny specks of black pollution dust embedded between apertures. This is what I fixate on while my tongue burrows deeper, spreading her wider, aching to reach further inward, to take on just a little more length, to get just slightly more immersed and involved. My electric taste buds buried against the walls of her shimmering vagina. If this is not propaganda then I do not know what is. Satisfaction in the narrow creases of her undoing, of razor burned skin and rounded orbital love. In my daydreams I penetrate you with unthinking and an unflinching flash, my sword hot through your flesh, my dagger buried, serrated, spent, bleeding out, exhausted and life threatening.

It was too easy, too smooth, too quick. I should have known better, I should have refrained. The colors dissolve when I close my eyes. I fight the counter insurgency, I aid in the economic collapse. I no longer attempt to mitigate whatever physical or psychological damage I may have caused, or been party to. The struggle will continue. The publications will continue to print. The airtime will not cease. It was all built for luxury, but now I tell you it is all about comfort. And the ramifications. I may have conquered this woman, on this night only, for a fleeting moment she was mine, when her labia was pinched between my teeth, when her pubic hair was entwined with my nose hair, when my tongue's tip was pressed against her clitoris. Even if only transitory and short-lived I still conquered—it could have been a country, it could have been a mountain, or a part of the sea, a colony taken back, but it was her, spread before me, an extension of my mouth, a prosthetic device, a puppet without the strings.

The trachea shave reduces the cartilage in the throat to make the shape and profile more feminine. Usually we perform this under local anesthesia and as an outpatient procedure. Go ahead and touch your throat. You will feel several horizontal ridges of cartilage there. Feel for the V-shaped protrusion of the cartilage. That is what we will reduce. We will begin by cutting a horizontal incision in the crease of the skin on the throat, then the vertical muscles in the throat will be separated to expose the cartilage. That is what will be shaved off. Targeting the notch at the top of the V. If you were younger it would be like slicing into refrigerated butter, but at your age it is much harder material. Using a scalpel, rongeurs, nippers, and a burror grinder, the deep cervical fascia will be incised and opened. The middle cervical fascia will be divided vertically. The sternothyroid and thyrohyoid muscles will be retraced laterally to expose the thyroid cartilage. The perichondrium will be incised on the superior rim of the thyroid. Then the perichondrium on the outside and the inside of the laminae will be elevated. The outwardly rolled superior notch will be obliquely excised. The two periochondrial flaps will be sutured together with dexon 5-0. Hematosis is made with electrocautery. We will add some light compressive dressing on the wound. The cartilage will have the consistency of a bar of soap. Our main concern at this point is to keep your voice the same. We don't want to shave off too much so that it affects your vocal chords and compromises the stability of your windpipes. What will remain for a week or so is a ropy scar with internal stitches that will have a small loop sticking on the end of the suture so that when you are healed we will simply pull out the stitches. The remaining raised scar will be completely unnoticeable after a few more days. You can cover it with face powder if you are feeling subconscious or insecure. If anyone asks what happened you can say you had thyroid surgery, they won't know the difference. You will need to rest your voice. You may experience a lowering of pitch, raspiness, and hoarseness. The more cartilage removed the greater the risk. You may experience pain and difficulty swallowing. It's none of my business but if you perform oral sex on men you may want to hold off while in recovery. You will need to avoid electrolysis immediately around the incision. Vitamin E oil will help with the healing of the scar. Your neck will be as flat as Lindsey Lohan's ass. Any questions?

From: caliph8@sharia4ever.org

When God created the world, He also created ten character types: faith, honor, courage, rebellion, pride, hypocrisy, riches, poverty, humility, and misery. Faith said I will accompany you. Honor and courage said I am right by your side. Rebellion said I am proud of you. Hypocrisy and riches said the West is where I reside.

Poverty and humility said they will rise up soon enough. Misery said I shall go into the desert and wait for the call to Paradise. You see, my friend, it is all here for us and for our making! The comfort in His creations that abound. Your pics just get better, so happy looking and relaxed. How you been? KK, bye for now... #inshallah

The admissions are numerous, the elation incalculable. The semblances and resemblances furthermore daunting and confusing. The doorbell rings as we argue across the room, my true whereabouts a mystery. Her crazed attributes something out of a Peruvian empire setting. Machu Picchu swarming with people...when they thrived, before the germs and the unprotected sex with Europeans. Unprotected sex with Europeans? Some things never change. The tap on the single pane window, the tear in the new luggage, the dreamlike homecoming. The impetus on you, forever on you, undying. Assume the position and it should be okay. Let me eat you like a buffet, do not be frightened by the stench, try not to focus on any one thing, refrain from reproach, play croquet in the park, your mind a busy Kasbah, your vagina as globetrotter, due to the military depletion…the telecommunications are failing, the guards are getting more torturous, her breasts appear more mature, the fascination in the squeals, the cleverness in the vindictiveness. As far as women are celebrated she is a keeper. Her wingspan in direct correlation with her height; the space between her eyes the exact size of a single eye; the ends of her mouth in vertical harmony with the center of her pupils. An asymmetrical jewel. With the box. With a minimum of training and a mere haphazard happenstance she assumed her own distinct right of entry...she lost her escorts, she blended in with the crowd, ditched the head scarf, her hair fell to her bony shoulders. If her magnificence were any brighter there would be more collective undoing and shame. This is all about control, of course. And jurisdiction. Was it a bad idea? Did it advance the cause? Were you hung out to dry? Did you like feeling so exposed? Espoused by your flailing ideas? Your skin-toned negligee pinned to the clothesline, the hot breeze blowing, the bewilderment in your limelight, the revelation too much, not enough, rewarding, sublime, painful, resuscitating, drowning you in your quandary, another day another sticky situation, remind me why I am here, plant another tree for prosperity, you can only go so far before you will need rest, it begins with an idea, and ends with detainment...look how far they have come, the outcome of your life is best seen when you are old, that sort of thing, you can only go so far as you can persuade, open your legs for a feeding, my skeletons are locked in the closet, forgiveness is easier attained than permission, if you dwell in the past it will cost you in the present, a drowning woman will grab for the short hairs, would you blame her, let your fear melt in the sunshine, she always felt judged by the company she kept, I want to be the first at your feast, it is not often that I have the pleasure of giving a medical exam so be happy that you are the one, did you have your guardian sign the waiver, are you ready for it, do you need a little more time, always make sure that any medical professional that is going to touch you washes thoroughly with soap, this is the best way to avoid staph infections and other unnecessary ills, like toxic shock syndrome or endocarditis, remain where you are, I don't think you will need your sister to help, please turn on your side, it was good you removed your underwear, that makes it much easier, I could go on and on about prevention but you truly do seem fine, you're ready for it, you are not alone here, no abnormal leakage or irregularly colored discharge, don't try to cover it, remember, *I am a professional*, you can trust me, there is no reason to resist, I am also a gentleman, you do possess remarkably good qualities in several departments, if only I could be for you what nobody else could be for you...strong, honorable, decent, noble and gallant, I could go on and on here, we all may have two legs but we still fall sometimes, if needed I would ask for your forgiveness, but likely it would never get to that, there is no reason for us to lose time for a false cause, I notice you chew your nails, is there a reason, don't waste energy on the irreducible, think: *your enemies will one day all be slain*, I will need to take a photo now, this is purely to document progress, it has to do with potential side effects, it is for your own good, plus I am required to do this by my oaths to the profession, there we go, all done, you are finished, do you have any questions…so it goes, not too far-fetched and still within the realm of possibilities, *oh the possibilities*, I can be so flagrant and brazen, one day it may all catch up to me, they may find the things I hid, or interview my other lady friends, they may try to paint a picture of me, to formulate a profile and connect the dots. They can try.

As we fall in love, a high free fall, an even deeper nose dive. Perhaps we can just agree to call it desire. Yours, mine, ours. I want to explore your hush-hush crawl space. At your earliest convenience. It would be the best way to get to know one another. It is dark and quiet and I could go there sometimes to meditate or make needed repairs. I could install a camera, but then all I would do is watch you. Twenty-four seven three sixty five. My time would be lost, I would no longer do my chores, have free time, take care of myself physically and mentally. But I would be entertained. I would throw it all away for you. There are no restrictions in place. What confines and limitations? This is our own private precinct, where the rules are limited and are adjudicated by us alone. We draw the lines where the children play and where the sound of the music box ends. The border town at the edge of the frequencies. Uncovered you radiate and emit the glow of an emir's concubine, void of mistakes and flaws, your shape better viewed sideways, nothing is lost, your intrinsic beauty more than cultural, your grandeur life threatening under the right circumstances, the rhythm of your heart a slow walk through the desert heat, the calm on your vaginal wall, the peace of having you inside my mouth, if only a small piece of you...I pluck your fringe pubic with a causal roman empire flare, I hope it does not hurt, let me know and I will change positioning, I could survive off your flesh, a virtual cannibal, when finished I could embalm you, fix you permanent for all time, not a mere trophy but more of a prized decoration, but I am off topic now, you may be getting confused, disoriented, the ether will do that when administered in high doses, and let's not forget the Tranxene you took earlier, that takes two to three hours to work, and more than eight to wear off, there is a reason the pharmacists warn you about the dangers of driving and alcohol when taking this, especially sixty milligrams, but you are a big girl, you can handle more than the recommended dosage. Not BBW. Don't take it as an insult. You just are a big woman with curves where they count.

From: caliph8@sharia4ever.org

You see my friend, we will inflict damage on our missions here on Earth, but we must take absolute comfort in knowing that the punishment God will bring to the non-believers will be 1,000 times worse than anything we can inflict. Imagine 9/11 times 1,000...nice image, no? The best part is YOU will not suffer for eternity for these sinners because THEY are the ignorant ones, not you*! The Wrath of God will show no mercy. The truth has been revealed to you before His knife connects with the flesh. Merry Christmas bitches! #inshallah*

Anything that is any good is going to be hated by everybody who has a say. Dependability is knowing that this is where you are going to sit tomorrow and the next day. And that the first instructions will not require follow-ups. That your present focus is creating your regrets. Desire's proof is in the pursuit and sometimes you have to do what you hate to get what you love. If you respect her she will come. Her diligence is in the attention she puts forth. This is not as bad as it appears. Trust me, there's been worse. Her behavior permitted is her behavior repeated. Her focus determines her feelings. The proof of her loyalty is her unwillingness to betray. All the waves of yesterday's naughtiness splashed upon the shores of today, unrelenting. No one was better off than her. Most were much worse off. As if they were having difficulty breathing, as if they had been poisoned. Botulism, sedative-hypnotic, atropine, methanol, arsenic trioxide, Fowler's solution, beryllium, hydrogen sulfide, pesticides, and the like. In all of these instances all had been rescued. There was either an antidote or simply the subject was overly exhausted and the symptoms were understandably misdiagnosed as poisoning. It usually was the fattest of the lot. The ones with undiagnosed obstructive sleep apnea, the ones with enlarged hearts, borderline pulmonary embolisms, urinary incontinence, social stigmatization, gout, heartburn, liver disease, and so on.

Her words reverberated in the air long after she spoke them. The descriptions and excuses comical and ridiculous. The pause was welcome and none too soon. This is when I stared meditatively at the ceiling. Acting as if I was deep in thought, in trance, pensive and preoccupied, but I was not. I was simply trying to escape the embarrassment. You see, sometimes indifference is useful. I put on that I was on the edge of tears, with a white face, a look of shock, a glare of awestruck bewilderment. How could it have come to this. What does it matter. It is all just inside my head. Do you hear the wolves' voices. The full moon light. Can you feel the airwaves, the wireless digital cable transmission. Sorry, try your password again. The soundtrack an ensemble of hits, a catalogue of mischievous jewels, music to fall asleep to, music to fuck to. Survival is an option. The flip side is peace and quiet and repose. A respite from the noise and clatter.

Warming my hands in Pavlovian anticipation. She is there off in the fluorescent distance wearing white see through slacks, revealing a steeply cut white thong with an oblong label tag. I am getting lazy now. But it is natural and inglorious. There is a great deal from such a small piece of cotton. The forlorn of the loin. This is not the end but the beginning. There is no time better than now. For that matter there is no time other than now that matters. Back to the deal. I spy her bra strap from behind. Stretched white elastic pressed firmly against her back and shoulder fat. She is tan so the white juxtaposition is added fodder. This is the type of bra that clasps in the back. I do not mind, nor should I. Clasp in the front and when she takes it off there is a slow revelation, inside outward, of her cleavage, then the nipples, then the fall and subsequent playful bounce and play. Unhook from the back and you will see the breasts almost spring up and recoil outward as if freed from a straightjacket's confines, alert, happy to feel the room's air, you behold them more suddenly, the revelation in an instant. Either will do. Equally gratifying none the same. Size 38 C. This outfit a deliberate ploy for attention, a maneuver for interest, a scheme to notice. If she had wanted to taunt she would have gone without panties, or had a misplaced nipple ride above the top line cut of her bra, something amiss but impossible to avoid. She is too much in order. Perhaps later, but if it happens then it could very well be an accident, a ruffle in the day, a haggard slip on her part because of the time spent sitting. Maybe that will be calculated into her ploy—she will nipple slip it, or wet her pants with mild incontinence, or remove her thong completely, an outline of dark pubic hair exposed, a landing strip, a Hitler stache above the pubis majora, or a freshly placed maxi pad front and center, something anew that would then get my attention. It would be clever and teasing. She would make me proud. I would be vexed and the game would be on.

I see the way you look at me. I think I have a pretty good idea of what is going on behind those gorgeous eyes of yours. I know why you dress so provocatively. You are a tease anyway but when you have a subject or theme and then an undivided audience you thrive. You blossom. You are radiant. With that confused coworker look, the gleaming eyes, the gaze as if you had spent too much time in front of the computer screen but in reality your mind has run wild and you are lost in blurring thoughts and imagery of our hot skin excreting salty seawater sweat, I tickle you with my chest hair, you cradle your tilted head against my neck, I snack on your earlobe, I lick dried wax from your inner ear, I taste the alkaline on your faux gold hoops, I lick the blush off of your upper cheek, I press my flattened tongue lengthwise along the length of your nose, my taste buds covering your open pores, I notice the cracked filling on your first molar, tooth number 4 lower left, the swollen gum line along the top of your front teeth, the periodontitis in its early stages, bone loss or just poor hygiene, no halitosis; your trimmed nose hair, your laugh line wrinkles deeper and more apparent; what anti-aging cream you use, if it is Biotherm or Zirh or another brand for which I am not familiar, is Botox your backup plan, do you do an alpha hydroxide acid peel from time to time. I focus in on the crumbling black dust of your mascara, is it 24 hour mascara, is it liquid or cake form, was it applied with rayon or nylon, you have applied it to the top eyelashes only for a heavy lidded look, could I suggest lower lash only for a wider eye look, is it waterproof.

The simultaneous destruction and liberation overcome me, I am left alone without the help of others, to fight the local resistance. I cannot be held accountable any more. It is the subtle give and take that has become problematic. Everything before seemed all about preventative measures. That is no longer the case. Like a straight twelve hours of sleep. Like the relaxing effects of fellatio to completion. I can see it now: *someday has arrived.* I am drawn into her motion by the slow moon tides. A failed addiction, a disappointing craving, a botched infatuation. I must level with myself as I will not be too happy with the outcome. Only the task, the struggle, the fight and pre-surrender bliss of not knowing, of ignorance, of denial, of first morning light...the humming, genitalia, diaspora, the mind games, psychodrama and babble, the first born, glory onto myself, memories of the deceased, cordial embraces, the pleasure of your conversation, when tomorrow becomes yesterday, the soap opera being played out, the passion untwisted, the scar on your knee, the rug burns, the carpet particles too small to see with the human eye, trapped and smashed, one with your skin...a stroll along the edge of insanity, you must resist the urge to rewrite history, time is a circle, nothing more to it, and then there are the reflections, of her in the hours of darkness, of her at first light, of her in a naked and vulnerable position, of her dressed for dinner out, of her defenseless and ill, of her under a fluorescent glow…within these circumstances she is right, right to not succumb, right to not yield, right to not touch herself in ways that will transpire fleeting blood flow emotions, one on one confessionals, scary blood work results and the like.

If I could fly backward into yesterday, even further still. I am no longer connected to my past, to where I once was. Where there was a plenitude of grace now is a dark shadow, a void waiting to be filled yet comfortable in its own awkwardness of incompleteness and deficiency. And I am considered one of the successful ones. From time to time it did feel right, that what I did was the best thing to do. Still I move on, I rotate, I advance and find myself back here again. I have tried to water my life yet still failed. The pain is miserable and wretched. To fail is to succeed, I try to console myself. Every struggle brings growth and healing. A depression overcomes me and I feel only her gloom and hopelessness for a bleak future of meaninglessness and insignificance. I know better than that but still I lay down on the dark and wet concrete and give in to the victimhood, hoping for a hand up, knowing that even if it came I might want to pass some time here. To know pleasure is to be familiar with pain, to know glory is to know tedium. I will persevere and learn, I will hurt and tear and cry and heal and extend for new time, lost at a quickened pace, it is fleeting and there is no recapture, it has disappeared and will remain gone. *Oh, to be a successful one.* My ambitions have been misled and are now mislaid. These are the politics of destiny. This is darker than jealousy, it is love without trust, not love for another but for yourself, it is encapsulated and the release date is unknown. The ultimate lesson of self-delusion and unbound love not too soon forgotten. I have lesser understandings of only a handful of things. This is a concept term: *understanding*. A brain pattern or lack thereof. Best explained through vicarious living and showtime. Perceived information, right or wrong, correct or incorrect, I am vulnerable to the environment, a victim to the neurochemistry, immovable by the genetics. At any one moment I could claim bouts of delirium, schizophrenia, mood disorders, anxiety, Munchausen's syndrome, delusional disorder, anorexia nervosa (for reasons other than weight loss), gender identity disorder, adjustment disorders, a Messianic complex, somatization disorder, transient ischemic attacks, potential neoplasms, encephalopathy, dyslexia, hemiballismus and hypersomnia. Ideas written in pencil on the back of a receipt, a venerable what-not-to-do list.

From: caliph8@sharia4ever.org

My friend, I want you to know more about me. I have a certain imagination. I love fine words for their own sake, and poetry the most of all the arts. I love heroic gestures and see my own deeds as befitting the noblest of occasions. I see myself as an important link in a chain of cause and consequence. My vision of the world has a hardness of outline. It is a vision in black and white. Loyalty to friends (you), family and tribe (you, again). My ethical beliefs exalt heroic virtues. I think this is why I like you so much. And likewise I believe your attraction to me is from the same vein. I hope I haven't said too much, LOL! #inshallah

We weep warm tears of pain. We suffer like the best of them. We take it head on, a dance into the flames. This is before the infusion of mistrust and loyalty. Before the doubt and suspicions. Glorified in the remembrances, brilliant in the reminiscences. She could lead her own empire, a grand duchess on the throne, a revolutionary with scary cleavage. A patient woman scorned and out for slow revenge. Yet calm and balanced, like the earth to the moon. I press her chest against mine, the soft billowing flesh a reminder of what is eternally important. She tells me that she wanted to fall. I tell her that this love is now focused. There is no right or wrong. There is no misplaced word or feeling. You can do no misdeeds, I remind her. You either play the game or at least pretend to play it. Her breasts are spread wide against my upper body, their circumference ample, their substance overflowing. Treasures only discovered whilst being acknowledged. I am in the throes of elation, a panicked frenzy, with the thought of her hard nipples in my mouth. I am resigned to a deferential kneeling at her lap, a thirsty traveler at her fountain to drink, a famished vagabond there to eat from her banquet of undoing. I know full well that I had been forewarned. But this is a new kind of rejection, a new kind of abandonment, a new kind of desertion. I inhale her soft smells and am inebriated by the chemical release. Endorphins, opioids, peptides, opiates, hormones, analgesia...loose into the room's conditioned and confined air. Her long hair obscures her privileged parts, access is restricted to only the extremely fortunate, and even then on seldom occasions.

I cannot recall her name. I become transfixed by the darkened mole on her upper thigh. Is it malignant or benign. Has it grown since the last checkup. Should I measure it now. Should I bring it up in conversation. Does she even know it is there. I want to lick it. I want to pinch it between my front teeth. Like a pimple ready to burst its puss into my mouth. A miniature version of her cumming, in silence or out loud, gushing with juice. I bookmark this for later reflection. You can do whatever you see fit, she tells me, opening her legs. I am confused by the eagerness and welcome gesture, but focused nonethesame, ready for whatever the unraveling moments bring me, whatever positioning seems best. The anticipation and hope, the long days and nights of border patrol and reconnaissance, a slow adaptation to your new surroundings...a protracted response to not knowing any better. I tell you this now: *try to get it over with as quickly as possible*. Even though it seems like heaven. And please do not be nervous. Nobody is here to judge you. The plan is to have no plan. It should not involve anything beyond an untreated appreciation of her. Her scale is undeniable. Her confidence not lacking for anything. She is elusive yet ubiquitous. At this point I do not know what to say. Is it simply that I have forgotten or did I readjust, fail...left mired in my own malfunction? I do not study for the knowledge. I do not read for the information. I do not gaze for the sake of appreciation. Everyone here gets a prize. I want to take it to the streets, expose myself for the violent rebellion within, open to all, my honesty bleeding onto the floor, the puddles of blood proof that I am still me, and that tending to others' wounds left me partially whole. I swallow and know it should soon be over. This is not transitional change. I am homesick for the intrigue. Walking in from the welcome, toward the containment. I watch the reflection in blue and green. I attain to live in the past and lick behind her earlobes and the other salty regions. The nether regions, the forbidden zones. I behold her through the bullet-proof Plexiglas. A prisoner with a visitor. Locked up, out of touch, imprisoned by my own demise, a security guard gone rogue, I have the key but I do not use it, I have the gun but I do not pull the trigger.

There are lucid moments of glorified eminence and brilliance. Times best left for the deceased, times better sealed up and stashed away, times that explode. We cordially shake hands but I know deep down that is not the end of it. I find no more pleasure in your conversation. It all seems like yesterday or further back in the past, in my memory line, in my recollection of things best left alone. I was at first disconcerted with myself and with my conduct and frame of mind. There were additional forces, of course, and the obligatory apprehension, like the returning sea tide or baby chatter. I knew I was being played. But I did not know if it was her or myself that was doing the playing. I saw the passion wasted figure, a tragic one at times, especially when I saw the scars. How dare you bring this up now. Watch what I do. Such concession is abnormal, but necessary nonethesame. I admire a good fight, a person willing to take their blows, but sometimes succumbing is the only way out. Someone has to win. There always needs to be a victor. There is not much left out there anymore. Anything is quite possible at this juncture.

The rise and fall of the man.

The emergence and tumble of one of God's children.

Do it for the love, not the money.

Faster still, she said. Time and time again, it was her mantra. I was not too concerned but I was careful. Careful not to let these things get to her head, careful not to let it get too out of control, careful to keep it from the point of no return. Her pants were soiled and the stain lingered, only slightly faded by the three consecutive warm-water washings. Again, this is what the police report read. I am paraphrasing as to not be accused of plagiarism. But then again what could they have known about the actual event. It is all just conjecture on their part. A consensus among the collective reconstruction. Applied to and by theories from textbooks, other crime scenes, interviews with killers, forensics, etc. What can definitely be surmised from the evidence is that the visit was quick. Her smell lives on. Her organs eternalized in jars of formaldehyde. The memories of her parted lips against my lips, forever burned to my mind's hard drive. The taste of her folds, alive, perspiring, giving juice, shedding invisible skin. She will live on. In her own way. In her own indelible legacy. I will forever hear her soft voice, her cooing in the night, her laugh. Her moans. The humanity in her lingering and enduring fiber. Her blood stains in the grout lines. The place where her head met the ceramic tile. I feel like I rescued her, only to abandon her in a time of need. Her most precious hours of destitution. But all of this is now just an afterthought. Should have. Would have, could have.

The devices were everywhere. They permeated the room. Much like the noise and distortion rumbling and bouncing within my mind. At times there was that wondrous feeling, that tinged euphoria. That *je ne sais quoi* appeal to things. But then again it was just another aspect of the investigation. And again there should be nothing to bury. At least that is the hope. What do you see when you look down into the water. There are portions that suffer and portions that only suffer from the execrable translation. There still remained only one thing that I did not like. And it only took short seconds-long intervals to elapse. To start again, to start anew. This is when I would leave her to figure it out on her own. I would be a fool not to leave you to your gold. And with that I swiftly departed, at least emotionally. Left to her own devices to consider her own case. So grim she had become that it was her solitude left to survive and/or die.

Then there was a silence. But that too seemed menacing. If she was any nearer I would be able to smell her. It was different when she menstruated. On the short days just before. I could tell it was coming on by the imminent rage. Careful now, she is getting closer. The birds are in flight. She did seem happy to see me. But this pleasant frame of mind is just an illusion. It is reluctantly produced for the benefit of sanity. I never did consider myself shy. I assure you that I can handle this too. Cursing was at a minimum. This is when I thought about sick leave. And about acting as if I had terminal cancer.

For the attention and for the time off. Maybe for the sympathy blow job, if that still exists. I would have to lose weight. I would have to lose my tan. I would have to recover at one point. There would be new terminology to learn. There would be elaborate stories needed to be fabricated: chemo treatments, radiation, medicine, doctors, insurance, fundraisers, wheelchairs, valet parking.

From: caliph8@sharia4ever.org

We are floating, swimming in the feeling that we are about to enter eternity. We have no doubts. We have made an oath on the Qu'ran, in the presence of Allah...a promise not to waver. This pledge of jihad is called bayt al-ridwan, *after the garden in Paradise that is reserved for the Prophets and Martyrs. I know there are many ways to do jihad but this, my friend, is the sweetest. Muhammad once said, "I brandished a sword and its edge broke off...I brandished it a second time and it became again the best of what it had been." You see my friend, all martyrdom operations, if done for Allah's sake, end with the most glorious entry into Paradise! Are you ready for what awaits us my friend? #inshallah*

She is special and unduplicatable, an oasis in the distance. There is no exchange value. She is a transient image moment. She is cut in black. She is there, alive...pull up, forward, back, backside, from behind, her ass there upward and upright, spread wide, wider still. The protocols have been blown wide open. These are the spectacles of everyday life. There remains the question of public sex acts and the last day of the month. All of the tropical oils and her feminine esthetics. I am trapped in recall. I am the blurry, she is the clean. Dizzy, I fall down again and chew on her earlobe for the sake of legacy. The reasons are threefold, often fourfold. She is part of a dream, a perfect dream for me. I imagine her black bikini bottoms pushed to the side, her bent over in the bush, her knees against the fallen eucalyptus leaves, her tan lines currently red but brown tomorrow. We are alone in our own world, the outside tuned way out, we hump to the rhythm of our own drums, we exist below the tempo. There will be nothing controversial about this outcome. We will be undone and it will be noted. I feel her now more than ever. She pushes back at me, her ebbing wave currents, the river's overflowing banks. I ride the small waves in the warm desert air. In harmony, a feign for restraint, she has mastered all savoir faire. She puts a new spin on words that have yet to be invented. These are the softer melodramatic undertones that hush the mind and pacify the heart. In throes of rapid response, her widened and spread ass a shadow looking for sun. She is so very wet there. Far from sated, yet close to unruffled. This is the unfiltered view of her that not many see but it is the truest definition of her, her essence bared bare for me, for the invited, for the select few, for the initiated. There is no subplot here. Nor a waning religious cult. This is truth and veracity on full glorious display. Her hips a throwback to a simpler time. A time when my mind did not race, a time when my heart did not hurt, a time when those that I miss now were there for me.

I disregard the imperfections, though few, like the mole on the upper left, or the ass acne near her crevasse, or the stretch mark up near her waist, or the sand that lingers along the lower fold of her right ass cheek. I am willing to overlook it all since she is willing to display—unfettered, uninhibited, abandoned and candid. She is wrapped around me tight in the sunlight, my nethers buried in a darkened bunker of soft folds and even softer fur. Her lips a warm ocean which I allow to drown me. Take me out to sea, rob me of my direction, get me lost so I can be found. I would advocate colonization if it meant frolicking like this with the natives. I will not be taken by surprise nor will I miss one moment of the unfolding action. I summon her mouth to mine. It is death and rebirth with each plunging of her tongue into my cavity, my teeth pressing firmly against her upper lip, the contact a hallucination of saccharine ambitions. Her saliva the taste of nihilism, the abyss on the horizon, the chasm of one. Her nipples pressed between my fingers. My pubic hair entwined with hers. Undistinguished words of sounds and moans echoed back and forth. Her knees weak. Her kneecaps with small cuts from the debris on the ground. Her bottom covered in her own cum. The soles of her feet black from the asphalt trail. Her hands dirty, her nails full of fallen skin, pussy juice, juice from the papaya she ate at lunch, beach sand, Purell, fructose syrup from the soda she couldn't finish, her own feces from when she used the public toilet. We lock stares and this is when I pull her hard against me, and hold her tighter still, and come as deep inside of her as I can. We had discussed that when I was ready she would take me in her mouth. But that is not what happened. She wanted me to remain inside of her, there. To utter the completion.

She drops into the carefree, unrelenting as she stokes the fuel of a familiar fire. We come together through clenched jaws. A hibernation coming out of sorts. We circle the runways then slowly land on top of these emotions. Exhaled relaxation, concentrated focus, on you, on me. I warm my throat with your discharge. This mythic age of an enduring epoch is redefined with new ways, new means, new adventures, new taboos. What we have is a classic relationship, in a traditional sense. We howl like wild animals behind the muted echoes of hands over mouths, of tongues buried in wet flesh. I may not be able to talk but I can still breathe. The red lines of indentation, where the tight elastic of her too small panties pulled snug for the last twelve hours. Her flesh pink, untouched by the harmful rays of the sun, or by bad genetics. Her skin pure and supple, like summer rain and velvet cushioning. We twirl our tongues under the dream night sky as if we did not care where the incident took place, or the eventual outcome, the cause and effect, the irreparable repercussions, the consequences, dire or magnificent. With each breath of air I am cast anew. These are the times and this is the place. What was once pornographic is now only art, that for which the beholder beholds. Beholden I submit to the simplicity, to the cause and to the effect. Her tits are milky, pale, a sprinkling of blue veins. Breastfeeder large. A fullness unmatched. Nipples simple but conglomerates in their own right, a cartel if you will. Darker than expected, a pleasant surprise for the uninitiated. Firm and erect as if the room were cold. My eyes curve with their shape. A sublime rendition of full breast fat in profile, of how the female breast should look, how it could not look any better. I collapse into her touch. It will be impossible to say goodbye to this moment. I navigate her manicured plains. I lick her playground pallet of love. Fading faint recollections of the taste of others', the similarities, the dissimilarities. The bad ones, the medium ones. This is of the best kind. Her looks match her taste. I could identify her only by her flavor. She mutters under her breath. She was talking to me. It was to herself, a reaffirmation, a solitary mind game, psychoanalytical discourse. Her angles are my despair. Back and forth, forward, backward, backside, neckline, the sweat between the cracks and the folds, and the drying out on the lips, the bones and muscles under her hips. The seldom lone hair. I want to crawl underneath her skin. I want to go ever deeper inside. I want to inhabit her. I want to become her. I want to fall into her perfection.

A stare into her eyes...a crystal palace glitter, light blue hues, the sublime over achievement. The wattage, the tonnage, the flowage. Texture free, like the best linens. She is so well adjusted, so well heeled, so one step out of the mire. She defies gravity in many ways, beyond clichés and melodramatics. Her upward pointed nose, her upward pointed breasts, her upward pointed nipples, slight yet very there, hiding on display under the nylon top. Her clothing a tapestry draped over a yet-to-be unveiled bronze lifelike statue, without wax (*sincerely*). There is nothing mediocre about the taste on her tongue. In the midst of a series of impromptu lulls, try not to forget what it is that you are fighting for. Her mood enhances colors of magenta and rouge when we press firmly against one another. This must be the place, a place weary of the lies and the illusions, of the shams and the fabrications. A place where I will remain misunderstood, world weary and world wise. A place where I can imagine her just so, a picture perfect nude body bent slightly forward over the wrought iron railing, exposing just enough danger to intrigue and/or mortify. I want to eat her cake. I want to fuck royalty. I want to break this compass that guides me errantly and off track. Break my rib, dig my grave, cleanse my mind with sleep. It is yours not just mine. Help me get the others out while there still is a chance. But not until after a few more groans.

Your honeysuckle flavor still lingers on my tongue. A reminder of what has been, what has gone, what will stay with me in my dark days, in my darker thoughts. I will remember you like that. Honey's suckle. There could be no better biological method for arousal, for memory and for reminiscence. The pressures on the periphery, the yellow drip stain in your panties, the infection, the cure, the limits of vulgarity and charm, the skills and techniques, the lint in your navel, that time in the toilet, the tan lines, the soft lines, your cheeks big and small, the crust in your ears, on your scalp, under your nails...all for which I eat like wartime shrapnel.

On the horizon I spy a break in the infinite texture. A mushroom cloud of sex and breath. I walk barefoot across the fire now. Everything is anything. The pathogens underneath us. She pervades my thoughts. She seeps into everything I do. She crawls slowly across my mind, traversing my dreams, lingering in my nightmares. Holding onto every last entanglement. Like a fraudulent life insurance policy. Like the pre-enjoyment of a passing kiss. Or a daylong nap with wet dreams of her there waking you with her hot mouth stroking your semi hard cock. Like food sickness or perjury. The glimpse of the chambermaid half dressed, her reflection through several mirrors. Her breast gravity flattened against her rib cage torso. The dying tundra animal and the disco lights in my mind, unable to turn off. Like when she wore the black cape, just the cape, her brown bush coiffed up and outward, untamed like a Victorian madam. Like when she told me to put away the money. *This one is on the house.* The time I chose the darkness over the light. She consumes me nonethesame. Unfair, daft, nonlinear, her rumble penetrated my everything and last fading essence, of being, of sleep, of deprivation and cause. With her, there is no common ground, nor common law. Nor common sensibilities and senses of the mind, only of the body politic that rules with each throbbing pulse of the tender slice of fruit between her legs. Within the guidelines you have some idea of what is coming next but on the whole the results are unexpected. Call it trifle enthusiasm but I am a simple man. Soon she will fold into my history, thread against thread, skin upon skin, electrons pulsating through the mind waves and the microwaves of a semi-forgotten existence, a mind frame from a simpler time of elapsed innocence. But I assure you I am not finished here. Do you feel me now. Do you feel my fluids pouring into you like sweltering molten metals into the form. Pinch, suck, pinch, suck. Your body a carcass in my mouth. The wounded prey, the hungry predator. I look through the nothingness and it is only her that I behold. Save the occasional intrusion, I wish this would never stop. That there would be no end to this perpetual and invited nightmare of vibrating stares and rubbing down flesh to the point that you can no longer feel the pleasure, the point where the pain overcomes and succeeds.

All told we tread water through our dreams and love. We wrap the pain with the glee. It all becomes one brief raw meaning of rescue, of recovery, of eclipse and relapse. She always brings her sex and her fashion. And she always liked to use her own equipment. The strategies were left to the analytics. The policies to the politicians. We were trained and we were trained well. Her tongue would be idle no more. Outside the helicopters waited her arrival. She had the stuff of illusion, of artifice and lure. Her breasts seemed real but were too close to perfection. Same for the tan, the hairline, her hips, legs, nails, eyebrows. Right this way, with every new idea comes a new paranoia. The resolutions no longer mattered. I back track, I digress, I investigate. She is a mere contribution to the whole of consciousness, awareness and responsiveness. She melts into my periphery, fading to a lost silhouette in the blaze. Red on red. She is the source of communication and this conscious effort at perpetual rebellion. A regurgitation of light and substance. She holds my eyes. I do not have to breath to inhale her toxins. The smile behind the mask of irony, a revelation of the scarring of yesterday's malaise and abandoned endeavors at chivalry. Allow the parallel motion to drop into place. It was here under her spell that everything became disjointed. It is now that it all fell apart. It has become brighter and the shadows have become unfamiliar. It was crusade each time I went for her. A revolution of sorts, the winner and loser undefined or one in the same.

The shape of the cheek bones, essentially the maxilla and zygomatic arch, are the most important determinant of the prominence of appearance, be it beauty or femininity. To emphasize the cheeks we will place a solid implant over the cheekbone, paired with injections of fat harvested from your love handles. The implant will consist of Gore-Tex and Medpo, ensuring integration and ingrowth with the underlying tissue. This will lock in more permanence. If revisions are ever needed to be made it will be nearly impossible to remove them. We will top that off with soft tissue fillers, in this case Restylane. In the event of an emergency we will make a small incision into the zygomatic bone. The shape is to consist of a combo of malar and submalar, providing a higher contour to the side of the face, and more projection and less of a sunken or gaunt look, extending from mid face upward, a la Jessica Biel. The incision will take place in the upper mouth near the top of the gum line, and the implants will be slid into place. This intraoral approach carries a higher risk of infection as the mouth contains more bacteria but this technique involves no visible scarring. Postoperative bleeding and formations of blood clots are the main risks. Asymmetry can occur due to uneven resorption, implant displacement and shifting. This can result from any minor trauma. A temporary loss of sensation is common and expected. We will maintain the look with autologous fat injections in a few months. The final result will be defined cheeks that will provide better balance to your face. Your other features will stand out. Full cheeks are a facial trait that never goes out of style. It is a quintessential sign of youth, beauty, femininity and even fidelity. They are associated with higher estrogen which suggests reproductive success.

She is a marble sculpture and my sanctuary. You are my wine and effort at rebellion. We are an illusion of progress. Your scars, blood stains and remnants remain despite the dry bath I gave you tonight. I press my ungloved hand against her moistness, attempt to find the moon in the night through a threshold of stars. There are no guarantees here, only certain connections. Her failed resistance began too late, the slow desire overcomes. Watching her empire slowly collapse, there were fleeting moments of freedom...free of thought, of want, of worry and shame. Slightly closer to death now freed from her cage. She is coming back around, with the warm glow of the sun and the buffer against the wind. I must suspend judgment. There is no recollection, only style. There is no recovery, only ash. As the water slowly rose she sat there staring...no more hopes, no more dreams, no more fears. Nothing left to recall and no false attributions.

At a cornerstone of time, the view from an angle of neither precision, nor luck, nor destiny. The outlook bleak for this century of imperialism. The doctors did sense that something was amiss. This is a new type of warfare. They said they could smell it in the drinks, but they chose not to say anything. That it was their duty to not get involved. She had nearly forgotten where she came from. Save for the conception of guarantee. Another workday, low lying clouds but no marine layer. The ever glow and her eager willingness. When the proper chemicals flowed in her brain. I taste her foreign tongue and it is distinct and fresh and zesty. I feel abandoned at a vacant all night motel. On the outskirts of town. *You are not alone*, she whispers to me. There is a phantom in this reality. I forget to feel. Back away? Walk away? Turn your head? Pull out, bust your nut on her backside. Remember, I still believe in God. And it has become harder to influence me. In my world of mind there is stop, pause, mute, rewind and fast-forward. As I see her eyes light up in little girl wonderment. *I am not a feign, but your friend*, she reminds me. Consider that every direction has its consequences. You will not know which way to turn until the end. And then it will be inconsequential. The topic at hand is delusion. The mirage of life. What do you make of the silence. What do you make of the pain. What do you make of the lack of focus and regret. I wanted to nibble on her tongue. Wrap my lips around her ears, play dirty, talk dirty. But I did not know what to say. I did play down the possibilities of damages. And scar tissue. How will I ever forget this and not remember it. How can I purge my mind like my stomach into the porcelain. Pause. Breath. Swallow. Try to get off the machine. I want to explode into tribalism and wildness unseen before. I want to shock myself, I want to scare myself. I want to feel needed, wanted, desired, *necessary. This is what I need.*

From: caliph8@sharia4ever.org

And you shall strive and thrive in His cause, with devotion and dedication, for He has chosen you, and has made no hardships for you. This is the religion of our father Ibrahim. It is He who named us Muslims, both before and in this Revelation of the Qu'ran. So the Messenger may be witness to you, and to all mankind! So perform regular prayer, give regular charity, and hold strongly to Allah! He is your Protector and it is best to be protected. In everything He does there is rhythm and rhyme, the effect is what I like to call "lawful magic." How have you been friend? Keep those pics coming! #nohomo Write soon please! I miss it! #inshallah

She is simplicity incarnate. Everything trimmed down to the fundamentals and vitals. No more body hair and no wrinkles. She developed slowly and she now ages slower still. She is at a place where perfection is revealed and reviled. A place where time is regarded in profile, in the shadows on the sand dollar, in the wax in her ears, in the space between the lines. She is all about the propaganda and the propaganda is all about her. Her quietness like closed door solitude. Locked away shortly, uninterrupted. The remnants on her lips. Those lips. The ratio of real life versus dreams. Reconstruction over time. And time is narrow and limited. Our collective predicament. We wait for our liberation in a crowded town square. We shed away the false promises to arrive at a truthful juncture of need, of release, of chagrin...for the feeling of raw life. I read her lips and they tell me where to go, they tell me how to feel. I whisper to her, *look me in the eye and tell me that it's through*. I look around and it is all whitewashed and there are no corners and there is no lingering fear and I feel more and more empty. I have hunted, I have stalked, I have preyed. She commands different distractions, new commotions, *nuevo* turmoil. She was more to me than a habitual reaction, or distraction or reaction. She was a masquerade on an infinite scale, a machine you cannot turn off, a dead harvest winter. It was all about the half moments, the slivers in time when you pull from past experience, from the hurt, from former longings, historical data, bygone aches and lust. Things started to look brand new again. I wanted the big house, the fancy car. Time at the beach, unfiltered and sober. Nothing could eclipse my moon. I had been pushed too far and had my diction forever altered. A series of points of no return. The stains remained but they were no longer random.

She had decided to grow her hair out. She looked wiser that way. I would give anything for some silence. I stayed inside a little too long, unable to withdraw, to pull out...she told me I could come in her mouth, just to let her know when I was ready, but I did not heed the offer, instead I came inside as deep as I could, in the hottest nether regions. I saw surprise on her face but it did subside and I think it is because she knew that if this was going to happen that this is probably the best time of the month. And as well it felt good to feel the ejaculation inside down there rather than in her mouth for a change. There is no narrative that can carry this along except the imagery of her barren body, opaque and cloudy white, strewn collapsed at ease across the 1,700 thread count sheets, my ejaculate dripping with calculated viscosity from within her shriveled sheer cliff walls forming a creamy wet spot puddle of love and desolation. Deeper than her wounded hole is the blue in her eyes and the fading in and out of sleep time slumber. She is no more than a little girl in these vulnerable moments. A princess dreaming of hosting a tea party.

I immediately had a feeling that I was wanted back. Looking behind I saw a fire in the distance and made for it. So now you know everything about me. My fears, my wants, my ideals, my ideas, my tastes, my dislikes. Please be a little more guarded in what you say, what you tell people. What about the armed guards? What about laughing out loud? I used to get upset by such things. Now I could not be bothered. The situation is very simple. You keep quiet and I will not turn you into the authorities. You think this is a game? Believe what you want. There are no deals made here. Only inference that she will do as she is told. And you did not know why but she was there all along. In the slivers, in the small hours. She later told of how her mind was cluttered with all things indistinct. And at this moment someone somewhere ascends to heaven. And this moment again. She recalls of how she couldn't quiet the dragon inside of her. Her pathos trying to distance itself from itself—a difficult task made harder still. She had always prided herself on her approachability, her accessibility. But now that is no longer retrievable, it is all post haste in a post everything world. It wasn't my business but I made it mine—it was her last addiction. She always did save the best for last. Her exposed body there, my hand running along, lengthwise, from rough to smooth, dry to wet. She seeps from every hole. Her ambitions certainly admirable if not bleak and prone to failure. At least she is trying. At least she is doing something. If not for herself, for others. I anticipated gushing rain from her pussy but that will wait, if it even comes. Your mind goes there and envisions the scene in cinematic opulence—professional lighting, water props, theatrical makeup and hair. It gushes and flows and I do not know what to say. I am at a total loss for words. I do not squint and I cannot look away. I am afraid I may miss something. This is unreal and I am processing it in the most deliberate ways to try and burn these images eternal in my mind. She does not move and I do not readjust. I wonder when she will run dry. The way she smelled now, the way she must taste. I forget to think. I am lost in detouring non-thought. I can try to imagine her flavors but I am sure they are different tonight. With all of the fluids, and all of the discharge and the varying colors. She is not herself. I am not myself. The change is beautiful. If only it could remain perpetual. Her standing and straddling me and spraying by body, dousing out the flame under my clothes, and in my mind. My dirty mind all hot and bothered. The electrical charges bounding to and fro like wild banshees, so very feral and untamed. It is in these moments that I know I am mad. A mad man with mad ideas and thoughts and illogical reasoning prone to almost anything short of violence.

The rows and lines around her body were perpetual still. It was Tuesday morning and it was slightly raining and we made love under the white cotton sheets. When she dressed I could still see the outline of her nipples, not just the shape but the coloring too. I could still feel their texture in my mouth, their rough skin edges against the smooth of my lips. Playing over again and again in my mind is your voice whispering, *this is a gift do not forget it.* As if this was a mercy fuck or I was the subject of her pity and philanthropy. I pay the voices in my head no mind. I zero in on the idea of her womanhood wrapped tight and hot and wet around the girth of my boyhood, sliding up and down, twisting side to side, gnawing at me, trying to hurt and injure me, testing how far she can take the acrobatics before someone is impaired. She almost looks even better in Capri jeans. When you see her bare ass you want to bury your face in it, stick your nose in deep and breath her essence in. She gets going and leans forward, opening herself up to you. *Go deeper* you hear her say. But in Capris she draws you just as hard. She looks naked when dressed. Her body is so well outlined. Her tight cleavage in that skin colored brassiere, too tight but chic. The bumps of her nipples shine proudly through the polyester. The brassiere underwire rigid against the fold below, where the massive weight of her tits meet the wall of her stomach. Her jaw line feminine and strong, her hair naturally dark but highlighted with blonde, an amazing semi widow's peak. Piercing aqua eyes, tiny blue seas. The size of her nipples in direct correlation to her eyes' footprint, what a pleasant image to be fixated on. The feel of her moist lips sliding along the edge of my undoing. Her ankles like wrists around my neck, her short leg hair stubble—where she deliberately missed when she shaved—riding rough against my ears. How she would look away when she came. How she would clamp down harder with her muscles on my shaft, a flirtatious pinch, as if she was trying to decapitate me there. These were all variations on her style. Her signature moves, likes, dislikes and positions. I believed her when she said she liked to suck dick. I believed her that one of her favorite positions was from behind, because she would finger herself at the same time and not have to look at me. Occasionally she would grab for my balls.

She is an adventure for no particular reason. I am grateful to have heroes like her, to be able to calculate her mass, her self-assurance, the gleam when she looks away, the saliva dripping from her nipple tip when she pulls up and tells me to change what I am doing. Her manipulation and supremacy over me. I am entitled to know how she feels but do I really want to. She is a blanket I cover over my face. She could suffocate me with her trimmed bush and dampened lips against mine, the weight of her entire body over my nimble head and I would be content. I would not struggle or whimper. It would be like summertime. Humid, her flesh afire, awake most of the night.

I watched the sound of her on my wall. The reflection dim and fainter still. Like our love, fading into the night, waning with the lost libido after quick sex. She is full-fledged motion through and through. A one woman petting zoo. I feel like excavating her skin, pulling back the layers, planting my lips against the cartilage, licking the muscles and fat with unparalleled enthusiasm. But this is not what I will do, of course. But I will certainly become a small part of her history. Maybe a one-off moment or a lingering thought, smell or image. A lasting player in her mental custody. The only controversy surrounding her outcome will be when she strikes next. Another unwilling and unknowing casualty, preyed upon by her soft breaths and fermented obfuscation. There is charm in her primal etiquette. She is at one with who she is. She rarely got distracted from the task, rarely looked away, a fervent glance in the wrong direction, a look at something that should not be looked at. Her see-through white pants another public indoctrination. The smell of coconut between her fingers. The smell of ass under her fake fingernails. I look at her wild land tundra backside and wonder where all the good has gone, where all the love has vanished to...a space and time no longer familiar to me, a place of solitude with no conjugal visitors. She made a point of telling me that she was glad to see me. It helped with the heartache and pain. And it was made more believable on the pretense that there was absence of malice and a tone of miraculous improvisation. But this could have been for her own sake and her own shame. Amiable indeed. And it put me in a pleasant frame of mind. It took me back to the old country, to a better time, a time when my mind was less cluttered by neurosis, by apprehension, by confusion, by ambition and dirty thoughts and ideas. This is where I would like to stop if it is her that I cannot obtain. I know you know what is best for you. It may not be what is best for me but that is my problem. *When I return from Europe*, is how she liked to preface sentences. She said it with a low level growl as if exhaling smoke.

This news travels slowly. I want to spread your legs and lean forward and drink from your elixir of life. I want to take aim. I want to detect the fire. I become paranoid, a detective in my own failed story, a botched attempt at additional physical cravings. Eat here now. I am a coward yet brave, suffering through the pain, silent but eloquent. My awareness of such things like rapture, like euphoria, like cocaine binges, drinking benders, falling into the category of a meantime history. A secular place where I go for relapsed parody, a heaven and a hell, testing limits by proxy rule of thumb, where I am unwise and sometimes vicious. I weep tepid tears for her, for us and for myself. I have lost track and I no longer keep score. I am resigned and forgotten. If only I could forget myself, lose myself. In these moments I wish it would all go away, that the void would be a vacuum that blares in my mind and drowns out the noise and filters the pollen and loose dust that clogs the pores of my mind and mental wellbeing. If not for the better memories and fading souvenirs then I would be a completely ruined man. Close is still not done, so my imminent demise may be greatly exaggerated should I come around again, bounce back, reinvent myself, spend some qualitative time alone, think new thoughts, play out new fantasies and undress new women in my head.

I read the article about her today. About her being the first woman to_________. Last night I dreamt that at 4am a man in a blue car parked in front of my house, got out and walked away then pulled out a cell phone and texted *69* and that detonated the bomb in the car and the explosion blew out all the windows in my house and set fire to my palm trees. This was a so called dream. This is what I dream about. Or the nightmare of watching my dead cold body in a basement morgue naked on a stainless steel gurney, two people I do not know looking at me and agreeing that no autopsy will be needed. This is when I unravel, at these weak points in time when I feel like everything is post- something or other. That the interweb is my only friend. That pacific standard time is the only zone. That animal slaughter makes sense. That any drug that you can smoke should be legalized. That currency conversion is a rigged art form. That the more volatile the solvent the better the finish. That childhood is another word for freedom. That pleasure outside of normal human behavior can be both wonderful and wrong for all the right reasons.

Being alive is to enjoy. Remember that expression. Being alive is to joy. To joy being a verb. If groping were legal I would have a clearer conscious. Better access equals better living. Still, sometimes she does speak to me, and not just in my dreams, but in real time, in hushed whisper tones like a virgin tepid before the first time. Or before the first failed attempt. Is it not all just failure then you die. I cannot afford to be too confident. I am in the throes of semi lucid logical theories which mean nothing and everything, a baseline from where to jump, a zero point from where to leap. My enriched awareness is not new but shaky nonethesame. If I could just keep hold of her in my grasps for slightly longer I would be a rapturous euphoric mess. The cure is in the disease, the doctors like to reassure me. There is no patent for that type of medicine. The panacea is in your mind. Enjoy the access to the unknown when you realize that yourself self is unnecessary and the meaning has slipped from your grasp long ago. Are you listening now? The effects stop working once you no longer allow them to affect you. It is nature taking its cruel course. The unique power circles and their power trips all lined up one after the other with their metaphorical genitalia whipped out waiting for their sloppy turn at you. This is why you succumbed long ago. It was not worth the fight. Imagine, you against the electrified fence. I do not think so. The anxiety has morphed into valid paranoia. No more joking about paranoia. This is as real as it gets. And the physical craving continues. You are not unique. You are not the only one to have survived such a potentially devastating crash. You are at a point way beyond the rule of thumb yet clinging onto the idea that all humans are not so vicious. That to be alive is to joy. That such access does not necessarily mean you have access to the devil. In the meantime you take the secular over the parody. And hope that you have chosen the least long path. A pathway leading to anywhere but here and now. A place where your thoughts and id may play second fiddle to your actual wellbeing without being too much of a distraction in the ringing head commotion.

She was going through each semi-lit room of my mind. The very act felt like scavenging and felt wrong and I tasted a tinge of premeditated violation in the ways and means for which she made her way around. My heaving desire was to apply myself to the cause, to any cause, to a just cause or even an unjust cause. I would often imagine her straddling me like a tamed animal and unhurriedly rocking back and forth. The weight of her pressed hard against my smashed crotch, I bestow her above me and I reach to touch her hanging tits but they are not there. A dreamlike black and white sequence: she is not to be obtained and she is not to be referred to in general terms. I could not let her go. I consider myself well educated, well dressed, bright, easy to fool. I tend to fit in and my charm and general charisma are more often than not *notable*. But now I feel as if I am on sick leave from myself, away from who I am and who I have become, a provision to further advancement, void of miracles amid an abyss of non-phenomenon. I do not know how to navigate in such stormy waters. I wish someone could take the controls.

The cold rain and dark skies are overwhelming at times. The choppy water portside is all too inviting as a last resort death mission. But I choose not to drown. I choose not to revolt. I choose not to lead a mutiny of one against my oppressor. I stand here and peer out off of this cliff of despondent desolation, gazing at the blurred horizon, your ship long gone, at sea, wild, untraceable, free. My mind and imagination lack the information in this state of utter in-definition and perplexity. I long for the calm, but if I ever get there again I do not know how I will fare. I close my eyes and am sustained by the thought that the storm is yours and not mine. The violence is manifested regardless of me.

I refrain from passing my slowly dragging hand along the length of her nude and polished body, a body riddled with orifices of bleached ivory whites and plucked black hair. I want to evolve the mind's eye. I was made quite unwell by being obliged to eat at her feet but without permission to swallow. My third and fourth instances of undoing. I want to be her friend in spite of her. Not just a fuck boy but a friend in the conventional sense of the word. If I awake in twelve hours I will be resolute to declare my staunch passion to the unknown of tomorrows. The forgiveness in *nuevo* beginnings, the calm of her arched backside pressed against my balmy flesh, the silence in her heartbeat at rest. Soon I will be sold. And soiled by the confines of my own mind. A prisoner in my own skin. The sign said welcome. She was barely legal when we first met. This I do remember. *Friends first*, she always liked to say. A contained flirt, always on the go, somewhere to get to, brief pauses between outbursts. She did travel poorly, and since she had stopped smoking her mood would get dark and foul and she would crave certain foods and her ass started to get fatter which was welcome, and her tits fuller which provided a new surprise each time she pulled her bra off. And I suffered the pain all along in silence. My capacity for alienation grew and I spent less time around people I knew. I started to frequent places that consisted of only strangers and awkward situations where it was not easy to talk nor would others be prone to meet you. Like gas stations and discount retail stores. My receptors were burning out, I was finishing my mission.

I am haunted by the façade of a normal existence. She invades my sleep with omniscient intentions, a demon in the half light, an ardent fiend in the nightfall shadows. She passes from the cracked leaded glass window panes and the failing enigmatic electric fixture dimness, she is my reflection and all is quiet and right when she is dry bathed and powdered in moneyed moon beam light. Her voice, a velvety wind through a forest of trees, beckoning me to a cool place for which I am unfamiliar, where the odors are overwhelming and crushing, where the hole in the damp earth makes me think of my premature grave, dug, prepared, and ready for me. These are the effects of her essence and quintessence, my nocturnal mistress and phantom demi-lover. She is lust incarnate. She is the source for the wet spot on the bed. As the sapphire morning sky hints of dawn I find myself alone and awake befuddled and fatigued from the lies, the deceit, the *mentiras*, the fabrications of my life and the falsehood in her eyes. She is a magical drug that can cure or backfire. I daydream of chewing on her fat, that there is leakage of some sort and I lick it clean and swallow the small amounts. That my tongue is her bandage. That her medical problems are vague and she doesn't like to talk about them but I can tell that they are serious enough and she is concerned. I want to be soaked in her filth, a drowning victim to the benign. A Spanish conquistador at shore, an outlaw in pain and sorrow, my own death rather imminent, her folds in my hungry mouth being devoured as the ultimate rush. I want to burrow deep into her cavern, a gaping hole to get lost in, to hibernate eternally within, to succumb to the disaster that is myself, the catastrophe which is me, on my better days, in my better moods, under an improved disposition. I lay reluctant victim to the femininity brigade display of her standing above me, her spiked heel against my throat, her black fishnet panties torn, ripped open and pulled to the side, her crotch wide agape and in full frontal art house view, a sight to remember, a sight to replay one thousand times, over and over. She makes me claustrophobic and I tremble. If there shall be bloodshed then bleed me out now. Dry my veins like a hunted trophy wild animal slaughter. Let me bathe in her hot box of wrinkles of pink and damp secretion befit a king in medieval times, dirty still, youthful and vigorous yet. If she denies me I will only despise her further. If she relents and permits me the ultimate in forfeit I will be forever indebted to the journey of each day, to the wondrous circumstances, to the escape hatch, to the glow on her face when I clinch her neck firmer and tighter to the point where she begs for more. If not for moral victory then at least for the appearance of summer rain in a darkened fire sky.

She played everything off as if it were not more than an erotic parlor game, in flesh tones and shades of black and satin red. She was my girl then and the stranger things got the better off we were. There was little to no intention in the inflections of her voice when she whispered her commands. How she wanted to be propped up a certain way, how she liked to be fondled like an unwilling passenger on a crowded metro train, how she liked to be licked between the lips, how she liked her hair pulled tight. If we got off track she would hold my hands down and whisper gently, *we need to start from zero*. There was that trained eye, a fixed stare from the curator to the art. She was always the recipient but the selection varied. Seamless, encased in her perfect shell, protected from the veil of onlooking strangers, guarded from the degradation of unannounced visitors. She had become my methodology and I had lost track of the reality that there would always be other options. My infatuation and zeal had expanded while my intellect had suffered, stifled by the oppressive and all-encompassing visions of her on all fours crawling in circles on the bed, a caged polar bear who had lost its mate. Her pussy drenching without being touched. The eagerness brought on by my undoing with each passing failed glance. A rising tide within and an expanding jungle below. She pulls me in against the gravitational logic. I try to walk away from the faint childhood recollections of differences between right and wrong, the dark and the light. I am brought back in by the commotion. The upheaval another reason to flounder and give in, resign to the antithesis of better judgment and walk out on achievement. *Pay the devil and he might leave you alone*, she liked to murmur. She twists underneath me, I see the sky night in her eyes, her limp body a floating mansion at sea. There is a cosmic relation but it cannot be defined, I mistrust the undercut factions of lust and greed, more, more, more, me, me, me. I try to run from it but find myself abandoned in it, a baby that fell into a well, a rat that ate the poison. My tongue now is ensconced in her. I burrow it deeper still, as if the more I can get into her the better off we will be.

In this truth there are moments of freedom. Breaks and lapse time from the hyperventilation, from the body shakes and trembling hands. Her sublimation beyond definition, into a realm of hypotheticals and insignificance. If it were not my tongue buried so deeply into her muff, then whose? It is not worth pretending to play the game, it is only worth when you actually do, when your tongue is tightly held firm between two hot walls of the most sensitive of flesh, eager and damp, salty and musky. Your intake breath filtered by the musk of her secretion. Am I not to deduce that from this moment forward she will forever refer back to this as her time, her hot moment of total worship and devotion, a period and place when she was not judged nor her pussy smelled, or her ass put out some off-putting odor, or the ingrown hair along the edges of her triangle were not so ugly, nor the flab of her upper inner thigh, nor the spidering stretch marks of her upper leg, nor the tattered appearance of her off brand panties which are worn out in the crotch and needed to be replaced a very long time ago but now rest leisurely around her right ankle while she gets off.

This is why I reinvent myself with a new name. I climb inside of her and twirl like a ballerina or Sufi mystic. I am guilty for staring and there is nothing but shame on my face. I am lost with my head buried in the pillow between her legs. I am no longer me. I am getting closer to becoming the person I have always wanted to become...the solo warrior, the unaccompanied wanderer. There will be no gynecological exam this visit, we will leave that climax for a better day. Leave it as it stands for now, the low hum vibrations of a life undone further made disheveled by the confines of one's undiagnosed illness, the verbosity in the design, the abandonment in the details. I am not me and I am not well. But all things will end, like everything before me. I could do better without the noise. The violence in her shrills, the hostility in her strident screams from the demons within and the chemical imbalances. I just want to stick it in her and pump away my problems, let the friction excite me to a climaxed ultimatum of my seed dripping into her hole, any hole. I am incensed by her rants, by her raves of misbegotten strife, the throbbing clitoris hidden under the hood, dying to get out, striving for sunlight, wanting to be licked and massaged, maneuvered just so, manipulated by two fingertips, rubbed the wrong way, pounded and pressed against hard and harder still. Let's imagine for one moment that this is the end and it is now that you will come and at that pinnacle culmination moment you suddenly die.

From: caliph8@sharia4ever.org

You see, my friend, the Arabs and their lands have always been under occupation and we have had as a result a fighting mood, if you will. It is a chronic mental condition that has become a national sport LOL. It is our duty to make raids on the enemy, on our neighbors, on our brothers. We actually have a name for it, ghazw. *Blood only gets shed in extreme cases of necessity. Well, my friend this is where we are at here and now. But you are my fam bro! You and I against the enemy... #inshallah*

There is no truth to the rumors, the gossip and chitchat in my rumbling numb mind of soft deceit and fabrication. Only the specter of a phantom-like existence, obscured by half-light, mum and silenced to proverbial nonsense otherwise known as discourse. It is sickening really. The incarceration of my essence strapped down, tied to a chair, abused, embarrassed, humiliated in front of a live studio audience. In some such ways I am better off. They were all faceless in my dreams, like you now. Naked on the white sheets of the bed, on your side, in the fetal position. I am lying with you now, against your backside. My body and parts molding into yours. The valley between your thighs from behind, a receptacle for my hardened parts. I reach around and cup your falling breast which fills my hand, spilling over only symbolically, your nipple nestled between two fingers. I reach down and stroke your abundant bush, pressing I feel your shape and lines. I kiss the nape of your neck then nibble your earlobe, breathing through my nose into your ear. I roll back into you. I want to eat you into a moonlight seascape, dream certain dreams behind curtains of collapse, ruined by you running through fields of altered space-time, a future bereft of this troubling fatigue, a future all my own which I control and which I destined. Your nonsense is troubling, but I stand to gain the most and to win in the end. The lips of uncertainty envelop me, a stranglehold on my advancement, a grappled grip to mark all of time, for I am no longer me, I am now a visage of a former self, all memories twisted and diluted by the angst of today.

It is about time now that she arrives. I am watching from the backseat of my car. The windows are slightly fogged over but I can see beyond, into the parking lot. She had better hurry and arrive before the automatic lot lights go off for the evening. Last night she wore black Lululemon yoga pants which accentuated the sublime lines of her child-bearing hips. The car smells of worn leather and musk. A man must be clean to impress the ladies. I see her now, her rounded ass thighs, her puffy shapes squeezed and stuffed into what appears to be the same pants as yesterday. I have a perfect vantage point for viewing this delectable woman. I want to touch her, shuddering I hold myself back, I reach down and feel my own stiffening mound confined under tight slacks. I should have worn something looser. She is listening to her iPod. One of her better qualities is her carefree ness. She does not know I am watching her, or if she knows she is playing it off, playing the game, flirting back at me. She is not aware of my car either. I have been here most of the day. I feel no shame for feeling this way, for watching her from the shadows (she likely knows and enjoys every minute of it). She can be mine at any time. The tension is almost too thick now. Contact between us is long overdue and when the time finally comes it may be too much of a good thing. Behind my eyes I stroke her elastic and warm flesh underneath the stretch pants, then quickly I envision her nude and I am licking her thighs like they are lollipops and I am famished, I lick the workout salt off of her skin, I feel the short hair against the rough surface of my tongue, her thighs never ending. She does not notice me. I press harder and closer still, her skin is nearly unbearable, I quiver.

The surface of her is a wonderfully alternate story. She is the object at its pinnacle, the chasm and occasional spasm responding to the flicking of a slowly dragging fingertip. The sound of her whimper when I stop and focus and massage one area as concentrated as concentration can be. The crescendo in her exhalation. She is there, laying still on the plush white linens in a sleek mother of pearl bodice, her gem swollen and throbbing, wet and darkened. The exhilaration and impatience for the warmth of an undulating tongue. If it could speak it would cry for a lifetime of attention and the face for learning the longing of a soul. My dreams start out with a passing vision of her naked breast, just one, in profile, a very guilty pleasure and even guiltier conscience. We were never friends per se, and I do not think we will ever be. But the easy comfort I feel with her leads my mind astray. I have been fighting it for a long time. Sometimes I worry that she will pick up on it. I am not sure I could live down the mortification. It is not love in the romantic sense. I am lusting for a stranger, for a potential enemy, for someone I do not know, for someone who is not necessarily good for me.

Currently: we are in a room, in an apartment building high above a busy city street, this is a place I have been to before, I am sitting on the bed, I tilt my head in a gesture of compliance, and she bends down to kiss me, her mouth in the perfect shape and I can feel her gentle and urging push into mine...gentle for a moment, but tenderness is not something she is fond of, hunger is much more her speed, I can feel her tongue pushing against mine, I feel my teeth scraping against that billowy bottom lip, the heat flares in my body, pushing against her, her hand rakes through my hair, pulling my head back, aggressive, forceful, forthcoming, I can feel her chest and those tits under my hands as I tug at her shirt, I want her clothes off, everything's happening so fast now, this is the only way it can happen, forceful and fast, if we slow down we will think, and if we think we will realize that this is a bad idea gone horribly wrong...we are now mostly naked, my dick is out, her yoga pants pulled off, her panties pulled to the side, her top and bra are off and her tits are up against my mouth, the noises are stifled, the sound of grinding has waylaid into motion noises of humming and slapping flesh, I slide inside of her and she collapses onto me, her heat is intense as she washes over me a soothing focus of drowning in the night, of distant sounds and touches that sooth and transplant me to a better place, I am helpless now, my instincts fail me, I do not know how to proceed, I sigh as we lay down on the carpet, she is on her back, the flesh of her ass spread wide, the carpet fibers against the dripping ooze between her legs, her tongue trails down my body, she dismantles me with each traversing passage, she teases me, she smiles, no intentions or plan, she is pure, she is dark, my breathing picks up, I am thrilled now, she traces my torso, she brands my mind with her commitment to the cause, she reaches forward now with an arching neck and I raise my body up and she takes me whole into her mouth. My blood is throbbing, I am robbed of my consciousness and I am lost.

It was just like this that I sat that night, feeling myself tense for a strike that would never fall and imagining the fingers running lengthwise along my trembling body. I tossed my head back with every thrust, I could swear it was real again, all over again, it is then that I felt the charges running up and down my spine, a current of electricity skipping across a rain-streaked excuse of a man, as my head tilted to the side I felt her bite caress my neck, I could swear that there were fingers running over my skin. The pain was unexpected but welcome as it greeted me. I felt the rush, a slowly growing desire, arousing waves washing over me as her hand lands again. I am driven into war, self-pride and needed battle. I want to fill her. I cry out, anything and everything, wishing for more and less at the same time, my blood itself is throbbing as my cheeks burn and I know that all of this is a lost cause. These memories would remain, torturing me and touching me in their intimacy every night that I returned to sleepy slumber. However, there was never a fight; I always surrendered to her. The temptation to feel it again would never stop; it was born of my stubbornness. I knew the memories would follow. You hold me beside you, fondly, as if you will never let me go. Your lips press to mine and I close my eyes. The heat envelopes me. She whispered my name and I chose to take that as an invitation and trailed slow kisses up her throat. I encircled her face with tiny pecks, taking eternity to reach her lips. Yes, those lips. She resisted for an instant, one crazed instance, where she did not know what she wanted. Then she surrendered and sank against me. And then, I stepped away. And I granted her a smile so wicked that her breath was stolen away. There was a dangerous glint in my eyes that warned her. But before she could respond, I had caught her within my grasp, drawing her hard against my chest. My mouth had closed determinedly over hers, once again. And then it was too late to retreat. This kiss was different from my first salute. It was no less thrilling, and awakened no less heat, but this kiss was possessive and demanding. It called for her not to surrender, but to join me in the pursuit of pleasure. She was left breathless, teased and tempted, cajoling her to venture with me deeper into the woods. She closed her eyes and surrendered to my touch. When I finally lifted my head, she could not look away from me, nor could she draw a full breath. She broke the kiss suddenly and I was ashamed of how far we had gone, ashamed of the way she tasted, ashamed of how close I was to simply claiming her. But she was far from sorry. Her cheeks were flushed and her eyes sparkled. Her breath came quickly in small pants. The proposition in her gaze was one that no man with blood in his veins could refuse.

The warning came in a passing lucid moment: *this was madness*. And I knew it but I couldn't stop. I was helpless to draw back from her. As she whirled me into deeper waters, to a place where the currents ran strong, to where the tug of desire became a physical force, pulling me under. We were not safe. Some relic of my mind screamed, battling to remind me that we had better stop. Now. Deliberately. Before she dropped her guard and let everything she had held back and had pent up now surge through her. She poured every ounce of her frustrated emotions into the act. And for the first time in our lives she knew she had shocked me, rocked me enough to have me falter, then struggle to follow her lead, to regain the reins, to win control back again. But she didn't want to give it up that easy.

From: caliph8@sharia4ever.org

If I may get a little graphic here I need to tell you something. Here it goes. We are all about self-esteem and self-respect. The most important factor on which the preservation of this self-esteem depends is the sexual behavior of women. Specifically our sisters and girlfriends. I must admit there is an obsessive intensity behind this, in fact there is a word for women's honor "ird" because it is so central in our beliefs. You see, a woman only has her chastity. Our sisters cannot whore around. And our girlfriends must only defer to us. This is all about serving the larger community and promoting our collective interests. That is why it is our duty to keep them on a straight line and if they falter it is our same duty to personally hand down punishment. A good flogging or whipping, strong enough that she doesn't get excited from it. On a lighter note we further sustain our reputations through courage and bravery, which you my friend are very good at. And hospitality and generosity which you are getting closer to still. Women have few roles, and they must answer to you always. #inshallah

I could no longer find solid ground. She had cut it out from under me. The only thing my worn down senses could find that was real was the desire that flamed between us, hotter and more powerful, more intense, shockingly more intoxicating—so much more than I had felt before. She was passion and desire, heat and longing, incarnate in a dimension never before explored. She rocketed both of us into it, then sent us adrift, floating on a familiar tide, one of subtle warmth, simple pleasure and gentle waves of delight. I had no idea how to return to the real world, and no real wish to do so. She was fuel to my fire, and I needed her as she needed me. The exchange became a heated duel and she held the upper hand, yet I was still a master, and she a simple apprentice. Step by step I reclaimed the control and I reclaimed her senses, as we dragged each other down into a sea of wanting. Of needing. Of having to have more than I ever offered to give, and for once I was uncertain. Her defenses vaporized beneath my onslaught, beneath that hard, fast, scorching kiss, hard enough to knock her wits from her head, fast enough to send her whirling, scorching enough to cinder any resistance. If time could stand still, in that instant, it did. Then reality came crashing back. We were both reeling. Both fighting to breathe, both struggling to regain our common ground and some measure of control. To hold against the fiery tide that had surged around us. She concentrated on her breathing again. On trying to ignore the way the heat flared wherever we touched.

She looked me in the eyes, aware of the impulse rising in her veins, that had always afflicted her when in my arms. Her senses might leap, but only in expectation. The more time we spent together, the more she was tempted and the less resistance she could muster. What she saw in my eyes nearly made my heart stop, sent a lick of fear down her spine. She had seen desire blaze in my eyes before. She knew how it affected me. I wasn't trying to hide what I felt. Her behavior had been a revelation until she had stopped holding everything back, she had not appreciated how much she had been concealing, how much was bottled up inside her. Until that moment, she hadn't fully understood how much she felt for me. Or more particularly, the nature of what she felt for me. She had told herself it would be just a kiss, something she could simply take and enjoy.

It wasn't worth it.

It.

Was.

Not.

Worth.

A touch of skin soft and slippery, with the hint of sweat. We fought our resistance beneath the cool sheets, as the wind flowed from the window above us. Eyes met briefly and begged for the chance to abandon all of our uncertainties. You began your work on my lips, probing gently as if drawing sex from a deep well of longing and need. Then heated tongues met in the midst of hot and quickening breath. And greedily we drank the wine of our lusts. Then intoxicated with those spirits, our clothes found their resting place on the floor. Piece by piece, until there were no hiding places, for the two glistening and wanting bodies. Hunger revealed in this hot moment. Then skin meshed with skin, as the floor became the stage. You moved atop of me easily, and lowered yourself gently. Kissing me as I was filled with you. As a gasp broke the kiss, your hands stroked the stray strands, away from my forehead. Our slow rhythm gave way to urgent and demanding thrusts of passion, as I arched my body for your comfort, and you threw me into ecstasy, with the strength of your blows. You left me screaming and soaked, in oblivion again and again, as you growled my name from the back of your throat, and our bodies both demanded more, each giving to the other, high on the fluids of foreign substance. I grasped, then released you, in an effort to relieve you of your control. The taste of your skin between my lips was like no other. To hear your cry of mercy, when my teeth met your warm skin, was more breathtaking than you knew. Yet I still released the control to you. As you wound your hands in my hair, and pulled until the flesh on my neck was taut, you moved with one final and breaking blow, forcing our way to the peaks of bliss, leaving our screams to echo on like battle cries. I welcomed the weight of you to crush me, as you collapsed on top of me, still hot and burning, glowing like an ember and casting a welcome light should you seek my gifts again.

The cheat sheets for a better code of release, lifestyle living in the past, a videotape sizzle reel downloaded long ago by a next generation member of a preferred club, quality is not an issue, the means to remove is used to your advantage the more you work at it the more you wear yourself down, into the confines, into the simulation world once on display but now forgotten, the license recently surfaced then revoked, all systems deployed and declined to an already forgotten implementation of patchwork and updates, the beast within your mind, the grueling progress concealed and concerned with the giving and the parables of shaken psyches and the truth in the psychosis, you must be insane by now...the classics taking aim and zeroing in on your fragile existence, the anecdote a famed and notorious rumination on self-doubt and textured density, the portrait a notion bigger than itself, the symbolism of a society based on medicine and staged tension, the equal opportunity employer in us all, the epiphany and the epitaph, hot versus ugly, boy versus girl, cock versus pussy...the body politics of disease and contamination, the amoral subject matter of policy from infancy, of ancient symbolism and burnout, this began in a very early period piece of time, circa Henry VIII, a stunner who shunned himself from the knife fight, who grew to disdain and divorce, a better style of living in a darker ages day, the people knew him by his hands, *click here now*, the exploited scams of how-to-stop-wetting-the-bed, or war memorial funding, the salvaged Lexus, the immigration debate, the six steps to salvation, the toxic shock syndrome, the fallacy of top secret data on a stolen laptop, the trees of Canada providing all our Sunday papers.

A newer version for a better past, something out on the vista, something exploited, a real scam by definition; the motel room stains on the twin beds, the purple markings for the luminal, the toxic waste sifting through your mind, the twelve steps to a brighter tomorrow: self-matters, the security in the data, the migrating shadow passwords, the ctrl alt delete, the return to a kinder and gentler self, the upside to pooling the unseen knowledge, the what's-in-it-for-me attitude, the building access codes, the secrecy in the secretary's stories, the prison sentence, the impact of election day, the trash talk behind bars, the bishop's call for prayer, the baby folds where your thighs meet your stomach, the crisis in everything you do, the hunt for c u next Tuesday, the nursery worker charged with selling newborns, the new fines for DUIs, the price hikes on lap dances and girlfriend experiences, the crackdown awaiting my fate, the steroid test, the girls with the shaved beavers that call themselves *the trim posse*, college chicks buying into bisexuality, liking to kiss other girls, having a harder time going down on them, west Nile virus, zika, cruising the deep web, aphrodisiacs in Chinese root mythology, the fungi between your toes, reading tarot cards to small children, pleading guilty to anything and everything, disease free zones, hot chicks with wide asses mooning you from a distance, your allies drifting away, when surgery is finally underway, the sedatives set in, the dreams wash ashore, the smell of ass on your hand, the hardship in the process, for god's sake, the new rules past city limits, the crowd watching, the imagined screwing of that girl with the mental condition, the thankless wedgie, the blowhard who claims to give the best blow jobs, the lone star deluxe, her latest reincarnation, sunrise nude yoga, her Nordic features, we all want the same thing, think of this as a bargain, the strength in your ideology, the hubris in your disorder, the profit in your lies, the recap of your morning, the disenchantment in her smile, the vertical smile, the hairy clam, the pink taco, the whistling kettle, the acquired taste, for coffee, for tea, for me, for soiled panties, test drive your future, scan the world, the red on her face when she blushes from the excitement, the loss of anonymity, the start and the end, her pores slowly tightening, the someday implosion that is you…the ideology of your slimming walls of red lips, moist, fluffy, swollen, the one way in with no return, the placed strength of your diversity backlit by a reasoned field trip, thrown into the pit of hungry vipers hell bent on revenge for something you did not do, if Jeffrey Dahmer says it is ok then it must be ok, run and do not look back, my dried out eyeball flooded with memories of all I have loved that are now gone, the futility in showing up, the agelessness between her legs when the room is lit only by candles, the codex ruminations between January and February, the months to start anew, the blue gene code, the rose garden in my mind, the church beyond my ordinary grasp, the cough that won't go away, the possible cancer, the possible asthma, long term lease agreements, entering the matrix, your forgotten email accounts, the flowers left on the porch, the photos on the dashboard, the media omnipresent, your golden box, half dressed in pirate gear, the non-visuals that can still get you off, the motif in your layers, the new protocols, the virtual machine that you have become, the weakness when I see your layering, role playing to the extreme, awkward exercise moves involving smoothed out crotches, breaking ground, packing sand, pushing envelopes, her density, her length, her so forth, the rumors validated by the silence, all that is upcoming, the hopeful improvements, beware, and be very afraid, the voices and the echo, the exchange rate, the lucky money, for love only, believe the hype, at this point go black and never go back, you are forever kinder, gentler, less average and more ordinary, I am a huge fan of yours, I have almost licked her dry at this point, I know this is your favorite position, your favorite motion, a simpler dialogue, between a man and a woman and conducted in one language, refreshing for a change, the whisper, a confused modem in the dark of night, the multiple angles of your behind in all of its imperfect glory, I do want to believe, reduce speed ahead, you have been forewarned, tuck me in for the big sleep, is it not all overrated, art, travel, tourism, every month another freak out session, the blues, choose your poison, what was your worst moment, another proven hurdle to overcome, your kind grace, do you feel alive today, is that stardom working out for you, is that a sequence on your neckline, to be immortal, I cherish your useful comments, please do not crucify me, cuddle me and pet my throbbing member, the errors and omissions, upon further examination, *click here now*, the verdict is still out, you are my wizard, I want to release in your mouth, when you have run out of aliases, talk about future plans, it will be announced today, we launch at four, we muff dive at five, my gutter mind and gutter logic, don't chance an opportunity to exploit by not explaining your stage name, sneak a peek, you are bare for the stare, leave your halo at home, save your thoughts now, you are so full yet so empty, your optimism, your pessimism, you are a cowardly narcissist, but I still like you nonethesame…the aftertaste of you, mad at myself for thinking, swept up in the current of your ocean, the body of water that nearly drowned my beliefs, how could I allow you to be such a thief, a nighttime raid on my heart. Get a new gimmick. Get a new trick. A love story to remain untold until I find my queen. I will not let this fairy tale die.

So that you can spend a longer amount of time to attain a deeper understanding of how and why to use them and when and under what types of applications, of varying patterns, of changeable moods, of assorted colors and characters, all the while with those who want to learn and who have faced the in between sips of a martini or other libation and the lessons which are always forthcoming, you know, learned by those whom you want to learn about, people like the decorator or the gardener or the bank teller in the almost too-tight mohair sweater, somewhere in the world, and this too is short, to spend the free time doing something fun, focusing on better derived solutions, so that the next time you are at someone's house and you think about asking where is the restroom, you should really ask where is the bathroom, because houses do not have restrooms, and when you get in there and have successfully locked the door you try to resist the urge to quietly look in all the drawers and the medicine chest and under the sink, but go ahead and do it anyway because there is often a good amount of clues about a person among their toiletries and their prescription and/or over-the-counter medicine, your Ambiens and Tetrasils and Ritalin and Excedrin Migraines, and fallen hair both long and short and the hair stuck in the brush and the blood or blood-looking red nail polish stained stainless steel trash can and leaking cleaning products like cobalt blue toilet bowl cleaners and soft scrub soaps or lack thereof, or opened boxes of hair dye (reds and brunettes) and douche kits, a jar of Vaseline, generic nail polish remover, an unopened value box of extra-absorbent tampons, a box of thong cut panty liners, see how it is that other people set up, the preparation for work or for the gym or for a trip to the supermarket or a night out with friends or an actual date, or strip down and wipe down before going to bed, *please remove the makeup otherwise you will stain your pillowcase*, how others put their face on, imagine in your mind your friend standing right there, naked in front of the mirror, lit by three 60-watt soft touch bulbs in a vanity track lighting system, doing her hair and makeup, a hair dryer in one hand and the aforementioned brush in the other, or applying transparent unscented roll-on deodorant under the arms, in the just shaven pits still a bit raw and uneven, then under the folds of each hanging boob as she lifts the 5 pound weighted mass and runs the roller along the horizontal crease wrinkle, or cleaning out her wax-laden ears with a non-brand name q-tip, or flexing her feeble bicep muscles ignoring the hanging underfat, or sucking in her gut and holding her breath long enough to rotate a side view and take in the concave profile of her lower torso, her boobs proudly projected on display, mounds mounted on her proud rib cage, or playing with herself with her fingertips and her unkempt jagged fingernails, careful not to let her uneven nails injure the soft lip lining, tenderly combing her pubic hair with the brush or trimming it back with the scissors from the kitchen drawer and letting the soft cut hair fall into the wastebasket or into the sink where she will wash it away but not all of it, some of it will remain on the edge of the basin, or popping zits on her shoulder, or squeezing blackheads on her nose, or plucking nose hair with tweezers, or pulling strands of gray hair from her head, or gripping onto her love handles, or applying Preparation H to her burning hemorrhoid-ridden asshole, or masturbating right there with the aid of the brush handle looking at her own front side, getting turned on by her own body, her own tits, her own pussy, her own silky skin, her own thighs and hips and tummy, or turning around and bending her ass toward the direction of the mirror to see what it looks like from behind, what a man would see if he took her from behind, but it would be darker than this now, or even candlelit, she sees the ass pimples, she sees the dark hair protruding from the crack and she is not sure what to do, how to get to it, what should be done about it, complete removal at a day spa or some self-pruning to make it all more subtle and less provocative and in your face, the pre-varicose veins behind the knees, the short cellulite lines around the orbit of her hips, the delicate struggle in the suggestion that there is still a lot of work to do and what needs to be done and in what triage center order, and how to go about it in the stark face reality of aging and time's inevitable advancing regression. You will try to avoid the challenge. You will want to give in, to surrender and relinquish. Something inside you will warn you against the deviation. Your time is better spent on something else. Take care of the business at hand and then leave the room. As you left it, like it was before. As if you had never been here.

A woman's breasts are a symbol of her femininity and fertility. In fact, they are the second thing we look at on a woman after her eyes. If you desire more voluminous breasts we may suggest AirSculpt "Up A Cup." How does it work you ask. It is essentially transferring your own fat to your breasts, for the most natural look and feel. This is the best in class technology. It looks and feels more natural. Painless, minimally invasive and no scarring. You can even return to work within 48 hours.
How is it done you ask. The breast tissue matrix consists of engineered tissues of complex, implanted, biocompatible

scaffolds seeded with the appropriate fat cells. The in-situ creation of a tissue matrix in the breast mound is begun with the external vacuum expansion of the mastectomy defect tissues, for subsequent seeding within the autologous fat grafts of adipocyte tissues. The autologous fat graft replacement of implants, be it saline or silicone, resolves possible medical complications such as capsular contracture, implant shell rupture, filler leakage, silent ruptures, device deflation and silicone-induced granulomas.

Is it going to look good you ask. Outcome depends on proper preparation and correct technique along with the harvesting and refining, and finally the injection of the breast filler fat. This we will harvest from your abdomen, thighs and buttocks. We will inject large volume grafts, to the tune of 220-650 cc. After harvesting by liposuction, the filler fat is obtained by low G-force syringe. The filler is then injected to the pre-expanded recipient site. Post-procedure will consist of a continual vacuum expansion therapy upon each injected breast. Operating time will be two hours. Our hope is no infections. No cysts, no seroma, no hematoma, no tissue necrosis. Our goal is 60-80 percentage increase of the breast volume. So not too big but no longer small. Despite its relative technical simplicity, the injection (grafting) technique is accompanied by post-op complications, like damage to the underlying breast structures, including the milk ducts, blood vessels and nerves. Sometimes the injected fat tissues can die and result in necrotic cysts.

What are the upsides to this procedure you ask. Well we are avoiding medical complications that other procedures tend to result in, like filler leakage, deflation, scar visibility, palpability, and capsular contracture. Yes, the achievable breast volume is limited with your procedure, but the large-volume, worldwide breast augmentations realized with implants—if not feather-layered into adjacent pectoral areas—will not achieve your desired ski slope contour and smaller mass. It will not translate into the stereotypical buxom big tit model but will augment one brassiere cup-size in one session! Think J Lo versus Pam Anderson. Shall we begin?

She is transcendence. In those camel colored riding pants. She is resistance to the plight of a more meager man, someone with nothing to lose, someone willing to go down under any circumstance and not deterred by the smell. She is paranoia. In a good way, in a cautious way, a way that saves lives and fortunes. She is morality, and the antithesis of a bad idea. She is moonlight and the soft curve of the lighted cast projection over shadows and dark. She is the silence you arrive at after a spent escapade, lost in the fermentation of a bad decision, of a bad thought, something perverse that you do not act upon, only think about and dwell on. She is the horizon, and what is beyond. The dark of night that never ceases. She will die just like you. An epiphany, a symphony incomplete but enough there to delight and cause demise. She is contagious indeed. A luxury that comforts, from the warm fold grip of her womanhood, and the comfort in that, to the collection of shoes she refuses to wear.

Swallow, I ask.

She is appropriations for appropriations' sake. She is satisfaction in no particular order. She is the messenger and the message. This is when she pushes back, in a slowing manner, in the warm desert air. Stretched out across the seam of my undoing. A pathway between lost and stolen. She is property that cannot be owned. She is dampness, where it counts. She is the threshold to the sanctuary and revolution in the flavoring. She is what is behind the curve. She is the behind. And she is the curve. She is motion, in gentle gliding fashion. Up, down, up, down. There you go, right there. Now don't move. Don't change. Don't stop. You found it. She is the intervals and the in betweens. She is the dominant species and the essence of life. She is sunshine revealed for final dissolution. She is society and all of its inclusion. She is the archive of my soul. She is what comes next. She is in this moment whispering *I love you*. She is liberation and spontaneity. She is forward thinking and attractive like beachfront property. She is lingering and remaining. She is unleashed. She is the underground and the truth here in my hands. She is stripped and given way to the platitudes of grace. She is nurturing and all honesty. She is honey. She is gold and ritual and reputation. She is history and romance and discovery. She is all about ancient yore, free flow and timeless. She is the afternoon siesta. She is the smell of light. She is wet at the edges and shielded by the one-way mirror.

She is walking backwards again, only to regard her ass in in-coming glory. Her dislikes: to make you feel sick, health officials, brand name designer drugs and knock off sunglasses, recalled products, posers, feigned outrage, overseas porn, foreign prisons, babies without mothers, gender identification disorders, politics, non-disclosure agreements, market woes, FDA warnings, fake laughs with fake friends, searching for love, webcam live links, FBI interviews, delayed broadcasts, E coli, star power, HIV, child abduction, the captors, mentoring and menopause.

With it the taste will come.

Try to keep your head elevated for the duration.

You may feel like you are getting a cold but this is normal.

Only the best for the better.

I hear the gurgle and your throbbing throat pitch black against the backlight. You come back toward me as a reflection, a warm glowing sun. You are a captured buffer against the wind and all that is ill. I continue to watch you closely from the far side of the room. Your beauty is contextual. You are beginning to work out very well for me. There is a silent hum when you pause to whisper: *it is hard to let go*. There were moments of discontinuation, moments of lapsed logic and awkwardness. Sometimes they stayed behind like fingerprint oils on a door. If it is okay I will start without you. Is this a bad time. Is this a bad angle. Is the lighting satisfactory for you. Why are there no clocks in the room, you ask. It will remain a mystery. Like most things. Even though this moment will pass, your statuesque silhouette form will remain burned into my memories. The curves. The bumps and humps. The delicate imprints. You draw me in from the periphery. You make a fool of me with my single mindedness, a simple man with a simple focus. I am determined to delve deeper but if I am to do so I will need your blessing. What is that on your tongue. My lips burn for yours. Beginning at zero I imagine only briefly a snapshot of my cock in your mouth, your lips sealed around the base of my shaft. You are looking at me with those innocent eyes. I know it is an act but it is effective all the same. The picture fades and I am back to the present. I wish now that I could live out such things. Even though they are innocent and nobody gets hurt they are a trap that pulls me under its spell. These cerebral attempts at taste and feeling, forgetting what it feels like to feel, a warm mouth along the length of my dick, the comfort in the humid timing. The images of you going down tailspin into my memory oblivion, a faded glory holed up in pent up anger and love life dementia. Is it not lovelier on this side of the room. You sweet little plaything. You can choose to not be difficult. You can choose the easier path. You can choose righteousness. I study on your backside the red lines where the straps cut into your flesh. A reminder of the under garments and their effects. By necessity or by design. Your reluctance prevails through the veiled misty glow of a woman coming undone in soft wattage light, in cheap lingerie, the musky smell of an unwashed crotch, the lost gaze of a drug addict awaiting her next fix. You, there, abandoning yourself. The peak of our love state or a mere transitional moment. There are adjustments to make and new identities to assume. I hear you calling out to me in silent screams. I can taste how you feel. Your aftertaste settling into the dying undulations of my frail taste buds, slowly melting to the lower ground and filling the crevasses as it runs out.

I want to become you, even if only partially.
I want to eat you, even if only figuratively.
I want to devour you, even if only in my mind.

From: caliph8@sharia4ever.org

The issue of sex in our religion can be best explained with the story of the sorcerer's apprentice and the pink elephant. The master of alchemy, after explaining to his apprentice the complex steps to be followed in making gold, said: "And, most importantly, throughout the entire process you must not think of the pink elephant."

Having been duly impressed by this warning, the apprentice tried desperately to heed it, but, of course, was unable to keep the forbidden subject out of his thoughts. At last he had to give up his attempts at making gold and sadly approached his master: "Why, my master, did you have to tell me not to think of the pink elephant? If you had not, I would have never thought of it." You see my friend, the pink elephant is the sex taboo. Do we need to find distraction in such triviality? Do we need to be led astray from our most righteous path by false temptation? You wonder why everyone is so preoccupied and withdrawn all the time. Sex is everywhere! Time to reign it in bro! #inshallah

Your fingerprints linger longer, the trace of you a mere remembrance of how bad things had gotten. *Te quiero*, she worded with a hint of sexual undertone aggression. I will not be played again. Unaccustomed to the seasons I wait in hibernation. A rising tide motion of exiled non-splendor. An in between time. And unfortunately yes there is a pause in my mind and during that lapse I do see through the clarity to a better place, a softer landing, a simpler time. Does the conversation always need to turn so dark. I would like to keep your panties for a while, to remember you, and to not forget your smell. Until the next time. If there is ever a next time. It is all about the scenery. And the landscapes. Your body on its side and regarded in silhouette, the high curve of your hip, the slope toward your feet, the narrowness of your waist. What was the question. This is universal in any language. If it is written then it is made to be forgotten. The trenches have been dug, the enemy awaits the orders. I wish that I could see through you, and through the deception and fondness. Not that it matters anymore. And remember that this is of little consequence to history. I know how you wanted it to be. Sometimes you can blend it all into the background noise, but often it jumps right back at you. I want to unplug the chords, I want to cut the ties, disconnect, and leave it all behind. Except for you. At least a semblance of you. In the afterthought of the afterglow. An afterlife guise waiting to be reborn. We can circumnavigate this impending storm or enter through the front door and hope to make it to the exit. In one piece, together, conjoined. We could do it for the sheer sake of privacy or collaboration. The suspicions subsiding with each changed cliché, insight into the worldwide and internal battlements, this war without end, under these apocalyptic terms, the new outposts of decadence, another setback, another winner amid the slow decline of our ambitions. We can hide behind the fluorescent glow of retail neon brilliance or stare down the spying satellites with conviction and insight, nude to the audience, skinny dipping outside the water. Who should be surprised. I always wanted to be a productive member of society. You can overcome this. This will not be another setback.

Slowly revealed, the intense fragility of perfection.

Her perfection.

My perfection.

Proper maintenance, grooming, product launches, fragrances, natural, organic and chemical. She slowly speaks: *the world is here for your own construction.* I am flattered and flustered. What was I thinking when I thought that this was such a good idea. I am on your side in this. Have you considered the harder questions. The placebo drugs. The radiation and the peel treatments. You will look the same but feel quite different.

There were too many opportunities for missed communication. Failed attempts at trying to understand one another, like any unwanted responsibility it weighs you down. One day this should be forgotten, handed over to the non-functioning parts of our minds. A cloud within a cloud, an elapsed chamber in an abandoned mansion just outside of town. We are all simply character studies of our own fallacies and myths. Science in your sway, progress in your pout. I imagine you as a baby, at different stages of development, but I return to the now. You are grown and full figured. Developed, legal, ripe, ready to be consumed and savagely devoured. Comfortable now in your leisure suit but when you are nude from the waist down and your important female parts are being commanded by the close proximity confines of my mouth and its trickery your comfort will give way to sublimation and the most sanguine of outlooks. I promise. There is a process to this authentication. Trust me, I have done this before. We can wait for your skin to dry. We can properly hang your athleisure on a rod. They are wrinkle-free you say. Still, I want you to be at ease. The revolution is all about you. I am happy you chose to make yourself available. I will count your breathing now, the tempo and cadence. I will slip underneath and beat along with it, unassumingly and inconspicuously. At one point you will not even know I am there. Until I take you in my mouth. It will be subtle and will feel natural, as if I belong attached to you. The anti-parasite apparatus. Something you can believe in. Something you can call a friend. An aid, a device, something that makes you feel warmer, wanted and sated. I telephoned you-know-who for permission. Your engagements have been set back a few days. This is best given the current circumstances. Your red lips now talk to me and tell me where to go. They send their warmest regards. You are now about to forever alter the soundtrack of my life. I am lost in the confusion of the explosion of shadows. In the room, against your skin, between your legs. I no longer remember the solitude. The loneliness multiplied several fold. The distinction between the store bought and the homemade. If you scream now I will have to take proper measures. Please do not make me slit my own tongue. Your heart beat breath releases the only measurement of time in these dark corner margins and precincts of slow motion continuum. The initiative initiated. We avoid eye contact, and for good reason. This is that leap of faith moment, if only briefly, suspended in the movements, held up in the gridlock of your shame. Please try to inhale, if not for me then for the sake of safety and investment. This induction into a more secure place.

The icon and the warning. Waning, I wrap my spirit around you, behold you in 360 degree fashion, a film camera on a boon, gliding in and out of focus. Lost in the labyrinth of your devastation. Sea sick in my mind trying to stay afloat while I swim toward the ripples of your spasms. The warm cold whimpers from the wreckage. I am not you but if I could become you I would. You are the solitary bee and I am the nectar. You approach me tentatively then land. You feed off of me. In me you find protection from the elements. The motions become habitual. Throbbing and raw we collide. Our next actions are uncertain. We lose all decision making, we suspend verdict for belief. A new kind of paranoia sets in, with it a new resolve. If I am to be taken it will be on my own terms, my own decree. I am wet now and the drain is slowly leaking, the water level descending along the sheer wall of my impairments. I am a bandit and you are my gypsy lover. We will walk alone, lost, disillusioned, under a muted silence, words and metaphors and analysis will serve no purpose. You will be even more exquisite. Your face lit by the morning sun, your skin aglow like an entranced child. Nothing abrupt, nothing appalling, only common language, lips against lips, your white pants as symbol, your limbs in slow motion playing now in the mirror's reflection. We will not be held accountable any more. The uneasiness of the day melts away with the forgotten obligations, to the world, to our health and to our future. I cannot see yet what I believe. Look me in the eye and tell me you are not okay. These brief moments of authenticity and the loss in self. Your wrinkle free white pants with no panty line nor hint of surplus. The heat from the smell, the exhaust, exhausted and beat, beat down by the zealous thought of you coming over again tonight. There are times when the best and only thing to do is to wait. The unfolding blossom of the trees, the slow bite of your tongue and the awaiting plague. The looped video in your mind of everything you had not done and everything you did not intend on doing. You, the product of your own regret.

From: caliph8@sharia4ever.org

Hello friend. I know you asked before about female circumcision, so here it is. The main purpose is to prevent the girl from wanting to engage in illicit premarital sex. This would be the case for clitoridectomy surgery. Now, if you want it to be altogether impossible for her to even have sex then we would go with infibulation, which involves stitching together the vulva. You see my friend, this all goes way back into the days before Islam. The old tribes considered it a requirement for marriage. I personally don't see anything wrong with it. We cannot allow fervent whoredom from our sisters. So anything to help out in this day and age of sluts on parade! My friend, while we are on the topic of sex, let me explain the eros of Islam. It is quite simple. We see women as an erotic subject to pursue. This is true, that we cannot hide. But here is the hook, are you ready? If we pursue them and conquer them then it is our duty to condemn them! You see it is ok from a distance to have a certain erotic viewpoint but you should never consummate it. And women have the attitude and knowledge that sex is shameful and this is the most righteous thought they can possess. You see my friend, this western thought of free love and pornos and women in bikini thongs in advertisements, well this is all good for your horny culture, but not for us on the righteous path. Can you feel me on this one my brother? #inshallah

You casually email me that you could not find your vibrator and you were asking me if I knew where it was or if I accidentally took it home with me last weekend, and that since you could not find it you ended up using your roommate's and that worked out just fine, it was more worn in, so that was special. You were not sure if you were going to tell her about borrowing it but you thought that it might bring you two closer if you were to be honest and forthright with her and sometimes were able to borrow it, and if you ever found your own that she could use it too. Maybe they could be kept in the bathroom that way either one of you could access the one of choice at their time of pleasing.

If I wore panties they would be wet by now.

I try to cling to the last threads of composure before I rescind my fore sworn dignity. I will remain calm in public if I see you again but inside I will feel like acting out on my impulses, like jumping you, pulling your skirt up, being a little too rough, ravaging you short of rape. Of course if when you see me again you do not want to go all out or be part of the very intense sexual exploration ride along with me then please remember and try to do the following: no direct eye contact with me; do not smile; do not glance in my direction even when you think I am not looking; do not laugh at my jokes; do not be helpful; do not be thoughtful; do not lick your lips; do not bite your lips; do not stand close enough to me so that I can smell you; do not try to look any certain staged way, like *put together hot* or *lazy couch chic*; do not do anything with your mouth like eating or drinking, anything to trigger thoughts of oral sex; do not make any sounds that could be construed as sexual in any way...and, most importantly, do not touch me.

I was bored and horny so I went online and searched for you by name and I came across a document that mentioned you had another last name because you had gotten married. You were four years older than I thought. Also it has been eleven years since I saw you. I wondered briefly if you ever thought of me. It does not matter. I imagine your huge tits in my hands, your warm pussy in my face, licking you there just as you liked it. I saw your email address and I thought of emailing you but then thought that it would be pointless. I then searched with your new married name for images of you. The only picture that came up of you was from last year and you are noticeably older and heavier or at least that is how you look in the photo because you are wearing a turtleneck. I was happy to see your face again. I right clicked on the picture and set it as my desktop wallpaper. The resolution was not the clearest but I could still tell it was you and if you could see me now I think you would find comfort in backgrounding my home screen.

The smell of the interstate cooling at night in the desert air, oil and humidity...sexual in its own rustic way, the sport utility parked on the shoulder, where I left it when I went to pee. You are asleep in the back and I think about you sucking me off here with the setting vista. Your ass the size of a continent, parted front and center and hot in the folds, wet to the touch, excited by the outdoor thrill of nowhere to go and the faded forgotten memories of where you have been. Redeeming in its shapeliness, a caricature of itself, free of cellulite. It is an exaggeration and I am in the mood for opulence.

The moon, a smile in the sky, the peach fuzz the color of flames…I lick the palm of your hand and run my open fingers along your delectable fruit…you drip into the smalls of my hand…they are inviting me to taste them as the sweet juice explodes on my tongue.

Another so called journey where you will either enjoy yourself or endanger yourself with the moribund aftertaste of spoiled produce, of failed scientific studies, of protested research of rank and foul odors and other pungent musings of who and why and where. Please be sure to read carefully your sworn statement before you sign on the dotted line. I can do you first if you prefer. Then it will be my turn to get off. The smells bring back the faded memories of that time. These treatments were not approved but they still seemed to work if at least for the psychosomatic effect. The combined protest of another medical freak, a feat left best unsaid, something for the books, something to not dwell on, something to try to suppress from your memory, to not only forget but to delete for all time from the canons of your mind. I think you might enjoy this.

From: caliph8@sharia4ever.org

Hello my friend. It has been a minute. You doing well with things? May I finish my thoughts on Islamic eros? There is a gap between belief and actuality. This is paralleled with the schism between public and private behavior. There is no public behavior in the sex department. Any and all PDA is abhorrent to the Muslim. You see, we like our women covered from head to toe. We want her body's outline and silhouette of curves concealed as well. Because of this we see Westerners as immodest and immoral. All of these fitted blouses with open necks showing cleavage, push-up bras, elaborate unveiled faces covered with painted makeup and fancy hair. The tight yoga pants revealing the outline of the buttocks and sometimes the lady parts, the camel toes. It is hard to look away but these sluts bring shame to their clan. Where is this whoredom headed my friend? What is the end game? Send some pics! Miss you! #inshallah

The Brazilian Butt Lift Miami surgery is a butt augmentation procedure that results in a more prominent, perky and attractive buttock area, a sensuous silhouette and an hourglass figure. An overall enhanced anatomic curvature of the region, establishing markedly feminine buttocks and hips that project more to the rear and more to the sides. Your own body fat is used to augment the buttocks in the most natural of ways.

With age the buttocks can drop. A Brazilian Butt Lift Miami helps fight the effects of aging. It is considered a safe form of plastic surgery because of the use of the patient's own fat. This helps in providing amazing, long-lasting results. Through the process of liposuction, fat from various other areas of the body (abdomen, back, flanks, hips and thighs) is removed, slimming those areas and providing a more contoured look. The removed fat is then processed and only the most pure and viable fat is injected into the buttocks. This is also known as a fat transfer. This enhances the size of the buttocks, which is massaged and reshaped to provide a more youthful appearance. The harvested fat cells are placed between the muscle layers and close to a blood supply where they have a greater chance at survival instead of being absorbed by the body. Fat transfers also create new collagen since fat contains stem cells that help create new tissue, improving the overall texture of skin. The fat transfer is made through very small incisions into the buttocks. The fat restores shape and volume and tightens the skin, all while providing a more youthful appearance and shape. It will not look anywhere masculine when I am done.

We will pay close attention to ensure that the buttock musculature results in a balanced walk, or stable gait, and not damage any muscles in the procedure. Not to get all technical, but the upper aspects of the buttocks end at the iliac crest and the lower aspects end at the horizontal gluteal crease, where the buttock's anatomy joins the rear and upper portions of the thighs. These are the two points of insertion. The left and right buttocks are divided by the intergluteal cleft (butt cheek) which contains the anus. The interior gluteal nerve structure divides into four or more fillets that travel in a crow's foot pattern across the gluteus to the anterior fascia. You see, it is a delta of nerve endings. This is why when you are spanked in certain areas it hurts, and in other areas it is pleasurable. This is the best alternate to actual buttock implants, which typically run the risk of rejection and complications from suture ruptures, implant exposure and infection. With BBLM there is minimal scarring and a much improved body contouring in the areas where the fat was harvested. Not to mention the intangible benefit of increased self-confidence. You will be far from your current state of gluteal hypoplasia, aka flat ass.

The procedure will be done with general anesthesia (a cocktail of lidocaine and apinephrine) and will take about two hours, depending on various factors such as the amount of fat that needs to be removed and the desired shape and size of the buttocks.

You will be placed in a state called operative plaxis. This will allow me to manipulate you into various positions. There are still risks to consider: discomfort, infection, asymmetry, capsular contracture, injury to the sciatic nerve, paresthesia, in other words, tingling of the skin, hematoma and excessive blood loss.

Post-op: You will need to wear a special compression garment, which is meant to support the buttocks tissue and compressed areas that have been lipo'd, to facilitate healing. You will need to wear adult diapers. You will need to refrain from putting too much weight on your buttocks for several weeks. Sitting should be done on something cushioned or padded and is not recommended for prolonged periods of time. We must prevent the fat from being absorbed or displaced. You should also refrain from sleeping on your back. You will need someone to massage your buttocks, this is in order to avoid the shrinking of the skin as it adapts to the new contours, and to resolve unevenness and localized swelling. You will need three weeks before you can return to work. It will be about two months before you fully recover from the bruising, swelling, soreness and pain. It is then that you can start working out, and partake in intense physical activity. The fat transfer will remain in your buttocks for the rest of your life. It will age with you just like the rest of your body tissues, which dictates the importance of a healthy lifestyle including exercise to help maintain the shape and size of the buttocks.

Your body image expectations may be different than the outcome. We are trying to avoid these unmet expectations now. We need to agree on a realistic and feasible outcome. Any resulting defects or deformities can usually be corrected with liposculpture, be it ultrasonic or not. Depressed scars and deep morphological defects are more difficult to correct because of the curvature of the buttocks as an anatomic unit. But for the sole purpose of looking like a woman, that desired Cameron Diaz ass in some leggings or tight size 10 jeans, I am more than confident we can get you there.

She was very womanlike with a breathy voice. Ready and willing to insult on the slightest impulse. At times I could not believe that she had taken it so far. The forensics of a meltdown on the verge of backing out. All the jovial banter, all the time-worn charming good looks, the professionally done makeup, the jazzy strut, the delayed matrimonial frenzy she deployed in well-timed staccato spurts. Our moments spent together short but effective. All the times we did it quote unquote wheelbarrow-style, as she liked to call it. Reminiscent of a rare hotness, a gorgeousness that does not come along too often. I avoided her schizophrenia as best I could and I think I did a fairly good job with that at the time. All of the returned purchases and dealing with the faked bank transfers. And then the fire and all of its ramifications. A rotating maze in my mind, a labyrinth of lost hope and slow motion demise, a spaceman without his ship, the intuition no longer compatible, the preoccupation no longer fun. There is not much left to do at this point. Except rotate the vortex in the prisms of light bouncing off the walls of your failing consciousness, a derided deviation of what is normal and to whom. And to think that this all started with a garter belt. It would have been better if I had never seen it at all. I would be better off. I did not enjoy it at the time and I certainly never thought that the repeating and reworking and remapping of the scene and what had transpired would ever get to an addictive level so toxic with additives, with what I wanted to remember, what I idolized, what I wished it to be, what I willed into being. Was she what I remember. Was she what I still sought out. Or was she no more than a morphed-out doll version, a simile of my own fantasy idealization. A one woman citizen of a nation state all my own. The perfect woman made up of perfect parts: extensive hips, slight legs, spongy feet, bulky ass, substantial tits, lithe shoulders, tapered neck, elegant hands, striking face, manicured nails and done-up hair. How else could one better define the ideal. The idle idea. Regardless of productivity and significance and worth. Self- and monetary. A void space of rejection.

Do not feel like you owe me anything, but I did crawl on all fours; I stalked; there was proper surveillance; I studied; I watched long into the night and often well into the mornings; I followed covertly so as not to alert you or cause you any harm or discomfort or concern; I preyed and I hunted—but all for the most noble of causes. I saw the faint recollections in your eyes and manners from the childhood paranoia. A resurgence of sentiments and emotions you buried long ago. There was fever in the revelation. I saw how you busied yourself with empty rituals of routine errands and tasks, to a newfound spiritualist's candle burning and the like. You seemed very together on the surface but inside you were becoming undone, threadbare. An invisible decomposition, amid mass distortion in the silence. You failed in the adaptation department. I know, I know, that was never a concern. There are lots of things best left undone and unsaid. I do not blame you nor does my respect wane. There is coherence in your thoughts and lucidity in the wind. Now I understand the whitewash and the dry baths. Your remnants and the scars will always remain. And if nothing is forever, they are at the least the most permanent of permanence that we will come across, splendid as they are. Like rose petals as metaphor, red lips swollen by lust and hunger. Curved and parted, flaccid but full of thrill. A red like no other red before it. A heavy and disturbing history, the illusion in progress. The parables of assumption and all of the certainty behind her. Her eyes failing to translate the storm within. The circumference in the shadows she cast unwanted and wanton, the slow preparation in her wait, in her impediments and delay. She was deliberate and nothing was going to change that. This is how it works, she would claim, and this need not extend beyond my own personal experience, nor leave this room. One must respect the physics. And the psychics. A new southbound direction, a new latitude, a new set of events to overcome. A reprieve from the bad posture and the metaphorical smoke lingering in the room, something to fill the wasted space. Redemption. On multiple levels, both above ground and underground. Nothing in particular out of the ordinary. Except perhaps everything. Which is nothing to cause alarm or prejudice. There is restraint in her silence. In her stillness and peace. Her flesh now smooth as satin, or velvet with the grain. Her lips less inflamed and inflated, the red deadening with each passing moment. Her notion of self-dissolving in deliberate slow motion. We cannot weep for the loss. There is sunlight in the blight. In context it is more than beautiful, ineffable and spiritual, as if she is cleansing for a sacrificial lamb, a surrender to the leaders and the gods. A slow dive to greater depths. Her carved out heart in her bloody hands. There were others but they will go unmentioned here. They would sometimes intrude and attempt to invade the psyche and hold my mental imagery hostage, a willing captive to the role playing. I look into her eyes and I only see the red. I do not look down because I am afraid of what her body may say. At this point the choice is not mine. I struggle with impromptu danger, of moonlight swimming, alone, fully clothed, in a canal along the roadway. Can you feel it. Can you smell it. As the high speed cars and dirty semis drive by. The sound of her squinting and whispering, *I cannot go on much further*.

I no longer knew what to make of her. Of the twitching. Of the stutters. It was no longer side acts to the passion, like it used to be. This was now more about an actual medical condition. Perhaps psychological but still physiological. I was too afraid to ask anyone, and I certainly was not going to bring up my observations with her, she would have none of that. That was for certain. But there was also the slurred speech. It was no longer only during the sex, but now it was more commonplace and in everyday situations. When she woke up, or on the telephone, in the car. It had to have been neurological. She also did not respond like she used to. It was not as if she did not care, rather it was more like she could not make the connection from one thing to the next, no cause and effect, no point A to point B. The string of logic had come unraveled, and she seemed under the weather, like in a dream space wonderland. At peace and still, half alive. Her tongue looser and less at will. Another small hill on a larger mountain, the visual of the bulging nipples on her mammary mounds. Should I just sit back and do nothing to enforce my litany for the orbits better known as her curves. As dangerous as they are. There should be a street sign warning. I fall inside and outside of you. All efforts by the authorities have been met, legalities and obscene obfuscations. Her body more an experiment than a work of art. What do we have here, a new piercing? I am surprised you never told me about this. Yet again I am surprised you tell me anything at all. If you ever remove it please let me be in the room. A concession to an audience of one. It is all just infotainment on an adult viewer level. Something slightly out of scale. The dimensions blurred like the raindrops that drip against the windshield of our awareness. I am not me and you are not you. At least at times. Those transcendent times of near catastrophe and reckoning. I visualize inappropriately a monsoon in your underpants. I sit back and regard it in full, playing out in real time, heating me, hardening me with each slight second that passes and another slice in time. A better now than never mindset of customized dreamscapes, of slideshow imagery of her ass naked and smashed up against the glass, her privates spread wide and wider still, in all of its glory and shame, it is hot and the lights are bright, the rendezvous has yet to take place, the drop spot yet to be determined, we are close to the timeout point, the requests have all been submitted, the code names set, the disguise is on but her identity remains certain, I long for the release, but am patient for the outcome, for the coming out, for coming out, for coming, out.

Enchanted you begin to see the ghosts in the room, you feel the pounding inside, the collective mapping of your sexual dysfunction making a turn for the better, the most savage of arguments, the domestic goddess condition, the subsequent marriage gone bad, the misinterpretation of this or that saga, of the suspicions in your borderline resentment, your refusal to believe that the abduction and ensuing rape scene were staged, the memories and reactions all interspersed, the questions lingering, the dreamy narrative maddening, you lose track of the accused, your coyness is delight in its own battered woman stylization, the tastes and smells overlapping into a sanguine half-allusion to the failing and flailing truth behind the one-way mirror, the plots and the secrets, the con, the twists, the underdog, the protagonist, the invitation list, the non-jokes, the curiosity in the slight runs of her pantyhose, her cleavage as the best humanity has to offer, the obsession with plastic surgery in the extreme, labiaplasty, buttock implants.

We are left to fend on our own: bite, munch, swallow, lick, grin, breathe, collapse. There were no guides, no compass, no lights to lead the proper way. All of this will be mentioned in the filing. There will be similar accusations. Daunting, in its arctic coolness. The dysfunction in the big wheel turning around and around. It is too hard to recall the course of events, however, there are hints and there are less than subtle souvenirs. The goal may not be admirable but it is oblique. We were not allowed to divulge any more than that. Not even less than that. The semblance was in the hard drive that I called my mind. The images kept coming back to me: her, there through the screen door, much younger than she is now, in her late teens, dirty and barefoot, dressed only in a too-small bikini, the lead-based turquoise paint on the door frame peeling, the light setting behind her, her silhouette accentuated, and duly noted are her erect nipples. I recall also a backyard behind her, it was full of junk and overgrown plants, a modern ruin, charming in its negligence. The perfect backdrop to her outline, tanned, shivering. I have said too much…I cannot recall anything else.

From: caliph8@sharia4ever.org

You might say that I am jealous by the American woman and her slutty ways and freedom to go outside. All I can say is that I am glad she is not my sister. Every night being allowed to party on the town, to entertain men, dress like sluts, to flaunt her sex onto anyone that pays attention. I quote from Qur'an 7:26, "O children of Adam, we have provided you with garments to cover your bodies as well as for luxury. But the best garment is the garment of righteousness. These are some of God's signs, that they may take heed." You see my friend, just because the clothes are there doesn't mean she can choose to dress like a whore. Our intention should be people of honor, held in high regard, with purpose and substance. Not push-up bras and thongs. Do we really need more temptations and distractions from the righteous path? #inshallah

She is tribalism exploded, the underdog, the anti-imperialist revolutionary. Always on the verge of collapse, threading in between dreams and love, washing away pain with purpose. An illusory sequence of wrapping limbs, love declarations and feigning instability. This is a new beginning from a somewhat older end. The implants are looking real and the soundtrack is more upbeat. Whatever it is about her cannot be named. She was the objective but now more a side player as I drift from the mooring. Unintentionally she will stay in my dream. She can remain the picture of love and forgetfulness, with those thick thighs and those troubled eyes. I quiet the hum in my mind to visualize her process, the shivers from the soul and her screams to get out. I feel her eyes upon me and the blood flow to the nothingness, the oblique failed attempts at temptation and lure. Exposed whole to her, I hold my breath as I swim in her vacant holes of warmth and wetness. No plans to resurface, she whispers inches from my ear, get up now, get…up…now. Her voice cascading a melting moonlit sky, a new kind of methodology. I regard her reflection in the blue and white impressions, contours outlined by the warm breezy sun, a picture of a more innocent time. Less complicated, less intricate, less dense.

She was holding in her stomach, arching and propelling her chest forward. She had her cheeks sucked in as well. She looked slimmer, tighter, easier to handle. Restored. It was my turn to comfort her. On occasion I would look up but mostly I fixed my eyes to her waist level. She would hold my hand. I acquiesced regardless, the willing participant, the reluctant disdainer. There will be a harvest after the labor. I slide my tongue along the rough edges of her skin. The tolls of time and the ravages of a lifetime of submission. She is mine now and nothing before has ever taken place except for what is remembered and even then our memories deceive. She is wetter now. She no longer wants to flee, she is courageous, bold and daring. Resistance has given way to fringe behavior, manners and conduct slightly out of the ordinary and norm. Edgy, ill conceived, daunting and frustrating. She is driven by the intent and by the inside motions, the conventional pulls and pushing. She is far from lost but is ruffled still, displaced in her own realm, entranced by the distant stares, quieted by the small discrete moments. I do not know what to say...in what cadence, what diction, what voice, what volume and level. And in another moment it will have changed, it will have not mattered.

Insignificance comes with the delay. I readjust in the light. The new perspective brings new measure, as I squint to see my only aspiration. The stimulation and release, the wander and wonder. The contagiousness in her airborne appeal, the hesitation in her step. The serenity of her soul and hardness of her core. The rippled calm on her sea of humiliation. The elsewhere that she never visits. The depth in her process. The indiscreet clutter in her mind. The aftertaste of her afterthought. Her walk without end.

From: caliph8@sharia4ever.org

Qur'an 7:80-84: "For ye who practices your lust on men in preference to women, ye are indeed a people transgressing beyond bounds, and we will rain down upon you a shower of brimstone." You see, my friend, the homo life is bad. When a man mounts another man the throne of God shakes a little. In my country, when we round up the gays we have these secret cops that do very bad things to them as fair punishment for their transgressions, like beat them up, flog them, lash them, stick things in their butts, humiliate them in public...very bad things. If these homos are caught in the act usually in some clans it means immediate death sentence. The Sharia is pretty clear about this. It is all very dirty stuff. I am just happy you like women and are on the righteous path my friend. More pics boo! #inshallah

The amazement.

The nothing at all.

Her reflection in the glass table, the marble base underneath. Her bosom like a large umbrella flared out to protect. The beggar in us all. That moment when you first go down, the unknown and the propensity for utter surprise. The obligations that come with the view. The comfort in not knowing. Her fairness, her coloring, her pretensions. All in all, time to time, a reason to look up, an occasion to check the merchandise and quality of the goods.

She had been standing all night. It has been fourteen days. She complained that it felt like labor pains. I felt a waning pity for her, the slavery to the circumstances. The poetry in the glass of water. An affinity to the attention. I observed her hair was harsh and that she wanted to return home. The gateways and the getaways and the possibilities in her genial countenance. Her figure no longer hidden from me. That long brown hair, brushed out, full and thick. She was very emphatic and impatient and all of the things that you would suspect of a woman of her demographics. She was still reserved in many ways. The virtual forthrightness in the way she touched herself. The trembling like a fiend, the subtle anxiety in her voice. The insignificance of the price when she never looks at the tag. The teenager inside of her, the girl just behind the eyes. The release when her thumb presses firmly against you there. The lost thoughts of a shower scene, of steam and the sound of falling water and weakened knees. Her popularity lost to a wishful existence, the latest maneuver in her play book. The choice of remaining clothing to remove. Her bra or panties. Her weakness for certain vices. Her questions of where she would be ranked if she were ever ranked. Her willingness to welcome you at any hour of the day. The theft that is embedded in her heart. Her next move. Her tight pants. Her forlorn member on partial display. Her choice of opening statements. Her submission to romance and its ideals. The pirate inside of her. Remember to smile. All of the recommendations. The next big deal, the next breakthrough, the next excuse to call it all off. As I sit next to her I give in to a small touch. A trick from the rule book. I smell her perfume. An expensive jasmine. An excuse to move in closer still. Do not hesitate. Remind me to reach behind her and to keep my shirt on. Good things happen with patience. Do you prefer the new version or the old. The good behavior or the bad. She is a weapon unaware. I could use the better details but I have had enough of waiting. The magic games, the catalog pictures torn out and taped to the wall, for inspiration, for the muse, for the sake of the passing fad. She told me she was branded but she would not say where. Her zest was synonymous with her appetite, equally voracious, equally endearing. The way she dropped her panties, a telegram of deceit, a ploy at my undoing, a stroke at the fire of my madness, further weakening my cause, the effect unrelenting and tender. The magic in her breath, the rapid processing of the thrill and rush running downstream, a one way street late at night and we were driving without the headlights on.

This is not how it was originally advertised, this was not the Natasha that I knew. This was not the Nathalie that I knew. This was not the Katja that I knew. Or the Holly, or the Kimberly, or the Pippa that I was so fond of. This was another level and another game. You can take back your catalogs of smooth lines and sleek colors and pages that smell of perfume and warehouses, all those chicks with their outfits denoted by As and Bs and Cs and F and occasionally up to L or M. The sizes from small to double extra-large. The cups from A to DD. The DDs for the heavy girls. The edges all smoothed out and the rough stuff brushed out. A finer polishing for a silkier final product. I want what is in there, dressed or naked, fat or thin, clean or dirty, blonde or brunette, curvy or plain, expensive or cheap, in stock or backordered. The savagery of failed mental and menial attempts thereof. Scale the vector, escape the reservation, ride the conveyor belt to nowhere, this material is not for show.

Please consider yourself forewarned: it gets much worse. And then it all came to be a long and comprehensive flashback with an attention to detail rivaled only by immediate reality. Look no further I told myself, there is nothing worthwhile behind that door. Nothing particularly special about that one girl on page 64 other than the fact that she is young and her tits are solid and firm under that camisole, and that she is exotic in a Brazilian meets German way, but sex with her would be a nightmare that results in cataclysmic ramifications. You can fantasize all you want and dream of her trimmed pubic, and when she bends forward and tells you *take me from behind, please*, or how her hard nipples fit perfectly in the cup that is your mouth when she is propped up over you with her size Cs suspended in fruitful animation, or how she sucks you off like a pro, like a porn star but with more realistic passion, like she really likes what she is doing and she really likes being there and that the longer it takes you to come the better because she has all the time in the world and her neck doesn't hurt and her mouth gets hotter with effort, or you imagine that she obliges your pass to go *there* and she tells you just don't go fast or any sudden movements, nothing that would hurt because it has been a minute since you let someone do that to you, and all of this with a Portuguese accent, or the smells that emit from under her arms or between her legs, those dark brown and full eyebrows, those swollen lips and crisp white teeth with slight imperfections, the stranger in her eyes and the lost girl look, that gaze of suspense, of hanging in the in between, this close to knowing, the black marks on the soles of her feet from the dirty floor, the feel of manicured nails running the length of your shoulders, the delicate lobes of her ears you nibble endlessly, her fluids you swallow and the waning flavors from sweet to a bitter bland but still delightful and desirable...page 64 dog eared, that lace trimmed 100 percent cotton elastic-free pink thong, how it comes to rest between her legs, the relaxed look, the framed painting, the captured art, poised in the best of lighting, hovering in a controlled environment, the curve of her spine, the arc to the treasure map of her back, the small bump reminders of the skeleton within, an agelessness to her as a whole, an homage to the ones before me, a deference to what may come, we walk the tightrope of playful deceit and treachery, hoping to not fall off, to not lose the pathway to the common ambition, the flashback imagery, a flickering dying projector bulb, of her there doing unspeakable things, all the while her splendor a virtual doll figurine given in to the corruption, a revelation of her inner side, the darker half, the bleaker depending on the audience, the ability to shock, the propensity to awe, to pound like thunder, to deconstruct her filmmaker, to take the dare, to expose anything and to freeze-frame it on command and request of you your ejaculate, to be beyond vulgar and bare none of the shame, to succumb to foreign dreams of perfection and precision, to yield to the undercut lust and allow you to bevel the edges, to light up her ultraviolet aura of unshakability, the rock star, the film star, the dying star on your last night in town, you Cinderella, your nurse in the short skirt, your teacher with a hair bun, your librarian with the wire rims, your mother's friend with all that mother's milk, the woman in the car at the red light, her sunglasses covering up the story she is trying to tell, the girl from page 64 and all of the other girls that came before her and the ones to come…and then you are brought back to that moment, a transcendental magical pause defying gravity and logic, back to the waiting and the clutching and holding onto whatever it is that is left, the slow low rumble vibrations, that moment when you realize that I am watching you, the touching and feeling, the reeling and the recovery, you admit to the imminent, to what is going to happen next, with the submission of a zealot, the fervor of a fanatic, no revisionist history here, no more distractions and loose ends, no more dirty clothes, no more failed relationships, no more hating of the game, no more hating the player, only connections along the outer walls of the confines that have set us free, new nuances, new shapes and sizing, with a new agreement with time, a new stage name, Jacqueline or Jenna...detoxify, an effort at cleaning up the scene, of the evidence, the forgetfulness of the stage fright, and the better resolution...yes, you come through better in this light, the flaws are more apparent but equally thrilling in their own imperfections, you the myth of science and discipline, she paves her own road to self-domination and unwarranted condemnation, a side effect to the forethought and night patrol detail, no ground beneath her feet, no handwritten note left on the nightstand, no left behind hair or whiskers from when she shaved there last night, her last night in this room, a fiasco in logistics, a cruel reminder of the ill-fated effects of space time and conspiracy, the benchmark for dogmatic injustice, of high art concepts, of atrophy and full moons...the way the night is lit, the costume of the assailant, she is lost in the gaze of the rising foam in the bath water, thoughtless, emotionless, free of want, free of hope, free of dreams and of fears.

A scapegoat for the inquisition, curvaceous as an acrobat in flight, deferring to the befallen, the real woman behind the mask, the lifting of the veils, losing the ship's registry, anonymous and unidentified, quality over quantity, your turn to order, your turn to choose, your turn to sort it all out, your turn to succumb, your turn to die and then live new again…take two a day, don't forget your password(s), an active shooter, in your pants, when you wake in the morning, during a hot shower, in the parked car, in a crowded store, in line to pay, numb to the deaths and the carnage that segue to hope and better planning, the increase in insurance premiums, all for one low monthly fee, our favorite song, do not be surprised if the impossible is asked of you, for the good of the fight, for the good of the team, for the good of the group, the collective mentality, nothing too perverse but it may require sex acts…the obligations and the slavery that drag you deeper and under from the mild lust, the forfeited hope for a better day and a better way, the questions of the whatnots and the with who's, and the Japanese market for such filth, and the size of her rack, and the calculated amount of curls in her hair, better luck next time, you are a ticking time bomb for the most part, an obligation to the betterment of virtually everything that disgusts and insults, but there is a ray of hope in you, a beforehand comment of warm up penance and atonement, of skill on display, of ability on exhibit, a showman for the minute few that care or dare to stare at your evolving acts of defiance and undoing, a marked life of failure and disgust, in who you may ask, in yourself and all that you represent and all that you do not represent...disembowelment or disguise, your segments on obsession to the other sex and her anus and all that you can fixate there, the tight bowels of collapse and defeat, hers and yours, get real, get a life, this craving will pass too, stay sane and try to stay clean, your mind is filthy friend.

The side show, the slide show, the freak show, the beforehand and the afterward, the prologue and the epilogue, fluency in the segments of one two three, the staccato rhythm of the counts, an illustrious disembowelment, the sensations and the larceny, a horror show horoscope of dismal forewarnings, the difficulty in the quasi-ness and the high faith moments of delusional grandeur, the blackmail and the theft, the perks and the decipher, the key to her heart and confessional clarity, the glamour in her mammaries, the perks to the trade, the confession to the hope and the postponement in the delayed gratification, the fun games with her fun bags, the thrill in the murder plot theme, the convention and convection in the crowd, a lost focus agenda, reprimanded, penalized...her revealing ways and refusal to succumb to the average-ness, she is the right bet, the wasteful pretense of a childlike wonder and wanderer, she violated more than her own rules, no need for a constitutional amendment, a gift to the reform, captured in perpetual atonement, an erotic terrorist rambunctious by even her own means, another violation and another act of abuse, civil disobedience, a lack of taxation and foresight, caving into the pressure, her failed attempt at makeup to hide the scars and stretch marks, the nothing woman, the enthusiasm in the packaging, all of the conspiracies and all of the conspirators, a new element to the equation, the logic in the sound and the waves in her tremble, are you ready to do time for my sins, to blow up this stable existence, to throw all caution into a furnace of shame.

I am ready for the slide.

From: caliph8@sharia4ever.org

The fourth Caliph once said: "The entire woman is evil. And what is worse is that it is a necessary evil." LMFAO. Did you know that women have a period once a month and that this makes them deficient in their religious practices? Did you know that the Prophet says the real contract of marriage is a license to play with the women's private parts, what's between the legs? Yes, sir, my friend. Did you know hell is full of whorish women, and in Paradise are only righteous men and the purest of virgins? I know it all sounds too good but you need to jump the leap with me my friend. A bit of faith to get us there. #inshallah

Her trifle enthusiasm was less contagious than the last time. She was simpler then. A better version than the now. I would speak directly to her, in soft tones and clear annunciations of every syllable and vowel. There was no need for interpretation, or analysis or grouping. We were as we were. Before the recent disintegration, a crumbling with exponential ramifications. Deliver us from evil. I gave her the time and the space and the understanding and she took it and ran with it and never quite returned...from the future, from the hiatus, from the other side. Until I could not find her. The only consistency was the continuance in her beauty. She aged well and is softer out of the shadows. That is what got us here. To this day, a woman of danger, courting trouble with each moment of unwrapped marvel and grandeur. The only thing I ever wanted, the pounding, the crashing, the metaphorical fractured spine. Should I wear a wire. Prepare for a shootout. The kind of breakdown that is inevitable when things get too good. For reason, for hope, for future anticipation. Beyond hypothesis, this is in the realm of freak show submission. I never imagined her so lovely. And compounding the pressing issue was her impetus and blind ambition for first rate results. In the byproducts, in the comments, in the dwindling belief that not all is alright. This had become personal and I was here to see to it, to see to the large areas, to see to her fruity smell and taste, to back up the files before they are destroyed. She shone in the rare spotlight. A mindless and emotional mess of lifted forgiveness and descent. I was not made for you, she liked to remind me. From here on out only the virtue of love continues, I countered back her way. In that white top I did not realize that your breasts were so big. Or is it the brassiere. Or are you swollen for any particular reason. Another failed diversion. The love is the only surviving remnant, it is the undercurrent, under the waves and the abyss, close to the ocean floor, close to the bottom of my heart and the stillness that exists there.

I want to start new and try it all over again but I cannot. I want it all to be simpler and younger but I cannot. I look in the mirror and see the age and the atrophy and come to the cold hard realization that time is traveling faster and faster and there is no way out of it. And nothing will be left behind to remind others of my former self. Of things I had done that affected people, of women I had known who specifically remembered me in their older years...the nothingness amid the stillness and the dark. And then I wish that I could wake up and continue living. I have had enough rest, now let me go at it again. I promise I will behave. And I will not commandeer the busy intersection when I get there. I just want to see less, to think less, to feel less, to be safely kept by the numbness and the anesthetized ethos of a marked man with some time to spare. No more semi-pornographic thoughts of her with that wide ass in front of me bending over in skimpy panties and tights and prodding me on, her center of gravity flaring open like a blooming flower in fast forward, inviting me to take her from behind, to do what I will on her, to offer me her services free of charge, to talk to me about her friend and how her friend's ass is even finer and that she could call her up. Or the dirty thoughts of sucking on lactating breasts, her angry at me for nibbling with my teeth. But she welcomes the relief. Or when she offers me her butt hole and tells me *do what you will just do it gently.* I think it, I visualize it, I create it. I manifest it in my mind.

Be prolific for a change and change the topic for once. She tastes so much grown across my lips. Her ambition wet and sodden. Translucent to my adulation of her soft gyrations and moaning. She plays the younger part, the innocence before the unspeakable acts. The symbolic virgin before the rape. Deserving of the solicitation, justified in the compensation.

From: caliph8@sharia4ever.org

What is the attraction to martyrdom you ask? Well I can tell you this, the power of the spirit and my faith in Him pulls me upward, while the power of the material world pulls me downward. I am hell bent on martyrdom and am immune to the material pull. Even if the operation fails I will meet the Prophet and His companions. You see my friend it is all good and righteous. Nothing to fear my friend. #inshallah

The way the soft breeze blows gently through the muslin and the small sounds of the branches tapping against the house. Reminders of a simpler approach, a revelation on slow time display, the antithesis of a quickie. The next addiction, the next crime. I will be damned, I can hear her say. *Mais oui, mais oui.* Those torpedo nipples, the rotation of the falling disregard for those around you, the compatibility in the scope and the nighttime cover. From the shadows, from the fog, from the indiscretion, of hope, of anticipation and expectancy. This is simply beyond us at this point, and it is deserving of history and encouragement. Another slice of the pie. The hair pie, the clam, the taco. A piece of history in the making, primped and tasting like ripe fruit. The same color as last time. Wearing a poker face, a disguise to cover the arrangement, a campaign for further legacy. A barren canvas of waxed skin, tender to the touch and slightly discolored from the abuse and over usage. As we search out another undisclosed location, a solicitation for donations. Your wish is not mine. You are deserving regardless, and I am more than a sponsor. I feel drugged and blinded in more ways than one. A willing victim to whatever crime you may fancy. I admit to being heavily medicated, mostly over the counter stuff, lightweight narcotics, expired painkillers. I cannot break free from the chain gang mentality holding me down like a boot to my throat, the troubled images that return time and again to my feeble and vulnerable mind, an escape postponed, a life half lived. Water board drowning me in the void of you. Sustaining me only enough to keep me alive, edging my release, thrilling me enough to keep me hard in the waning moments of a man lost to the fog of slow demise, a lab rat fed poison, destined to an eternity of solitude and semi-vague boredom. One for the ages and then some.

There is always more, mostly hatched from the fate, the underbelly and the undercurrent, the soft breath from the long pause. Awake in the sunny shadows of her smile, unhindered by the indecision. The recollections in the curves of her lines and the tonality of her voice, when she was angry or scared or timid. The blend of the nostalgia and the melancholy, the never ending affection that lingers to this day, in the interwoven textures of life and the gentle steps. There is more than relevance in her wide angled silhouette. There is integrity and insolence. I trail the perfume of your love, the scent of your being, the movement of your words and haze. The sideways aesthetics and the half time spent sliding the key through your hole. The life-size cakewalk. The varying levels of income and outcome. The ability disguised as difference, and those soft tits. And those small fingertip sized nipples, pink with excitement, erect with abandonment. Another amazing level of intoxication without the bad conduct unbecoming.

You are amazing and you are not even programmed. How is that for better living. Every way possible and then some more. This initiative of futile demise. I am under your guidance. I am under your spell. Steeped in unreaped benefits from this and that, the misrepresentations of a formal investigation into detachment and other qualities not unique to you but part of your guise, a component to your costuming. A wide ranging disguise at that. Your undergarments and the well-maintained manifest destiny in the front yard. All green and lush and well-watered and so very inviting. The detachment in the favoritism of this latest representation of an attempt at sublimation gone awry. No need for any of the acts to be deemed illegal. Call it avant-garde or cutting edge, a slow ballad building to a crescendo thumping bass line. The dramatics of a yesterday twisted by memories in your favor, a better kind of souvenir. There is something wrong with the angling, something wrong with the lighting and something off with the wardrobe. But the show goes on in my mind, the theater rolls on, the drama unfolding in the soft folds of infatuation and happenstance. I shall remind you that I am no longer me. The me that you once knew, the one stifled in the face of caution. I am the new dangerous version, a stalker out for prey, a diseased porn star with no regard for others just a big dick that he is going to stick into whatever he fancies. But I digress.

This is a date. This is no way to proceed. My apologies. Your name is Helen, *amirite*?

From: caliph8@sharia4ever.org

There is a rumor that Arabs are addicted to sex more frequently than their neighbors in more northerly climates. Are we just more sensuous and prone to indulge in our pleasurable ways? Does sex play a more active role in the Arab mind than say the mind of a German? The hot climate brings all the boys to the yard. LOL! Can you blame us for being so deliberate in our appeal? There is a sumptuousness and lusciousness to the desert and it reflects in our ways. Shhh, don't tell the Prophet. LMFAO. #inshallah

An end to space and time and the beginnings of estate-like living. A brighter kind of woman, a closer type of friend. O, where art thou when I need you the most. In the dark of night, in the back recesses of my fizzling mind. The safe place for unsafe activity. Your voice the bonus track when I have nothing left. The front-scape and the landscape an escape into the enchanted fields, a place to hide, a place to call home in the shady times, when lost in the forest like a hunter without his dog, the options minimal, survival questionable, your death a welcome possibility. No need for more time, or angst or turmoil or second and third guessing of yourself and your choice or lack thereof. The quiet time that can come of it. The easy out. The cancellation of the campaign. The end of the discussion and the concussion, that I suffer every time. The list grows and gets longer, and my longing advances the same. For a new solution, for an easier way out. Someone who will allow me, someone who will commit and permit me the intrusion, or the marketing campaign of a maestro, something more than the industry standard, something more along the lines of low-level perversion. A more appropriate escape plan to hatch and implement, in your soft folds staring at your soft lines. A reason for the reasoning. The discharge from your pores the seasoning of my downfall. The nervousness and the misrepresentation. The feeling that you have to pretend that you are someone that you are not.

Perhaps I will never hear from you again. Please do not ditch me. I will behave. Do not feel obligated. There are no rules to play by. No checklists. Just you and I and the countdown. The count up. The pent up anger and energy and horniness. You want to explode right about now. And then you stall. I will show you mine even if you don't show me yours. I have goals and ambition. The ramifications, the self-help tricks, the magical exertions at release and liberation. I am a multi-faceted player in a game that has no sides, no teams, no uniforms or cheerleaders.

Your love a campaign for the struggle, good news for a dark day, the industry standard, I will be the guest if you will be the hostess, a newer kind of white, a newer kind of Anglo Saxon depravity and just cause for a just crime, lifted by your loftiness, harvested opium in golden fields, the latest fashion wear, the latest in undergarments and disguise, more easily managed from the rear, the solution letting itself in languidly and easily, like slowed down morning light infiltrating the room. I will try to accommodate as many of you as possible, but as always, no guarantees and no lasting interface.

The slipstream side swiped undoing of skin against skin, slippery when wetter, the appetite, the smell, the imagery, the reality—of too much too soon, of authenticity in question and backlit shadows of foregone dreams for a bit of peace, a bit of quiet, when it is all just too much. The gushing of your waterways drowning me out, the domestic pet that cannot swim. The upskirt photo in your mind that you cannot shake. Real or a fake, staged amid the bright fluorescent lighting at the mall to keep you from getting sleepy so you will buy more, the soft techno beats to keep your spirits up. The plaid, the Burberry, the pleats. The soft of her inner thigh, the bleached cotton smashed against the plump package. The black lint or pubic, that which cannot be distinguished. The slight wrinkles and folds, the blemishes and red spots, fleshy and round. Spent and uneasy, a lost species, one of a kind, alone in my dark thoughts and perversions, my mouth a wasteland of wasted talent. On the brink I wait for the deluge. A conduit to the other side of this soon to be allocated time space sliver of my life, of preferences in tastes or lack thereof. There are no drawbacks only experiences gone awry. Feel free to be clumsy; it is less contrived that way. You are too neat, break free from the confines that hold you back. The lightning in your cavern, waiting for the air and room light. All of this because of the upskirt angle. Nude, on your side, in spoon positioning, deep asleep I enter you from behind. I do not move you, I try not to rock the bed. Only short slow strokes, aligned just right for minimal interference. I hold you by the hips. And smell the conditioner in your hair. And the cotton sheet against my ass. You are reliable like that, and it is appreciated. I am tenacious and I know that you admire that about me. The movements are bionic, mechanical, clean, neat. Any handicaps disappear with the repetitive motion of erotic defeat. I am the victim as well as the attacker. The prisoner and the guard. Your rash has subsided in the dark and is smooth to the touch, your imperfections bleed away with heightened craving for your backside spread and enlarged: wide hips vertical, warm lips opened for want, soft short hair for protection from the elements. The nectar behind your ears. The transcript of stretch marks along your curvilinear sides. Feverish I burrow into your canal of charitable fervor. Undone but much closer still. Closer than ever before. A good distance from the fantasies. I acquiesce to the ludicrous lovebird Beaujolais tastes of her lips and resign myself to the volcanic overflow petitioning of today to keep the image alive for future reference.

From: caliph8@sharia4ever.org

My friend, I admit there is so much sexual frustration in Islam but I can tell you that when we allow the social controls to break down, we can allow the repressed aggression to surface...and it is then that we can act upon the urges and sort out the bad women among us! Sometimes we take the heat for being a verbally abusive culture but won't you agree that verbal abuse is better than a bunch of actual gang raping? Sometimes it is in the form of secret built-in threat of punishment on the unknowing. Like here in a big city, where I can find a woman online and seduce her for a minute, get her alone, and administer punishment on her. You see, the Prophet affords us these licenses of justice in the form of poisonous arrows. Every eye shall cry on the Day of Resurrection except those of the few who cast down against the deeds made forbidden by Allah! #inshallah

The love portico.
A rudderless boat adrift at sea.

A sea of loss and grief and love and hope.

Please allow me the abandonment. A new set of clothes, a new volume, a new alias. No dwelling on the inhibitions, or the consecration of a new smell. The taste is in the agony. The new girl at the counter in the duty free. Together we can foil the plans, reinvent ourselves as new collaborators, love spies, alter egos, lions and tigers, the anti-stigma, the antiseptic, the unflinching deep throated kiss, unending. A weather forecast of high pressures and low jet streams. Pulling you closer, pulling you in, pulling you down. A promising new remix for a new century. Gone bad, gone wild, forgotten, a constant reminder that you are not me and I am not you. Satisfying the doubters with their infected doubt and suspicions. Call it a genre choice. A cry for help silenced by the muffled dull of lull time between thrusts, this is why I like you and still you could be trying harder. There will be no false attributions or ascriptions, only the burning scented flavor of a forgotten candle in a corner room, a briefcase full of toys, a keychain flash drive memory of a long ago night recalled in sideways perspective. You are not me and I am not you. Demoralized, walking wounded, seeking amnesty and discounted detox. Can you smell the jasmine. We stroll hand in hand on the edge of sanity, nude to our inhibitions and drunk from the juice of our bodies. Time warped and inebriated—all about the small things, the whimper, the tremble, the shakes and the smallest of body parts.

A reminder: *you are not me and I am not you.*

We resist the urge to rewrite our destiny. Our twofold heroic effort at demystifying the mysteriousness between us, in the ether, in the small particles, in the fairy dust. I spy the small folds of your shriveled self. The small wrinkles within the cracked skin under a more watchful eye. You are not me and I am not you. The lines tell a story, a secret note passed across the room, of lust and thrill and time well spent. Whatever may have been once secret is now revealed in this poem of flesh. A desertscape void of water, void of life, left to be abused and misused, all simply indicative of a fresher time in the past. Always something in the past, something better than now. The present is not like before and the before is not like now. Then the silence, and the short breaths. Nothing left to dismiss, only metaphor and circumstance.

A fervent glance in itself an indoctrination, I am not you and you are not me. The subtle cosmic give and take, the mind games in the shadows. The sounds from the inbound train. The rumbling on the tracks and the tremble in her voice. The aural trepidation as the march continues on. The volume level ascends. It comes through as crashing glass until suddenly a quieted silence. A new day, a new friend, a new outlook, another angle. Past all of the vigilance and yellow caution tape. You thought that you had already played this out through your mind several times. But it is not unfolding as planned. You are less concerned. Your excitement is waning. This is a new start. Between transitional moments, the segments, the loose ends, the sweet nothings, the lies. It is all for your own good, you remind yourself. You are not her and she is not you. Far from it, far removed, onto other things. Then the letdown and the meltdown. The conspicuous trail in the gravel path. The indicators and tell-tale signs. If there was a crowd or an audience it would be hushed right about now. By the melodrama on display, the bad acting, the forgetting of lines. Her engines revved, the slow rumble tumble of two lost souls entwined in superfluous interplay at the interchange of their relationship. No more straight forward enticing. Just a peek around the corner, a tug here, a nip there. The great dying, an extinction of sorts. Something to soothe the soul, to give you new meaning. A retail therapy upper. Buy now, pay later. A slow release epidemic waiting to happen. The sickness befalls you and you become weak in the knees. She is not you. You are not her. Life after the obliteration, the eradication of something foreign, something minimal and primal. The innocence, the pattern of the migrating birds, the volunteers gathering to search for the missing girl. You plug in, you attach the belt, you become one with the machine for better living. You are inside her but not her. It has become the new way, the way it was not supposed to be. Nonstop action and thrill, a dramatized rift between what you should have done and what you actually did. Your judgment in reserve. You have bravely tackled the bitter sophistication, overcome the storm with its rain and hail and tornado. Illusive yet ubiquitous it is a reminder of the old days, a simpler time, alive and transparent. Her source of communication a breath every once in a while, a drooping fingertip, dirt under the nail. You advocate further colonization of her body. She relents and you proceed. You feel her breaths beside your own and you realize once again that you are not her and she is not you. That umbilical cord is cut. A harmony of rhythms and structures, music on a sheet, a map to get from there to here, a mystery logo on the tag of her underpants. What of the connection between the strained language and the execution. What of the correlation between sleep and hallucinations. Of bright light and shadows. Of being tied up and left to your own devises and thrill. These shadows are unfamiliar, these names mean nothing. No longer a common language only touch, while the impressions await you in the layaway.

From: caliph8@sharia4ever.org
Hello my friend did you miss me? I know it has been a hot minute. You may wonder why my obsession with the decadence of the West. It all started not very long ago. In fact the Arabs and the Middle East were very stagnant and content in our blissful ignorance to advancement around us. Then we started getting conquered. The US and Europeans began bringing in its cultures, its science, its mercantile goods, its politics, its missionaries and its values! We were like WTF is going on here? And we started to unite against the monster. So here we are a hundred years later, a blink of time to the Prophet! The Caliphate is the end game. Everyone who ever controlled us will ultimately be under Islamic rule. If they want to impose their will on us we want to impose back our Sharia and we will be the victors, not the victims! You see my friend, when I do what is right because I observe the commandments I am inwardly protected from serious harm by God, in whom I trust, for He keeps an eye on me. Because of this, my sense of security is extraordinary and I am able to reserve my calm. If one's heart is sealed one cannot comprehend...but you, my friend, do get it. He who is blind here will be blind in the hereafter. Our God is the knower of all things! #inshallah

An ostentatious way to do things, the unshakable treachery, the rejoining at the hips, the celebration in postcard picture portions. Your conscious on trial, and losing badly. Let me watch you dig yourself out of this grave. All of this infighting cannot be of any good, to either side. The slow motion outtakes a sharp and shiny blade slowly running lengthwise down your arm, parallel to the veins and the arteries but close enough still to cause alarm, picture a fishtailing car speeding down a freeway.

New perspectives and new definitions for disgust and shame and indignity.

But I digress.

Your predominant ancestors, the carefree and erudite. The big skulls for the big heads. All of this because of a befallen kiss. Where it mattered, when it counted. A new love bandage. The flank and flack of the kiss abhorred, your coworker in tow. In silence, suffering through too much already. Can we go home now. A new ancestral pedigree. How could you. How could they. It is all tied together too nicely. A hand job you won't ever receive. A little extra something you weren't expecting and you certainly hadn't paid for. Or the smell of Chanel 19 on expensive beige cashmere. In a department store, your tits handprint-sized, the latest in vogue couture. My fingerprints still lingering on your milky skin with those small spidery blue veins that enlarge when you get excited. Precocious and/or pre-varicose. Oh how you would most like to breastfeed. The future beauty in your stretch marks, your flaws on display, window dressing during the holidays. Call me an addict and bad names for my bad thoughts. Curse me out because I deserve it. Something extra for good measure. *Enter keyword here*. Specify type. Mid to late 20s, brunette, light eyes (green or blue), busty, not BBW but just busty, naturally endowed—is it too much to ask. Spiritually non-denominational. Pretend to be looking at the paper, here she comes. Reboot after installation. It will be launched soon enough, but never before the beta. Save traffic feature monitor. There's gonna be a whole lotta lovin' come spring time. A solo artist unknown, working for the next meal. Holding tight until the breakthrough. Her nipples at rest in my mouth. A pit stop in transit, suspended indefinitely. Her interface composed of varying shades of Ulta grey. A cacophony of cornucopia grandeur. She knows that I like surprises. It's either too much makeup or not enough, no in-between. And I wonder why you do not color that colorless mole. An observation from an admirer of the opposite sex, I prefer the fatter version of you. You are not as sexy when you are the thin you. A comment from the suggestion box of my mind. The pattern of what you shaved, or rather the hair you spared. It could become a part time job of mine. Where do I apply. I am hot for you, the embers of September to December. Always surprised by how marvelous you look in the flesh. My thoughts are drawn back to the afterlife.

Then the beforelife.

The pre-conception.

The neo neo-natal.

And all that there is before it started.

The moonlight moments of soft dusk.

The give and take and what will be attested to and what will be denied. My conscience drawn in closer until the small trace of accountability. Gloriously inappreciable yet still full of love and want. As the flood gates of the aqueduct get thrown open. Please don't brag. Her aerobics are amazing, her flexibility top level. The moves she can pull off. I tell you, *startling*. I want to be her cameraman. I want to be her set lighting guy. I want to do her makeup as I do her in my mind. For all eternity. Together we are time crossed lovers. A glorious prelude to the capsizing of this ocean liner. This vessel of throbbing flesh and muscle, of pumping blood with nowhere to run. She has been miscast as the betrayer. Beyond consensus, beyond the dropout, beyond the squashed illusion, beyond the mechanics and inner-workings, beyond the agony and the directorial debut. Expel me from this life.

The terrace overlook of your being.

The sheer essence of what could have been.

The defiant dictator on the stand.

The genocide in your coup.

Please repeat and spell out your name for the record.

Let's try to go over this again. A smooth velvet glove running the length of your nude body, the peach fuzz on alert and at attention. Your nipples hard as if exposed to the biting chill of a January evening. Your lips moist like a sliced mango or guava. Please don't forget me when I am gone. If the memories are lost so is the person. To eternity. Less ornery and less complicated. Your body ready for consumption. Ripe, matured, grown. After market. The corruption in the kiss. What I like to call the point of no return action. When you do something that changes things indelible and for which there is no rewind. I am a despotic time warped paranoid. Lost to the desire to turn you over and enter you from behind...fast, without constraint and finesse, a mad man on a very important mission. You are no longer autonomous. I want to be inside of you and test out jet propulsion theory. I want to lay claim to your homestead of flesh, the flat of your back, the ripples of your rib cage, the geography of your skin peel. As I graze for that which I can swallow. The taste of chlorine behind your ear. The lint of white cotton in your belly button I swallow after letting it linger on my tongue. The preamble to the amble. New definitions of terminology and the lack thereof. Your shortage of incestuous experience and domestic abuse. That attractive quality about you. The randomness in your censors, the acerbic inflow and the lack of gauges and controls.

You are a survivor after all. Even if you have never really been put to the test. This is when you decided to stop wearing thongs and started to not wear panties altogether. An act that is commonly referred to as *commando*. Is it the egalitarian in you, or the equal opportunity forbearer of fruits and treats. The thrill you spread when you bend down in public and expose what is commonly referred to as butt cleavage. Your glistening skin opaque with an aura otherworldly. The minimalist approach. A mental keepsake in modern day baroque proportions. Amplified and near extinction such forthrightness and zeal. You have come to conquer but have left only fields of fire and ruin. You devastate with that delineation somewhere between a slow motioned kiss on the cheek and full blown dialysis. There is no middle ground with you, no middle earth escape, no heaven, no hell. Only the pulse, and the evaporating microwave heat. Warm and warmer still, rising unseen. The image of being bent down, across that well-lit department store, eating away at my mind, a cavity that goes neglected until it is beyond repair. I am the goldfish and you are the bowl. This thing that is going on between us, that's the water. The uniformed formation that your veins make entwined with your bone shapes and your hips' orbital flex, space ship-like, flying saucer-ish. The future-ism in the hope that dwells between your legs. I will step back before I venture into the vulgar again. The refrain is not an adequate substitute but it will have to do.

The wax that builds up in the deltas of your ears, they are part of me.

The nasal mucus held tight by your nose hairs, they are part of me.

The yellow discharge in your jeans, your homemade yellowcake, that is part of me.

The enzymes of your saliva, they are part of me.

The nail fungus alive under those beautiful toenails, they are part of me.

The fluids you secrete through your apocrine sweat glands, they are part of me.

The microorganisms that emit from your underarms, they are part of me.

The scab on your knuckle about to fall off, has become part of me.

The plaque on the enamel of your teeth, it is part of me.

The dandruff and redness and irritation on your scalp, it is all part of me.

The oil filling the open pores of your nose, it is part of me.

Your pubic hair between my canine and first molar, they have become part of me.

The glucose and fructose you ejaculate and now rest within the taste buds of my tongue, they are part of me.

From: caliph8@sharia4ever.org

No reply back my friend? Are you ghosting me? Where is the love? LOL Here in the USA exists a spiritual vacuum, a progressing decay of spiritual belief replaced with false self-reliance, narcissism, selfie culture, and materialism on steroids. Why does the USA have a space program? Is it for lack of spirituality? You have to ask yourself, we look up into space when we do not even look within. Qur'an (2:165): "Some people set up idols to rival God, and love them as if they are God. But those who believe love God the most." You see, it is very simple, love Allah and no other false prophets. It is so easy I do not know why not everyone is doing it LOL. When we are summoned to Paradise Allah is going to be like "Where are my idol worshippers at now?" #inshallah

This was to have been the point that I go off. A little forbearance killjoy action of the fractured moment, a new nanny, a new play thing, a new build up to another arms race. The tepidity is carefully dispensed. Her nipples like ICBMs. She calls them her *assistants*. It is all very conspicuous and eye-catching, idea and thought provoking. She could be called an enchantress. Someone who likes to play people even more than she likes to play herself. A role in a low budget film, beholding herself cinematically with a light pop soundtrack of jungle beats and quiet guitar solos played out while she goes about her mundane daily routines of mailing letters, doctor visits, B12 shots, four hand massages and picking up dry cleaning. The cinema verite she likes to call it. The truth in her life and its movements. The smell of perfumed alcohol in her wake as she passes through the café door to pick up another chocolate truffle to satisfy her pre-diabetic sweet tooth.

That thing right here between us, that's the time bomb. You see it. Sifting through the sphere of electrons and electrodes of invisible-to-the-eye particles, right there between us, in the six inch space between the tips of our noses. Shall we spend the weekend at the zoo, then the park, cocktails of homemade sangria, maybe some oral in the bushes. I know of a particularly safe spot. You are at the top of your game, the top module of model behavior and looks. I will let you leave to the store as long as you agree to return. Swear to god? Swear on your mother's grave? I feel like I can smell the radiation leaking from the nuclear reactor in my pants. Save me from this massacre of one, from the coup leader dictator that overwhelms me and guides all my urges. Yes, you know him. And all too well. LOL. My drive for you is epidemic and pandemic, immune to the panacea and the sugar pill placebos. If this gets botched I want you to know that the accusations were not all true. Now please help me to contain the tidal wave. I am claustrophobic to your compelling charms, your sexy accusations, the contempt in your voice, the distrust and suspicion. You are a very dangerous little girl and I like that about you. I want to be your future ex that you talk about when you have had too many mimosas, the one you think about hovering over you naked while you finger yourself to sleep. The one your mother still asks about.

From: caliph8@sharia4ever.org

I want you to allow a wave of intolerance wash over you. I want you to let a wave of hatred wash over you. Yes, hate is good. Our goal is sharia. We have a Quranic duty. We are called by God to conquer. Our goal must remain simple, we must have an Islamic nation built on our Prophet's laws. No apologies. #inshallah

The danger in the colorless smell.

The quarter of an hour now past two.

The minutes that we waited, in the dark and in the confusion that set in.

Her genuine regard for your fondness.
The key to the storage room.
The combination to the lock on the gate.
Today should differ from no other.
Her additional elements on display.
The sparkle shine luminescence of the nose stud cubic zirconia.
The unfinished business.
At hand and future tense.
No filtering or alterations.
Birth control.
Foreplay.
Blow job.
Kimberley.
Katja.
Lisa.
Angela.
Nathalie.
Panty line through the polyester.
Undulations and adorations.
Arousal in the erosion.
The smell of Pantene in the air.
No filtering.
No alterations.
Thrust forward, back.
Repeat.
No disguises.
No games.

I waited some time for her to regard me. With fondness or without, a simple wish denied. Another longing unfulfilled. The partiality no longer mutual. But now I face the stark reality that it was one-way. Yes, she is shrewd. But who that is worth a damn isn't? And how does this day differ from any other. I wish I could make the call. Could she be playing me. Playing at my emotional triggers, blasé or unaffected, secretly longing for me but very cautious with her approach. When our eyes met the first time, she was there in the back of the crowded elevator, with a small child in an expensive stroller, she was wearing that very snobbish red and grey argyle sweater. No makeup and no affects to her beauty. After all, she was just going for a quick trip to the mall to return a couple items. Perhaps panties that were gifted her but she did not like the fit. Perhaps designer soaps or bath salts that would induce allergic reactions.

I read her diary of the unfulfilled. Contrary to her perfected appearance she is unrepaired, her thoughts malignant, her surroundings confined, her desires spinning out like runaway wheelchairs of the mind. Can she be a better looking woman with a better smelling scent? Can this happen from within or from without? The Nest cam red light flickers in the corner of the nursery as I walk backwards to the door.

From: caliph8@sharia4ever.org

All wisdom, direction and good success consists in that which the Messengers of God have spoken. The rest is delivered by the Divine Laws of Sharia. There is no other way besides this. There is nothing that can be added to it. You see my friend, the whole world is ours, the Middle East and the United States of Unbelievers. Do I rely on God? Yes, very much so. Do I believe in my predestination? Yes, absolutely. And so should you. Allah is wise and exalted in might. He is the Lord of the Throne (of the Glory) Supreme. You see, the strong believer is better and more beloved to Allah than the weak believer. Do not feel helpless. Do not let Satan instill thoughts that could weaken your faith. Ignore "the Man." You can trust me boo. LOL #nohomo #inshallah

The tears of the moon and the epic stare of her thunder tits, me the star crossed lover amid the digital divide...the lack of want and wont, the end-user always in mind...the oral history all but got it wrong, she was well groomed and it was opening night, the freestyle in the freak style, so loyal, so dishonest...so the story goes...a showcase namesake keepsake, a princess among women, for I am the king of kings...I guessed her password on the second try...for I am a kept man...as the sanctions loom, here comes the trouble...she is scary crazy, scary sexy...her muff as tapestry, the most glorious overshot...it is all part and parcel to this path to attainment, tapping the reserves. Another well-positioned device, as she goes uncounted...unnoticed breaking wind and breaking tradition, a fetish for the breakdown of this and that as we watch and allow...the bluebirds at play in puddles of formaldehyde...her ass spread seated or standing the outward form is always there...do not worry nor fret...it still feels good for me...rubbing all over the big mamma panties...fucking A your ass makes my neck veins pop...*spank this with all you've got*...swollen ass laying bare, that ass up in the grass...animal planet hot damn it.

The loincloths and girdles, giddy girlies for the everyday touch...master and slave imprisoned, morphing from the mundane to the insane, a noble attempt at redemption and hope...another pioneer at a crossroads between phenomena and chatter...she is Russian or Hungarian, a prostitute of sorts...here at last, top quality pubic fleece...golden, silver, bronze...the carpet fibers, the truth in the DNA...responds well to shampoo, you could make yarn with it, or a soft sweater something to keep you warm on a cold night with a cup of hot cocoa...the fringes of the photograph, a distillery of hope and redemption...for the lost and undocumented and the demented, those expecting a child or another sting operation...simple commands...all rights reserved.

In order to go "all in" your testicles will be removed, the skin of your penis will be inverted and used as a flap to preserve blood and nerve supplies to the new vagina. A clitoris is made from the glans of the penis. This will be fully functional and sensitive as any natural female clitoris. You have been circumcised so when we build the labia minora we will use some of your scrotal tissue, of course removing completely the pubic hair follicles. Your testes seem rather large so we should have enough to graft, but if not we can harvest from your thighs or hips. The aesthetic, sensational and functional results vary greatly. Your skin ranges in elasticity and is affected by your age, nutrition, physical activity and smoking. Because the human body treats the new vagina as a wound your care of it will require regular douching, as there are no natural lubricants for self-cleaning. Maintenance of the volume means you need to keep it occasionally dilated with use of dildos or suitable substitutes. Basically keep it open. Sexual intercourse is not an adequate method of dilation. We will administer regular applications of estrogen into the vagina, but this must be calculated into your total estrogen dose. I am assuming you are on an estrogen regimen. Some surgeons like to go deep, they think it causes tightness. I do not practice this method. Too deep can cause vaginal stenosis, which will require stretching it out again, either gradually or in extreme instances under anesthetic. You do not have ovaries or uteri so you will need to keep on the hormone therapy to maintain female status. We will begin with the removal of both balls. A simple subcapsular castration. You will be lying face up on an operating table. Your penis will be taped against your abdomen. The nurse will shave a small area for the incision. I do notice you are already well groomed there. After anesthetics have been administered I will make an incision in the midpoint of the scrotum and cut through the underlying tissue. I will then remove the testicles and parts of the spermatic cord from the superficial inguinal ring through the incision. I will then make a circular cut around the skin of the shaft of the penis under the glans and separate the urethra from the erectile tissue. Then perform a bilateral resection of the erectile tissue. Next, I will separate the neurovascular bundle from the erectile tissue, creating a space for the neovagina between the rectum and urethra and prostate as I see yours is still intact. At this point I will invert the skin of the shaft of the penis and close the distal end. Next will be to insert a placeholder into the neovagina while I create passages for the neoclitoris and urethra and then fix it all into place. At this point I will inject fibrin glue into the neovagina and position it into its final position, along with last adjustments to the labia majora. During your follow up procedure in six weeks we will better construct the vaginal entrance.

Surgery will last 3.5 hours. We aim for the best preservation of the neurovascular bundle which will result in a sensitive clitoroplasty. The most common complications in short-term post op recovery include superficial wound healing around the external sutures. We

will closely monitor for loss of depth or breadth of the neovagina. These problems can result from inconsistent dilation. So be sure to work it out.
Short term complications: bleeding requiring reoperation, wound infection requiring antibiotic treatment, wound dehiscence, clitoral flap necrosis, rectovaginal fistula, pulmonary emboli, deep vein thrombosis, and finally mortality.
Your sex drive may diminish. Rates of masturbation steeply decline after surgeries like this. You may not be able to reach orgasm. Right away or never. I realize you may not be doing this for the sex life. On physical, emotional and social levels you may do great and thrive. The euphoria of your true identity being realized after all these years is an exalted state of elation for many. I can assure you that you will eventually figure out your new body and how to get off. Any questions?

Weaving in and out of the traffic flows of your mind, the servers blocked or severed, nobody to contact, no assistance from a help desk. The emergency number unlisted. Only the hospital to call. If they answer. The double entendre of the word(s) head count. The anti-piracy in the conspiracy of double standards and double penetration, metaphorically and literally with some scary dudes you didn't properly meet or with some choice toys purchased with your daddy's credit card. Built up to break down. The remedy in the elucidation. Your problems were always my problems. Do not be led to believe differently. Compared to last year's numbers we are at a disadvantage. Pretty and petty standard fare. Do not contact me until you can put out and shut up. I have been a bad man and I have a lot to do still. This brash ambition, this crass choosing of yet another route not taken, a new path with new consequences, dire and otherwise. The prescription you just financed may cause bleeding, dry mouth, cramps, impotence, irritability, insomnia, nausea and suicidal thoughts.

I dream sleep slumber into the forward thinking thoughts of being injured and rushed to the hospital for some unknown and un-diagnosable ailment or disease or broken limb or viral infection and when I get there I get my nurse of choice and it's the one I was thinking about, the one I always request, the tall busty blonde, I think her name is Heather or Jocelyn, she has mild halitosis but I do not let it bother me, and I think the reason I like her so much is how she brushes her large tits against my arm, or my shoulder, when she is taking my blood pressure or adjusting my pillow, it is all just a game we play and I know she likes it too.

There are these thoughts always resulting in the same outcome throughout. The apartheid moment between. The unseen but viscerally felt. When the minority feelings suddenly take over the controls of the majority. A full-fledged egg hunt, in the shadow of the fourth dimension. It feels so much better. The politics of destiny, the point where the propaganda ends and the revolution begins. But there is still something else there, and it smells like old wine or stale flowers, faint, musky, half-alive. It contains a different message, a kind of foresight and forethought. Something to hold in higher regard. A new kind of conclusion. Aren't you happy you chose option number two? And if you really think about it there is a lesser understanding of any given one thing, yet it all remains the same.

From: caliph8@sharia4ever.org

Hello my friendly ghost, how you been! I hope things are good on your end. I want to convey to you the fact that the ultimate aim with all of this is the knowledge of God. That is it, nothing more nothing less! We must search out God's essence and the deepest secrets of our faith. Mind and heart, knowledge and duty. The ills of this society are the failures of weak imperialistic men and the devil himself. Their passivity and corruption are at fault as they have brought all of this upon themselves. You see my friend, our actions will be justified. In Him hope is never dead, in Him love is never lost. I bear witness that there is no god but Allah and the Prophet Muhammad (peace be upon Him) is the last and final messenger. #inshallah

The struggle was set. It was as if she watered your grave for you. Keeping the appearance up, letting everyone know that it was alright. Keeping this up for days. A noteworthy performance. She was there with thoughts on empty, nothing to look forward to, nothing to recall, simply existing nerveless and emotionless. She was there with no ideation at all, just a simple woman with dire intentions. Picking away at the charred remains of you. The victim in a victimless world. Someone who is in a better place. No longer suffering. It is all very macabre and you can tell she is getting off on it, not just a bit but a lot. Significantly, like she was made for this shtick. In her eyes if you look closely you can see the violent rebellion. You cannot help but laugh when you see her choke on her accumulated saliva, then swallow...the grief in the small acts. You think to yourself, this will all be over soon enough. All of the unanswered questions, the quick cut away shots and zoom outs to wider angles where the details get lost. You are onto the next thing, then the next thing still. Everything becomes lost by design and by intention. The disintegration and disruption in her most feminine voice. For all of her nonexistent externalities and vacant expressions she still breaks you free from the anchor, adrift she sets fire to all the paintings ever painted, knocking down all the sculptures ever sculpted. And all that is left in the wake, like tears in the eyes of a child. You walked through the invisible streets crumbled in future ruins, broken stone, overgrown plants, a perpetual victim to the disarray. You cannot take it anymore. You no longer let her envelope you, you cannot let the sleeping beauty sleep. Your only salvation is without her. Your only liberation exists in a crowded street or marketplace, where strangers smile when they pass, where your shoulder may brush that of another, the small moments on a grander scale.

Her functional molecules work sideways, upside down and intermittently. A new kind of woman. A new smell of breath. In her voice one can hear the coexistence of the between now and the not quite then.

The cyanide's flavor was waning.

You bite her flesh in your dreams for fun. Another rudimentary exercise at hope, at longing, at fermentation and cleanliness. Her own name defies her. The reasoning and the protocols beyond simple logic, into a realm not quite worth fighting for but still safe from abandonment. A fresher kind of you. She shivers and comes off as undernourished. You do not fall victim to her game. Her shapes and lines bring with them their own kind of geometry. She still believes in the ancient human longings, of desire first and naïve truths. The paranoid exposure of a threatened muse. As if she had been descending the grand ballroom staircase of your mind for hours, then suddenly the elongated pause. The shallow breath. You still are not deterred. She is more a phantom than reality. She forgets how you feel and you feel for her, within, without, enduringly and endearingly. Now is not the time, you think. Maybe later, another day, another frame of mind. You cling to the moral fortitude and to the distant fading memories that are all you have left for recall. Slices of your impressions, genetic snapshots of moments consummated and spit up. Allegorical blow jobs where she would oblige but would not swallow. The small rejection in her regurgitation and muffled inaudible excuse. Your essence left to expire in the tissue now flushed into mainline oblivion. The fulfillment in the abandonment, the achievement in the leaving behind. You long to touch the technology. The joy ride that is her in these moments of desolation and desecration. It is now that you know more than ever that you are you and not somebody else.

Oh, please help me come.

You close your eyes and gently raise your hips, a sign of encouragement, a precursor to hope and advancement. You will not get out of here without it. The colorless light flashes in your mind, in the dark shadows of nothingness, it is warmer the deeper you go, fast, then easy. You have ignored all of the signs to this point now. What you take from her is unrequited and unanswered. This is the way she prefers it to be. She is found this way. She giggles and you know why. Her long hair sways wavelike from behind. You act like you do not notice the proximity and the sounds. You tell yourself not to remember. It is as if it hurts to open your eyes, to behold what spreads out before you, what is displayed, what lingers and longs. Beyond the confines and the false pretenses, toward the console and placation of a warm embrace, be it with limbs or unspoken members. These are the parenthetical moments, the bookmark instances of life to recall a better day or a more hopeful hour. Times that we all need but that we all do not know. If only they could be encapsulated and then time released, like non-formulary drugs, like top shelf pharmaceuticals. In overlapping 36-hour durations. So you never feel the pain and the loneliness.

From: caliph8@sharia4ever.org

I was an apostle sent from myself to myself, and my essence was led to me by the evidence of my own signs. And when I sold my soul to the possession of the kingdom of Paradise for an eternity it is then that He soared with me, in the consequence of my union, beyond everlasting life in Heaven, no darkness in my days, no harms in my path, no fears in my actions. The mercy of His light has fueled the fire of my vengeance. You are with me on this path my bro fam. You are of the chosen, from the infidels. How intoxicating is that? Talk soon, kk bye now! #inshallah

Colors that last up to ten hours...look five years younger or your money back...if you don't love what you see we'll give it to you absolutely free...unleash your style and erase years in minutes...the body language of lust to the primal point...the lean in on the morning after, the walk of shame...always hit the spot then lock in your next date...a kick-ass good-bye kiss because you know she will tell her friends everything...let your lips steal the spotlight and embrace of-the-moment shapes...be impossible to resist, show off your cleavage, beauty starts here girl...v-zone safe scent tips, your moan zone, the post-sex leakage...when the deed is done...in the cropped faux-fur jacket and the satin evening clutch...that lace-trimmed blouse, and high-waisted trousers...ruffles everywhere, and ready to come off...your cherry red thong and garter...the peek-a-boo pumps...together a drop-dead dazzling number through the night vision goggles, you the sweet stunner...my sophisticated siren, the ever trendsetter...yes, I could use some advice on love and sex...I fail you by not always allowing super deep penetration...the definitive mood wrecker...restricted blood flow to the genitals...when your down-there region is damn near numb...amp my anticipation and touch me in two places at once...give me the joystick grasp, the big bang buildup...lick the tip for an allover explosion...a hot and heavy holding pattern, don’t stop yet...this total body rapture...I will never back off...all I want now is payback...I’d just as soon go down in flames if it meant taking you out on the way….I know where you were last night.

As if there was anything left of me, in the burnt seared ruins of my previous self, the former spirit that no longer shines, that whimpers in the corner of my blurred vision, through my burning eyes, fighting for time and attention with all the other thoughts that occupy my every waking and sleeping moment, momentous and subtle, passive and aggressive, the perversion in my relapse and desire to blow it all up and start anew.

The bedtime hour unhurried.
More fiery than our luminary daystar.
Enduring these untainted intentions of arousal.
I see you there in the moonlight bent at the waist.

Glowing, overflowing with your femininity, charming with your damp flesh.

I unveil myself slipping through your luxury. In a sex shop. When we emerge the size of superstars.

From: caliph8@sharia4ever.org

Certainly Allah does not look at your bank accounts or flashy Rolexes, but instead he stares closely to your heart and intentions. You see, my friend, nobody is telling you to worship Him. No, it is simply being suggested to you that there are glorious consequences and rewards if you shall so choose the most good of deeds. Sincere intention of the Mujahid is the highest form of self and it does not go unnoticed by Him. For those who do the righteous deeds awaits Paradise and Everlasting Gardens of Delight, where rivers flow underneath your reclined body in raised thrones...what a resting place! I have to go now, let me know if you have any questions. #inshallah

Into a non-blurry landscape of clear lights and controlled temperatures, of her shapely figure, of her bubble gum breath. A safer place to swim. A place of new empires and newer ghettos. A place for the more fortunate in an on-the-surface unfortunate time. We are all just victims here. A jaded man with nothing to lose…without intentions, without inflections in his voice and no swagger in his step. You have been forewarned. A deed is not dirty until I say so. An opportunity is not missed until I have forgone the conclusions to this story.

More outgoing or aggressive behavior than normal, confusion, strange conduct, agitation, hallucinations, worsening of depression, suicidal thoughts, allergic reactions including swelling of the face, lips, tongue, and/or throat that may cause difficulty in breathing or swallowing which may or may not require treatment right away or in the least *soon*...rashes, hives, joint pain, muscle pain, alterations in some laboratory blood tests, liver problems, inflammation of the pancreas, nausea, gallstones, inflammation of the gallbladder. You are of childbearing age, experience night sweats, cognitive difficulties, tension headaches, fluctuations in weight, ear-nose-throat complications, vestibular abnormalities, heartburn, palpitations, mitral valve prolapse, syncope, and mood disorders. You feel run down, experiencing problems with short term memory, problems finding the right word when speaking, like verbal dyslexia, you feel excessively tired after doing normal mundane activities, activities that you once did without problem, you feel fatigued after sleep, even after long periods of sleep, you never feel refreshed, you feel depressed by life and your new found difficulties just getting by at work or at home, you have frequent headaches and muscle aches and even a consistent mild fever.

Passivity is the new aggression.

Lost is the new found.

Flaccid the new hard.

Insular is the new cosmopolitan...the unexpected is the new planned, the convened the new dispersed...ethos is the new pathos, famine the new satiation...when the refugees are the only homeowners…imaginary friends make the best lovers...*cultivate your gardens*, the best advice from a long-dead Frenchman...narcotics in the new hope...panty line is the new commando...decadence is the new depravity while your areolas are the new bull's-eye...the fishnet webbing of the new aesthetic amid the promises in the new lies.

From: caliph8@sharia4ever.org

You made a covenant with me that you would remain faithful to Allah. You have gained possession of my heart. I conjure you by Allah if I die before you that you let the world know that I was a slave of love, and that the same flame of passion may be passed on to any of the mourners who so shall choose the Righteous Path. Make not your own hands to contribute to your own destruction, but do good, for Allah loves those who do good. A day will come when bargaining is off the table, when no friendships exist, when those without faith will be rejected. You see, my friend, these are the foundations of hope, and there is tranquility in all aspects of your good deeds. #inshallah

It is as if she wanted to cross more than her fingers. The imagery surreal and lost to the panic of a man who had gone from innocence to loss and pain and grief so fast that he no longer knew himself, he no longer had his own identity, only shame and regret and self-doubt, the lingering questions of how and why did I get here, and so fast to boot. A wounded gypsy wanderer but without the romantic connotations, without the dreamy flare. A sad story gone bad with a pathetic end. Delirium and debilitating pain, dementia and self-inebriation, forgetting what it all meant to begin with, about the cause, about the effect, about being affected and broken. Down and further downward, a spiral staircase to a dark nowhere. The ultimate destination. Manic footage for a depressive reprieve. The pain in my head dissipating at the skull, maybe that was the point, a conceptual piece of art, an intangible piece of ass, framed by turquoise spandex, glistening with butter cocoa oil, wide and large, a fortress forbidden in the forest, a last point of refuge in a forlorn and forgotten timepiece. I dream of fluorescent lit nights when I can stroll through her aisles, tossing the produce and dairy into her basket, whimsical this and that, banter to the girls behind the counter, flirty smiles and smirks to the ones across the way that you catch looking at you, within you, the bionic stare from the nearsighted girl. The dulled twinkle in her semi-glistening brown eyes, the slight over-caking of milky film on the eyeball. The pre-glaucoma in the straining, the bloodshot sprinkle shotgunned across the whites of her eyes. An overcast doorway entry to her soul, the pathway unwinding, the prism losing light, debauched in its finality.

I am a man without a face.

Without the guile left to do the job. All I can think of is those lips, and their brown coloring against the tan of her skin, and her tits and their brown nipples, supple and pleasant and sometimes distraught and often game. This is what I think about and you think I am not mad. An ego out of body, an afterlife experience of hovering over the room, regarding myself on a hospital bed, pail, naked and gone. Oh how it would all be so much simpler if I were not me. Take away all of the baroque illusions, all the fairy dust, all the glitter splashed across her body and face, take away the smells and the warmth, the extreme heat emanating from down there, take away the inaudible words she whimpers into my ear when it is late and dark and she needs to be held, take away the acceptance in her embrace, take away the gaze in her eyes when she is not of right mind, take away the inhibitions to indulge, take away your thong and the teasing factor of the hidden, take away those tattoos and what they once stood for, take away the stretch marks, take away the eye makeup, take away your trust in men, take away the fire in your crotch, take away the come hither smell you emit monthly on the regular, take away your instances of moral dilemma, take away your cautious reticence, take away the dormant disease, take away the quivering act, take away your mixed race fantasies, take away the mourning and the regret and the after thoughts, take away those white teeth and big lips, take away the thought of you taking me wholly in your mouth, take away the naughty invitations, take away innuendo and ennui, take away bruising on your knees, take away nylons and stockings, take away high heels and the inherent dangers, take away cuddling and sweet nothings, take away occupational hazards, take away chemical imbalance, take away my impulses unmet and unconsummated, take away the taste of sugar between her thighs and in her armpits, take away the currency of beauty and the trappings of loveliness, take away her fake groans, take away her fake accent, take away her guilty charge, take away her limp, take away her fat calves, take away her hair extensions, take away her birth and take away her death, take away the gash and all that it stands for, take away citizen's arrest, take away yeast infections and the subsequent blame, take away endorphins and the longing I have for you, take away the fact that this will never come to be, take away the gleam in my eye before it takes me away, take away premonitions and belief in conspiracies, take away that movement you make when you turn around and the look back with that lost girl act, the façade fronting the pretense, take away my skin and its sensations, take away by bones and their aches, take away palliative care, take away faint sounds and spells, take away aftertaste, take away daybreak and the cracks in your skin, take away propaganda and lubrication, take away torture and naiveté, take away erosion and love's by-product waste, take away curiosity and science, take away the ball and chain and cock and ball torture, take away clitoral piercing, take away adult incontinence, take away irregularity, take away your title, your gender, your education, your height and weight, your inclinations, take away your comfort zone, take away gravity and your impatience, take away the embedded star in the soul cast in your eye, take away your legal problems, the car wrecks you caused, the bills you never paid, the calls you never returned, the family you estranged, take away the sacrifices you made for love and pleasure, take away self-hate, take away that contour on your butt cheek in profile, take away gossip and hate and spite, take away your negative vibes, take away the small silent curiosity, take away this monstrosity of dis-ingenuity, take away my collapsed lungs, take away this paranoia, take away this child of god and this unwashed soul, take away this future that is burned, take away my better days, take away the greed and the empathy, take away the fairy tales, take away this century of imperialism, take away the evidence and the reasonable doubt, take away those panty lines that make my mind run rampant, take away the sake of clarity, take away the low hum background sound, take away the avant-garde, take away this kept man from his comfort zone, take away the Spanish inquisition, take away horses and steel and syphilis, take away her green eyes, take away rejection and abandonment, take away the hole in the tip of your black nylons, take away the chipped red paint from your toenail, take away the imagery of you backing up into me, take away the stains on the sheets, take away the wet spot and comfort in the remains, take away the reflection and the heavy rain, take away the narration and the reflection, take away the statutes that enslave us eternal, take away the confines that bind the mind, take away the mire that stifles ephemeral, take away the stigmata, take away the pathos infected in dissonance, take away this motionless chatter, take away these moments cast upon themselves, take away conscious effort at rebellion, take away the regurgitation of motion and light, take away nipples and all that nipples stand for, take away those leg crossing motions that distract me to the tilt, take away that robe that covers those gasps of perfection, take away the wires and the lines and the lies, take away the re-direction, take away discretion and indiscretions, take away crotch shots, take away the fast pace of the revolution, take away the slight curves of your hips in silhouetted half-light, take away the smirks and the gasps and the jealousy, take away the intentional and unintentional, take away the brush strokes and the fingers in the gash, take away rebellion and certifiable insanity, take away the concrete walls and steel doors, take away my passport and my birth records, take away my credit scores, take away my name and rename me, take away chemicals and freshness, take away innovation and places of prayer, take away the fake news and the saturation, take away slow motion and fast forward, take away pause and mute, take away junk mail, take away big pharma, take away liberation and independence and unity of cause, take away the aftertaste of your discharge, take away the clit rings and the toe rings, take away pseudo bourgeois sophistication, take away the chronic fatigue, take away the dawn and the sunset, take away soiled motel comforters, take away broken half memories, take away the tether and the tempo, take away the darkness in the textured light, take away this undercurrent ambiguity between you and me, take away these quasi truisms and allusions of us together again, take away the accent marks and the hyphenations, take away the condensed moisture in the comforts of your folds, take away the seams in your cheap undergarments, take away the fantasy of you hovering over me, nude, unhinged, take away the conjugal visits, take away this lonesome aesthetic, take away the penetration and the withdrawals, take away the FBI agents in my mind, take away the bouncer at the doorway to my enlightenment, take away this smash and grab job for the loot treasure left behind, my only solace in a consolation-free world, take away the victimization and the aggressor, take away this cage of death and the slow collapse of the empire that exists in between your cleavage, take away what happens behind the farmhouse, take away the rope and the sleeping pills and the gun, take away the devices of diversion for a better day, take away the crutches and the enablers, take away the helicopters, take away the stairs to the rooftop, take away the addictions that keep me afloat, take away your flavoring and the hushed tones in the dark, take away the murmurs and the crawl space in your heart, take away the cameras and the surveillance, take away revulsion in the rhythm and motion, take away the bittersweet aftertaste in her mouth, take away these lost years, take away the longitudes and the latitudes, take away the maps and coordinates, take away the gimmicks and soft white lies, take away the fantasies of you bent over a sofa, take away the dark of night and its loose indiscretions, take away the freshness of the scent, take away the dissemination and the fragmentation, take away those heavy lids that hide the heaven in your eyes, take away the point where the conversation began, take away the slow walks in the desert heat, take away the forgotten ancient melodies of soul, in your wounds and in your unmentionables, take away the blood test results, take away the mystery of the tides and the mist emanating from your sacred area, take away the unwavering thoughts and the undeterred actions, for I am not me today and I may not be myself much longer, no longer that one self, a new direction with new tools, take away this renegade prosperity, take away the time loop on my life, take away the drifting halo, take away my dirty soul after I have fallen asleep, take away the echoing sentiments better left untold, take away these rewound thoughts and misgivings of how it should have been, if only it had been like that, take away the elements for better ease tonight when I leave without you, take away this silence that keeps me in the drought, take away the death mask and the seduction, take away her red lips suspended in an instant of motion, take away the realism in the crime, take away the cover of night and let the truth out, take away the last time I ever saw you, take away the misleading impressions of how you really are not.

Somewhere in the echo's displacement and the innermost point of my reason's cosmos is a surf that disobeys the habitual laws of our crowning consummation amid the landscape of our days, of the drumming on the nothingness, in the harmony of your laughing gas, in the pulsation of a thrashing beast among the particles of our grinning optics of the space elaborately engraved within the nature of scenic fashion from the smiling ether in the distance on the cornerstone of our preparation. We indulge in the unblemished and find the truth is verified by the design of the sensation and the zeal for exposure for with each method we inherit the light and inhabit chronic chastity and find judgement to be the tragedy indulging in the chic of virtue and viciousness strewn with the ashes of gloom, we dwell in the decency of allusions to affluence delivering the decorations of perfected sweetheart scheme, as you find me nestling on the inside of your celestial sphere paying off the travel agent of my ascension as the celebration has befallen the blooming tropics of Eden Paradise forever. *All perfect praise be to Allah, the Lord of the Worlds. I testify there is none worthy of worship except Allah, and that Muhammad is His Slave and Messenger. Lord of Mankind remove this affliction as You are the Only Healer, none can be healed unless healed by You. Heal me so completely that when I enter Paradise my servings of wine and honey will be bountiful as I stroll the gardens of perpetual bliss. The groves of shade and every fruit waiting for me. The full grown virgins with swelling pear-shaped breasts and most appetizing vaginas. White skinned and hairless except the eyebrows and head. Splendid, pure, non-menstruating, never dissatisfied and all praising. Their libidinous sex organs and an ever-erect penis. In the Name of Allah, the Most Beneficent, the Most Merciful. All the praises and thanks be to Allah, the Lord of all Mankind. The Only Owner of the Day of Resurrection. You alone I worship, and You alone I ask for help. Guide me to the Straight Way. The Way of those on whom You have bestowed Your Grace, not the way of those who earned Your anger, nor of those who went astray.*

"Excuse me my friend, can you tell me which ferry goes to Sausalito, *inshallah*?"

Made in the USA
San Bernardino, CA
15 November 2018